For Owen
from Clara

March 10th 1973

"Happy birthday to you"

G. K. CHESTERTON
Selected Stories

G. K. CHESTERTON

A Selection from his Non-Fictional Prose

Selected by W. H. Auden

G. K. CHESTERTON
Selected Stories

Edited by Kingsley Amis

FABER AND FABER
3 Queen Square
London

First published in 1972
by Faber and Faber Limited
3 Queen Square London WC1
Printed in Great Britain by
Latimer Trend & Co Ltd Plymouth

ISBN 0 571 09914 9

ACKNOWLEDGEMENTS

Grateful acknowledgement is made to the owner of the Chesterton copyrights, Miss D. E. Collins, c/o Messrs. A. P. Watt & Son; to Messrs. Cassell & Co. Ltd., for permission to reprint the ten stories taken from their collection edition of *Father Brown Stories* comprising 49 tales in all; and to Messrs. Darwen Finlayson of Beaconsfield for permission to reprint the remaining stories.

Contents

Introduction   *page* 11

From THE CLUB OF QUEER TRADES (1905)
The Tremendous Adventures of Major Brown   22

From THE INNOCENCE OF FATHER BROWN (1911)
The Blue Cross   46
The Secret Garden   67
The Invisible Man   88
The Honour of Israel Gow   106

From THE WISDOM OF FATHER BROWN (1914)
The Perishing of the Pendragons   122

From THE MAN WHO KNEW TOO MUCH (1922)
The Bottomless Well   142

From THE INCREDULITY OF FATHER BROWN
   (1926)
The Oracle of the Dog   159
The Dagger With Wings   182

From THE SECRET OF FATHER BROWN (1927)
The Mirror of the Magistrate   206

From THE POET AND THE LUNATICS (1929)
The Yellow Bird   226

From THE SCANDAL OF FATHER BROWN (1935)
The Blast of the Book   246
The Green Man   262

9

Introduction

Chesterton is often spoken of as being out of favour, though to be often spoken of as being anything at all (he might have said) is a kind of favour. He, or a large part of him, has never been out of favour with me, nor with a high proportion of literates over thirty-five or forty. It is tempting to conclude that the disfavour, if any, must reside among junior age-groups; at the same time, a great deal of Chesterton's work and public personality must be directly antipathetic, for reasons of varying cogency, to the standard liberal intellectual of any generation.

To begin with, he wrote a lot: over fifty books and innumerable ephemera in a not especially long life. And what he wrote was diverse: short stories, novels, a couple of plays, verse of all lengths and weights, biography, autobiography, history (of a sort), polemic (of most sorts), literary criticism, and almost anything that can be ranged under the general—and, these days, unattractive—heading of belles-lettres. (Why, I wonder, is a writer who produces a large and varied body of work felt to be suspect, whereas a similarly prolific composer is thought of as showing things like inexhaustible fecundity?) Well: more vaguely, to those who have read him long ago, inattentively or not at all, Chesterton can appear as a fat buffoon, an unthinking optimist, a wielder of empty and facetious paradox, one who praised beer and pubs as though nobody else was ever going to have done so, a Roman Catholic propagandist and an antisemite.

This is not in all points an unfair picture. He did write too much. The breadth of his output is a token not so much of versatility as of restlessness and dissatisfaction: his friend Ronald

Knox said of him that "he never really found his medium". He could be silly, unfunny and verbose; his devotion to paradox became an addiction that sometimes drove out even his abundant common sense. And, as can be seen in "The Bottomless Well" and a few other places, he was anti-semitic, though never, I think, actively. Against this charge, it will not really do to plead that so were plenty of his contemporaries, from Belloc to Sapper, nor that his objection was not to Jews as such, but to the world of high finance, in which Jews had been noticeable at the time in question. However, it must be said in his defence that he was quick to speak out against the rise of Hitlerism, rather quicker, in fact, than some social democrats of the period.

Real acquaintance with the bulk of Chesterton's writing uncovers a figure no more congenial to progressive thinkers of our day than he was to those of his own. (Until I re-read "The Secret Garden", I had not realized that thinkers could be called progressive, and gently derided on that score, sixty years ago.) Not that he fits into any stereotype of the reactionary: he was too much his own man for that, inveighing against imperialism and the power of the rich as stoutly as any liberal, if not quite from that standpoint. But, to give a few examples, he was against rationalism, the spread of science, sociology (partly for its scientific pretensions), introspection, what might be called unmorality, and George Moore. He was for the normal man, doctrine, vulgar conviviality, the past, England and Sherlock Holmes. And much more besides: in particular, his patriotism was qualified by a deep respect for other nationalities, such that no other English writer I know has written about Americans or Frenchmen with so much perceptive generosity.

Chesterton's stance on most matters could be summed up very roughly as follows. What is simple, generally agreed, old and obvious is not only more likely to be true than what is complex, original, new and subtle, but much more interesting as well: a prescription calculated to alienate almost any type of progressive thinker. His work is full of celebrations of the commonplace, from the descriptive passages in his fiction that show us we have never properly looked at a suburban street before, to critical insights like the one enabling him to see that the distinctive genius of Shakespeare lay in his being sublimely ordinary. No clever paradox, this, but triumphantly argued out, and incidentally carrying the uncomfortable rider that what we think of as the artistic temperament is a hallmark of the second-rate.

As a critic, Chesterton is always provocative, perhaps too regularly so. Perhaps he did too much use the work of other writers as raw material for the exposition of his own ideas. But at his best, on Browning or Dickens, he passes with honours the first test of any critic, that of being able to praise convincingly, to extend the grounds on which some author or work can be enjoyed. He writes with an energy and humour that remain fresh even when his subject has become faded by time. So, too, in his polemical essays, where the dust overlying one or another long-defunct controversy will suddenly be blown away by a joke, a gust of insight—often of the chillier sort—or the force of a prediction: religion and reason (to take a case), conventionally thought of as foes, are to Chesterton really cousins and allies, allies seen as withering and dying side by side in a welter of assorted superstitions—a truism in 1972, but surely a remarkable forecast in 1908. In an age of prophets, he stands up adequately when measured against Shaw and Wells; indeed, if a prophet's prophecies are supposed to bear some relation to the event, rather better than adequately.

Even to (I should guess) the majority of his admirers, Chesterton's verse has become reduced to a handful of anthology pieces, at the head of which stands "Lepanto"—as an exhilarating battle poem a major sin of his against the progressive light, though it does avoid the aggravating offence of being also patriotic: no Englishmen were present when the forces of the Papal League under Don John of Austria defeated the Turks and their allies by sea in 1571. However: it is in his fiction that I find Chesterton's genius best and most characteristically displayed. (Here I am far from sure I have the majority with me.) The novels and stories, especially the stories, dramatize virtually the whole range of the themes and interests met with in his other work. Further, the polemical tone and forensic style of much of that other work reappear—modified, to be sure—in the fiction, alongside the elements of narrative, in which he was only periodically interested, and of description, at which he was a master.

Lack of concern to narrate, readiness to depict or argue or float paradoxes instead, are the twin flaws of his less successful fictional efforts. In his later novels, these non-narrative and non-dramatic concerns, together with perished satire on fashionable fads of his day, reduce the story to a mere vehicle, and a boneshaker at that. Implausibility and facetiousness abound. His worst volume, *Tales of the Long Bow* (1925), chronicles the escapades of a group of friends set on bringing about the enactment of common sayings. Thus Colonel Crane literally eats his hat (he has taken to wearing a scooped-out cabbage on his head), Captain Pierce literally gets pigs to fly (well, he has some dropped on parachutes). The result is quite as painful as it sounds.

Such faults are much rarer in Chesterton's earlier fiction. They mar, but they could never come near ruining, his first novel, *The Napoleon of Notting Hill* (1904), that vivid and haunting fantasy of a future London—by a truly odd coincidence, a London of 1984—in which the boroughs turn into rival, warlike city-states of medieval constitution, weaponry and costume, the outcome being resolved on the cloudy day when the Provost of Notting Hill goes down to die with all his army in Kensington Gardens, and the pastoral chiefs of Shepherd's Bush with their spears and fleeces, aided by such allies as the rude clans from Paddington Green, destroy his empire.

The London ostensibly portrayed is a mixture of the remote past and the dim future; what we actually see and feel is the Edwardian London of Chesterton's own time. Here, as in "The Blue Cross" and others of his stories, he brings to vigorous life the old and accurate cliché (who coined it?) about London being not so much a city as a series of villages, each with its own special landscape and atmosphere, and, to this day, its own unexpected remnants of countryside. Chesterton was the passionate and learned poet of the town he had come to know intimately by what is still the only method: a favourite walk of his was from the family house in Kensington to St. Paul's Cathedral.

The other feature of *The Napoleon of Notting Hill* that links it to its author's other fiction is its use of a kind of rhetoric, stylized almost to the point of the theatrical, in both dialogue and narration. A sufficient example from the novel would need a solid page or more of prefatory explanation, so I will point instead to the closing few sentences of "The Blue Cross" and of "The Yellow Bird", and to any of Father Brown's periodic tirades. There is something vulgar and faintly absurd about this effect, which, to my taste, comes an embarrassing cropper at the end of "The Oracle of the Dog", but there is something rather grand as well, qualities which co-exist happily and naturally enough in a Chestertonian universe.

The type of rhetoric I mean is all over *The Man Who Was Thursday* (1908), which fully earns its subtitle, A Nightmare—indeed, it would be hard to find any other short description for its brilliantly original blending of relatively straightforward cloak-and-dagger elements with the metaphysical and even the apocalyptic. What I will risk calling nightmarishness is another characteristic Chestertonian effect, an air of unreality that is not the same thing as implausibility (though there is implausibility here and there as well), a feeling that the world we see and hear and touch is a flimsy veil that only just manages to cover up a deeper and far more awful reality, a sense, in fact, of impending "apocalypse" in the literal meaning of "uncovering". Many of the stories distil this impression, most notably, perhaps, that little masterpiece, "The Honour of Israel Gow" —a masterpiece in other ways too, as I hope to show.

When I sat down to compile this selection I fully intended to throw in substantial extracts from *The Man Who Was Thursday*, but found soon enough that the only fair procedure would have been to quote the entire volume, which is after all separately available. I had forgotten how undetachable even the most internally dramatic scenes must prove to be, how cumulative are all the effects of a good novel. So here is a baker's dozen of short stories, cast at that moderately ample length in which Chesterton was most at home. Just under half of them date from that first and best period of his career in fiction, 1904–14, roughly corresponding to the fourth decade of his life. After the later date his output became more uneven, though Father Brown sustained his merits to the last.

That dumpy, short-sighted little Essex priest, with his moon face and his perpetual umbrella, is one of the greatest of all great-detective figures. For many, he will always be *the* greatest, largely because he does without those adventitious eccentricities—solitary violin-playing, obsessive orchid-growing—that other contenders need in order to stiffen their personalities. He also scorns his rivals' tendency to happen to be an expert in whatever specialized field of knowledge is required for solving the case. His field of knowledge is human nature, and his skills are observation, reason and common sense. I have heard it said that he is sometimes too much a mouthpiece for his author's religious beliefs; their shared enemy, however, is not any kind of Protestantism nor even atheism as such, but bogus mysticism, superstition and folly. To have such nuisances spiritedly and accurately denounced is, in our day quite as much as in theirs, a little better than endurable.

To revert: whatever else he may or may not be, Brown is a detective, not (of course) a professional, just someone who happens to be about when a crime has been committed, but a detective none the less; and all these stories, like most of the ninety-odd stories Chesterton wrote, are detective stories. They are, very arguably, detective stories "with a difference"—a qualifying label that puts the experienced reader on his guard at once. Nearly all the time, the main difference about a thriller "with a difference" turns out to be that it fails to thrill; science fiction "with a difference" will differ from science fiction by being unscientific in all senses, and more than likely, in the last few years, unfictional into the bargain. To be respectable, the difference in this sense must be an addition, not a subtraction, and not, or preferably not, a substitution.

Some sort of defining gesture seems called for at this point. Most people would probably agree that a detective story without a difference, so to speak, involves a crime, normally murder, of which the perpetrator is not immediately apparent, some clues to his identity, method, etc., some deduction from these, and the exposure of the criminal. Where such people divide is over the deduction part, how valid it needs to be and how important it should be made. To the more permissive wing, form rather than substance—a bit of speculation about why the body was moved, a couple of minutes' pondering about those footsteps in the snow—is all that is required; the author can deceive the reader, withhold vital information, proceed by revealing totally new facts instead of linking established ones together, and get away with it if his story moves well, his detective is fun and his dénouement sufficiently unexpected. To the more rigorous party, in whose moderately liberal section I myself belong, deduction is of the essence, whatever else may be stirred in: the author may mislead the reader, but he must not cheat him or lie to him; the detective is entitled to a certain amount of luck, but not to second sight; the unravelling must be consequential; and no twin brothers, poisons unknown to science, previously undisclosed secret passages or other conjuror's rabbits are permitted.

I have said I favour the second view; but holders of the first could certainly plead that their kind of story has always been far more widespread and popular than mine, and further, by way of starting to move back to the main issue, that at the time when Father Brown entered on his career the deduction-before-everything school of writing hardly existed: none of the supposedly marvellous chains of reasoning devised by Poe's Dupin stands up to scrutiny, and Dupin's great successor, Sherlock Holmes, went on about deduction far more regularly than he used it. Only a very few of his exploits, "The Red-Headed League" and "Silver Blaze" among them, satisfy my criteria; Holmes was much likelier to produce the criminal out of nowhere at all in the last couple of pages.

Chesterton never descended to that kind of thing, but there

is a nasty rabbit in "The Secret Garden", and he does annoyingly withhold clues that he could have slipped in easily and unobtrusively. "Didn't you notice," asks Brown towards the end of one of the stories in this collection, "the [murderer] played with a pen and not with a paper-knife; though he had a beautiful bright steel paper-knife [on his desk]? . . . There are limits to the irony of assassins." No, I didn't notice, because I wasn't told about the knife at the time. Elsewhere, there is a piece of implausibility or illogic nearer the heart of the plot, vulnerable to a simple question or two, as follows.

"The Secret Garden"—how could the murderer have been so certain that one of the other characters was going to bring a vitally important object with him on the fatal evening? And, even if the murderer was just gambling on a good chance, how could he expect to find the object unattended exactly when he needed it?

"The Invisible Man"—would not at least one of the witnesses simply have happened to mention seeing the man?

"The Oracle of the Dog"—what would have happened to the game on the beach if Miss Druce had cried out a little later than she did?

And so on. Nevertheless, others of the stories, apart from everything else they do, will satisfy the strictest deductive precisian—or rather should make him cheer. Brown's apparently insane, but really pedantically accurate, answers to sane questions; his own apparently insane, but really vitally relevant questions; the clue in four words that identifies a murderer at once and unmistakably—to Brown, though to very few of us; the desert well that indicated the solution of a crime by having nothing to do with it; all such strokes take their place in what I see as the finest detective-story tradition. They do more than that: they are models, helping to shape that tradition as well as adding lustre to it.

"The Honour of Israel Gow" (to specify further) would have been a remarkable story in any era. Its Edwardian date makes it astonishing. The deductive rules and limitations, at that time still only half-shaped, are more than adhered to, they are exploited with the panache of a master. The setting-up of the main body of clues—the strange assortment of objects littering Glengyle Castle—is skilful and inventive enough; the profusion of the false explanations suggested by Father Brown sustains that level; the process whereby it is the most macabre event that establishes the rationality of the true explanation ascends higher; the explanation of that explanation is a kind of wild, spendthrift bonus, and the way in which the most essential clue of all is not merely introduced, but spotlighted, on the second page has the impudence of genius.

In short, here is a detective story as well as a detective story with a difference, or several differences. One of these I will leave it to the reader to discover. Another is the emphatic presence of that air of unreality I alluded to earlier, leading Brown, no hysteric, to suggest in the middle of a violent storm that "the great devil of the universe may be sitting on the top tower of this castle at this moment, as big as a hundred elephants, and roaring like the Apocalypse". Yet another difference—an addition, not a subtraction or a substitution—lies in the use of Chesterton's descriptive gift, most notably as regards the landscape surrounding the castle. The painter he at first intended, but failed, to become could hardly have bettered his prose depictions of the effects of light.

This particular difference also distinguished the story that, to me, shares first place in this volume, "The Blue Cross". Chesterton was fascinated not just by light, but by changes in light, as also by the changes in feeling that accompany them. This overriding interest leads him, here as elsewhere, to play ducks and drakes with the passage of time. He wants a busy, sunlit, prosaic morning joined on to a mysterious evening twilight that leads into a sinister darkness under the stars, so that his characters have to move at snail's pace while these changes come about. Poor Valentin and his policemen are condemned to take what I compute as six hours to cover the six or so miles from Victoria to somewhere near Hampstead: unbelievably slow going even by horse-omnibus.

I find it hard to care, while sternly refusing any comfort

along the lines of, "Well, it all helps to build up the atmosphere of fantasy". Such helps are gross, and fantasy, in the sense of abandonment of reasonableness, is out of place in a tale that, among other things, celebrates reason. My consolation, or distraction, lies in Chesterton's bold use of a different sort of unlikelihood that manages (for once: it could only be done once) to use million-to-one-against coincidence—Valentin's finding and following of Father Brown's trail—as its strategy, and to pull it off. And who could forget that sublimely rhetorical moment at which Brown tells the great thief Flambeau that there is no escape from God's laws anywhere in the universe?— "On plains of opal, under cliffs cut out of pearl, you would still find a notice-board, 'Thou shalt not steal.' "

Other Chestertonian differences include his exaltation of now tattered virtues like honour, courage, loyalty and chivalry, or chivalrousness; his capacity to go on demonstrating that murder or other violence is not an indispensable ingredient of the detective story—in five of these thirteen, no crime ever gets committed; his constant ability to suggest, without ever repeating himself, that the crime, or apparent crime, has been committed with the aid of magic. This last regularly leads into a characteristic rebuke to superstitious credulity, though in one case the rebuke takes the lenient form of a practical joke. The story referred to embodies yet another difference by being a skit on the detective story that is also a true detective story.

What above all pervades these pieces, indeed the whole of his fiction, is Chesterton's inexhaustible fascination with the outward appearance of things, not only with the effects of light upon them, but with the things in themselves: landscape and seascape, streets, shops, gardens, the outsides and insides of houses, ornaments, knick-knacks of every possible kind, details of dress and costume—and, more than any of these, the lineaments of the human being inside the costume. Nobody, I think, would call Chesterton a great characterizer of the inner selves of men and women, but one would have to turn to a writer on the scale of his beloved Dickens to find a better representer of how they look. Of all the thousands of people who appear in his

20

fiction, even those with the merest walk-on parts, not one recalls another in his face or body. Every time, the author rises exultantly to the occasion and draws someone new.

If Chesterton was an optimist (no bad thing to be anyway, I should have thought, if it can be managed), it was largely because he loved the world his God had made, and never ceased to enjoy that vitally important aspect of the entire creation: its surface.

The Tremendous Adventures of Major Brown

Rabelais, or his wild illustrator Gustave Doré, must have had something to do with the designing of the things called flats in England and America. There is something entirely Gargantuan in the idea of economizing space by piling houses on top of each other, front doors and all. And in the chaos and complexity of those perpendicular streets anything may dwell or happen, and it is in one of them, I believe, that the inquirer may find the offices of the Club of Queer Trades. It may be thought at the first glance that the name would attract and startle the passer-by, but nothing attracts or startles in these dim immense hives. The passer-by is only looking for his own melancholy destination, the Montenegro Shipping Agency or the London office of the *Rutland Sentinel*, and passes through the twilight passages as one passes through the twilight corridors of a dream. If the Thugs set up a Strangers' Assassination Company in one of the great buildings in Norfolk Street, and sent in a mild man in spectacles to answer inquiries, no inquiries would be made. And the Club of Queer Trades reigns in a great edifice hidden like a fossil in a mighty cliff of fossils.

The nature of this society, such as we afterwards discovered it to be, is soon and simply told. It is an eccentric and Bohemian Club, of which the absolute condition of membership lies in this, that the candidate must have invented the method by which he earns his living. It must be an entirely new trade. The exact definition of this requirement is given in the two principal rules. First, it must not be a mere application or variation of an existing trade. Thus, for instance, the Club would not admit an insurance agent simply because instead of insuring men's furniture against being burnt in a fire, he insured, let us say, their trousers against being torn by a mad dog. The principle (as Sir Bradcock Burnaby-Bradcock, in the extraordinarily eloquent and soaring speech to the club on the occasion of the question being raised in the Stormby Smith affair, said wittily and keenly) is the same. Secondly, the trade must be a genuine commercial source of income, the support of its inventor. Thus the Club would not receive a man simply because he chose to pass his days collecting broken sardine tins, unless he could drive a roaring trade in them. Professor Chick made that quite clear. And when one remembers what Professor Chick's own new trade was, one doesn't know whether to laugh or cry.

The discovery of this strange society was a curiously refreshing thing; to realize that there were ten new trades in the world was like looking at the first ship or the first plough. It made a man feel what he should feel, that he was still in the childhood of the world. That I should have come at last upon so singular a body was, I may say without vanity, not altogether singular, for I have a mania for belonging to as many societies as possible: I may be said to collect clubs, and I have accumulated a vast and fantastic variety of specimens ever since, in my audacious youth, I collected the Athenaeum. At some future day, perhaps, I may tell tales of some of the other bodies to which I have belonged. I will recount the doings of the Dead Man's Shoes Society (that superficially immoral, but darkly justifiable communion); I will explain the curious origin of the Cat and Christian, the name of which has been so shamefully misinterpreted; and the world shall know at least why the Institute of Typewriters coalesced with the Red Tulip League. Of the Ten Teacups, of course I dare not say a word. The first of my revelations, at any rate, shall be concerned with the Club of Queer Trades, which, as I have said, was one of this class, one which I was almost bound to come across sooner or later, because of my singular hobby. The wild youth of the metropolis call me facetiously "The King of Clubs". They also call me

"The Cherub", in allusion to the roseate and youthful appearance I have presented in my declining years. I only hope the spirits in the better world have as good dinners as I have. But the finding of the Club of Queer Trades has one very curious thing about it. The most curious thing about it is that it was not discovered by me; it was discovered by my friend Basil Grant, a star-gazer, a mystic, and a man who scarcely stirred out of his attic.

Very few people knew anything of Basil; not because he was in the least unsociable, for if a man out of the street had walked into his rooms he would have kept him talking till morning. Few people knew him, because, like all poets, he could do without them; he welcomed a human face as he might welcome a sudden blend of colour in a sunset; but he no more felt the need of going out to parties than he felt the need of altering the sunset clouds. He lived in a queer and comfortable garret in the roofs of Lambeth. He was surrounded by a chaos of things that were in odd contrast to the slums around him; old fantastic books, swords, armour—the whole dust-hole of romanticism. But his face, amid all these quixotic relics, appeared curiously keen and modern—a powerful, legal face. And no one but I knew who he was.

Long ago as it is, everyone remembers the terrible and grotesque scene that occurred in ——, when one of the most acute and forcible of the English judges suddenly went mad on the bench. I had my own view of that occurrence; but about the facts themselves there is no question at all. For some months, indeed for some years, people had detected something curious in the judge's conduct. He seemed to have lost interest in the law, in which he had been beyond expression brilliant and terrible as a K.C., and to be occupied in giving personal and moral advice to the people concerned. He talked more like a priest or a doctor, and a very outspoken one at that. The first thrill was probably given when he said to a man who had attempted a crime of passion: "I sentence you to three years' imprisonment, under the firm, and solemn, and God-given conviction, that what you require is three months at the sea-

24

side." He accused criminals from the bench, not so much of their obvious legal crimes, but of things that had never been heard of in a court of justice, monstrous egoism, lack of humour, and morbidity deliberately encouraged. Things came to a head in that celebrated diamond case in which the Prime Minister himself, that brilliant patrician, had to come forward gracefully and reluctantly, to give evidence against his valet. After the detailed life of the household had been thoroughly exhibited, the judge requested the Premier again to step forward, which he did with quiet dignity. The judge then said, in a sudden, grating voice: "Get a new soul. That thing's not fit for a dog. Get a new soul." All this, of course, in the eyes of the sagacious, was premonitory of that melancholy and farcical day when his wits actually deserted him in open court. It was a libel case between two very eminent and powerful financiers, against both of whom charges of considerable defalcation were brought. The case was long and complex; the advocates were long and eloquent; but at last, after weeks of work and rhetoric, the time came for the great judge to give a summing up; and one of his celebrated masterpieces of lucidity and pulverizing logic was eagerly looked for. He had spoken very little during the prolonged affair, and he looked sad and lowering at the end of it. He was silent for a few moments, and then burst into a stentorian song. His remarks (as reported) were as follows:

> "*O Rowty-owty tiddly-owty*
> *Tiddly-owty tiddly-owty*
> *Highty-ighty tiddly-ighty*
> *Tiddly-ighty ow.*"

He then retired from public life and took the garret in Lambeth.

I was sitting there one evening, about six o'clock, over a glass of that gorgeous Burgundy which he kept behind a pile of black-letter folios; he was striding about the room, fingering, after a habit of his, one of the great swords in his collection; the red glare of the strong fire struck his square features and his fierce grey hair; his blue eyes were even unusually full of dreams, and he had opened his mouth to speak dreamily, when the door was flung open, and a pale, fiery man, with red hair and a huge furred overcoat, swung himself panting into the room.

"Sorry to bother you, Basil," he gasped. "I took a liberty—made an appointment here with a man—a client—in five minutes—I beg your pardon, sir," and he gave me a bow of apology.

Basil smiled at me. "You didn't know," he said, "that I had a practical brother. This is Rupert Grant, Esquire, who can and does all there is to be done. Just as I was a failure at one thing, he is a success at everything. I remember him as a journalist, a house-agent, a naturalist, an inventor, a publisher, a school-master, a—what are you now, Rupert?"

"I am and have been for some time," said Rupert, with some dignity, "a private detective, and there's my client."

A loud rap at the door had cut him short, and, on permission being given, the door was thrown sharply open and a stout, dapper man walked swiftly into the room, set his silk hat with a clap on the table, and said, "Good evening, gentle*men*," with a stress on the last syllable that somehow marked him out as a martinet, military, literary and social. He had a large head streaked with black and grey, and an abrupt black moustache, which gave him a look of fierceness which was contradicted by his sad sea-blue eyes.

Basil immediately said to me, "Let us come into the next room, Gully," and was moving towards the door, but the stranger said:

"Not at all. Friends remain. Assistance possibly."

The moment I heard him speak I remembered who he was, a certain Major Brown I had met years before in Basil's society. I had forgotten altogether the black dandified figure and the large solemn head, but I remembered the peculiar speech, which consisted of only saying about a quarter of each sentence, and that sharply, like the crack of a gun. I do not know, it may have come from giving orders to troops.

Major Brown was a V.C., and an able and distinguished

26

soldier, but he was anything but a warlike person. Like many among the iron men who recovered British India, he was a man with the natural beliefs and tastes of an old maid. In his dress he was dapper and yet demure; in his habits he was precise to the point of the exact adjustment of a tea-cup. One enthusiasm he had, which was of the nature of a religion—the cultivation of pansies. And when he talked about his collection, his blue eyes glittered like a child's at a new toy, the eyes that had remained untroubled when the troops were roaring victory round Roberts at Candahar.

"Well, Major," said Rupert Grant, with a lordly heartiness, flinging himself into a chair, "what is the matter with you?"

"Yellow pansies. Coal cellar, P. G. Northover," said the Major with righteous indignation.

We glanced at each other with inquisitiveness. Basil, who had his eyes shut in his abstracted way, said simply:

"I beg your pardon."

"Fact is. Street, you know, man, pansies. On wall. Death to me. Something. Preposterous."

We shook our heads gently. Bit by bit, and mainly by the seemingly sleepy assistance of Basil Grant, we pieced together the Major's fragmentary, but excited narration. It would be infamous to submit the reader to what we endured; therefore I will tell the story of Major Brown in my own words. But the reader must imagine the scene. The eyes of Basil closed as in a trance, after his habit, and the eyes of Rupert and myself getting rounder and rounder as we listened to one of the most astounding stories in the world, from the lips of the little man in black, sitting bolt upright in his chair and talking like a telegram.

Major Brown was, I have said, a successful soldier, but by no means an enthusiastic one. So far from regretting his retirement on half-pay, it was with delight that he took a small neat villa, very like a doll's house, and devoted the rest of his life to pansies and weak tea. The thought that battles were over when he had once hung up his sword in the little front hall (along with two patent stew-pots and a bad water-colour), and betaken himself instead to wielding the rake in his little sunlit garden, was to him like having come into a harbour in heaven. He was Dutch-like and precise in his taste in gardening, and had, perhaps, some tendency to drill his flowers like soldiers. He was one of those men who are capable of putting four umbrellas in the stand rather than three, so that two may lean one way and two another; he saw life like a pattern in a freehand drawing-book. And assuredly he would not have believed, or even understood, anyone who had told him that within a few yards of his brick paradise he was destined to be caught in a whirlpool of incredible adventure, such as he had never seen or dreamed of in the horrible jungle, or the heat of battle.

One certain bright and windy afternoon, the Major, attired in his usual faultless manner, had set out for his usual constitutional. In crossing from one great residential thoroughfare to another, he happened to pass along one of those aimless-looking lanes which lie along the back-garden walls of a row of mansions, and which in their empty and discoloured appearance give one an odd sensation as of being behind the scenes of a theatre. But mean and sulky as the scene might be in the eyes of most of us, it was not altogether so in the Major's, for along the coarse gravel footway was coming a thing which was to him what the passing of a religious procession is to a devout person. A large, heavy man, with fish-blue eyes and a ring of irradiating red beard, was pushing before him a barrow, which was ablaze with incomparable flowers. There were splendid specimens of almost every order, but the Major's own favourite pansies predominated. The Major stopped and fell into conversation, and then into bargaining. He treated the man after the manner of collectors and other mad men, that is to say, he carefully and with a sort of anguish selected the best roots from the less excellent, praised some, disparaged others, made a subtle scale ranging from a thrilling worth and rarity to a degraded insignificance, and then bought them all. The man was just pushing off his barrow when he stopped and came close to the Major.

"I'll tell you what, sir," he said. "If you're interested in them things, you just get on to that wall."

"On the wall!" cried the scandalized Major, whose conventional soul quailed within him at the thought of such fantastic trespass.

"Finest show of yellow pansies in England in that there garden, sir," hissed the tempter. "I'll help you up, sir."

How it happened no one will ever know, but that positive enthusiasm of the Major's life triumphed over all its negative traditions, and with an easy leap and swing that showed that he was in no need of physical assistance, he stood on the wall at the end of the strange garden. The second after, the flapping of the frock-coat at his knees made him feel inexpressibly a fool. But the next instant all such trifling sentiments were swallowed up by the most appalling shock of surprise the old soldier had ever felt in all his bold and wandering existence. His eyes fell upon the garden, and there across a large bed in the centre of the lawn was a vast pattern of pansies; they were splendid flowers, but for once it was not their horticultural aspects that Major Brown beheld, for the pansies were arranged in gigantic capital letters so as to form the sentence:

"DEATH TO MAJOR BROWN"

A kindly-looking old man, with white whiskers, was watering them.

Brown looked sharply back at the road behind him; the man with the barrow had suddenly vanished. Then he looked again at the lawn with its incredible inscription. Another man might have thought he had gone mad, but Brown did not. When romantic ladies gushed over his V.C. and his military exploits, he sometimes felt himself to be a painfully prosaic person, but by the same token he knew he was incurably sane. Another man, again, might have thought himself a victim of a passing practical joke, but Brown could not easily believe this. He knew from his own quaint learning that the garden arrangement was an elaborate and expensive one; he thought it extravagantly improbable that anyone would pour out money like water for a joke against him. Having no explanation whatever to offer, he admitted the fact to himself, like a clear-headed man, and waited as he would have done in the presence of a man with six legs.

At this moment the stout old man with white whiskers looked up, and the watering-can fell from his hand, shooting a swirl of water down the gravel path.

"Who on earth are you?" he gasped, trembling violently.

"I am Major Brown," said that individual, who was always cool in the hour of action.

The old man gaped helplessly like some monstrous fish. At last he stammered wildly, "Come down—come down here!"

"At your service," said the Major, and alighted at a bound on the grass beside him, without disarranging his silk hat.

The old man turned his broad back and set off at a sort of waddling run towards the house, followed with swift steps by the Major. His guide led him through the back passages of a gloomy, but gorgeously appointed house, until they reached the door of the front room. Then the old man turned with a face of apoplectic terror dimly showing in the twilight.

"For heaven's sake," he said, "don't mention jackals."

Then he threw open the door, releasing a burst of red lamp-light, and ran downstairs with a clatter.

The Major stepped into a rich, glowing room, full of red copper, and peacock and purple hangings, hat in hand. He had the finest manners in the world, and, though mystified, was not in the least embarrassed to see that the only occupant was a lady, sitting by the window, looking out.

"Madam," he said bowing simply, "I am Major Brown."

"Sit down," said the lady; but she did not turn her head.

She was a graceful, green-clad figure, with fiery red hair and a flavour of Bedford Park. "You have come, I suppose," she said mournfully, "to tax me about the hateful title-deeds."

"I have come, madam," he said, "to know what is the matter. To know why my name is written across your garden. Not amicably either."

He spoke grimly, for the thing had hit him. It is impossible to describe the effect produced on the mind by that quiet and sunny garden scene, the frame for a stunning and brutal personality. The evening air was still, and the grass was golden in the place where the little flowers he studied cried to heaven for his blood.

"You must know I must not turn round," said the lady; "every afternoon till the stroke of six I must keep my face turned to the street."

Some queer and unusual inspiration made the prosaic soldier resolute to accept these outrageous riddles without surprise.

"It is almost six," he said; and even as he spoke the barbaric copper clock upon the wall clanged the first stroke of the hour. At the sixth the lady sprang up and turned on the Major one of the queerest and yet most attractive faces he had ever seen in his life; open, and yet tantalizing, the face of an elf.

"That makes the third year I have waited," she cried. "This is an anniversary. The waiting almost makes one wish the frightful thing would happen once and for all."

And even as she spoke, a sudden rending cry broke the stillness. From low down on the pavement of the dim street (it was already twilight) a voice cried out with a raucous and merciless distinctness:

"Major Brown, Major Brown, where does the jackal dwell?"

Brown was decisive and silent in action. He strode to the front door and looked out. There was no sign of life in the blue gloaming of the street, where one or two lamps were beginning to light their lemon sparks. On returning, he found the lady in green trembling.

"It is the end," she cried, with shaking lips; "it may be death for both of us. Whenever——"

But even as she spoke her speech was cloven by another hoarse proclamation from the dark street, again horribly articulate.

"Major Brown, Major Brown, how did the jackal die?"

Brown dashed out of the door and down the steps, but again he was frustrated; there was no figure in sight, and the street was far too long and empty for the shouter to have run away.

31

Even the rational Major was a little shaken as he returned in a certain time to the drawing-room. Scarcely had he done so than the terrific voice came:

"Major Brown, Major Brown, where did——"

Brown was in the street almost at a bound, and he was in time—in time to see something which at first glance froze the blood. The cries appeared to come from a decapitated head resting on the pavement.

The next moment the pale Major understood. It was the head of a man thrust through the coal-hole in the street. The next moment, again, it had vanished, and Major Brown turned to the lady. "Where's your coal cellar?" he said, and stepped out into the passage.

She looked at him with wild grey eyes. "You will not go down," she cried, "alone, into the dark hole, with that beast?"

"Is this the way?" replied Brown, and descended the kitchen stairs three at a time. He flung upon the door of a black cavity and stepped in, feeling in his pocket for matches. As his right hand was thus occupied, a pair of great slimy hands came out of the darkness, hands clearly belonging to a man of gigantic stature, and seized him by the back of the head. They forced him down, down in the suffocating darkness, a brutal image of destiny. But the Major's head, though upside down, was perfectly clear and intellectual. He gave quietly under the pressure until he had slid down almost to his hands and knees. Then finding the knees of the invisible monster within a foot of him, he simply put out one of his long, bony, and skilful hands, and gripping the leg by a muscle pulled it off the ground and laid the huge living man, with a crash, along the floor. He strove to rise, but Brown was on top like a cat. They rolled over and over. Big as the man was, he had evidently now no desire but to escape; he made sprawls hither and thither to get past the Major to the door, but that tenacious person had him hard by the coat collar and hung with the other hand to a beam. At length there came a strain in holding back this human bull, a strain under which Brown expected his hand to rend and part from the arm. But something else rent and parted; and the dim

32

fat figure of the giant vanished out of the cellar, leaving the torn coat in the Major's hand; the only fruit of his adventure and the only clue to the mystery. For when he went up and out at the front door, the lady, the rich hangings, and the whole equipment of the house had disappeared. It had only bare boards and whitewashed walls.

"The lady was in the conspiracy, of course," said Rupert, nodding. Major Brown turned brick red. "I beg your pardon," he said, "I think not."

Rupert raised his eyebrows and looked at him for a moment, but said nothing. When next he spoke he asked:

"Was there anything in the pockets of the coat?"

"There was sevenpence halfpenny in coppers and a three-penny-bit," said the Major carefully; "there was a cigarette-holder, a piece of string, and this letter," and he laid it on the table.

It ran as follows:

"Dear Mr. Plover,

I am annoyed to hear that some delay has occurred in the arrangements *re* Major Brown. Please see that he is attacked as per arrangement tomorrow. The coal-cellar, of course.

Your faithfully,
P. G. Northover."

Rupert Grant was leaning forward listening with hawklike eyes. He cut in:

"Is it dated from anywhere?"

"No—oh, yes!" replied Brown, glancing upon the paper; "14 Tanner's Court, North——"

Rupert sprang up and struck his hands together.

"Then why are we hanging here? Let's get along. Basil, lend me your revolver."

Basil was staring into the embers like a man in a trance; and it was some time before he answered:

"I don't think you'll need it."

"Perhaps not," said Rupert, getting into his fur coat. "One

c

33

never knows. But going down a dark court to see criminals——"

"Do you think they are criminals?" asked his brother.

Rupert laughed stoutly. "Giving orders to a subordinate to strangle a harmless stranger in a coal-cellar may strike you as a very blameless experiment, but——"

"Do you think they wanted to strangle the Major?" asked Basil, in the same distant and monotonous voice.

"My dear fellow, you've been asleep. Look at the letter."

"I am looking at the letter," said the mad judge calmly; though, as a matter of fact, he was looking at the fire. "I don't think it's the sort of letter one criminal would write to another."

"My dear boy, you are glorious," cried Rupert, turning round, with laughter in his blue bright eyes. "Your methods amaze me. Why, there *is* the letter. It *is* written, and it does give orders for a crime. You might as well say that the Nelson Column was not at all the sort of thing that was likely to be set up in Trafalgar Square."

Basil Grant shook all over with a sort of silent laughter, but did not otherwise move.

"That's rather good," he said; "but, of course, logic like that's not what is really wanted. It's a question of spiritual atmosphere. It's not a criminal letter."

"It is. It's a matter of fact," cried the other in an agony of reasonableness.

"Facts," murmured Basil, like one mentioning some strange, far-off animals, "how facts obscure the truth. I may be silly—in fact, I'm off my head—but I never could believe in that man— what's his name, in those capital stories?—Sherlock Holmes. Every detail points to something, certainly; but generally to the wrong thing. Facts point in all directions, it seems to me, like the thousands of twigs on a tree. It's only the life of the tree that has unity and goes up—only the green blood that springs, like a fountain, at the stars."

"But what the deuce else can the letter be but criminal?"

"We have eternity to stretch our legs in," replied the mystic. "It can be an infinity of things. I haven't seen any of them— I've only seen the letter. I look at that, and say it's not criminal."

"Then what's the origin of it?"

"I haven't the vaguest idea."

"Then why don't you accept the ordinary explanation?"

Basil continued for a little to glare at the coals, and seemed to be collecting his thoughts in a humble and even painful way. Then he said:

"Suppose you went out into the moonlight. Suppose you passed through silent, silvery streets and squares until you came into an open and deserted space, set with a few monuments, and you beheld one dressed as a ballet girl dancing in the argent glimmer. And suppose you looked, and saw it was a man disguised. And suppose you looked again, and saw it was Lord Kitchener. What would you think?"

He paused a moment, and went on:

"You could not adopt the ordinary explanation. The ordinary explanation of putting on singular clothes is that you look nice in them; you would not think that Lord Kitchener dressed up like a ballet girl out of ordinary personal vanity. You would think it much more likely that he inherited a dancing madness from a great grandmother; or has been hypnotized at a séance; or threatened by a secret society with death if he refused the ordeal. With Baden-Powell, say, it might be a bet—but not with Kitchener. I should know all that, because in my public days I knew him quite well. So I know that letter quite well, and criminals quite well. It's not a criminal's letter. It's all atmospheres." And he closed his eyes and passed his hand over his forehead.

Rupert and the Major were regarding him with a mixture of respect and pity. The former said:

"Well, I'm going, anyhow, and shall continue to think—until your spiritual mystery turns up—that a man who sends a note recommending a crime, that is, actually a crime that is actually carried out, at least tentatively, is, in all probability, a little casual in his moral tastes. Can I have that revolver?"

"Certainly," said Basil, getting up. "But I am coming with you." And he flung an old cape or cloak round him, and took a sword-stick from the corner.

35

"You!" said Rupert, with some surprise, "you scarcely ever leave your hole to look at anything on the face of the earth."

Basil fitted on a formidable old white hat.

"I scarcely ever," he said, with an unconscious and colossal arrogance, "hear of anything on the face of the earth that I do not understand at once, without going to see it."

And he led the way out into the purple night.

We four swung along the flaring Lambeth streets, across Westminster Bridge, and along the Embankment in the direction of that part of Fleet Street which contained Tanner's Court. The erect, black figure of Major Brown, seen from behind, was a quaint contrast to the hound-like stoop and flapping mantle of young Rupert Grant, who adopted, with childlike delight, all the dramatic poses of the detective of fiction. The finest among his many fine qualities was his boyish appetite for the colour and poetry of London. Basil, who walked behind, with his face turned blindly to the stars, had the look of a somnambulist.

Rupert paused at the corner of Tanner's Court, with a quiver of delight at danger, and gripped Basil's revolver in his greatcoat pocket.

"Shall we go in now?" he asked.

"Not get police?" asked Major Brown, glancing sharply up and down the street.

"I am not sure," answered Rupert, knitting his brows. "Of course, it's quite clear, the thing's all crooked. But there are four of us, and——"

"I shouldn't get the police," said Basil in a queer voice. Rupert glanced at him and stared hard.

"Basil," he cried, "you're trembling. What's the matter—are you afraid?"

"Cold, perhaps," said the Major, eyeing him. There was no doubt that he was shaking.

At last, after a few moments' scrutiny, Rupert broke into a curse.

"You're laughing," he cried. "I know that confounded, silent, shaky laugh of yours. What the deuce is the amusement,

Basil? Here we are, all four of us, within a yard of a den of ruffians——"

"But I shouldn't call the police," said Basil. "We four heroes are quite equal to a host," and he continued to quake with his mysterious mirth.

Rupert turned with impatience and strode swiftly down the court, the rest of us following. When he reached the door of No. 14 he turned abruptly, the revolver glittering in his hand.

"Stand close," he said in the voice of a commander. "The scoundrel may be attempting an escape at this moment. We must fling open the door and rush in."

The four of us cowered instantly under the archway, rigid, except for the old judge and his convulsion of merriment.

"Now," hissed Rupert Grant, turning his pale face and burning eyes suddenly over his shoulder, "when I say 'Four', follow me with a rush. If I say 'Hold him', pin the fellows down, whoever they are. If I say 'Stop', stop. I shall say that if there are more than three. If they attack us I shall empty my revolver on them. Basil, have your sword-stick ready. Now—one, two, three, four!"

With the sound of the word the door burst open, and we fell into the room like an invasion, only to stop dead.

The room, which was an ordinary and neatly-appointed office, appeared, at the first glance, to be empty. But on a second and more careful glance, we saw seated behind a very large desk with pigeon-holes and drawers of bewildering multiplicity, a small man with a black waxed moustache, and the air of a very average clerk, writing hard. He looked up as we came to a standstill.

"Did you knock?" he asked pleasantly. "I am sorry if I did not hear. What can I do for you?"

There was a doubtful pause, and then, by general consent, the Major himself, the victim of the outrage, stepped forward.

The letter was in his hand, and he looked unusually grim.

"Is your name P. G. Northover?" he asked.

"That is my name," replied the other, smiling.

"I think," said Major Brown, with an increase in the dark

glow of his face, "that this letter was written by you." And with a loud clap he struck open the letter on the desk with his clenched fist. The man called Northover looked at it with unaffected interest and merely nodded.

"Well, sir," said the Major, breathing hard, "what about that?"

"What about it, precisely," said the man with the moustache.

"I am Major Brown," said that gentleman sternly.

Northover bowed. "Pleased to meet you, sir. What have you to say to me?"

"Say!" cried the Major, loosing a sudden tempest; "why, I want this confounded thing settled. I want——"

"Certainly, sir," said Northover, jumping up with a slight elevation of the eyebrows. "Will you take a chair for a moment." And he pressed an electric bell just above him, which thrilled and tinkled in a room beyond. The Major put his hand on the back of the chair offered him, but stood chafing and beating the floor with his polished boot.

The next moment an inner glass door was opened, and a fair, weedy, young man, in a frock-coat, entered from within.

"Mr. Hopson," said Northover, "this is Major Brown. Will you please finish that thing for him I gave you this morning and bring it in?"

"Yes, sir," said Mr. Hopson, and vanished like lightning.

"You will excuse me, gentlemen," said the egregious Northover, with his radiant smile, "if I continue to work until Mr. Hopson is ready. I have some books that must be cleared up before I get away on my holiday tomorrow. And we all like a whiff of the country, don't we? Ha! Ha!"

The criminal took up his pen with a childlike laugh, and a silence ensued; a placid and busy silence on the part of Mr. P. G. Northover; a raging silence on the part of everybody else.

At length the scratching of Northover's pen in the stillness was mingled with a knock at the door, almost simultaneously with the turning of the handle, and Mr. Hopson came in again with the same silent rapidity, placed a paper before his principal, and disappeared again.

38

The man at the desk pulled and twisted his spiky moustache for a few moments as he ran his eye up and down the paper presented to him. He took up his pen, with a slight, instantaneous frown, and altered something, muttering—"Careless". Then he read it again with the same impenetrable reflectiveness, and finally handed it to the frantic Brown, whose hand was beating the devil's tattoo on the back of the chair.

"I think you will find that all right, Major," he said briefly.

The Major looked at it; whether he found it all right or not will appear later, but he found it like this:

Major Brown to P. G. Northover

	£	s.	d.
January 1, to account rendered	5	6	0
May 9, to potting and embedding of 200 pansies .	2	0	0
To cost of trolley with flowers	0	15	0
To hiring of man with trolley	0	5	0
To hire of house and garden for one day . .	1	0	0
To furnishing of room in peacock curtains, copper ornaments, &c.	3	0	0
To salary of Miss Jameson	1	0	0
To salary of Mr. Plover	1	0	0
Total . . £14		6	0

A remittance will oblige

"What," said Brown, after a dead pause, and with eyes that seemed slowly rising out of his head, "what in heaven's name is this?"

"What is it?" repeated Northover, cocking his eyebrow with amusement. "It's your account, of course."

"My account!" The Major's ideas appeared to be in a vague stampede. "My account! And what have I got to do with it?"

"Well," said Northover, laughing outright, "naturally I prefer you to pay it."

The Major's hand was still resting on the back of the chair as the words came. He scarcely stirred otherwise, but he lifted the chair bodily into the air with one hand and hurled it at Northover's head.

The legs crashed against the desk, so that Northover only got a blow on the elbow as he sprang up with clenched fists, only to be seized by the united rush of the rest of us. The chair had fallen clattering on the empty floor.

"Let me go, you scamps," he shouted. "Let me——"

"Stand still," cried Rupert authoritatively. "Major Brown's action is excusable. The abominable crime you have attempted——"

"A customer has a perfect right," said Northover hotly, "to question an alleged overcharge, but, confound it all, not to throw furniture."

"What, in God's name, do you mean by your customers and overcharges?" shrieked Major Brown, whose keen feminine nature, steady in pain or danger, became almost hysterical in the presence of a long and exasperating mystery. "Who are you? I've never seen you or your insolent tomfool bills. I know one of your cursed brutes tried to choke me——"

"Mad," said Northover, gazing blankly round; "all of them mad. I didn't know they travelled in quartettes."

"Enough of this prevarication," said Rupert; "your crimes are discovered. A policeman is stationed at the corner of the court. Though only a private detective myself, I will take the responsibility of telling you that anything you say——"

"Mad," repeated Northover, with a weary air.

And at this moment, for the first time, there struck in among them the strange, sleepy voice of Basil Grant.

"Major Brown," he said, "may I ask you a question?"

The Major turned his head with an increased bewilderment.

"You?" he cried; "certainly, Mr. Grant."

"Can you tell me," said the mystic, with sunken head and lowering brow, as he traced a pattern in the dust with his sword-stick, "can you tell me what was the name of the man who lived in your house before you?"

The unhappy Major was only faintly more disturbed by this last and futile irrelevancy, and he answered vaguely:

"Yes, I think so; a man named Gurney something—a name with a hyphen—Gurney-Brown; that was it."

"And when did the house change hands?" said Basil, looking up sharply. His strange eyes were burning brilliantly.

"I came in last month," said the Major.

And at the mere word the criminal Northover suddenly fell into his great office chair and shouted with a volleying laughter.

"Oh! it's too perfect—it's too exquisite," he gasped, beating the arms with his fists. He was laughing deafeningly; Basil Grant was laughing voicelessly; and the rest of us only felt that our heads were like weathercocks in a whirlwind.

"Confound it, Basil," said Rupert, stamping. "If you don't want me to go mad and blow your metaphysical brains out, tell me what all this means."

Northover rose.

"Permit me, sir, to explain," he said. "And, first of all, permit me to apologize to you, Major Brown, for a most abominable and unpardonable blunder, which has caused you menace and inconvenience, in which, if you will allow me to say so, you have behaved with astonishing courage and dignity. Of course you need not trouble about the bill. We will stand the loss." And, tearing the paper across, he flung the halves into the waste-paper basket and bowed.

Poor Brown's face was still a picture of distraction. "But I don't even begin to understand," he cried. "What bill? what blunder? what loss?"

Mr. P. G. Northover advanced in the centre of the room, thoughtfully, and with a great deal of unconscious dignity. On closer consideration, there were apparent about him other things beside a screwed moustache, especially a lean, sallow face, hawk-like, and not without a careworn intelligence. Then he looked up abruptly.

"Do you know where you are, Major?" he said.

"God knows I don't," said the warrior, with fervour.

"You are standing," replied Northover, "in the office of the Adventure and Romance Agency, Limited."

"And what's that?" blankly inquired Brown.

The man of business leaned over the back of the chair, and fixed his dark eyes on the other's face.

"Major," said he, "did you ever, as you walked along the empty street upon some idle afternoon, feel the utter hunger for something to happen—something, in the splendid words of Walt Whitman: 'Something pernicious and dread; something far removed from a puny and pious life; something unproved; something in a trance; something loosed from its anchorage, and driving free.' Did you ever feel that?"

"Certainly not," said the Major shortly.

"Then I must explain with more elaboration," said Mr. Northover, with a sigh. "The Adventure and Romance Agency has been started to meet a great modern desire. On every side, in conversation and in literature, we hear of the desire for a larger theatre of events—for something to waylay us and lead us splendidly astray. Now the man who feels this desire for a varied life pays a yearly or a quarterly sum to the Adventure and Romance Agency; in return, the Adventure and Romance Agency undertakes to surround him with startling and weird events. As a man is leaving his front door, an excited sweep approaches him and assures him of a plot against his life; he gets into a cab, and is driven to an opium den; he receives a mysterious telegram or a dramatic visit, and is immediately in a vortex of incidents. A very picturesque and moving story is first written by one of the staff of distinguished novelists who are at present hard at work in the adjoining room. Yours, Major Brown (designed by our Mr. Grigsby), I consider peculiarly forcible and pointed; it is almost a pity you did not see the end of it. I need scarcely explain further the monstrous mistake. Your predecessor in your present house, Mr. Gurney-Brown, was a subscriber to our agency, and our foolish clerks, ignoring alike the dignity of the hyphen and the glory of military rank, positively imagined that Major Brown and Mr. Gurney-Brown were the same person. Thus you were suddenly hurled into the middle of another man's story."

"How on earth does the thing work?" asked Rupert Grant, with bright and fascinated eyes.

"We believe that we are doing a noble work," said Northover warmly. "It has continually struck us that there is no element in modern life that is more lamentable than the fact that the modern man has to seek all artistic existence in a sedentary state. If he wishes to float into fairyland, he reads a book; if he wishes to dash into the thick of battle, he reads a book; if he wishes to soar into heaven, he reads a book; if he wishes to slide down the banisters, he reads a book. We give him these visions, but we give him exercise at the same time, the necessity of leaping from wall to wall, of fighting strange gentlemen, of running down long streets from pursuers—all healthy and pleasant exercises. We give him a glimpse of that great morning world of Robin Hood or the Knights Errant, when one great game was played under the splendid sky. We give him back his childhood, that godlike time when we can act stories, be our own heroes, and at the same instant dance and dream."

Basil gazed at him curiously. The most singular psychological discovery had been reserved to the end, for as the little business man ceased speaking he had the blazing eyes of a fanatic.

Major Brown received the explanation with complete simplicity and good humour.

"Of course; awfully dense, sir," he said. "No doubt at all, the scheme excellent. But I don't think——" He paused a moment, and looked dreamily out of the window. "I don't think you will find me in it. Somehow, when one's seen—seen the thing itself, you know—blood and men screaming, one feels about having a little house and a little hobby; in the Bible, you know, 'There remaineth a rest.' "

Northover bowed. Then after a pause he said:

"Gentlemen, may I offer you my card. If any of the rest of you desire, at any time, to communicate with me, despite Major Brown's view of the matter——"

"I should be obliged for your card, sir," said the Major, in his abrupt but courteous voice. "Pay for chair."

The agent of Romance and Adventure handed his card, laughing.

It ran, "P. G. Northover, B.A., C.Q.T., Adventure and Romance Agency, 14 Tanner's Court, Fleet Street."

"What on earth is 'C.Q.T.'?" asked Rupert Grant, looking over the Major's shoulder.

"Don't you know?" returned Northover. "Haven't you ever heard of the Club of Queer Trades?"

"There seems to be a confounded lot of funny things we haven't heard of," said the little Major reflectively. "What's this one?"

"The Club of Queer Trades is a society consisting exclusively of people who have invented some new and curious way of making money. I was one of the earliest members."

"You deserve to be," said Basil, taking up his great white hat, with a smile, and speaking for the last time that evening.

When they had passed out the Adventure and Romance agent wore a queer smile, as he trod down the fire and locked up his desk. "A fine chap, that Major; when one hasn't a touch of the poet one stands some chance of being a poem. But to think of such a clockwork little creature of all people getting into the nets of one of Grigsby's tales," and he laughed out aloud in the silence.

Just as the laugh echoed away, there came a sharp knock at the door. An owlish head, with dark moustaches, was thrust in, with deprecating and somewhat absurd inquiry.

"What! back again, Major?" cried Northover in surprise. "What can I do for you?"

The Major shuffled feverishly into the room.

"It's horribly absurd," he said. "Something must have got started in me that I never knew before. But upon my soul I feel the most desperate desire to know the end of it all."

"The end of it all?"

"Yes," said the Major. " 'Jackals,' and the title-deeds, and 'Death to Major Brown.' "

The agent's face grew grave, but his eyes were amused.

"I am terribly sorry, Major," said he, "but what you ask is impossible. I don't know anyone I would sooner oblige than you; but the rules of the agency are strict. The Adventures are confidential; you are an outsider; I am not allowed to let you know an inch more than I can help. I do hope you understand——"

"There is no one," said Brown, "who understands discipline better than I do. Thank you very much. Good-night."

And the little man withdrew for the last time.

He married Miss Jameson, the lady with the red hair and the green garments. She was an actress, employed (with many others) by the Romance Agency; and her marriage with the prim old veteran caused some stir in her languid and intellectualized set. She always replied very quietly that she had met scores of men who acted splendidly in the charades provided for them by Northover, but that she had only met one man who went down into a coal-cellar when he really thought it contained a murderer.

The Major and she are living as happily as birds, in an absurd villa, and the former has taken to smoking. Otherwise he is unchanged—except, perhaps, there are moments when, alert and full of feminine unselfishness as the Major is by nature, he falls into a trance of abstraction. Then his wife recognizes with a concealed smile, by the blind look in his blue eyes, that he is wondering what were the title-deeds, and why he was not allowed to mention jackals. But, like so many old soldiers, Brown is religious, and believes that he will realize the rest of those purple adventures in a better world.

From *The Club of Queer Trades*
(Darwen Finlayson)

The Blue Cross

Between the silver ribbon of morning and the green glittering ribbon of sea, the boat touched Harwich and let loose a swarm of folk like flies, among whom the man we must follow was by no means conspicuous—nor wished to be. There was nothing notable about him, except a slight contrast between the holiday gaiety of his clothes and the official gravity of his face. His clothes included a slight, pale grey jacket, a white waistcoat, and a silver straw hat with a grey-blue ribbon. His lean face was dark by contrast, and ended in a curt black beard that looked Spanish and suggested an Elizabethan ruff. He was smoking a cigarette with the seriousness of an idler. There was nothing about him to indicate the fact that the grey jacket covered a loaded revolver, that the white waistcoat covered a police card, or that the straw hat covered one of the most powerful intellects in Europe. For this was Valentin himself, the head of the Paris police and the most famous investigator of the world; and he was coming from Brussels to London to make the greatest arrest of the century.

Flambeau was in England. The police of three countries had tracked the great criminal at last from Ghent to Brussels, from Brussels to the Hook of Holland; and it was conjectured that he would take some advantage of the unfamiliarity and confusion of the Eucharistic Congress, then taking place in London. Probably he would travel as some minor clerk or secretary connected with it; but, of course, Valentin could not be certain; nobody could be certain about Flambeau.

It is many years now since this colossus of crime suddenly ceased keeping the world in a turmoil; and when he ceased, as they said after the death of Roland, there was a great quiet upon the earth. But in his best days (I mean, of course, his worst) Flambeau was a figure as statuesque and international as the Kaiser. Almost every morning the daily paper announced that he had escaped the consequences of one extraordinary crime by committing another. He was a Gascon of gigantic stature and bodily daring; and the wildest tales were told of his outbursts of athletic humour; how he turned the *juge d'instruction* upside down and stood him on his head, "to clear his mind"; how he ran down the Rue de Rivoli with a policeman under each arm. It is due to him to say that his fantastic physical strength was generally employed in such bloodless though undignified scenes; his real crimes were chiefly those of ingenious and whole-sale robbery. But each of his thefts was almost a new sin, and would make a story by itself. It was he who ran the great Tyrolean Dairy Company in London, with no dairies, no cows, no carts, no milk, but with some thousand subscribers. These he served by the simple operation of moving the little milk-cans outside people's doors to the doors of his own customers. It was he who had kept up an unaccountable and close correspondence with a young lady whose whole letter-bag was intercepted, by the extraordinary trick of photographing his messages infini-tesimally small upon the slides of a microscope. A sweeping simplicity, however, marked many of his experiments. It is said he once repainted all the numbers in a street in the dead of night merely to divert one traveller into a trap. It is quite cer-tain that he invented a portable pillar-box, which he put up at corners in quiet suburbs on the chance of strangers dropping postal orders into it. Lastly he was known to be a startling acro-bat; despite his huge figure, he could leap like a grasshopper and melt into the tree-tops like a monkey. Hence the great Valentin, when he set out to find Flambeau, was perfectly well aware that his adventures would not end when he had found him.

But how was he to find him? On this the great Valentin's ideas were still in process of settlement.

There was one thing which Flambeau, with all his dexterity of disguise, could not cover, and that was his singular height. If

Valentin's quick eye had caught a tall apple-woman, a tall grenadier, or even a tolerably tall duchess, he might have arrested them on the spot. But all along his train there was nobody that could be a disguised Flambeau, any more than a cat could be a disguised giraffe. About the people on the boat he had already satisfied himself; and the people picked up at Harwich or on the journey limited themselves with certainty to six. There was a short railway official travelling up to the terminus, three fairly short market-gardeners picked up two stations afterwards, one very short widow lady going up from a small Essex town, and a very short Roman Catholic priest going up from a small Essex village. When it came to the last case, Valentin gave it up and almost laughed. The little priest was so much the essence of those Eastern flats: he had a face as round and dull as a Norfolk dumpling; he had eyes as empty as the North Sea; he had several brown-paper parcels which he was quite incapable of collecting. The Eucharistic Congress had doubtless sucked out of their local stagnation many such creatures, blind and helpless, like moles disinterred. Valentin was a sceptic in the severe style of France, and could have no love for priests. But he could have pity for them, and this one might have provoked pity in anybody. He had a large, shabby umbrella, which constantly fell on the floor. He did not seem to know which was the right end of his return ticket. He explained with a moon-calf simplicity to everybody in the carriage that he had to be careful, because he had something made of real silver "with blue stones" in one of his brown-paper parcels. His quaint blending of Essex flatness with saintly simplicity continuously amused the Frenchman till the priest arrived (somehow) at Stratford with all his parcels, and came back for his umbrella. When he did the last, Valentin even had the good nature to warn him not to take care of the silver by telling everybody about it. But to whomever he talked, Valentin kept his eye open for someone else; he looked out steadily for anyone, rich or poor, male or female, who was well up to six feet; for Flambeau was four inches above it.

He alighted at Liverpool Street, however, quite conscientiously secure that he had not missed the criminal so far. He then went to Scotland Yard to regularize his position and arrange for help in case of need; he then lit another cigarette and went for a long stroll in the streets of London. As he was walking in the streets and squares beyond Victoria, he paused suddenly and stood. It was a quaint, quiet square, very typical of London, full of an accidental stillness. The tall, flat houses round looked at once prosperous and uninhabited; the square of shrubbery in the centre looked as deserted as a green Pacific islet. One of the four sides was much higher than the rest, like a dais; and the line of this side was broken by one of London's admirable accidents—a restaurant that looked as if it had strayed from Soho. It was an unreasonably attractive object, with dwarf plants in pots and long, striped blinds of lemon yellow and white. It stood specially high above the street, and in the usual patchwork way of London, a flight of steps from the street ran up to meet the front door almost as a fire-escape might run up to a first-floor window. Valentin stood and smoked in front of the yellow-white blinds and considered them long.

The most incredible thing about miracles is that they happen. A few clouds in heaven do come together into the staring shape of one human eye. A tree does stand up in the landscape of a doubtful journey in the exact and elaborate shape of a note of interrogation. I have seen both these things myself within the last few days. Nelson does die in the instant of victory; and a man named Williams does quite accidentally murder a man named Williamson; it sounds like a sort of infanticide. In short, there is in life an element of elfin coincidence which people reckoning on the prosaic may perpetually miss. As it has been well expressed in the paradox of Poe, wisdom should reckon on the unforeseen.

Aristide Valentin was unfathomably French; and the French intelligence is intelligence specially and solely. He was not "a thinking machine"; for that is a brainless phrase of modern fatalism and materialism. A machine only *is* a machine because it cannot think. But he was a thinking man, and a plain man at

D
49

the same time. All his wonderful successes, that looked like conjuring, had been gained by plodding logic, by clear and commonplace French thought. The French electrify the world not by starting any paradox, they electrify it by carrying out a truism. They carry a truism so far—as in the French Revolution. But exactly because Valentin understood reason, he understood the limits of reason. Only a man who knows nothing of motors talks of motoring without petrol; only a man who knows nothing of reason talks of reasoning without strong, undisputed first principles. Here he had no strong first principles. Flambeau had been missed at Harwich; and if he was in London at all, he might be anything from a tall tramp on Wimbledon Common to a tall toastmaster at the Hôtel Métropole. In such a naked state of nescience, Valentin had a view and a method of his own.

In such cases he reckoned on the unforeseen. In such cases, when he could not follow the train of the reasonable, he coldly and carefully followed the train of the unreasonable. Instead of going to the right places—banks, police-stations, rendezvous—he systematically went to the wrong places; knocked at every empty house, turned down every *cul de sac*, went up every lane blocked with rubbish, went round every crescent that led him uselessly out of the way. He defended this crazy course quite logically. He said that if one had a clue this was the worst way; but if one had no clue at all it was the best, because there was just the chance that any oddity that caught the eye of the pursuer might be the same that had caught the eye of the pursued. Somewhere a man must begin, and it had better be just where another man might stop. Something about that flight of steps up to the shop, something about the quietude and quaintness of the restaurant, roused all the detective's rare romantic fancy and made him resolve to strike at random. He went up the steps, and sitting down by the window, asked for a cup of black coffee.

It was half-way through the morning, and he had not breakfasted; the slight litter of other breakfasts stood about on the table to remind him of his hunger; and adding a poached egg to his order, he proceeded musingly to shake some white sugar into his coffee, thinking all the time about Flambeau. He remembered how Flambeau had escaped, once by a pair of nail scissors, and once by a house on fire; once by having to pay for an unstamped letter, and once by getting people to look through a telescope at a comet that might destroy the world. He thought his detective brain as good as the criminal's, which was true. But he fully realized the disadvantage. "The criminal is the creative artist; the detective only the critic," he said with a sour smile, and lifted his coffee cup to his lips slowly, and put it down very quickly. He had put salt in it.

He looked at the vessel from which the silvery powder had come; it was certainly a sugar-basin; as unmistakably meant for sugar as a champagne-bottle for champagne. He wondered why they should keep salt in it. He looked to see if there were any more orthodox vessels. Yes, there were two salt-cellars quite full. Perhaps there was some speciality in the condiment in the salt-cellars. He tasted it; it was sugar. Then he looked round at the restaurant with a refreshed air of interest, to see if there were any other traces of that singular artistic taste which puts the sugar in the salt-cellars and the salt in the sugar-basin. Except for an odd splash of some dark fluid on one of the white-papered walls, the whole place appeared neat, cheerful and ordinary. He rang the bell for the waiter.

When that official hurried up, fuzzy-haired and somewhat blear-eyed at that early hour, the detective (who was not without an appreciation of the simpler forms of humour) asked him to taste the sugar and see if it was up to the high reputation of the hotel. The result was that the waiter yawned suddenly and woke up.

"Do you play this delicate joke on your customers every morning?" inquired Valentin. "Does changing the salt and sugar never pall on you as a jest?"

The waiter, when this irony grew clearer, stammeringly assured him that the establishment had certainly no such intention; it must be a most curious mistake. He picked up the sugar-basin and looked at it; he picked up the salt-cellar and looked at that, his face growing more and more bewildered. At

51

last he abruptly excused himself, and hurrying away, returned in a few seconds with the proprietor. The proprietor also examined the sugar-basin and then the salt-cellar; the proprietor also looked bewildered.

Suddenly the waiter seemed to grow inarticulate with a rush of words.

"I zink," he stuttered eagerly, "I zink it is those two clergymen."

"What two clergymen?"

"The two clergymen," said the waiter, "that threw soup at the wall."

"Threw soup at the wall?" repeated Valentin, feeling sure this must be some Italian metaphor.

"Yes, yes," said the attendant excitedly, and pointing at the dark splash on the white paper; "threw it over there on the wall."

Valentin looked his query at the proprietor, who came to his rescue with fuller reports.

"Yes, sir," he said, "it's quite true, though I don't suppose it has anything to do with the sugar and salt. Two clergymen came in and drank soup here very early, as soon as the shutters were taken down. They were both very quiet, respectable people; one of them paid the bill and went out; the other, who seemed a slower coach altogether, was some minutes longer getting his things together. But he went at last. Only, the instant before he stepped into the street he deliberately picked up his cup, which he had only half emptied, and threw the soup slap on the wall. I was in the back room myself, and so was the waiter; so I could only rush out in time to find the wall splashed and the shop empty. It didn't do any particular damage, but it was confounded cheek; and I tried to catch the men in the street. They were too far off though; I only noticed they went round the corner into Carstairs Street."

The detective was on his feet, hat settled and stick in hand. He had already decided that in the universal darkness of his mind he could only follow the first odd finger that pointed; and this finger was odd enough. Paying his bill and clashing the glass doors behind him, he was soon swinging round into the other street.

It was fortunate that even in such fevered moments his eye was cool and quick. Something in a shop-front went by him like a mere flash; yet he went back to look at it. The shop was a popular greengrocer and fruiterer's, an array of goods set out in the open air and plainly ticketed with their names and prices. In the two most prominent compartments were two heaps, of oranges and of nuts respectively. On the heap of nuts lay a scrap of cardboard, on which was written in bold, blue chalk, "Best tangerine oranges, two a penny." On the oranges was the equally clear and exact description, "Finest Brazil nuts, 4d. a lb." M. Valentin looked at these two placards and fancied he had met this highly subtle form of humour before, and that somewhat recently. He drew the attention of the red-faced fruiterer, who was looking rather sullenly up and down the street, to this inaccuracy in his advertisements. The fruiterer said nothing, but sharply put each card into its proper place. The detective, leaning elegantly on his walking-cane, continued to scrutinize the shop. At last he said: "Pray excuse my apparent irrelevance, my good sir, but I should like to ask you a question in experimental psychology and the association of ideas."

The red-faced shopman regarded him with an eye of menace; but he continued gaily, swinging his cane. "Why," he pursued, "why are two tickets wrongly placed in a greengrocer's shop like a shovel hat that has come to London for a holiday? Or, in case I do not make myself clear, what is the mystical association which connects the idea of nuts marked as oranges with the idea of two clergymen, one tall and the other short?"

The eyes of the tradesman stood out of his head like a snail's; he really seemed for an instant likely to fling himself upon the stranger. At last he stammered angrily: "I don't know what you 'ave to do with it, but if you're one of their friends, you can tell 'em from me that I'll knock their silly 'eads off, parsons or no parsons, if they upset my apples again."

"Indeed?" asked the detective, with great sympathy. "Did they upset your apples?"

53

"One of 'em did," said the heated shopman; "rolled 'em all over the street. I'd 'ave caught the fool but for havin' to pick 'em up."

"Which way did these parsons go?" asked Valentin.

"Up that second road on the left-hand side, and then across the square," said the other promptly.

"Thanks," said Valentin, and vanished like a fairy. On the other side of the second square he found a policeman, and said: "This is urgent, constable; have you seen two clergymen in shovel hats?"

The policeman began to chuckle heavily. "I 'ave, sir; and if you arst me, one of 'em was drunk. He stood in the middle of the road that bewildered that——"

"Which way did they go?" snapped Valentin.

"They took one of them yellow buses over there," answered the man; "them that go to Hampstead."

Valentin produced his official card and said very rapidly: "Call up two of your men to come with me in pursuit," and crossed the road with such contagious energy that the ponderous policeman was moved to almost agile obedience. In a minute and a half the French detective was joined on the opposite pavement by an inspector and a man in plain clothes.

"Well, sir," began the former, with smiling importance, "and what may——?"

Valentin pointed suddenly with his cane. "I'll tell you on the top of that omnibus," he said, and was darting and dodging across the tangle of the traffic. When all three sank panting on the top seats of the yellow vehicle, the inspector said: "We could go four times as quick in a taxi."

"Quite true," replied their leader placidly, "if we only had an idea of where we were going."

"Well, where *are* you going?" asked the other, staring.

Valentin smoked frowningly for a few seconds, then; removing his cigarette, he said: "If you *know* what a man's doing, get in front of him; but if you want to guess what he's doing, keep behind him. Stray when he strays; stop when he stops; travel as slowly as he. Then you may see what he saw and may act as

54

he acted. All we can do is to keep our eyes skinned for a queer thing."

"What sort of a queer thing do you mean?" asked the inspector.

"Any sort of queer thing," answered Valentin, and relapsed into obstinate silence.

The yellow omnibus crawled up the northern roads for what seemed like hours on end; the great detective would not explain further, and perhaps his assistants felt a silent and growing desire for lunch, for the hours crept long past the normal luncheon hour, and the long roads of the North London suburbs seemed to shoot out into length after length like an infernal telescope. It was one of those journeys on which a man perpetually feels that now at last he must have come to the end of the universe, and then finds he has only come to the beginning of Tufnell Park. London died away in draggled taverns and dreary scrubs, and then was unaccountably born again in blazing high streets and blatant hotels. It was like passing through thirteen separate vulgar cities all just touching each other. But though the winter twilight was already threatening the road ahead of them, the Parisian detective still sat silent and watchful, eyeing the frontage of the streets that slid by on either side. By the time they had left Camden Town behind, the policemen were nearly asleep; at least, they gave something like a jump as Valentin leapt erect, struck a hand on each man's shoulder, and shouted to the driver to stop.

They tumbled down the steps into the road without realizing why they had been dislodged; when they looked round for enlightenment they found Valentin triumphantly pointing his finger towards a window on the left side of the road. It was a large window, forming part of the long façade of a gilt and palatial public-house; it was the part reserved for respectable dining, and labelled "Restaurant". This window, like all the rest along the frontage of the hotel, was of frosted and figured glass, but in the middle of it was a big, black smash, like a star in the ice.

"Our cue at last," cried Valentin, waving his stick; "the place with the broken window."

"What window? What cue?" asked his principal assistant. "Why, what proof is there that this has anything to do with them?"

Valentin almost broke his bamboo stick with rage.

"Proof!" he cried. "Good God! the man is looking for proof! Why, of course, the chances are twenty to one that it has *nothing* to do with them. But what else can we do? Don't you see we must either follow one wild possibility or else go home to bed?" He banged his way into the restaurant, followed by his companions, and they were soon seated at a late luncheon at a little table, and looking at the star of smashed glass from the inside. Not that it was very informative to them even then.

"Got your window broken, I see," said Valentin to the waiter, as he paid his bill.

"Yes, sir," answered the attendant, bending busily over the change, to which Valentin silently added an enormous tip. The waiter straightened himself with mild but unmistakable animation.

"Ah, yes, sir," he said. "Very odd thing that, sir."

"Indeed? Tell us about it," said the detective with careless curiosity.

"Well, two gents in black came in," said the waiter; "two of those foreign parsons that are running about. They had a cheap and quiet little lunch, and one of them paid for it and went out. The other was just going out to join him when I looked at my change again and found he'd paid me more than three times too much. 'Here,' I says to the chap who was nearly out of the door, 'you've paid too much.' 'Oh,' he says, very cool, 'have we?' 'Yes,' I says, and picks up the bill to show him. Well, that was a knock-out."

"What do you mean?" asked his interlocutor.

"Well, I'd have sworn on seven Bibles that I'd put 4s. on that bill. But now I saw I'd put 14s., as plain as paint."

"Well?" cried Valentin moving slowly, but with burning eyes, "and then?"

"The parson at the door he says, all serene, 'Sorry to confuse your accounts, but it'll pay for the window.' 'What window?' I says. 'The one I'm going to break,' he says, and smashed that blessed pane with his umbrella."

All the inquirers made an exclamation; and the inspector said under his breath: "Are we after escaped lunatics?" The waiter went on with some relish for the ridiculous story:

"I was so knocked silly for a second, I couldn't do anything. The man marched out of the place and joined his friend just round the corner. Then they went so quick up Bullock Street that I couldn't catch them, though I ran round the bars to do it."

"Bullock Street," said the detective, and shot up that thoroughfare as quickly as the strange couple he pursued.

Their journey now took them through bare brick ways like tunnels; streets with few lights and even with few windows; streets that seemed built out of the blank backs of everything and everywhere. Dusk was deepening, and it was not easy even for the London policemen to guess in what exact direction they were treading. The inspector, however, was pretty certain that they would eventually strike some part of Hampstead Heath. Abruptly one bulging and gas-lit window broke the blue twilight like a bull's-eye lantern; and Valentin stopped an instant before a little garish sweetstuff shop. After an instant's hesitation he went in; he stood amid the gaudy colours of the confectionery with entire gravity and bought thirteen chocolate cigars with a certain care. He was clearly preparing an opening; but he did not need one.

An angular, elderly young woman in the shop had regarded his elegant appearance with a merely automatic inquiry; but when she saw the door behind him blocked with the blue uniform of the inspector, her eyes seemed to wake up.

"Oh," she said, "if you've come about that parcel, I've sent it off already."

"Parcel!" repeated Valentin; and it was his turn to look inquiring.

"I mean the parcel the gentleman left—the clergyman gentleman."

"For goodness' sake," said Valentin, leaning forward with

57

his first real confession of eagerness, "for Heaven's sake tell us what happened exactly."

"Well," said the woman, a little doubtfully, "the clergymen came in about half an hour ago and bought some peppermints and talked a bit, and then went off towards the Heath. But a second after, one of them runs back into the shop and says, 'Have I left a parcel?' Well, I looked everywhere and couldn't see one; so he says, 'Never mind; but if it should turn up, please post it to this address,' and he left me the address and a shilling for my trouble. And sure enough, though I thought I'd looked everywhere, I found he'd left a brown-paper parcel, so I posted it to the place he said. I can't remember the address now; it was somewhere in Westminster. But as the thing seemed so important, I thought perhaps the police had come about it."

"So they have," said Valentin shortly. "Is Hampstead Heath near here?"

"Straight on for fifteen minutes," said the woman, "and you'll come right out on the open." Valentin sprang out of the shop and began to run. The other detectives followed him at a reluctant trot.

The street they threaded was so narrow and shut in by shadows that when they came out unexpectedly into the void common and vast sky they were startled to find evening still so light and clear. A perfect dome of peacock-green sank into gold amid the blackening trees and the dark violet distances. The glowing green tint was just deep enough to pick out in points of crystal one or two stars. All that was left of the daylight lay in a golden glitter across the edge of Hampstead and that popular hollow which is called the Vale of Health. The holiday makers who roam this region had not wholly dispersed: a few couples sat shapelessly on benches; and here and there a distant girl still shrieked in one of the swings. The glory of heaven deepened and darkened around the sublime vulgarity of man; and standing on the slope and looking across the valley, Valentin beheld the thing which he sought.

Among the black and breaking groups in that distance was one especially black which did not break—a group of two

58

figures clerically clad. Though they seemed as small as insects, Valentin could see that one of them was much smaller than the other. Though the other had a student's stoop and an inconspicuous manner, he could see that the man was well over six feet high. He shut his teeth and went forward, whirling his stick impatiently. By the time he had substantially diminished the distance and magnified the two black figures as in a vast microscope, he had perceived something else; something which startled him, and yet which he had somehow expected. Whoever was the tall priest, there could be no doubt about the identity of the short one. It was his friend of the Harwich train, the stumpy little *curé* of Essex whom he had warned about his brown-paper parcels.

Now, as far as this went, everything fitted in finally and rationally enough. Valentin had learned by his inquiries that morning that a Father Brown from Essex was bringing up a silver cross with sapphires, a relic of considerable value, to show some of the foreign priests at the congress. This undoubtedly was the "silver with blue stones"; and Father Brown undoubtedly was the little greenhorn in the train. Now there was nothing wonderful about the fact that what Valentin had found out Flambeau had also found out; Flambeau found out everything. Also there was nothing wonderful in the fact that when Flambeau heard of a sapphire cross he should try to steal it; that was the most natural thing in all natural history. And most certainly there was nothing wonderful about the fact that Flambeau should have it all his own way with such a silly sheep as the man with the umbrella and the parcels. He was the sort of man whom anybody could lead on a string to the North Pole; it was not surprising that an actor like Flambeau, dressed as another priest, could lead him to Hampstead Heath. So far the crime seemed clear enough; and while the detective pitied the priest for his helplessness, he almost despised Flambeau for condescending to so gullible a victim. But when Valentin thought of all that had happened in between, of all that had led him to his triumph, he racked his brains for the smallest rhyme or reason in it. What had the stealing of a blue-and-silver cross from a priest from Essex to do with chucking soup at wall-paper? What had it to do with calling nuts oranges, or with paying for windows first and breaking them afterwards? He had come to the end of his chase; yet somehow he had missed the middle of it. When he failed (which was seldom), he had usually grasped the clue, but nevertheless missed the criminal. Here he had grasped the criminal, but still he could not grasp the clue.

The two figures that they followed were crawling like black flies across the huge green contour of a hill. They were evidently sunk in conversation, and perhaps did not notice where they were going; but they were certainly going to the wilder and more silent heights of the Heath. As their pursuers gained on them, the latter had to use the undignified attitudes of the deer-stalker, to crouch behind clumps of trees and even to crawl prostrate in deep grass. By these ungainly ingenuities the hunters even came close enough to the quarry to hear the murmur of the discussion but no word could be distinguished except the word "reason" recurring frequently in a high and almost childish voice. Once, over an abrupt dip of land and a dense tangle of thickets, the detectives actually lost the two figures they were following. They did not find the trail again for an agonizing ten minutes, and then it led round the brow of a great dome of hill overlooking an amphitheatre of rich and desolate sunset scenery. Under a tree in this commanding yet neglected spot was an old ramshackle wooden seat. On this seat sat the two priests still in serious speech together. The gorgeous green and gold still clung to the darkening horizon; but the dome above was turning slowly from peacock-green to peacock-blue, and the stars detached themselves more and more like solid jewels. Mutely motioning to his followers, Valentin contrived to creep up behind the big branching tree, and, standing there in deathly silence, heard the words of the strange priests for the first time.

After he had listened for a minute and a half, he was gripped by a devilish doubt. Perhaps he had dragged the two English policemen to the wastes of a nocturnal heath on an errand no saner than seeking figs on thistles. For the two priests were talking exactly like priests, piously, with learning and leisure, about the most aerial enigmas of theology. The little Essex priest spoke the more simply, with his round face turned to the strengthening stars; the other talked with his head bowed, as if he were not even worthy to look at them. But no more innocently clerical conversation could have been heard in any white Italian cloister or black Spanish cathedral.

The first he heard was the tail of one of Father Brown's sentences, which ended: ". . . what they really meant in the Middle Ages by the heavens being incorruptible."

The taller priest nodded his bowed head and said:

"Ah, yes, these modern infidels appeal to their reason; but who can look at those millions of worlds and not feel that there may well be wonderful universes above us where reason is utterly unreasonable?"

"No," said the other priest; "reason is always reasonable, even in the last limbo, in the lost borderland of things. I know that people charge the Church with lowering reason, but it is just the other way. Alone on earth, the Church makes reason really supreme. Alone on earth, the Church affirms that God himself is bound by reason."

The other priest raised his austere face to the spangled sky and said:

"Yet who knows if in that infinite universe——?"

"Only infinite physically," said the little priest, turning sharply in his seat, "not infinite in the sense of escaping from the laws of truth."

Valentin behind his tree was tearing his finger-nails with silent fury. He seemed almost to hear the sniggers of the English detectives whom he had brought so far on a fantastic guess only to listen to the metaphysical gossip of two mild old parsons. In his impatience he lost the equally elaborate answer of the tall cleric, and when he listened again it was again Father Brown who was speaking:

"Reason and justice grip the remotest and the loneliest star. Look at those stars. Don't they look as if they were single diamonds and sapphires? Well, you can imagine any mad botany or geology you please. Think of forests of adamant with leaves of brilliants. Think, the moon is a blue moon, a single elephantine sapphire. But don't fancy that all that frantic astronomy would make the smallest difference to the reason and justice of conduct. On plains of opal, under cliffs cut out of pearl, you would still find a notice-board, 'Thou shalt not steal.' "

Valentin was just in the act of rising from his rigid and crouching attitude and creeping away as softly as might be, felled by the one great folly of his life. But something in the very silence of the tall priest made him stop until the latter spoke. When at last he did speak, he said simply, his head bowed and his hands on his knees:

"Well, I still think that other worlds may perhaps rise higher than our reason. The mystery of heaven is unfathomable, and I for once can only bow my head."

Then, with brow yet bent and without changing by the faintest shade his attitude or voice, he added:

"Just hand over that sapphire cross of yours, will you? We're all alone here, and I could pull you to pieces like a straw doll."

The utterly unaltered voice and attitude added a strange violence to that shocking change of speech. But the guarder of the relic only seemed to turn his head by the smallest section of the compass. He seemed still to have a somewhat foolish face turned to the stars. Perhaps he had not understood. Or, perhaps, he had understood and sat rigid with terror.

"Yes," said the tall priest, in the same low voice and in the same still posture, "yes, I am Flambeau."

Then, after a pause, he said:

"Come, will you give me that cross?"

"No," said the other, and the monosyllable had an odd sound.

Flambeau suddenly flung off all his pontifical pretensions. The great robber leaned back in his seat and laughed low but long.

"No," he cried; "you won't give it me, you proud prelate. You won't give it me, you little celibate simpleton. Shall I tell you why you won't give it me? Because I've got it already in my own breast-pocket."

The small man from Essex turned what seemed to be a dazed face in the dusk, and said, with the timid eagerness of *The Private Secretary*:[1]

"Are—are you sure?"

Flambeau yelled with delight.

"Really, you're as good as a three-act farce," he cried. "Yes, you turnip, I am quite sure. I had the sense to make a duplicate of the right parcel, and now, my friend, you've got the duplicate, and I've got the jewels. An old dodge, Father Brown—a very old dodge."

"Yes," said Father Brown, and passed his hand through his hair with the same strange vagueness of manner. "Yes, I've heard of it before."

The colossus of crime leaned over to the little rustic priest with a sort of sudden interest.

"*You* have heard of it?" he asked. "Where have *you* heard of it?"

"Well, I mustn't tell you his name, of course," said the little man simply. "He was a penitent, you know. He had lived prosperously for about twenty years entirely on duplicate brown-paper parcels. And so, you see, when I began to suspect you, I thought of this poor chap's way of doing it at once."

"Began to suspect me?" repeated the outlaw with increased intensity. "Did you really have the gumption to suspect me just because I brought you up to this bare part of the heath?"

"No, no," said Brown with an air of apology. "You see, I suspected you when we first met. It's that little bulge up the sleeve where you people have the spiked bracelet."

"How in Tartarus," cried Flambeau, "did you ever hear of the spiked bracelet?"

"Oh, one's little flock, you know!" said Father Brown, arching his eyebrows rather blankly. "When I was a curate in Hartlepool, there were three of them with spiked bracelets. So,

[1] This popular stage success of the late 19th century was adapted by the actor Charles Hawtrey from Von Moser's *Bibliothekar*.

63

as I suspected you from the first, don't you see, I made sure that the cross should go safe, anyhow. I'm afraid I watched you, you know. So at last I saw you change the parcels. Then, don't you see, I changed them back again. And then I left the right one behind."

"Left it behind?" repeated Flambeau, and for the first time there was another note in his voice beside his triumph.

"Well, it was like this," said the little priest, speaking in the same unaffected way. "I went back to that sweet-shop and asked if I'd left a parcel, and gave them a particular address if it turned up. Well, I knew I hadn't; but when I went away again I did. So, instead of running after me with that valuable parcel, they have sent it flying to a friend of mine in Westminster." Then he added rather sadly: "I learnt that, too, from a poor fellow in Hartlepool. He used to do it with handbags he stole at railway stations, but he's in a monastery now. Oh, one gets to know, you know," he added, rubbing his head again with the same sort of desperate apology. "We can't help being priests. People come and tell us these things."

Flambeau tore a brown-paper parcel out of his inner pocket and rent it in pieces. There was nothing but paper and sticks of lead inside it. He sprang to his feet with a gigantic gesture, and cried:

"I don't believe you. I don't believe a bumpkin like you could manage all that. I believe you've still got the stuff on you, and if you don't give it up—why, we're all alone, and I'll take it by force!"

"No," said Father Brown simply, and stood up also; "you won't take it by force. First, because I really haven't still got it. And, second, because we are not alone."

Flambeau stopped in his stride forward.

"Behind that tree," said Father Brown, pointing, "are two strong policemen and the greatest detective alive. How did they come here, do you ask? Why, I brought them, of course! How did I do it? Why, I'll tell you if you like! Lord bless you, we have to know twenty such things when we work among the criminal classes! Well, I wasn't sure you were a thief, and it would never do to make a scandal against one of our own clergy. So I just tested you to see if anything would make you show yourself. A man generally makes a small scene if he finds salt in his coffee; if he doesn't, he has some reason for keeping quiet. I changed the salt and sugar, and *you* kept quiet. A man generally objects if his bill is three times too big. If he pays it, he has some motive for passing unnoticed. I altered your bill, and *you* paid it."

The world seemed waiting for Flambeau to leap like a tiger. But he was held back as by a spell; he was stunned with the utmost curiosity.

"Well," went on Father Brown, with lumbering lucidity, "as you wouldn't leave any tracks for the police, of course somebody had to. At every place we went to, I took care to do something that would get us talked about for the rest of the day. I didn't do much harm—a splashed wall, spilt apples, a broken window; but I saved the cross, as the cross will always be saved. It is at Westminster by now. I rather wonder you didn't stop it with the Donkey's Whistle."

"With the what?" asked Flambeau.

"I'm glad you've never heard of it," said the priest, making a face. "It's a foul thing. I'm sure you're too good a man for a Whistler. I couldn't have countered it even with the Spots myself; I'm not strong enough in the legs."

"What on earth are you talking about?" asked the other.

"Well, I did think you'd know the Spots," said Father Brown, agreeably surprised. "Oh, you can't have gone so very wrong yet!"

"How in blazes do you know all these horrors?" cried Flambeau.

The shadow of a smile crossed the round, simple face of his clerical opponent.

"Oh, by being a celibate simpleton, I suppose," he said. "Has it never struck you that a man who does next to nothing but hear men's real sins is not likely to be wholly unaware of human evil? But, as a matter of fact, another part of my trade, too, made me sure you weren't a priest."

E   65

"What?" asked the thief, almost gaping.

"You attacked reason," said Father Brown. "It's bad theology."

And even as he turned away to collect his property, the three policemen came out from under the twilight trees. Flambeau was an artist and a sportsman. He stepped back and swept Valentin a great bow.

"Do not bow to me, *mon ami*," said Valentin, with silver clearness. "Let us both bow to our master."

And they both stood an instant uncovered, while the little Essex priest blinked about for his umbrella.

From *The Father Brown Stories*
(Cassell & Co. Ltd.)

The Secret Garden

Aristide Valentin, Chief of the Paris Police, was late for his dinner, and some of his guests began to arrive before him. These were, however, reassured by his confidential servant, Ivan, the old man with a scar and a face almost as grey as his moustaches, who always sat at a table in the entrance hall—a hall hung with weapons. Valentin's house was perhaps as peculiar and celebrated as its master. It was an old house, with high walls and tall poplars almost overhanging the Seine; but the oddity—and perhaps the police value—of its architecture was this: that there was no ultimate exit at all except through this front door, which was guarded by Ivan and the armoury. The garden was large and elaborate, and there were many exits from the house into the garden. But there was no exit from the garden into the world outside; all round it ran a tall, smooth unscalable wall with special spikes at the top; no bad garden, perhaps, for a man to reflect in whom some hundred criminals had sworn to kill.

As Ivan explained to the guests, their host had telephoned that he was detained for ten minutes. He was, in truth, making some last arrangements about executions and such ugly things; and though these duties were rootedly repulsive to him, he always performed them with precision. Ruthless in the pursuit of criminals, he was very mild about their punishment. Since he had been supreme over French—and largely over European—police methods, his great influence had been honourably used for the mitigation of sentences and the purification of prisons. He was one of the great humanitarian French freethinkers; and the only thing wrong with them is that they make mercy even colder than justice.

67

When Valentin arrived he was already dressed in black clothes and the red rosette—an elegant figure, his dark beard already streaked with grey. He went straight through his house to his study, which opened on the grounds behind. The garden door of it was open, and after he had carefully locked his box in its official place, he stood for a few seconds at the open door looking out upon the garden. A sharp moon was fighting with the flying rags and tatters of a storm, and Valentin regarded it with a witsfulness unusual in such scientific natures as his. Perhaps such scientific natures have some psychic prevision of the most tremendous problem of their lives. From any such occult mood, at least, he quickly recovered, for he knew he was late and that his guests had already begun to arrive. A glance at his drawing-room when he entered it was enough to make certain that his principal guest was not there, at any rate. He saw all the other pillars of the little party; he saw Lord Galloway, the English Ambassador—a choleric old man with a russet face like an apple, wearing the blue ribbon of the Garter. He saw Lady Galloway, slim and thread-like with silver hair and a face sensitive and superior. He saw her daughter, Lady Margaret Graham, a pale and pretty girl with an elfish face and copper-coloured hair. He saw the Duchess of Mont St. Michel, black-eyed and opulent, and with her her two daughters, black-eyed and opulent also. He saw Dr. Simon, a typical French scientist, with glasses, a pointed brown beard, and a forehead barred with those parallel wrinkles which are the penalty of superciliousness, since they come through constantly elevating the eyebrows. He saw Father Brown of Cobhole, in Essex, whom he had recently met in England. He saw—perhaps with more interest than any of those—a tall man in uniform, who had bowed to the Galloways without receiving any very hearty acknowledgement, and who now advanced alone to pay his respects to his host. This was Commandant O'Brien, of the French Foreign Legion. He was a slim yet somewhat swaggering figure, clean-shaven, dark-haired, and blue-eyed, and as seemed natural in an officer of that famous regiment of victorious failures and successful suicides, he had an air at once

68

dashing and melancholy. He was by birth an Irish gentleman, and in boyhood had known the Galloways—especially Margaret Graham. He had left his country after some crash of debts, and now expressed his complete freedom from British etiquette by swinging about in uniform, sabre and spurs. When he bowed to the Ambassador's family, Lord and Lady Galloway bent stiffly, and Lady Margaret looked away.

But for whatever old causes such people might be interested in each other, their distinguished host was not specially interested in them. Not one of them at least was in his eyes the guest of the evening. Valentin was expecting, for special reasons, a man of world-wide fame, whose friendship he had secured during some of his great detective tours and triumphs in the United States. He was expecting Julius K. Brayne, that multimillionaire whose colossal and even crushing endowments of small religions have occasioned so much easy sport and easier solemnity for the American and English papers. Nobody could quite make out whether Mr. Brayne was an atheist or a Mormon, or a Christian Scientist; but he was ready to pour money into any intellectual vessel, so long as it was an untried vessel. One of his hobbies was to wait for the American Shakespeare—a hobby more patient than angling. He admired Walt Whitman, but thought that Luke P. Tanner, of Paris, Pa., was more "progressive" than Whitman any day. He liked anything that he thought "progressive". He thought Valentin "progressive", thereby doing him a grave injustice.

The solid appearance of Julius K. Brayne in the room was as decisive as a dinner bell. He had this great quality, which very few of us can claim that his presence was as big as his absence. He was a huge fellow, as fat as he was tall, clad in complete evening black, without so much relief as a watch-chain or a ring. His hair was white and well brushed back like a German's; his face was red, fierce and cherubic, with one dark tuft under the lower lip that threw up that otherwise infantile visage with an effect theatrical and even Mephistophelean. Not long, however, did that *salon* merely stare at the celebrated American; his lateness had already become a domestic problem, and he was sent with all speed into the dining-room with Lady Galloway upon his arm.

Except on one point the Galloways were genial and casual enough. So long as Lady Margaret did not take the arm of that adventurer O'Brien her father was quite satisfied; and she had not done so; she had decorously gone in with Dr. Simon. Nevertheless, old Lord Galloway was restless and almost rude. He was diplomatic enough during dinner, but when, over the cigars, three of the younger men—Simon the doctor, Brown the priest, and the detrimental O'Brien, the exile in a foreign uniform—all melted away to mix with the ladies or smoke in the conservatory, then the English diplomatist grew very undiplomatic indeed. He was stung every sixty seconds with the thought that the scamp O'Brien might be signalling to Margaret somehow; he did not attempt to imagine how. He was left over the coffee with Brayne, the hoary Yankee who believed in all religions, and Valentin, the grizzled Frenchman who believed in none. They could argue with each other, but neither could appeal to him. After a time this "progressive" logomachy had reached a crisis of tedium; Lord Galloway got up also and sought the drawing-room. He lost his way in long passages for some six or eight minutes: till he heard the high-pitched, didactic voice of the doctor, and then the dull voice of the priest, followed by general laughter. They also, he thought with a curse, were probably arguing about "science and religion". But the instant he opened the *salon* door he saw only one thing—he saw what was not there. He saw that Commandant O'Brien was absent, and that Lady Margaret was absent, too.

Rising impatiently from the drawing-room, as he had from the dining-room, he stamped along the passage once more. His notion of protecting his daughter from the Irish-Algerian ne'er-do-well had become something central and even mad in his mind. As he went towards the back of the house, where was Valentin's study, he was surprised to meet his daughter, who swept past with a white, scornful face, which was a second enigma. If she had been with O'Brien, where was O'Brien? If she had not been with O'Brien, where had she been? With a sort of senile and passionate suspicion he groped his way to the dark back parts of the mansion, and eventually found a servants' entrance that opened on to the garden. The moon with her scimitar had now ripped up and rolled away all the storm-wrack. The argent light lit up all four corners of the garden. A tall figure in blue was striding across the lawn towards the study door; a glint of moonlit silver on his facings picked him out as Commandant O'Brien.

He vanished through the french windows into the house, leaving Lord Galloway in an indescribable temper, at once virulent and vague. The blue-and-silver garden, like a scene in a theatre, seemed to taunt him with all that tyrannic tenderness against which his worldly authority was at war. The length and grace of the Irishman's stride enraged him as if he were a rival instead of a father; the moonlight maddened him. He was trapped as if by magic into a garden of troubadours, a Watteau fairyland; and, willing to shake off such amorous imbecilities by speech, he stepped briskly after his enemy. As he did so he tripped over some tree or stone in the grass; looked down at it first with irritation and then a second time with curiosity. The next instant the moon and the tall poplars looked at an unusual sight—an elderly English diplomatist running hard and crying or bellowing as he ran.

His hoarse shouts brought a pale face to the study door, the beaming glasses and worried brow of Dr. Simon, who heard the nobleman's first clear words. Lord Galloway was crying: "A corpse in the grass—a blood-stained corpse." O'Brien at least had gone utterly from his mind.

"We must tell Valentin at once," said the doctor, when the other had brokenly described all that he had dared to examine. "It is fortunate that he is here"; and even as he spoke the great detective entered the study, attracted by the cry. It was almost amusing to note his typical transformation; he had come with the common concern of a host and a gentleman, fearing that some guest or servant was ill. When he was told the gory fact, he turned with all his gravity instantly bright and business-like; for this, however abrupt and awful, was his business.

"Strange, gentlemen," he said, as they hurried out into the garden, "that I should have hunted mysteries all over the earth, and now one comes and settles in my own backyard. But where is the place?" They crossed the lawn less easily, as a slight mist had begun to rise from the river; but under the guidance of the shaken Galloway they found the body sunken in deep grass— the body of a very tall and broad-shouldered man. He lay face downwards, so they could only see that his big shoulders were clad in black cloth, and that his big head was bald, except for a wisp or two of brown hair that clung to his skull like wet sea- weed. A scarlet serpent of blood crawled from under his fallen face.

"At least," said Simon, with a deep and singular intonation, "he is none of our party."

"Examine him, doctor," cried Valentin rather sharply. "He may not be dead."

The doctor bent down. "He is not quite cold, but I am afraid he is dead enough," he answered. "Just help me to lift him up."

They lifted him carefully an inch from the ground, and all doubts as to his being really dead were settled at once and frightfully. The head fell away. It had been entirely sundered from the body; whoever had cut his throat had managed to sever the neck as well. Even Valentin was slightly shocked. "He must have been as strong as a gorilla," he muttered.

Not without a shiver, though he was used to anatomical abortions, Dr. Simon lifted the head. It was slightly slashed about the neck and jaw, but the face was substantially unhurt. It was a ponderous, yellow face, at once sunken and swollen, with a hawk-like nose and heavy lids—the face of a wicked Roman emperor, with, perhaps, a distant touch of a Chinese emperor. All present seemed to look at it with the coldest eye of ignorance. Nothing else could be noted about the man except that, as they had lifted his body, they had seen underneath it the white gleam of a shirtfront defaced with a red gleam of blood. As Dr. Simon said, the man had never been of their party. But he might very well have been trying to join it, for he had come dressed for such an occasion.

Valentin went down on his hands and knees and examined with his closest professional attention the grass and ground for some twenty yards round the body, in which he was assisted less skilfully by the doctor, and quite vaguely by the English lord. Nothing rewarded their grovellings except a few twigs, snapped or chopped into very small lengths, which Valentin lifted for an instant's examination, and then tossed away.

"Twigs," he said gravely; "twigs, and a total stranger with his head cut off; that is all there is on this lawn."

There was an almost creepy stillness, and then the unnerved Galloway called out sharply:

"Who's that? Who's that over there by the garden wall?"

A small figure with a foolishly large head drew waveringly near them in the moonlit haze; looked for an instant like a goblin, but turned out to be the harmless little priest whom they had left in the drawing-room.

"I say," he said meekly, "there are no gates to this garden, do you know."

Valentin's black brows had come together somewhat crossly, as they did on principle at the sight of the cassock. But he was far too just a man to deny the relevance of the remark. "You are right," he said. "Before we find out how he came to be killed, we may have to find out how he came to be here. Now listen to me, gentlemen. If it can be done without prejudice to my position and duty, we shall all agree that certain distinguished names might well be kept out of this. There are ladies, gentlemen, and there is a foreign ambassador. If we must mark it down as a crime, then it must be followed up as a crime. But till then I can use my own discretion. I am the head of the police; I am so public that I can afford to be private. Please Heaven, I will clear every one of my own guests before I call in my men to look for anybody else. Gentlemen, upon your honour, you will none of you leave the house till tomorrow at noon; there are bedrooms for all. Simon, I think you know where to find my man, Ivan, in the front hall; he is a confidential man. Tell him to leave another servant on guard and come to me at once. Lord Galloway, you are certainly the best person to tell the ladies what has happened, and prevent a panic. They also must stay. Father Brown and I will remain with the body."

When this spirit of the captain spoke in Valentin he was obeyed like a bugle. Dr. Simon went through to the armoury and routed out Ivan, the public detective's private detective. Galloway went to the drawing-room and told the terrible news tactfully enough, so that by the time the company assembled there the ladies were already startled and already soothed. Meanwhile the good priest and the good atheist stood at the head and foot of the dead man motionless in the moonlight, like symbolic statues of their two philosophies of death.

Ivan, the confidential man with the scar and the moustaches, came out of the house like a cannon ball, and came racing across the lawn to Valentin like a dog to his master. His livid face was quite lively with the glow of this domestic detective story, and it was with almost unpleasant eagerness that he asked his master's permission to examine the remains.

"Yes; look, if you like, Ivan," said Valentin, "but don't be long. We must go in and thrash this out in the house."

Ivan lifted his head, and then almost let it drop.

"Why," he gasped, "it's—no, it isn't; it can't be. Do you know this man, sir?"

"No," said Valentin indifferently; "we had better go inside."

Between them they carried the corpse to a sofa in the study, and then all made their way to the drawing-room.

The detective sat down at a desk quietly, and even with hesitation; but his eye was the iron eye of a judge at assize. He made a few rapid notes upon paper in front of him, and then said shortly: "Is everybody here?"

"Not Mr. Brayne," said the Duchess of Mont St. Michel, looking round.

"No," said Lord Galloway, in a hoarse, harsh voice. "And not Mr. Neil O'Brien, I fancy. I saw that gentleman walking in the garden when the corpse was still warm."

"Ivan," said the detective, "go and fetch Commandant O'Brien and Mr. Brayne. Mr. Brayne, I know, is finishing a cigar in the dining-room; Commandant O'Brien, I think, is walking up and down the conservatory. I am not sure."

The faithful attendant flashed from the room, and before anyone could stir or speak Valentin went on with the same soldierly swiftness of exposition.

"Everyone here knows that a dead man has been found in the garden, his head cut clean from his body. Dr. Simon, you have examined it. Do you think that to cut a man's throat like that would need great force? Or, perhaps, only a very sharp knife?"

"I should say that it could not be done with a knife at all," said the pale doctor.

"Have you any thought," resumed Valentin, "of a tool with which it could be done?"

"Speaking within modern probabilities, I really haven't," said the doctor, arching his painful brows. "It's not easy to hack a neck through even clumsily, and this was a very clean cut. It could be done with a battle-axe or an old headsman's axe, or an old two-handed sword."

"But, good heavens!" cried the Duchess, almost in hysterics; "there aren't any two-handed swords and battle-axes round here."

Valentin was still busy with the paper in front of him. "Tell me," he said, still writing rapidly, "could it have been done with a long French cavalry sabre?"

A low knocking came at the door, which for some unreasonable reason, curdled everyone's blood like the knocking in *Macbeth*. Amid that frozen silence Dr. Simon managed to say: "A sabre —yes, I suppose it could."

"Thank you," said Valentin. "Come in, Ivan."

The confidential Ivan opened the door and ushered in Commandant Neil O'Brien, whom he had found at last pacing the garden again.

The Irish officer stood disordered and defiant on the threshhold. "What do you want with me?" he cried.

"Please sit down," said Valentin in pleasant, level tones. "Why, you aren't wearing your sword! Where is it?"

"I left it on the library table," said O'Brien, his brogue

deepening in his disturbed mood. "It was a nuisance, it was getting——"

"Ivan," said Valentin: "please go and get the Commandant's sword from the library." Then, as the servant vanished: "Lord Galloway says he saw you leaving the garden just before he found the corpse. What were you doing in the garden?"

The commandant flung himself recklessly into a chair. "Oh," he cried in pure Irish; "admirin' the moon. Communing with Nature, me boy."

A heavy silence sank and endured, and at the end of it came again that trivial and terrible knocking. Ivan reappeared, carrying an empty steel scabbard. "This is all I can find," he said.

"Put it on the table," said Valentin, without looking up.

There was an inhuman silence in the room, like that sea of inhuman silence round the dock of the condemned murderer. The Duchess's weak exclamations had long ago died away. Lord Galloway's swollen hatred was satisfied and even sobered. The voice that came was quite unexpected.

"I think I can tell you," cried Lady Margaret, in that clear, quivering voice with which a courageous woman speaks publicly. "I can tell you what Mr. O'Brien was doing in the garden, since he is bound to silence. He was asking me to marry him. I refused; I said in my family circumstances I could give him nothing but my respect. He was a little angry at that; he did not seem to think much of my respect. I wonder," she added, with rather a wan smile, "if he will care at all for it now. For I offer it him now. I will swear anywhere that he never did a thing like this."

Lord Galloway had edged up to his daughter, and was intimidating her in what he imagined to be an undertone. "Hold your tongue, Maggie," he said in a thunderous whisper. "Why should you shield the fellow? Where's his sword? Where's his confounded cavalry——"

He stopped because of the singular stare with which his daughter was regarding him, a look that was indeed a lurid magnet for the whole group.

"You old fool!" she said, in a low voice without pretence of

76

piety; "what do you suppose you are trying to prove? I tell you this man was innocent while with me. But if he wasn't innocent, he was still with me. If he murdered a man in the garden, who was it who must have seen—who must at least have known? Do you hate Neil so much as to put your own daughter——"

Lady Galloway screamed. Everyone else sat tingling at the touch of those satanic tragedies that have been between lovers before now. They saw the proud, white face of the Scotch aristocrat and her lover, the Irish adventurer, like old portraits in a dark house. The long silence was full of formless historical memories of murdered husbands and poisonous paramours.

In the centre of this morbid silence an innocent voice said: "Was it a very long cigar?"

The change of thought was so sharp that they had to look round to see who had spoken.

"I mean," said little Father Brown, from the corner of the room, "I mean that cigar Mr. Brayne is finishing. It seems nearly as long as a walking-stick."

Despite the irrelevance there was assent as well as irritation in Valentin's face as he lifted his head.

"Quite right," he remarked sharply. "Ivan, go and see about Mr. Brayne again, and bring him here at once."

The instant the factotum had closed the door, Valentin addressed the girl with an entirely new earnestness.

"Lady Margaret," he said, "we all feel, I am sure, both gratitude and admiration for your act in rising above your lower dignity and explaining the Commandant's conduct. But there is a hiatus still. Lord Galloway, I understand, met you passing from the study to the drawing-room, and it was only some minutes afterwards that he found the garden and the Commandant still walking there."

"You have to remember," replied Margaret, with a faint irony in her voice, "that I had just refused him, so we should scarcely have come back arm in arm. He is a gentleman, anyhow; and he loitered behind—and so got charged with murder."

"In those few moments," said Valentin gravely, "he might really——"

77

The knock came again, and Ivan put in his scarred face.

"Beg pardon, sir," he said, "but Mr. Brayne has left the house."

"Left!" cried Valentin, and rose for the first time to his feet.

"Gone. Scooted. Evaporated," replied Ivan, in humorous French. "His hat and coat are gone, too; and I'll tell you something to cap it all. I ran outside the house to find any traces of him, and I found one, and a big trace, too."

"What do you mean?" asked Valentin.

"I'll show you," said his servant, and reappeared with a flashing naked cavalry sabre, streaked with blood about the point and edge. Everyone in the room eyed it as if it were a thunderbolt; but the experienced Ivan went on quite quietly:

"I found this," he said, "flung among the bushes fifty yards up the road to Paris. In other words, I found it just where your respectable Mr. Brayne threw it when he ran away."

There was again a silence, but of a new sort. Valentin took the sabre, examined it, reflected with unaffected concentration of thought, and then turned a respectful face to O'Brien. "Commandant," he said, "we trust you will always produce this weapon if it is wanted for police examination. Meanwhile," he added, slapping the steel back in the ringing scabbard, "let me return you your sword."

At the military symbolism of the action the audience could hardly refrain from applause.

For Neil O'Brien, indeed, that gesture was the turning-point of existence. By the time he was wandering in the mysterious garden again in the colours of the morning the tragic futility of his ordinary mien had fallen from him; he was a man with many reasons for happiness. Lord Galloway was a gentleman, and had offered him an apology. Lady Margaret was something better than a lady, a woman at least, and had perhaps given him something better than an apology, as they drifted among the old flower-beds before breakfast. The whole company was more light-hearted and humane, for though the riddle of the death remained, the load of suspicion was lifted off them all, and sent flying off to Paris with the strange millionaire—a man they hardly knew. The devil was cast out of the house—he had cast himself out.

Still, the riddle remained; and when O'Brien threw himself on a garden seat beside Dr. Simon, that keenly scientific person at once resumed it. He did not get much talk out of O'Brien, whose thoughts were on pleasanter things.

"I can't say it interests me much," said the Irishman frankly, "especially as it seems pretty plain now. Apparently Brayne hated this stranger for some reason; lured him into the garden, and killed him with my sword. Then he fled to the city, tossing the sword away as he went. By the way, Ivan tells me the dead man had a Yankee dollar in his pocket. So he was a countryman of Brayne's, and that seems to clinch it. I don't see any difficulties about the business."

"There are five colossal difficulties," said the doctor quietly; "like high walls within walls. Don't mistake me. I don't doubt that Brayne did it; his flight, I fancy, proves that. But as to how he did it. First difficulty: Why should a man kill another man with a great hulking sabre, when he can almost kill him with a pocket knife and put it back in his pocket? Second difficulty: Why was there no noise or outcry? Does a man commonly see another come up waving a scimitar and offer no remarks? Third difficulty: A servant watched the front door all the evening; and a rat cannot get into Valentin's garden anywhere. How did the dead man get into the garden? Fourth difficulty: Given the same conditions, how did Brayne get out of the garden?"

"And the fifth," said Neil, with eyes fixed on the English priest, who was coming slowly up the path.

"Is a trifle, I suppose," said the doctor, "but I think an odd one. When I first saw how the head had been slashed, I supposed the assassin had struck more than once. But on examination I found many cuts across the truncated section; in other words, they were struck *after* the head was off. Did Brayne hate his foe so fiendishly that he stood sabring his body in the moonlight?"

"Horrible!" said O'Brien, and shuddered.

The little priest, Brown, had arrived while they were talking, and had waited, with characteristic shyness, till they had finished. Then he said awkwardly:

"I say, I'm sorry to interrupt. But I was sent to tell you the news!"

"News?" repeated Simon, and stared at him rather painfully through his glasses.

"Yes, I'm sorry," said Father Brown mildly. "There's been another murder, you know."

Both men on the seat sprang up, leaving it rocking.

"And, what's stranger still," continued the priest, with his dull eyes on the rhododendrons, "it's the same disgusting sort; it's another beheading. They found the second head actually bleeding in the river, a few yards along Brayne's road to Paris; so they suppose that he——"

"Great Heaven!" cried O'Brien. "Is Brayne a monomaniac?"

"There are American vendettas," said the priest impassively. Then he added: "They want you to come to the library and see it."

Commandant O'Brien followed the other towards the inquest, feeling decidedly sick. As a soldier, he loathed all this secretive carnage; where were these extravagant amputations going to stop? First one head was hacked off, and then another; in this case (he told himself bitterly) it was not true that two heads were better than one. As he crossed the study he almost staggered at a shocking coincidence. Upon Valentin's table lay the coloured picture of yet a third bleeding head; and it was the head of Valentin himself. A second glance showed him it was only a Nationalist paper, called *The Guillotine*, which every week showed one of its political opponents with rolling eyes and writhing features after execution; for Valentin was an anticlerical of some note. But O'Brien was an Irishman, with a kind of chastity even in his sins; and his gorge rose against that great brutality of the intellect which belongs only to France. He felt Paris as a whole, from the grotesques on the Gothic churches to the gross caricatures in the newspapers. He remembered the gigantic jests of the Revolution. He saw the whole city as one ugly energy, from the sanguinary sketch lying on Valentin's table up to where, above a mountain and forest of gargoyles, the great devil grins on Notre Dame.

The library was long, low, and dark; what light entered it shot from under low blinds and had still some of the ruddy tinge of morning. Valentin and his servant Ivan were waiting for them at the upper end of a long, slightly-sloping desk, on which lay the mortal remains, looking enormous in the twilight. The big black figure and yellow face of the man found in the garden confronted them essentially unchanged. The second head, which had been fished from among the river reeds that morning, lay streaming and dripping beside it; Valentin's men were still seeking to recover the rest of this second corpse, which was supposed to be afloat. Father Brown, who did not seem to share O'Brien's sensibilities in the least, went up to the second head and examined it with his blinking care. It was little more than a mop of wet, white hair, fringed with silver fire in the red and level morning light; the face, which seemed of an ugly, empurpled and perhaps criminal type, had been much battered against trees or stones as it tossed in the water.

"Good morning, Commandant O'Brien," said Valentin, with quiet cordiality. "You have heard of Brayne's last experiment in butchery, I suppose?"

Father Brown was still bending over the head with white hair, and he said, without looking up:

"I suppose it is quite certain that Brayne cut off this head, too."

"Well, it seems common sense," said Valentin, with his hands in his pockets. "Killed in the same way as the other. Found within a few yards of the other. And sliced by the same weapon which we know he carried away."

"Yes, yes; I know," replied Father Brown, submissively. "Yet, you know, I doubt whether Brayne could have cut off this head."

"Why not?" inquired Dr. Simon, with a rational stare.

"Well, Doctor," said the priest, looking up blinking, "can a man cut off his own head? I don't know."

F   81

O'Brien felt an insane universe crashing about his ears; but the doctor sprang forward with impetuous practicality and pushed back the wet, white hair.

"Oh, there's no doubt it's Brayne," said the priest quietly. "He had exactly that chip in the left ear."

The detective, who had been regarding the priest with steady and glittering eyes, opened his clenched mouth and said sharply: "You seem to know a lot about him, Father Brown."

"I do," said the little man simply. "I've been about with him for some weeks. He was thinking of joining our church."

The stare of the fanatic sprang into Valentin's eyes; he strode towards the priest with clenched hands. "And, perhaps," he cried, with a blasting sneer: "perhaps he was also thinking of leaving all his money to your church."

"Perhaps he was," said Brown stolidly; "it is possible."

"In that case," cried Valentin, with a dreadful smile: "you may indeed know a great deal about him. About his life and about his——"

Commandant O'Brien laid a hand on Valentin's arm. "Drop that slanderous rubbish, Valentin," he said: "or there may be more swords yet."

But Valentin (under the steady, humble gaze of the priest) had already recovered himself. "Well," he said shortly: "people's private opinions can wait. You gentlemen are still bound by your promise to stay; you must enforce it on your-selves—and on each other. Ivan here will tell you anything more you want to know; I must get to business and write to the authorities. We can't keep this quiet any longer. I shall be writing in my study if there is any more news."

"Is there any more news, Ivan?" asked Dr. Simon, as the chief of police strode out of the room.

"Only one more thing, I think, sir," said Ivan, wrinkling up his grey old face; "but that's important, too, in its way. There's that old buffer you found on the lawn," and he pointed without pretence of reverence at the big black body with the yellow head. "We've found out who he is, anyhow."

"Indeed!" cried the astonished doctor; "and who is he?"

"His name was Arnold Becker," said the under-detective, "though he went by many aliases. He was a wandering sort of scamp, and is known to have been in America; so that was where Brayne got his knife into him. We didn't have much to do with him ourselves, for he worked mostly in Germany. We've communicated, of course, with the German police. But, oddly enough, there was a twin brother of his, named Louis Becker, whom we had a great deal to do with. In fact, we found it necessary to guillotine him only yesterday. Well, it's a rum thing, gentlemen, but when I saw that fellow flat on the lawn I had the greatest jump of my life. If I hadn't seen Louis Becker guillotined with my own eyes, I'd have sworn it was Louis Becker lying there in the grass. Then, of course, I remembered his twin brother in Germany, and following up the clue——"

The explanatory Ivan stopped, for the excellent reason that nobody was listening to him. The commandant and the doctor were both staring at Father Brown, who had sprung stiffly to his feet, and was holding his temples tight like a man in sudden and violent pain.

"Stop, stop, stop!" he cried; "stop talking a minute, for I see half. Will God give me strength? Will my brain make the one jump and see all? Heaven help me! I used to be fairly good at thinking. I could paraphrase any page in Aquinas once. Will my head split—or will it see? I see half—I see only half."

He buried his head in his hands, and stood in a sort of rigid torture of thought or prayer, while the other three could only go on staring at this last prodigy of their wild twelve hours.

When Father Brown's hands fell they showed a face quite fresh and serious, like a child's. He heaved a huge sigh, and said: "Let us get this said and done with as quickly as possible. Look here, this will be the quickest way to convince you all of the truth." He turned to the doctor. "Dr. Simon," he said, "you have a strong head-piece, and I heard you this morning asking the five hardest questions about this business. Well, if you will now ask them again, I will answer them."

Simon's pince-nez dropped from his nose in his doubt and

wonder, but he answered at once. "Well, the first question, you know, is why a man should kill another with a clumsy sabre at all when a man can kill with a bodkin?"

"A man cannot behead with a bodkin," said Brown, calmly, "and for *this* murder beheading was absolutely necessary."

"Why?" asked O'Brien, with interest.

"And the next question?" asked Father Brown.

"Well, why didn't the man cry out or anything?" asked the doctor; "sabres in gardens are certainly unusual."

"Twigs," said the priest gloomily, and turned to the window which looked on the scene of death. "No one saw the point of the twigs. Why should they lie on that lawn (look at it) so far from any tree? They were not snapped off; they were chopped off. The murderer occupied his enemy with some tricks with the sabre, showing how he could cut a branch in mid-air, or what not. Then, while his enemy bent down to see the result, a silent slash, and the head fell."

"Well," said the doctor slowly, "that seems plausible enough. But my next two questions will stump anyone."

The priest still stood looking critically out of the window and waited.

"You know how all the garden was sealed up like an airtight chamber," went on the doctor. "Well, how did the strange man get into the garden?"

Without turning round, the little priest answered: "There never was any strange man in the garden."

There was a silence, and then a sudden cackle of almost childish laughter relieved the strain. The absurdity of Brown's remark moved Ivan to open taunts.

"Oh!" he cried; "then we didn't lug a great fat corpse on to a sofa last night? He hadn't got into the garden, I suppose?"

"Got into the garden?" repeated Brown reflectively. "No, not entirely."

"Hang it all," cried Simon, "a man gets into the garden, or he doesn't."

"Not necessarily," said the priest, with a faint smile. "What is the next question, Doctor?"

84

"I fancy you're ill," exclaimed Dr. Simon sharply; "but I'll ask the next question if you like. How did Brayne get out of the garden?"

"He didn't get out of the garden," said the priest, still looking out of the window.

"Didn't get out of the garden?" exploded Simon.

"Not completely," said Father Brown.

Simon shook his fists in a frenzy of French logic. "A man gets out of a garden, or he doesn't," he cried.

"Not always," said Father Brown.

Dr. Simon sprang to his feet impatiently. "I have no time to spare on such senseless talk," he cried angrily. "If you can't understand a man being on one side of the wall or the other, I won't trouble you further."

"Doctor," said the cleric very gently, "we have always got on very pleasantly together. If only for the sake of old friendship, stop and tell me your fifth question."

The impatient Simon sank into a chair by the door and said briefly: "The head and shoulders were cut about in a queer way. It seemed to be done after death."

"Yes," said the motionless priest, "it was done so as to make you assume exactly the one simple falsehood that you did assume. It was done to make you take for granted that the head belonged to the body."

The borderland of the brain, where all the monsters are made, moved horribly in the Gaelic O'Brien. He felt the chaotic presence of all the horse-men and fish-women that man's unnatural fancy has begotten. A voice older than his first fathers seemed saying in his ear: "Keep out of the monstrous garden where grows the tree with double fruit. Avoid the evil garden where died the man with two heads." Yet, while these shameful symbolic shapes passed across the ancient mirror of his Irish soul, his Frenchified intellect was quite alert, and was watching the odd priest as closely and incredulously as all the rest.

Father Brown had turned round at last, and stood against the window with his face in dense shadow; but even in that shadow

85

they could see it was pale as ashes. Nevertheless, he spoke quite sensibly, as if there were no Gaelic souls on earth.

"Gentlemen," he said; "you did not find the strange body of Becker in the garden. You did not find any strange body in the garden. In face of Dr. Simon's rationalism, I still affirm that Becker was only partly present. Look here!" (pointing to the black bulk of the mysterious corpse); "you never saw that man in your lives. Did you ever see this man?"

He rapidly rolled away the bald-yellow head of the unknown, and put in its place the white-maned head beside it. And there, complete, unified, unmistakable, lay Julius K. Brayne.

"The murderer," went on Brown quietly, "hacked off his enemy's head and flung the sword far over the wall. But he was too clever to fling the sword only. He flung the *head* over the wall also. Then he had only to clap on another head to the corpse, and (as he insisted on a private inquest) you all imagined a totally new man."

"Clap on another head!" said O'Brien, staring. "What other head? Heads don't grow on garden bushes, do they?"

"No," said Father Brown huskily, and looking at his boots; "there is only one place where they grow. They grow in the basket of the guillotine, beside which the Chief of Police, Aristide Valentin, was standing not an hour before the murder. Oh, my friends, hear me a minute more before you tear me in pieces. Valentin is an honest man, if being mad for an arguable cause is honesty. But did you ever see in that cold, grey eye of his that he is mad? He would do anything, *anything*, to break what he calls the superstition of the Cross. He has fought for it and starved for it, and now he has murdered for it. Brayne's crazy millions had hitherto been scattered among so many sects that they did little to alter the balance of things. But Valentin heard a whisper that Brayne, like so many scatter-brained sceptics, was drifting to us; and that was quite a different thing. Brayne would pour supplies into the impoverished and pugnacious Church of France; he would support six Nationalist newspapers like *The Guillotine*. The battle was already balanced on a point, and the fanatic took flame at the risk. He resolved to destroy the millionaire, and he did it as one would expect the greatest of detectives to commit his only crime. He abstracted the severed head of Becker on some criminological excuse, and took it home in his official box. He had that last argument with Brayne, that Lord Galloway did not hear the end of; that failing, he led him out into the sealed garden, talked about swordsmanship, used twigs and a sabre for illustration, and——"

Ivan of the Scar sprang up. "You lunatic," he yelled; "you'll go to my master now, if I take you by——"

"Why, I was going there," said Brown heavily; "I must ask him to confess, and all that."

Driving the unhappy Brown before them like a hostage or sacrifice, they rushed together into the sudden stillness of Valentin's study.

The great detective sat at his desk apparently too occupied to hear their turbulent entrance. They paused a moment, and then something in the look of that upright and elegant back made the doctor run forward suddenly. A touch and a glance showed him that there was a small box of pills at Valentin's elbow, and that Valentin was dead in his chair; and on the blind face of the suicide was more than the pride of Cato.

From *The Father Brown Stories*
(Cassell & Co. Ltd.)

The Invisible Man

In the cool blue twilight of two steep streets in Camden Town, the shop at the corner, a confectioner's, glowed like the butt of a cigar. One should rather say, perhaps, like the butt of a firework, for the light was of many colours and some complexity, broken up by many mirrors and dancing on many gilt and gaily-coloured cakes and sweetmeats. Against this one fiery glass were glued the noses of many gutter-snipes, for the chocolates were all wrapped in those red and gold and green metallic colours which are almost better than chocolate itself; and the huge white wedding-cake in the window was somehow at once remote and satisfying, just as if the whole North Pole were good to eat. Such rainbow provocations could naturally collect the youth of the neighbourhood up to the ages of ten or twelve. But this corner was also attractive to youth at a later stage; and a young man, not less than twenty-four, was staring into the same shop window. To him, also, the shop was of fiery charm, but this attraction was not wholly to be explained by chocolates; which, however, he was far from despising.

He was a tall, burly, red-haired young man, with a resolute face but a listless manner. He carried under his arm a flat, grey portfolio of black-and-white sketches which he had sold with more or less success to publishers ever since his uncle (who was an admiral) had disinherited him for Socialism, because of a lecture which he had delivered against that economic theory. His name was John Turnbull Angus.

Entering at last, he walked through the confectioner's shop into the back room, which was a sort of pastry-cook restaurant, merely raising his hat to the young lady who was serving there.

She was a dark, elegant, alert girl in black, with a high colour and very quick, dark eyes; and after the ordinary interval she followed him into the inner room to take his order.

His order was evidently a usual one. "I want, please," he said with precision, "one halfpenny bun and a small cup of black coffee." An instant before the girl could turn away he added, "Also, I want you to marry me."

The young lady of the shop stiffened suddenly, and said: "Those are jokes I don't allow."

The red-haired young man lifted grey eyes of an unexpected gravity.

"Really and truly," he said, "it's as serious—as serious as the halfpenny bun. It is expensive, like the bun; one pays for it. It is indigestible, like the bun. It hurts."

The dark young lady had never taken her dark eyes off him, but seemed to be studying him with almost tragic exactitude. At the end of her scrutiny she had something like the shadow of a smile, and she sat down in a chair.

"Don't you think," observed Angus absently, "that it's rather cruel to eat these halfpenny buns? They might grow up into penny buns. I shall give up these brutal sports when we are married."

The dark young lady rose from her chair and walked to the window, evidently in a state of strong but not unsympathetic cogitation. When at last she swung round again with an air of resolution, she was bewildered to observe that the young man was carefully laying out on the table various objects from the shop window. They included a pyramid of highly coloured sweets, several plates of sandwiches, and the two decanters containing that mysterious port and sherry which are peculiar to pastry-cooks. In the middle of this neat arrangement he had carefully let down the enormous load of white sugared cake which had been the huge ornament of the window.

"What on earth are you doing?" she asked.

"Duty, my dear Laura," he began.

"Oh, for the Lord's sake, stop a minute," she cried, "and don't talk to me in that way. I mean what is all that?"

"A ceremonial meal, Miss Hope."

"And what is *that*?" she asked impatiently, pointing to the mountain of sugar.

"The wedding-cake, Mrs. Angus," he said.

The girl marched to that article, removed it with some clatter, and put it back in the shop window; she then returned, and, putting her elegant elbows on the table, regarded the young man not unfavourably, but with considerable exasperation.

"You don't give me any time to think," she said.

"I'm not such a fool," he answered; "that's my Christian humility."

She was still looking at him; but she had grown considerably graver behind the smile.

"Mr. Angus," she said steadily, "before there is a minute more of this nonsense I must tell you something about myself as shortly as I can."

"Delighted," replied Angus gravely. "You might tell me something about myself, too, while you are about it."

"Oh, do hold your tongue and listen," she said. "It's nothing that I'm ashamed of, and it isn't even anything that I'm specially sorry about. But what would you say if there were something that is no business of mine and yet is my nightmare?"

"In that case," said the man seriously, "I should suggest that you bring back the cake."

"Well, you must listen to the story first," said Laura, persistently. "To begin with, I must tell you that my father owned the inn called the 'Red Fish' at Ludbury, and I used to serve people in the bar."

"I have often wondered," he said, "why there was a kind of Christian air about this one confectioner's shop."

"Ludbury is a sleepy, grassy little hole in the Eastern Counties, and the only kind of people who ever came to the 'Red Fish' were occasional commercial travellers, and for the rest, the most awful people you can see, only you've never seen them. I mean little, loungy men, who had just enough to live on, and had nothing to do but lean about in bar-rooms and bet on horses, in bad clothes that were just too good for them. Even these wretched young rotters were not very common at our house;

90

but there were two of them that were a lot too common—common in every sort of way. They both lived on money of their own, and were wearisomely idle and overdressed. But yet I was a bit sorry for them, because I half believe they slunk into our little empty bar because each of them had a slight deformity; the sort of thing that some yokels laugh at. It wasn't exactly a deformity either; it was more an oddity. One of them was a surprisingly small man, something like a dwarf, or at least like a jockey. He was not at all jockeyish to look at, though he had a round black head and a well-trimmed black beard, bright eyes like a bird's; he jingled money in his pockets; he jangled a great gold watch chain; and he never turned up except dressed just too much like a gentleman to be one. He was no fool, though, though a futile idler; he was curiously clever at all kinds of things that couldn't be the slightest use; a sort of impromptu conjuring; making fifteen matches set fire to each other like a regular firework; or cutting a banana or some such thing into a dancing doll. His name was Isidore Smythe; and I can see him still, with his little dark face, just coming up to the counter, making a jumping kangaroo out of five cigars.

"The other fellow was more silent and more ordinary; but somehow he alarmed me much more than poor little Smythe. He was very tall and slight, and light-haired; his nose had a high bridge, and he might almost have been handsome in a spectral sort of way; but he had one of the most appalling squints I have ever seen or heard of. When he looked straight at you, you didn't know where you were yourself, let alone what he was looking at. I fancy this sort of disfigurement embittered the poor chap a little; for while Smythe was ready to show off his monkey tricks anywhere, James Welkin (that was our squinting man's name) never did anything except soak in our bar parlour, and go for great walks by himself in the flat, grey country all round. All the same, I think Smythe, too, was a little sensitive about being so small, though he carried it off more smartly. And so it was that I was really puzzled, as well as startled, and very sorry, when they both offered to marry me in the same week.

"Well, I did what I've since thought was perhaps a silly thing. But, after all, these freaks were my friends in a way; and I had a horror of their thinking I refused them for the real reason, which was that they were so impossibly ugly. So I made up some gas or other of another sort, about never meaning to marry anyone who hadn't carved his way in the world. I said it was a point of principle with me not to live on money that was just inherited like theirs. Two days after I had talked in this well-meaning sort of way, the whole trouble began. The first thing I heard was that both of them had gone off to seek their fortunes, as if they were in some silly fairy tale.

"Well, I've never seen either of them from that day to this. But I've had two letters from the little man called Smythe, and really they were rather exciting."

"Ever heard of the other man?" asked Angus.

"No, he never wrote," said the girl, after an instant's hesitation. "Smythe's first letter was simply to say that he had started out walking with Welkin to London; but Welkin was such a good walker that the little man dropped out of it, and took a rest by the roadside. He happened to be picked up by some travelling show, and, partly because he was nearly a dwarf, and partly because he was really a clever little wretch, he got on quite well in the show business, and was soon sent up to the Aquarium, to do some tricks that I forgot. That was his first letter. His second was much more of a startler, and I only got it last week."

The man called Angus emptied his coffee-cup and regarded her with mild and patient eyes. Her own mouth took a slight twist of laughter as she resumed: "I suppose you've seen on the hoardings all about this 'Smythe's Silent Service'? Or you must be the only person that hasn't. Oh, I don't know much about it, it's some clockwork invention for doing all the housework by machinery. You know the sort of thing: 'Press a button—A Butler who Never Drinks.' 'Turn a handle—Ten Housemaids who Never Flirt.' You must have seen the advertisements. Well, whatever these machines are, they are making pots of money; and they are making it all for that little imp whom I knew down in Ludbury. I can't help feeling pleased the poor little chap has fallen on his feet; but the plain fact is, I'm in terror of his turning up any minute and telling me he's carved his way in the world—as he certainly has."

"And the other man?" repeated Angus with a sort of obstinate quietude.

Laura Hope got to her feet suddenly. "My friend," she said, "I think you are a witch. Yes, you are quite right. I have not seen a line of the other man's writing; and I have no more notion than the dead of what or where he is. But it is of him that I am frightened. It is he who is all about my path. It is he who has half driven me mad. Indeed, I think he has driven me mad; for I have felt him where he could not have been, and I have heard his voice when he could not have spoken."

"Well, my dear," said the young man, cheerfully, "if he were Satan himself, he is done for now you have told somebody. One goes mad all alone, old girl. But when was it you fancied you felt and heard our squinting friend?"

"I heard James Welkin laugh as plainly as I hear you speak," said the girl, steadily. "There was nobody there, for I stood just outside the shop at the corner, and could see down both streets at once. I had forgotten how he laughed, though his laugh was as odd as his squint. I had not thought of him for nearly a year. But it's a solemn truth that a few seconds later the first letter came from his rival."

"Did you ever make the spectre speak or squeak, or anything?" asked Angus, with some interest.

Laura suddenly shuddered, and then said with an unshaken voice: "Yes. Just when I had finished reading the second letter from Isidore Smythe announcing his success, just then, I heard Welkin say: 'He shan't have you, though.' It was quite plain, as if he were in the room. It is awful; I think I must be mad."

"If you were really mad," said the young man, "you would think you must be sane. But certainly there seems to me to be something a little rum about this unseen gentleman. Two heads

93

are better than one—I spare you allusions to any other organs—
and really, if you would allow me, as a sturdy, practical man,
to bring back the wedding-cake out of the window——"

Even as he spoke, there was a sort of steely shriek in the
street outside, and a small motor, driven at devilish speed, shot
up to the door of the shop and stuck there. In the same flash of
time a small man in a shiny top hat stood stamping in the outer
room.

Angus, who had hitherto maintained hilarious ease from
motives of mental hygiene, revealed the strain of his soul by
striding abruptly out of the inner room and confronting the new-
comer. A glance at him was quite sufficient to confirm the savage
guesswork of a man in love. This very dapper but dwarfish
figure, with the spike of black beard carried insolently forward,
the clever unrestful eyes, the neat but very nervous fingers, could
be none other than the man just described to him: Isidore
Smythe, who made dolls out of banana skins and matchboxes:
Isidore Smythe, who made millions out of undrinking butlers
and unflirting housemaids of metal. For a moment the two
men, instinctively understanding each other's air of possession,
looked at each other with that curious cold generosity which is
the soul of rivalry.

Mr. Smythe, however, made no allusion to the ultimate
ground of their antagonism, but said simply and explosively:
"Has Miss Hope seen that thing on the window?"

"On the window?" repeated the staring Angus.

"There's no time to explain other things," said the small
millionaire shortly. "There's some tomfoolery going on here
that has to be investigated."

He pointed his polished walking-stick at the window, recently
depleted by the bridal preparations of Mr. Angus; and that
gentleman was astonished to see along the front of the glass a
long strip of paper pasted, which had certainly not been on the
window when he had looked through it some time before.
Following the energetic Smythe outside into the street, he
found that some yard and a half of stamp paper had been
carefully gummed along the glass outside, and on this was

written in straggly characters: "If you marry Smythe, he will die."

"Laura," said Angus, putting his big red head into the shop, "you're not mad."

"It's the writing of that fellow Welkin," said Smythe gruffly. "I haven't seen him for years, but he's always bothering me. Five times in the last fortnight he's had threatening letters left at my flat, and I can't even find out who leaves them, let alone if it is Welkin himself. The porter of the flat swears that no suspicious characters have been seen, and here he has pasted up a sort of dado on a public shop window, while the people in the shop——"

"Quite so," said Angus modestly, "while the people in the shop were having tea. Well, sir, I can assure you I appreciate your common sense in dealing so directly with the matter. We can talk about other things afterwards. The fellow cannot be very far off yet, for I swear there was no paper there when I went last to the window, ten or fifteen minutes ago. On the other hand, he's too far off to be chased, as we don't even know the direction. If you'll take my advice, Mr. Smythe, you'll put this at once in the hands of some energetic inquiry man, private rather than public. I know an extremely clever fellow, who has set up in business five minutes from here in your car. His name's Flambeau, and though his youth was a bit stormy, he's a strictly honest man now, and his brains are worth money. He lives in Lucknow Mansions, Hampstead."

"That is odd," said the little man, arching his black eyebrows. "I live myself in Himalaya Mansions round the corner. Perhaps you might care to come with me; I can go to my rooms and sort out these queer Welkin documents, while you run round and get your friend the detective."

"You are very good," said Angus politely. "Well, the sooner we act the better."

Both men, with a queer kind of impromptu fairness, took the same sort of formal farewell of the lady, and both jumped into the brisk little car. As Smythe took the wheel and they turned the great corner of the street, Angus was amused to see a gigantesque poster of "Smythe's Silent Service," with a picture of a huge headless iron doll, carrying a saucepan with the legend, "A Cook Who is Never Cross."

"I use them in my own flat," said the little black-bearded man, laughing, "partly for advertisement, and partly for real convenience. Honestly, and all above board, those big clock-work dolls of mine do bring you coals or claret or a time-table quicker than any live servants I've ever known, if you know which knob to press. But I'll never deny, between ourselves, that such servants have their disadvantages, too."

"Indeed?" said Angus, "is there something they can't do?"

"Yes," replied Smythe coolly; "they can't tell me who left those threatening letters at my flat."

The man's motor was small and swift like himself; in fact, like his domestic service, it was of his own invention. If he was an advertising quack, he was one who believed in his own wares. The sense of something tiny and flying was accentuated as they swept up long white curves of road in the dead but open daylight of evening. Soon the white curves came sharper and dizzier; they were upon ascending spirals, as they say in the modern religions. For indeed, they were cresting a corner of London which is almost as precipitous as Edinburgh, if not quite so picturesque. Terrace rose above terrace, and the special tower of flats they sought, rose above them all to almost Egyptian height, gilt by the level sunset. The change, as they turned the corner and entered the crescent known as Himalaya Mansions, was as abrupt as the opening of a window; for they found that pile of flats sitting above London as above a green sea of slate. Opposite to the mansions, on the other side of the gravel crescent, was a bushy enclosure more like a steep hedge or dyke than a garden, and some way below that ran a strip of artificial water, a sort of canal, like the moat of that embowered fortress. As the car swept round the crescent it passed, at one corner, the stray stall of a man selling chestnuts; and right away at the other end of the curve, Angus could see a dim blue policeman walking slowly. These were the only human shapes in that high suburban solitude; but he had an irrational sense that they expressed the speechless poetry of London. He felt as if they were figures in a story.

The little car shot up to the right house like a bullet, and shot out its owner like a bomb shell. He was immediately inquiring of a tall commissionaire in shining braid, and a short porter in shirt sleeves, whether anybody or anything had been seeking his apartments. He was assured that nobody and nothing had passed these officials since his last inquiries; whereupon he and the slightly bewildered Angus were shot up in the lift like a rocket, till they reached the top floor.

"Just come in for a minute," said the breathless Smythe. "I want to show you those Welkin letters. Then you might run round the corner and fetch your friend." He pressed a button concealed in the wall, and the door opened of itself.

It opened on a long, commodious ante-room, of which the only arresting features, ordinarily speaking, were the rows of tall half-human mechanical figures that stood up on both sides like tailors' dummies. Like tailors' dummies they were headless; and like tailors' dummies they had a handsome unnecessary humpiness in the shoulders, and a pigeon-breasted protuberance of chest; but barring this, they were not much more like a human figure than any automatic machine at a station that is about the human height. They had two great hooks like arms, for carrying trays; and they were painted pea-green, or vermilion, or black for convenience of distinction; in every other way they were only automatic machines and nobody would have looked twice at them. On this occasion, at least, nobody did. For between the two rows of these domestic dummies lay something more interesting than most of the mechanics of the world. It was a white, tattered scrap of paper scrawled with red ink; and the agile inventor had snatched it up almost as soon as the door flew open. He handed it to Angus without a word. The red ink on it actually was not dry, and the message ran: "If you have been to see her today, I shall kill you."

There was a short silence, and then Isidore Smythe said quietly: "Would you like a little whisky? I rather feel as if I should."

"Thank you; I should like a little Flambeau," said Angus, gloomily. "This business seems to me to be getting rather grave. I'm going round at once to fetch him."

"Right you are," said the other, with admirable cheerfulness. "Bring him round here as quick as you can."

But as Angus closed the front door behind him he saw Smythe push back a button, and one of the clockwork images glided from its place and slid along a groove in the floor carrying a tray with syphon and decanter. There did seem something a trifle weird about leaving the little man alone among those dead servants, who were coming to life as the door closed.

Six steps down from Smythe's landing the man in shirt sleeves was doing something with a pail. Angus stopped to extract a promise, fortified with a prospective bribe, that he would remain in that place until the return with the detective, and would keep count of any kind of stranger coming up those stairs. Dashing down to the front hall he then laid similar charges of vigilance on the commissionaire at the front door, from whom he learned the simplifying circumstance that there was no back door. Not content with this, he captured the floating policeman and induced him to stand opposite the entrance and watch it; and finally paused an instant for a pennyworth of chestnuts, and an inquiry as to the probable length of the merchant's stay in the neighbourhood.

The chestnut seller, turning up the collar of his coat, told him he should probably be moving shortly, as he thought it was going to snow. Indeed, the evening was growing grey and bitter, but Angus, with all his eloquence, proceeded to nail the chestnut man to his post.

"Keep yourself warm on your own chestnuts," he said earnestly. "Eat up your whole stock; I'll make it worth your while. I'll give you a sovereign if you'll wait here till I come back, and then tell me whether any man, woman, or child has gone into that house where the commissionaire is standing."

He then walked away smartly, with a last look at the besieged tower.

"I've made a ring round that room, anyhow," he said.

"They can't all four of them be Mr. Welkin's accomplices."

Lucknow Mansions were, so to speak, on a lower platform of that hill of houses, of which Himalaya Mansions might be called the peak. Mr. Flambeau's semi-official flat was on the ground floor, and presented in every way a marked contrast to the American machinery and cold hotel-like luxury of the flat of the Silent Service. Flambeau, who was a friend of Angus, received him in a rococo artistic den behind his office, of which the ornaments were sabres, harquebuses, Eastern curiosities, flasks of Italian wine, savage cooking-pots, a plumy Persian cat, and a small dusty-looking Roman Catholic priest, who looked particularly out of place.

"This is my friend, Father Brown," said Flambeau. "I've often wanted you to meet him. Splendid weather, this; a little cold for Southerners like me."

"Yes, I think it will keep clear," said Angus, sitting down on a violet-striped Eastern ottoman.

"No," said the priest quietly; "it has begun to snow."

And indeed, as he spoke, the first few flakes, foreseen by the man of chestnuts, began to drift across the darkening window-pane.

"Well," said Angus heavily. "I'm afraid I've come on business, and rather jumpy business at that. The fact is, Flambeau, within a stone's throw of your house is a fellow who badly wants your help; he's perpetually being haunted and threatened by an invisible enemy—a scoundrel whom nobody has even seen." As Angus proceeded to tell the whole tale of Smythe and Welkin, beginning with Laura's story, and going on with his own, the supernatural laugh at the corner of two empty streets, the strange distinct words spoken in an empty room, Flambeau grew more and more vividly concerned, and the little priest seemed to be left out of it, like a piece of furniture. When it came to the scribbled stamp-paper pasted on the window, Flambeau rose, seeming to fill the room with his huge shoulders.

"If you don't mind," he said, "I think you had better tell me the rest on the nearest road to this man's house. It strikes me, somehow, that there is no time to be lost."

"Delighted," said Angus, rising also, "though he's safe enough for the present, for I've set four men to watch the only hole to his burrow."

They turned out into the street, the small priest trundling after them with the docility of a small dog. He merely said, in a cheerful way, like one making conversation: "How quick the snow gets thick on the ground."

As they threaded the steep side streets already powdered with silver, Angus finished his story; and by the time they reached the crescent with the towering flats, he had leisure to turn his attention to the four sentinels. The chestnut seller, both before and after receiving a sovereign, swore stubbornly that he had watched the door and seen no visitor enter. The policeman was even more emphatic. He said he had had experience of crooks of all kinds, in top hats and in rags; he wasn't so green as to expect suspicious characters to look suspicious; he looked out for anybody, and, so help him, there had been nobody. And when all three men gathered round the gilded commissionaire, who still stood smiling astride of the porch, the verdict was more final still.

"I've got a right to ask any man, duke or dustman, what he wants in these flats," said the genial and gold-laced giant, "and I'll swear there's been nobody to ask since this gentleman went away."

The unimportant Father Brown, who stood back, looking modestly at the pavement, here ventured to say meekly: "Has nobody been up and down stairs, then, since the snow began to fall? It began while we were all round at Flambeau's."

"Nobody's been in here, sir, you can take it from me," said the official, with beaming authority.

"Then I wonder what that is?" said the priest, and stared at the ground blankly like a fish.

The others all looked down also; and Flambeau used a fierce exclamation and a French gesture. For it was unquestionably true that down the middle of the entrance guarded by the man in gold lace, actually between the arrogant, stretched legs of that colossus, ran a stringy pattern of grey footprints stamped upon the white snow.

"God!" cried Angus involuntarily; "the Invisible Man!"

Without another word he turned and dashed up the stairs, with Flambeau following; but Father Brown still stood looking about him in the snow-clad street as if he had lost interest in his query.

Flambeau was plainly in a mood to break down the door with his big shoulder; but the Scotsman, with more reason, if less intuition, fumbled about on the frame of the door till he found the invisible button; and the door swung slowly open.

It showed substantially the same serried interior; the hall had grown darker, though it was still struck here and there with the last crimson shafts of sunset, and one or two of the headless machines had been moved from their places for this or that purpose, and stood here and there about the twilit place. The green and red of their coats were all darkened in the dusk, and their likeness to human shapes slightly increased by their very shapelessness. But in the middle of them all, exactly where the paper with the red ink had lain, there lay something that looked very like red ink spilled out of its bottle. But it was not red ink.

With a French combination of reason and violence Flambeau simply said "Murder!" and, plunging into the flat, had explored every corner and cupboard of it in five minutes. But if he expected to find a corpse he found none. Isidore Smythe simply was not in the place, either dead or alive. After the most tearing search the two men met each other in the outer hall with streaming faces and staring eyes. "My friend," said Flambeau, talking French in his excitement, "not only is your murderer invisible, but he makes invisible also the murdered man."

Angus looked round at the dim room full of dummies, and in some Celtic corner of his Scotch soul a shudder started. One of the life-size dolls stood immediately overshadowing the blood stain, summoned, perhaps, by the slain man an instant before he fell. One of the high-shouldered hooks that served the thing for arms, was a little lifted and Angus had suddenly the horrid fancy that poor Smythe's own iron child had struck him down. Matter had rebelled, and these machines had killed their master. But even so, what had they done with him?

"Eaten him?" said the nightmare at his ear; and he sickened for an instant at the idea of rent, human remains absorbed and crushed into all that acephalous clockwork.

He recovered his mental health by an emphatic effort, and said to Flambeau: "Well, there it is. The poor fellow has evaporated like a cloud and left a red streak on the floor. The tale does not belong to this world."

"There is only one thing to be done," said Flambeau, "whether it belongs to this world or the other, I must go down and talk to my friend."

They descended, passing the man with the pail, who again asseverated that he had let no intruder pass, down to the commissionaire and the hovering chestnut man, who rightly reasserted their own watchfulness. But when Angus looked round for his fourth confirmation he could not see it, and called out with some nervousness: "Where is the policeman?"

"I beg your pardon," said Father Brown; "that is my fault. I just sent him down the road to investigate something—that I just thought worth investigating."

"Well, we want him back pretty soon," said Angus abruptly, "for the wretched man upstairs has not only been murdered, but wiped out."

"How?" asked the priest.

"Father," said Flambeau, after a pause, "upon my soul I believe it is more in your department than mine. No friend or foe has entered the house, but Smythe is gone, as if stolen by the fairies. If that is not supernatural, I——"

As he spoke they were all checked by an unusual sight; the big blue policeman came round the corner of the crescent running. He came straight up to Brown.

"You're right, sir," he panted, "they've just found poor Mr. Smythe's body in the canal down below."

Angus put his hand wildly to his head. "Did he run down and drown himself?" he asked.

"He never came down, I'll swear," said the constable, "and he wasn't drowned either, for he died of a great stab over the heart."

"And yet you saw no one enter?" said Flambeau in a grave voice.

"Let us walk down the road a little," said the priest.

As they reached the other end of the crescent he observed abruptly: "Stupid of me! I forgot to ask the policeman something. I wonder if they found a light brown sack."

"Why a light brown sack?" asked Angus, astonished.

"Because if it was any other coloured sack, the case must begin over again," said Father Brown; "but if it was a light brown sack, why, the case is finished."

"I am pleased to hear it," said Angus with hearty irony. "It hasn't begun, so far as I am concerned."

"You must tell us all about it," said Flambeau, with a strange heavy simplicity, like a child.

Unconsciously they were walking with quickening steps down the long sweep of road on the other side of the high crescent, Father Brown leading briskly, though in silence. At last he said with an almost touching vagueness: "Well, I'm afraid you'll think it so prosy. We always begin at the abstract end of things, and you can't begin this story anywhere else.

"Have you ever noticed this—that people never answer what you say? They answer what you mean—or what they think you mean. Suppose one lady says to another in a country house, 'Is anybody staying with you?' the lady doesn't answer 'Yes; the butler, the three footmen, the parlour-maid, and so on,' though the parlour-maid may be in the room, or the butler behind her chair. She says: 'There is *nobody* staying with us,' meaning nobody of the sort you mean. But suppose a doctor inquiring into an epidemic asks, 'Who is staying in the house?' then the lady will remember the butler, the parlour-maid, and the rest. All language is used like that; you never get a question answered literally, even when you get it answered truly. When those four quite honest men said that no man had gone into the Mansions, they did not really mean that *no man* had gone into them. They meant no man whom they could suspect of being your man. A man did go into the house, and did come out of it, but they never noticed him."

103

"An invisible man?" inquired Angus, raising his red eyebrows.

"A mentally invisible man," said Father Brown.

A minute or two after he resumed in the same unassuming voice, like a man thinking his way. "Of course, you can't think of such a man, until you do think of him. That's where his cleverness comes in. But I came to think of him through two or three little things in the tale Mr. Angus told us. First, there was the fact that this Welkin went for long walks. And then there was the vast lot of stamp paper on the window. And then, most of all, there were the two things the young lady said—things that couldn't be true. Don't get annoyed," he added hastily, noting a sudden movement of the Scotsman's head; "she thought they were true all right, but they couldn't be true. A person *can't* be quite alone in a street a second before she receives a letter. She can't be quite alone in a street when she starts reading a letter just received. There must be somebody pretty near her; he must be mentally invisible."

"Why must there be somebody near her?" asked Angus.

"Because," said Father Brown: "barring carrier-pigeons, somebody must have brought her the letter."

"Do you really mean to say," asked Flambeau, with energy, "that Welkin carried his rival's letters to his lady?"

"Yes," said the priest. "Welkin carried his rival's letters to his lady. You see, he had to."

"Oh, I can't stand much more of this," exploded Flambeau. "Who is this fellow? What does he look like? What is the usual get-up of a mentally invisible man?"

"He is dressed rather handsomely in red, blue and gold," replied the priest promptly with decision, "and in this striking, and even showy costume he entered Himalaya Mansions under eight human eyes; he killed Smythe in cold blood, and came down into the street again carrying the dead body in his arms——"

"Reverend sir," cried Angus, standing still, "are you raving mad, or am I?"

"You are not mad," said Brown, "only a little unobservant.

104

You have not noticed such a man as this, for example."

He took three quick strides forward, and put his hand on the shoulder of an ordinary passing postman who had bustled by them unnoticed under the shade of the trees.

"Nobody ever notices postmen, somehow," he said thoughtfully; "yet they have passions like other men, and even carry large bags where a small corpse can be stowed quite easily."

The postman, instead of turning naturally, had ducked and tumbled against the garden fence. He was a lean fair-bearded man of very ordinary appearance, but as he turned an alarmed face over his shoulder, all three men were fixed with an almost fiendish squint.

Flambeau went back to his sabres, purple rugs and Persian cat, having many things to attend to. John Turnbull Angus went back to the lady at the shop, with whom that imprudent young man contrives to be extremely comfortable. But Father Brown walked those snow-covered hills under the stars for many hours with a murderer, and what they said to each other will never be known.

From *The Father Brown Stories*
(Cassell & Co. Ltd.)

The Honour of Israel Gow

A stormy evening of olive and silver was closing in, as Father Brown, wrapped in a grey Scotch plaid, came to the end of a grey Scotch valley and beheld the strange castle of Glengyle. It stopped one end of the glen or hollow like a blind alley; and it looked like the end of the world. Rising in steep roofs and spires of seagreen slate in the manner of the old French-Scottish châteaux, it reminded an Englishman of the sinister steeple-hats of witches in fairy tales; and the pine woods that rocked round the green turrets looked, by comparison, as black as numberless flocks of ravens. This note of a dreamy, almost a sleepy devilry, was no mere fancy from the landscape. For there did rest on the place one of those clouds of pride and madness and mysterious sorrow which lie more heavily on the noble houses of Scotland than on any other of the children of men. For Scotland has a double dose of the poison called heredity; the sense of blood in the aristocrat, and the sense of doom in the Calvinist.

The priest had snatched a day from his business at Glasgow to meet his friend Flambeau, the amateur detective, who was at Glengyle Castle with another more formal officer investigating the life and death of the late Earl of Glengyle. That mysterious person was the last representative of a race whose valour, insanity, and violent cunning had made them terrible even among the sinister nobility of their nation in the sixteenth century. None were deeper in that labyrinthine ambition, in chamber within chamber of that palace of lies that was built up around Mary Queen of Scots.

The rhyme in the country-side attested the motive and the result of their machinations candidly:

"As green sap to the simmer trees
Is red gold to the Ogilvies."

For many centuries there had never been a decent lord in
Glengyle Castle; and with the Victorian era one would have
thought that all eccentricities were exhausted. The last Glengyle, however, satisfied his tribal tradition by doing the only
thing that was left for him to do; he disappeared. I do not mean
that he went abroad; by all accounts he was still in the castle, if
he was anywhere. But though his name was in the church register
and the big red Peerage, nobody ever saw him under the sun.

If anyone saw him it was a solitary man-servant, something
between a groom and a gardener. He was so deaf that the more
business-like assumed him to be dumb; while the more pene-
trating declared him to be half-witted. A gaunt, red-haired
labourer, with a dogged jaw and chin, but quiet black-blue
eyes, he went by the name of Israel Gow, and was the one silent
servant on that deserted estate. But the energy with which he
dug potatoes, and the regularity with which he disappeared
into the kitchen gave people an impression that he was provid-
ing for the meals of a superior, and that the strange earl was
still concealed in the castle. If society needed any further proof
that he was there, the servant persistently asserted that he was
not at home. One morning the provost and the minister (for
the Glengyles were Presbyterian) were summoned to the castle.
There they found that the gardener, groom and cook had added
to his many professions that of an undertaker, and had nailed
up his noble master in a coffin. With how much or how little
further inquiry this odd fact was passed, did not as yet very
plainly appear; for the thing had never been legally investigated till Flambeau had gone north two or three days before.
By then the body of Lord Glengyle (if it was the body) had lain
for some time in the little churchyard on the hill.

As Father Brown passed through the dim garden and came
under the shadow of the château, the clouds were thick and the
whole air damp and thundery. Against the last stripe of the
green-gold sunset he saw a black human silhouette; a man in a

chimney-pot hat, with a big spade over his shoulder. The combination was queerly suggestive of a sexton; but when Brown remembered the deaf servant who dug potatoes, he thought it natural enough. He knew something of the Scotch peasant; he knew the respectability which might well feel it necessary to wear "blacks" for an official inquiry; he knew also the economy that would not lose an hour's digging for that. Even the man's start and suspicious stare as the priest went by were consonant enough with the vigilance and jealousy of such a type.

The great door was opened by Flambeau himself, who had with him a lean man with iron-grey hair and papers in his hand: Inspector Craven from Scotland Yard. The entrance hall was mostly stripped and empty; but the pale, sneering faces of one or two of the wicked Ogilvies looked down out of the black periwigs and blackening canvas.

Following them into an inner room, Father Brown found that the allies had been seated at a long oak table, of which their end was covered with scribbled papers, flanked with whisky and cigars. Through the whole of its remaining length it was occupied by detached objects arranged at intervals; objects about as inexplicable as any objects could be. One looked like a small heap of glittering broken glass. Another looked like a high heap of brown dust. A third appeared to be a plain stick of wood.

"You seem to have a sort of geological museum here," he said, as he sat down, jerking his head briefly in the direction of the brown dust and the crystalline fragments.

"Not a geological museum," replied Flambeau; "say a psychological museum."

"Oh, for the Lord's sake," cried the police detective, laughing, "don't let's begin with such long words."

"Don't you know what psychology means?" asked Flambeau with friendly surprise. "Psychology means being off your chump."

"Still I hardly follow," replied the official.

"Well," said Flambeau, with decision; "I mean that we've only found out one thing about Lord Glengyle. He was a maniac."

The black silhouette of Gow with his top hat and spade passed the window, dimly outlined against the darkening sky. Father Brown stared passively at it and answered:

"I can understand there must have been something odd about the man, or he wouldn't have buried himself alive—nor been in such a hurry to bury himself dead. But what makes you think it was lunacy?"

"Well," said Flambeau; "you just listen to the list of things Mr. Craven has found in the house."

"We must get a candle," said Craven, suddenly. "A storm is getting up, and it's too dark to read."

"Have you found any candles," asked Brown smiling, "among your oddities?"

Flambeau raised a grave face, and fixed his dark eyes on his friend.

"That is curious, too," he said. "Twenty-five candles, and not a trace of a candlestick."

In the rapidly darkening room and rapidly rising wind, Brown went along the table to where a bundle of wax candles lay among the other scrappy exhibits. As he did so he bent accidentally over the heap of red-brown dust; and a sharp sneeze cracked the silence.

"Hullo!" he said; "snuff!"

He took one of the candles, lit it carefully, came back and stuck it in the neck of the whisky bottle. The unrestful night air, blowing through the crazy window, waved the long flame like a banner. And on every side of the castle they could hear the miles and miles of black pine wood seething like a black sea around a rock.

"I will read the inventory," began Craven gravely, picking up one of the papers, "the inventory of what we found loose and unexplained in the castle. You are to understand that the place generally was dismantled and neglected; but one or two rooms had plainly been inhabited in a simple but not squalid style by somebody; somebody who was not the servant Gow. The list is as follows:

"First item. A very considerable hoard of precious stones,

nearly all diamonds, and all of them loose, without any setting whatever. Of course, it is natural that the Ogilvies should have family jewels; but those are exactly the jewels that are almost always set in particular articles of ornament. The Ogilvies would seem to have kept theirs loose in their pockets, like coppers.

"Second item. Heaps and heaps of loose snuff, not kept in a horn, or even a pouch, but lying in heaps on the matelpieces, on the sideboard, on the piano, anywhere. It looks as if the old gentleman would not take the trouble to look in a pocket or lift a lid.

"Third item. Here and there about the house curious little heaps of minute pieces of metal, some like steel springs and some in the form of microscopic wheels. As if they had gutted some mechanical toy.

"Fourth item. The wax candles, which have to be stuck in bottle necks because there is nothing else to stick them in. Now I wish you to note how very much queerer all this is than anything we anticipated. For the central riddle we are prepared; we have all seen at a glance there was something wrong about the last earl. We have come here to find out whether he really lived here, whether he really died here, whether that red-haired scarecrow who did his burying had anything to do with his dying. But suppose the worst in all this, the most lurid or melodramatic solution you like. Suppose the servant really killed the master, or suppose the master isn't really dead, or suppose the master is dressed up as the servant, or suppose the servant is buried for the master; invent what Wilkie Collins's tragedy you like, and you still have not explained a candle without a candlestick, or why an elderly gentleman of good family should habitually spill snuff on the piano. The core of the tale we could imagine; it is the fringes that are mysterious. By no stretch of fancy can the human mind connect together snuff and diamonds and wax and loose clockwork."

"I think I see the connexion," said the priest. "This Glengyle was mad against the French Revolution. He was an enthusiast for the *ancien régime*, and was trying to re-enact literally the family life of the last Bourbons. He had snuff because it was the eighteenth-century luxury; wax candles, because they were the eighteenth-century lighting; the mechanical bits of iron represent the locksmith hobby of Louis XVI; the diamonds are for the Diamond Necklace of Marie Antoinette."

Both the other men were staring at him with round eyes. "What a perfectly extraordinary notion!" cried Flambeau. "Do you really think that is the truth?"

"I am perfectly sure it isn't," answered Father Brown, "only you said that nobody could connect snuff and diamonds and clockwork and candles. I give you that connexion off-hand. The real truth, I am very sure, lies deeper."

He paused a moment and listened to the wailing of the wind in the turrets. Then he said: "The late Earl of Glengyle was a thief. He lived a second and darker life as a desperate housebreaker. He did not have any candlesticks because he only used these candles cut short in the lantern he carried. The snuff he employed as the fiercest French criminals have used pepper: to fling it suddenly in dense masses in the face of a captor or pursuer. But the final proof is in the curious coincidence of the diamonds and the small steel wheels. Surely that makes everything plain to you? Diamonds and small steel wheels are the only two instruments with which you can cut out a pane of glass."

The bough of a broken pine tree lashed heavily in the blast against the window-pane behind them, as if in parody of a burglar, but they did not turn round. Their eyes were fastened on Father Brown.

"Diamonds and small wheels," repeated Craven ruminating. "Is that all that makes you think it the true explanation?"

"I don't think it the true explanation," replied the priest placidly; "but you said that nobody could connect the four things. The true tale, of course, is something much more humdrum. Glengyle had found, or thought he had found, precious stones on his estate. Somebody had bamboozled him with those loose brilliants, saying they were found in the castle caverns. The little wheels are some diamond-cutting affair. He had to do the thing very roughly and in a small way, with the help of a few shepherds or rude fellows on these hills. Snuff is the one great luxury of such Scotch shepherds; it's the one thing with which you can bribe them. They didn't have candlesticks because they didn't want them; they held the candles in their hands when they explored the caves."

"Is that all?" asked Flambeau after a long pause. "Have we got to the dull truth at last?"

"Oh, no," said Father Brown.

As the wind died in the most distant pine woods with a long hoot as of mockery, Father Brown, with an utterly impassive face, went on:

"I only suggested that because you said one could not plausibly connect snuff with clockwork or candles with bright stones. Ten false philosophies will fit the universe; ten false theories will fit Glengyle Castle. But we want the real explanation of the castle and the universe. But are there no other exhibits?"

Craven laughed, and Flambeau rose smiling to his feet and strolled down the long table.

"Items five, six, seven, etc.," he said, "are certainly more varied than instructive. A curious collection, not of lead pencils, but of lead out of lead pencils. A senseless stick of bamboo, with the top rather splintered. It might be the instrument of the crime. Only, there isn't any crime. The only other things are a few old missals and little Catholic pictures, which the Ogilvies kept, I suppose, from the Middle Ages—their family pride being stronger than their Puritanism. We only put them in the museum because they seem curiously cut about and defaced."

The heady tempest without drove a dreadful wrack of clouds across Glengyle and threw the long room into darkness as Father Brown picked up the little illuminated pages to examine them. He spoke before the drift of darkness had passed; but it was the voice of an utterly new man.

"Mr. Craven," said he, talking like a man ten years younger: "you have got a legal warrant, haven't you, to go up and examine that grave? The sooner we do it the better, and get to the bottom of this horrible affair. If I were you I should start now."

"Now," repeated the astonished detective, "and why now?"

"Because this is serious," answered Brown; "this is not spilt snuff or loose pebbles, that might be there for a hundred reasons. There is only one reason I know of for *this* being done; and the reason goes down to the roots of the world. These religious pictures are not just dirtied or torn or scrawled over, which might be done in idleness or bigotry, by children or by Protestants. These have been treated very carefully—and very queerly. In every place where the great ornamented name of God comes in the old illuminations it has been elaborately taken out. The only other thing that has been removed is the halo round the head of the Child Jesus. Therefore, I say, let us get our warrant and our spade and our hatchet, and go and break open that coffin."

"What *do* you mean?" demanded the London officer.

"I mean," answered the little priest, and his voice seemed to rise slightly in the roar of the gale, "I mean that the great devil of the universe may be sitting on the top tower of this castle at this moment, as big as a hundred elephants, and roaring like the Apocalypse. There is black magic somewhere at the bottom of this."

"Black magic," repeated Flambeau in a low voice, for he was too enlightened a man not to know of such things; "but what can these other things mean?"

"Oh, something damnable, I suppose," replied Brown impatiently. "How should I know? How can I guess all their mazes down below? Perhaps you can make a torture out of snuff and bamboo. Perhaps lunatics lust after wax and steel filings. Perhaps there is a maddening drug made of lead pencils! Our shortest cut to the mystery is up the hill to the grave."

His comrades hardly knew that they had obeyed and followed him till a blast of the night wind nearly flung them on their faces in the garden. Nevertheless they had obeyed him like automata; for Craven found a hatchet in his hand, and the warrant in his pocket; Flambeau was carrying the heavy spade of the strange gardener; Father Brown was carrying the little gilt book from which had been torn the name of God.

The path up the hill to the churchyard was crooked but short; only under the stress of wind it seemed laborious and long. Far as the eye could see, farther and farther as they mounted the slope, were seas beyond seas of pines, now all aslope one way under the wind. And that universal gesture seemed as vain as it was vast, as vain as if that wind were whistling about some unpeopled and purposeless planet. Through all that infinite growth of grey-blue forests sang, shrill and high, that ancient sorrow that is in the heart of all heathen things. One could fancy that the voices from the underworld of unfathomable foliage were cries of the lost and wandering pagan gods: gods who had gone roaming in that irrational forest, and who will never find their way back to heaven.

"You see," said Father Brown in low but easy tone, "Scotch people before Scotland existed were a curious lot. In fact, they're a curious lot still. But in the prehistoric times I fancy they really worshipped demons. That," he added genially, "is why they jumped at the Puritan theology."

"My friend," said Flambeau, turning in a kind of fury, "what does all that snuff mean?"

"My friend," replied Brown, with equal seriousness, "there is one mark of all genuine religions: materialism. Now, devil-worship is a perfectly genuine religion."

They had come up on the grassy scalp of the hill, one of the few bald spots that stood clear of the crashing and roaring pine forest. A mean enclosure, partly timber and partly wire, rattled in the tempest to tell them the border of the graveyard. But by the time Inspector Craven had come to the corner of the grave, and Flambeau had planted his spade point downwards and leaned on it, they were both almost as shaken as the shaky wood and wire. At the foot of the grave grew great tall thistles, grey and silver in their decay. Once or twice, when a ball of thistle-down broke under the breeze and flew past him, Craven jumped slightly as if it had been an arrow.

Flambeau drove the blade of his spade through the whistling

grass into the wet clay below. Then he seemed to stop and lean on it as on a staff.

"Go on," said the priest very gently. "We are only trying to find the truth. What are you afraid of?"

"I am afraid of finding it," said Flambeau.

The London detective spoke suddenly in a high crowing voice that was meant to be conversational and cheery. "I wonder why he really did hide himself like that. Something nasty, I suppose; was he a leper?"

"Something worse than that," said Flambeau.

"And what do you imagine," asked the other, "would be worse than a leper?"

"I don't imagine it," said Flambeau.

He dug for some dreadful minutes in silence, and then said in a choked voice: "I'm afraid of his not being the right shape."

"Nor was that piece of paper, you know," said Father Brown quietly, "and we survived even that piece of paper."

Flambeau dug on with a blind energy. But the tempest had shouldered away the choking grey clouds that clung to the hills like smoke and revealed grey fields of faint starlight before he cleared the shape of a rude timber coffin, and somehow tipped it up upon the turf. Craven stepped forward with his axe; a thistle-top touched, and he flinched. Then he took a firmer stride, and hacked and wrenched with an energy like Flambeau's till the lid was torn off, and all that was there lay glimmering in the grey starlight.

"Bones," said Craven; and then he added, "but it is a man," as if that were something unexpected.

"Is he," asked Flambeau in a voice that went oddly up and down, "is he all right?"

"Seems so," said the officer huskily, bending over the obscure and decaying skeleton in the box. "Wait a minute."

A vast heave went over Flambeau's huge figure. "And now I come to think of it," he cried, "why in the name of madness shouldn't he be all right? What is it gets hold of a man on these cursed cold mountains? I think it's the black, brainless repetition; all these forests, and over all an ancient horror of unconsciousness. It's like the dream of an atheist. Pine-trees and more pine-trees and millions more pine-trees——"

"God!" cried the man by the coffin; "but he hasn't got a head."

While the others stood rigid the priest, for the first time, showed a leap of startled concern.

"No head!" he repeated. "*No head?*" as if he had almost expected some other deficiency.

Half-witted visions of a headless baby born to Glengyle, of a headless youth hiding himself in the castle, of a headless man pacing those ancient halls or that gorgeous garden, passed in panorama through their minds. But even in that stiffened instant the tale took no root in them and seemed to have no reason in it. They stood listening to the loud woods and the shrieking sky quite foolishly, like exhausted animals. Thought seemed to be something enormous that had suddenly slipped out of their grasp.

"There are three headless men," said Father Brown: "standing round this open grave."

The pale detective from London opened his mouth to speak, and left it open like a yokel, while a long scream of wind tore the sky; then he looked at the axe in his hands as if it did not belong to him, and dropped it.

"Father," said Flambeau in that infantile and heavy voice he used very seldom, "what are we to do?"

His friend's reply came with the pent promptitude of a gun going off.

"Sleep!" cried Father Brown. "Sleep. We have come to the end of the ways. Do you know what sleep is? Do you know that every man who sleeps believes in God? It is a sacrament; for it is an act of faith and it is a food. And we need a sacrament, if only a natural one. Something has fallen on us that falls very seldom on men; perhaps the worst thing that can fall on them."

Craven's parted lips came together to say: "What do you mean?"

The priest turned his face to the castle as he answered:

"We have found the truth; and the truth makes no sense."

He went down the path in front of them with a plunging and reckless step very rare with him, and when they reached the castle again he threw himself upon sleep with the simplicity of a dog.

Despite his mystic praise of slumber, Father Brown was up earlier than anyone else except the silent gardener; and was found smoking a big pipe and watching that expert at his speechless labours in the kitchen garden. Towards daybreak the rocking storm had ended in roaring rains, and the day came with a curious freshness. The gardener seemed even to have been conversing, but at sight of the detectives he planted his spade sullenly in a bed and, saying something about his breakfast, shifted along the lines of cabbages and shut himself in the kitchen. "He's a valuable man, that," said Father Brown. "He does the potatoes amazingly. Still," he added with a dispassionate charity, "he has his faults; which of us hasn't? He doesn't dig this bank quite regularly. There, for instance," and he stamped suddenly on one spot. "I'm really very doubtful about that potato."

"And why?" asked Craven, amused with the little man's new hobby.

"I'm doubtful about it," said the other, "because old Gow was doubtful about it himself. He put his spade in methodically in every place but just this. There must be a mighty fine potato just there."

Flambeau pulled up the spade and impetuously drove it into the place. He turned up, under a load of soil, something that did not look like a potato, but rather like a monstrous, overdomed mushroom. But it struck the spade with a cold click; it rolled over like a ball, and grinned up at them.

"The Earl of Glengyle," said Brown sadly, and looked down heavily at the skull.

Then, after a momentary meditation, he plucked the spade from Flambeau, and, saying: "We must hide it again," clamped the skull down in the earth. Then he leaned his little body and huge head on the great handle of the spade, that stood up stiffly in the earth, and his eyes were empty and his forehead full of wrinkles. "If one could only conceive," he muttered, "the meaning of this last monstrosity." And leaning on the large spade handle, he buried his brows in his hands, as men do in church.

All the corners of the sky were brightening into blue and silver; the birds were chattering in the tiny garden trees; so loud it seemed as if the trees themselves were talking. But the three men were silent enough.

"Well, I give it all up," said Flambeau at last boisterously. "My brain and this world don't fit each other; and there's an end of it. Snuff, spoilt Prayer Books, and the insides of musical boxes—what——"

Brown threw up his bothered brow and rapped on the spade handle with an intolerance quite unusual with him. "Oh, tut, tut, tut, tut!" he cried. "All that is as plain as a pikestaff. I understood the snuff and clockwork, and so on, when I first opened my eyes this morning. And since then I've had it out with old Gow, the gardener, who is neither so deaf nor so stupid as he pretends. There's something amiss about the loose items. I was wrong about the torn mass-book, too; there's no harm in that. But it's this last business. Desecrating graves and stealing dead men's heads—surely there's harm in that? Surely there's black magic still in that? That doesn't fit in to the quite simple story of the snuff and the candles." And, striding about again, he smoked moodily.

"My friend," said Flambeau, with a grim humour, "you must be careful with me and remember I was once a criminal. The great advantage of that estate was that I always made up the story myself, and acted it as quick as I chose. This detective business of waiting about is too much for my French impatience. All my life, for good or evil, I have done things at the instant; I always fought duels the next morning; I always paid bills on the nail; I never even put off a visit to the dentist——"

Father Brown's pipe fell out of his mouth and broke into three pieces on the gravel path. He stood rolling his eyes, the exact picture of an idiot. "Lord, what a turnip I am!" he kept saying.

"Lord, what a turnip!" Then, in a somewhat groggy kind of way, he began to laugh.

"The dentist!" he repeated. "Six hours in the spiritual abyss, and all because I never thought of the dentist! Such a simple, such a beautiful and peaceful thought! Friends, we have passed a night in hell; but now the sun is risen, the birds are singing, and the radiant form of the dentist consoles the world."

"I will get some sense out of this," cried Flambeau, striding forward, "if I use the tortures of the Inquisition."

Father Brown repressed what appeared to be a momentary disposition to dance on the now sunlit lawn and cried quite piteously, like a child: "Oh, let me be silly a little. You don't know how unhappy I have been. And now I know that there has been no deep sin in this business at all. Only a little lunacy, perhaps—and who minds that?"

He spun round once, then faced them with gravity.

"This is not a story of crime," he said, "rather it is the story of a strange and crooked honesty. We are dealing with the one man on earth, perhaps, who has taken no more than his due. It is a study in the savage living logic that has been the religion of this race.

"That old local rhyme about the house of Glengyle——

> " 'As green sap to the simmer trees
> Is red gold to the Ogilvies'——

was literal as well as metaphorical. It did not merely mean that the Glengyles sought for wealth; it was also true that they literally gathered gold; they had a huge collection of ornaments and utensils in that metal. They were, in fact, misers whose mania took that turn. In the light of that fact, run through all the things we found in the castle. Diamonds without their gold rings; candles without their gold candlesticks; snuff without the gold snuff-boxes; pencil-leads without the gold pencil-cases; a walking-stick without its gold top; clockwork without the gold clocks—or rather watches. And, mad as it sounds, because the haloes and the name of God in the old missals were of real gold, these also were taken away."

The garden seemed to brighten, the grass to grow gayer in the strengthening sun, as the crazy truth was told. Flambeau lit a cigarette as his friend went on.

"Were taken away," continued Father Brown; "were taken away—but not stolen. Thieves would never have left this mystery. Thieves would have taken the gold snuff-boxes, snuff and all; the gold pencil-cases, lead and all. We have to deal with a man with a peculiar conscience, but certainly a conscience. I found that mad moralist this morning in the kitchen garden yonder, and I heard the whole story.

"The late Archbishop Ogilvie was the nearest approach to a good man ever born at Glengyle. But his bitter virtue took the turn of the misanthrope; he moped over the dishonesty of his ancestors, from which, somehow, he generalized a dishonesty of all men. More especially he distrusted philanthrophy or free-giving; and he swore if he could find one man who took his exact rights he should have all the gold of Glengyle. Having delivered this defiance to humanity he shut himself up, without the smallest expectation of its being answered. One day, however, a deaf and seemingly senseless lad from a distant village brought him a belated telegram; and Glengyle, in his acrid pleasantry, gave him a new farthing. At least he thought he had done so, but when he turned over his change he found the new farthing still there and a sovereign gone. The accident offered him vistas of sneering speculation. Either way, the boy would show the greasy greed of the species. Either he would vanish, a thief stealing a coin; or he would sneak back with it virtuously, a snob seeking a reward. In the middle of the night Lord Glengyle was knocked up out of his bed—for he lived alone—and forced to open the door to the deaf idiot. The idiot brought with him, not the sovereign, but exactly nineteen shillings and eleven-pence three-farthings in change.

"Then the wild exactitude of this action took hold on the mad lord's brain like fire. He swore he was Diogenes, that had long sought an honest man, and at last had found one. He made a new will, which I have seen. He took the literal youth into his huge, neglected house, and trained him up as his solitary servant and—after an odd manner—his heir. And whatever that queer creature understands, he understood absolutely his lord's two fixed ideas: first, that the letter of right is everything; and second, that he himself was to have the gold of Glengyle. So far, that is all; and that is simple. He has stripped the house of gold, and taken not a grain that was not gold; not so much as a grain of snuff. He lifted the gold leaf off an old illumination, fully satisfied that he left the rest unspoilt. All that I understood; but I could not understand this skull business. I was really uneasy about the human head buried among the potatoes. It distressed me—till Flambeau said the word.

"It will be all right. He will put the skull back in the grave, when he has taken the gold out of the tooth."

And indeed, when Flambeau crossed the hill that morning, he saw that strange being, the just miser, digging at the desecrated grave, the plaid round his throat thrashing out in the mountain wind; the sober top hat on his head.

From *The Father Brown Stories*
(Cassell & Co. Ltd.)

The Perishing of the Pendragons

Father Brown was in no mood for adventures. He had lately fallen ill with over-work, and when he began to recover, his friend Flambeau had taken him on a cruise in a small yacht with Sir Cecil Fanshaw, a young Cornish squire and an enthusiast for Cornish coast scenery. But Brown was still rather weak; he was no very happy sailor; and though he was never of the sort that either grumbles or breaks down, his spirits did not rise above patience and civility. When the other two men praised the ragged violet sunset or the ragged volcanic crags, he agreed with them. When Flambeau pointed out a rock shaped like a dragon, he looked at it and thought it very like a dragon. When Fanshaw more excitedly indicated a rock that was like Merlin, he looked at it, and signified assent. When Flambeau asked whether this rocky gate of the twisted river was not the gate of Fairyland, he said "Yes". He heard the most important things and the most trivial with the same tasteless absorption. He heard that the coast was death to all but careful seamen; he also heard that the ship's cat was asleep. He heard that Fanshaw couldn't find his cigar-holder anywhere; he also heard the pilot deliver the oracle "Both eyes bright, she's all right; one eye winks, down she sinks". He heard Flambeau say to Fanshaw that no doubt this meant the pilot must keep both eyes open and be spry. And he heard Fanshaw say to Flambeau that, oddly enough, it didn't mean this: it meant that while they saw two of the coast-lights, one near and the other distant, exactly side by side, they were in the right river-channel; but that if one light was hidden behind the other, they were going on the rocks. He heard Fanshaw add that his country was full of such quaint fables and idioms; it was the very home of romance; he even pitted this part of Cornwall against Devonshire, as a claimant to the laurels of Elizabethan seamanship. According to him there had been captains among these coves and islets compared with whom Drake was practically a landsman. He heard Flambeau laugh, and ask if, perhaps, the adventurous title of "Westward Ho!" only meant that all Devonshire men wished they were living in Cornwall. He heard Fanshaw say there was no need to be silly; that not only had Cornish captains been heroes, but that they were heroes still: that near that very spot there was an old admiral, now retired, who was scarred by thrilling voyages full of adventures; and who had in his youth found the last group of eight Pacific Islands that was added to the chart of the world. This Cecil Fanshaw was, in person, of the kind that commonly urges such crude but pleasing enthusiasms; a very young man, light-haired, high-coloured, with an eager profile; with a boyish bravado of spirits, but an almost girlish delicacy of tint and type. The big shoulders, black brows and black mousquetaire swagger of Flambeau were a great contrast.

All these trivialities Brown heard and saw; but heard them as a tired man hears a tune in the railway wheels, or saw them as a sick man sees the pattern of his wall-paper. No one can calculate the turns of mood in convalescence: but Father Brown's depression must have had a great deal to do with his mere unfamiliarity with the sea. For as the river-mouth narrowed like the neck of a bottle, and the water grew calmer and the air warmer and more earthly, he seemed to wake up and take notice like a baby. They had reached that phase just after sunset when air and water both look bright, but earth and all its growing things look almost black by comparison. About this particular evening, however, there was something exceptional. It was one of those rare atmospheres in which a smoked-glass slide seems to have been slid away from between us and Nature; so that even dark colours on that day look more gorgeous than bright colours on cloudier days. The trampled earth of the river-banks and the peaty stain in the pools did not look drab but glowing umber, and the dark woods astir in the breeze did not look, as usual, dim blue with mere depth or distance, but more like wind-tumbled masses of some vivid violet blossom. This magic clearness and intensity in the colours was further forced on Brown's slowly reviving senses by something romantic and even secret in the very form of the landscape.

The river was still well wide and deep enough for a pleasure boat so small as theirs; but the curves of the country-side suggested that it was closing in on either hand; the woods seemed to be making broken and flying attempts at bridge-building—as if the boat were passing from the romance of a valley to the romance of a hollow and so to the supreme romance of a tunnel. Beyond this mere look of things there was little for Brown's freshening fancy to feed on; he saw no human beings, except some gipsies trailing along the river bank, with faggots and osiers cut in the forest; and one sight no longer unconventional, but in such remote parts still uncommon: a dark-haired lady, bare-headed, and paddling her own canoe. If Father Brown ever attached any importance to either of these, he certainly forgot them at the next turn of the river which brought in sight a singular object.

The water seemed to widen and split, being cloven by the dark wedge of a fish-shaped and wooded islet. With the rate at which they went, the islet seemed to swim towards them like a ship; a ship with a very high prow—or, to speak more strictly, a very high funnel. For at the extreme point nearest them stood up an odd-looking building, unlike anything they could remember or connect with any purpose. It was not specially high, but it was too high for its breadth to be called anything but a tower. Yet it appeared to be built entirely of wood, and that in a most unequal and eccentric way. Some of the planks and beams were of good, seasoned oak; some of such wood cut raw and recent; some again of white pinewood, and a great deal more of the same sort of wood painted black with tar. These black beams were set crooked or criss-cross at all kinds of angles, giving the whole a most patchy and puzzling appearance. There were one or two windows, which appeared to be coloured and leaded in an old-fashioned but more elaborate style. The travellers looked at it with that paradoxical feeling we have when something reminds us of something, and yet we are certain it is something very different.

Father Brown, even when he was mystified, was clever in analysing his own mystification. And he found himself reflecting that the oddity seemed to consist in a particular shape cut out in an incongruous material; as if one saw a top-hat made of tin, or a frock-coat cut out of tartan. He was sure he had seen timbers of different tints arranged like that somewhere, but never in such architectural proportions. The next moment a glimpse through the dark trees told him all he wanted to know, and he laughed. Through a gap in the foliage there appeared for a moment one of those old wooden houses, faced with black beams, which are still to be found here and there in England, but which most of us see imitated in some show called "Old London" or "Shakespeare's England". It was in view only long enough for the priest to see that, however old-fashioned, it was a comfortable and well-kept country-house, with flower-beds in front of it. It had none of the piebald and crazy look of the tower that seemed made out of its refuse.

"What on earth's this?" said Flambeau, who was still staring at the tower.

Fanshaw's eyes were shining, and he spoke triumphantly. "Aha! you've not seen a place quite like this before, I fancy; that's why I've brought you here, my friend. Now you shall see whether I exaggerate about the mariners of Cornwall. This place belongs to Old Pendragon, whom we call the Admiral; though he retired before getting the rank. The spirit of Raleigh and Hawkins is a memory with the Devon folk; it's a modern fact with the Pendragons. If Queen Elizabeth were to rise from the grave and come up this river in a gilded barge, she would be received by the Admiral in a house exactly such as she was accustomed to, in every corner and casement, in every panel on the wall or plate on the table. And she would find an English Captain still talking fiercely of fresh lands to be found in little ships, as much as if she had dined with Drake."

"She'd find a rum sort of thing in the garden," said Father Brown, "which would not please her Renaissance eye. That Elizabethan domestic architecture is charming in its way; but it's against the very nature of it to break out into turrets."

"And yet," answered Fanshaw, "that's the most romantic and Elizabethan part of the business. It was built by the Pendragons in the very days of the Spanish wars; and though it's needed patching and even rebuilding for another reason, it's always been rebuilt in the old way. The story goes that the lady of Sir Peter Pendragon built it in this place and to this height, because from the top you can just see the corner where vessels turn into the river mouth; and she wished to be the first to see her husband's ship, as he sailed home from the Spanish Main."

"For what other reason," asked Father Brown, "do you mean that it has been rebuilt?"

"Oh, there's a strange story about that, too," said the young squire with relish. "You are really in a land of strange stories. King Arthur was here and Merlin and the fairies before him. The story goes that Sir Peter Pendragon, who (I fear) had some of the faults of the pirates as well as the virtues of the sailor, was bringing home three Spanish gentlemen in honorable captivity, intending to escort them to Elizabeth's court. But he was a man of flaming and tigerish temper, and coming to high words with one of them, he caught him by the throat and flung him, by accident or design, into the sea. A second Spaniard, who was the brother of the first, instantly drew his sword and flew at Pendragon, and after a short but furious combat in which both got three wounds in as many minutes, Pendragon drove his blade through the other's body and the second Spaniard was accounted for. As it happened the ship had already turned into the river mouth and was close to comparatively shallow water. The third Spaniard sprang over the side of the ship, struck out for the shore, and was soon near enough to it to stand up to his waist in water. And turning again to face the ship, and holding up both arms to Heaven—like a prophet calling plagues upon a wicked city—he called out to Pendragon in a piercing and terrible voice, that he at least was yet living, that he would go on living, that he would live for ever; and that generation after generation the house of Pendragon should never see him or his, but should know by very certain signs that he and his vengeance were alive. With that he dived under the wave, and was either drowned or swam so long under water that no hair of his head was seen afterwards."

"There's that girl in the canoe again," said Flambeau irrelevantly, for good-looking young women would call him off any topic. "She seems bothered by the queer tower just as we were."

Indeed, the black-haired young lady was letting her canoe float slowly and silently past the strange islet; and was looking intently up at the strange tower, with a strong glow of curiosity on her oval and olive face.

"Never mind girls," said Fanshaw impatiently; "there are plenty of them in the world, but not many things like the Pendragon Tower. As you may easily suppose, plenty of superstitions and scandals have followed in the track of the Spaniard's curse; and no doubt, as you would put it, any accident happening to this Cornish family would be connected with it by rural credulity. But it is perfectly true that this tower has been burnt down two or three times; and the family can't be called lucky, for more than two, I think, of the Admiral's near kin have perished by shipwreck; and one at least to my own knowledge, on practically the same spot where Sir Peter threw the Spaniard overboard."

"What a pity!" exclaimed Flambeau. "She's going."

"When did your friend the Admiral tell you this family history?" asked Father Brown, as the girl in the canoe paddled off, without showing the least intention of extending her interest from the tower to the yacht, which Fanshaw had already caused to lie alongside the island.

"Many years ago," replied Fanshaw; "he hasn't been to sea for some time now, though he is as keen on it as ever. I believe there's a family compact or something. Well, here's the landing-stage; let's come ashore and see the old boy."

They followed him on to the island, just under the tower, and Father Brown, whether from the mere touch of dry land, or the interest of something on the other bank of the river (which he stared at very hard for some seconds), seemed singularly improved in briskness. They entered a wooded avenue between two fences of thin greyish wood, such as often enclose parks or gardens, and over the top of which the dark trees tossed to and fro like black and purple plumes upon the hearse of a giant. The tower, as they left it behind, looked all the quainter, because such entrances are usually flanked by two towers; and this one looked lopsided. But for this, the avenue had the usual appearance of the entrance to a gentleman's grounds; and, being so curved that the house was now out of sight, somehow looked a much larger park than any plantation on such an island could really be. Father Brown was, perhaps, a little fanciful in his fatigue, but he almost thought the whole place must be growing larger, as things do in a nightmare. Anyhow, a mystical monotony was the only character of their march, until Fanshaw suddenly stopped, and pointed to something sticking out through the grey fence—something that looked at first rather like the imprisoned horn of some beast. Closer observation showed that it was a slightly curved blade of metal that shone faintly in the fading light.

Flambeau, who like all Frenchmen had been a soldier, bent over it and said in a startled voice: "Why, it's a sabre! I believe I know the sort, heavy and curved, but shorter than the cavalry; they used to have them in artillery and the——"

As he spoke the blade plucked itself out of the crack it had made and came down again with a more ponderous slash, splitting the fissiparous fence to the bottom with a rending noise. Then it was pulled out again, flashed above the fence some feet farther along, and again split it halfway down with the first stroke; and after waggling a little to extricate itself (accompanied with curses in the darkness) split it down to the ground with a second. Then a kick of devilish energy sent the whole loosened square of thin wood flying into the pathway, and a great gap of dark coppice gaped in the paling.

Fanshaw peered into the dark opening and uttered an exclamation of astonishment. "My dear Admiral!" he exclaimed, "do you—er—do you generally cut out a new front door whenever you want to go for a walk?"

The voice in the gloom swore again, and then broke into a jolly laugh. "No," it said; "I've really got to cut down this fence somehow; it's spoiling all the plants, and no one else here can do it. But I'll only carve another bit off the front door, and then come out and welcome you."

And sure enough, he heaved up his weapon once more, and, hacking twice, brought down another and similar strip of fence, making the opening about fourteen feet wide in all. Then through this larger forest gateway he came out into the evening light, with a chip of grey wood sticking to his sword-blade.

He momentarily fulfilled all Fanshaw's fable of an old piratical Admiral; though the details seemed afterwards to decompose into accidents. For instance, he wore a broad-brimmed hat as protection against the sun; but the front flap of it was turned up straight to the sky, and the two corners pulled down lower than the ears, so that it stood across his forehead in a crescent like the old cocked hat worn by Nelson. He wore an ordinary dark-blue jacket, with nothing special about the buttons, but the combination of it with white linen trousers somehow had a sailorish look. He was tall and loose, and walked with a sort of swagger, which was not a sailor's roll, and yet somehow suggested it; and he held in his hand a short sabre which was like a navy cutlass, but about twice as big. Under the bridge of the hat his eagle face looked eager, all the more because it was not only clean-shaven, but without eyebrows. It seemed almost as if all the hair had come off his face from his thrusting it through a throng of elements. His eyes were prominent and piercing. His colour was curiously attractive, while partly tropical; it reminded one vaguely of a blood-orange. That is, that while it was ruddy and sanguine, there was a yellow in it that was in no way sickly, but seemed rather to glow like gold apples of the Hesperides. Father Brown thought he had never seen a figure so expressive of all the romances about the countries of the Sun.

When Fanshaw had presented his two friends to their host he fell again into a tone of rallying the latter about his wreckage of the fence and his apparent rage of profanity. The Admiral pooh-poohed it at first as a piece of necessary but annoying garden work; but at length the ring of real energy came back into his laughter, and he cried with a mixture of impatience and good humour:

"Well, perhaps I do go at it a bit rabidly, and feel a kind of pleasure in smashing anything. So would you if your only pleasure was in cruising about to find some new Cannibal Islands, and you had to stick on this muddy little rockery in a sort of rustic pond. When I remember how I've cut down a mile and a half of green poisonous jungle with an old cutlass half as sharp as this; and then remember I must stop here and chop this matchwood, because of some confounded old bargain scribbled in a family Bible, why, I——"

He swung up the heavy steel again; and this time sundered the wall of wood from top to bottom at one stroke.

"I feel like that," he said, laughing, but furiously flinging the sword some yards down the path, "and now let's go up to the house; you must have some dinner."

The semicircle of lawn in front of the house was varied by three circular garden beds, one of red tulips, a second of yellow tulips, and the third of some white, waxen-looking blossoms that the visitors did not know and presumed to be exotic. A heavy, hairy and rather sullen-looking gardener was hanging up a heavy coil of garden hose. The corners of the expiring sunset which seemed to cling about the corners of the house gave glimpses here and there of the colours of remoter flower-beds; and in a treeless space on one side of the house opening upon the river stood a tall brass tripod on which was tilted a big brass telescope. Just outside the steps of the porch stood a little painted green garden table, as if someone had just had tea there. The entrance was flanked with two of those half-featured lumps of stone with holes for eyes that are said to be South Sea idols; and on the brown oak beam across the doorway were some confused carvings that looked almost as barbaric.

As they passed indoors, the little cleric hopped suddenly on to the table, and standing on it peered unaffectedly through his spectacles at the mouldings in the oak. Admiral Pendragon looked very much astonished, though not particularly annoyed; while Fanshaw was so amused with what looked like a performing pigmy on his little stand, that he could not control his laughter. But Father Brown was not likely to notice either the laughter or the astonishment.

He was gazing at three carved symbols, which, though very worn and obscure, seemed still to convey some sense to him. The first seemed to be the outline of some tower or other building, crowned with what looked like curly-pointed ribbons. The second was clearer: an old Elizabethan galley with decorative waves beneath it, but interrupted in the middle by a curious jagged rock, which was either a fault in the wood or some conventional representation of the water coming in. The third represented the upper half of a human figure, ending in an escalloped line like the waves; the face was rubbed and featureless, and both arms were held very stiffly up in the air.

"Well," muttered Father Brown, blinking, "here is the legend of the Spaniard plain enough. Here he is holding up his arms and cursing in the sea; and here are the two curses: the wrecked ship and the burning of Pendragon Tower."

Pendragon shook his head with a kind of venerable amusement. "And how many other things might it not be?" he said. "Don't you know that sort of half-man, like a half-lion or half-stag, is quite common in heraldry? Might not that line through the ship be one of those *parti-per-pale* lines, *indented*, I think they call it? And though the third thing isn't so very heraldic, it would be more heraldic to suppose it a tower crowned with laurel than with fire; and it looks just as like it."

"But it seems rather odd," said Flambeau, "that it should exactly confirm the old legend."

"Ah," replied the sceptical traveller, "but you don't know how much of the old legend may have been made up from the old figures. Besides, it isn't the only old legend. Fanshaw, here, who is fond of such things, will tell you there are other versions of the tale, and much more horrible ones. One story credits my unfortunate ancestor with having had the Spaniard cut in two;

and that will fit the pretty picture also. Another obligingly credits our family with the possession of a tower full of snakes and explains those little, wriggly things in that way. And a third theory supposes the crooked line on the ship to be a conventionalized thunderbolt; but that alone, if seriously examined, would show what a very little way these unhappy coincidences really go."

"Why, how do you mean?" asked Fanshaw.

"It so happens," replied his host coolly, "that there was no thunder and lightning at all in the two or three shipwrecks I know of in our family."

"Oh!" said Father Brown, and jumped down from the little table.

There was another silence in which they heard the continuous murmur of the river; then Fanshaw said, in a doubtful and perhaps disappointed tone: "Then you don't think there is anything in the tales of the tower in flames?"

"There are the tales, of course," said the Admiral, shrugging his shoulders; "and some of them, I don't deny, on evidence as decent as one ever gets for such things. Someone saw a blaze hereabout, don't you know, as he walked home through a wood; someone keeping sheep on the uplands inland thought he saw a flame hovering over Pendragon Tower. Well, a damp dab of mud like this confounded island seems the last place where one would think of fires."

"What is that fire over there?" asked Father Brown with a gentle suddenness, pointing to the woods on the left river-bank. They were all thrown a little off their balance, and the more fanciful Fanshaw had even some difficulty in recovering his, as they saw a long, thin stream of blue smoke ascending silently into the end of the evening light.

Then Pendragon broke into a scornful laugh again. "Gipsies!" he said; "they've been camping about here for a week. Gentlemen, you want your dinner," and he turned as if to enter the house.

But the antiquarian superstition in Fanshaw was still quivering, and he said hastily: "But, Admiral, what's that hissing noise quite near the island? It's very like fire."

132

"It's more like what it is," said the Admiral, laughing as he led the way; "it's only some canoe going by."

Almost as he spoke, the butler, a lean man in black, with very black hair and a very long, yellow face, appeared in the doorway and told him that dinner was served.

The dining-room was as nautical as the cabin of a ship; but its note was rather that of the modern than the Elizabethan captain. There were, indeed, three antiquated cutlasses in a trophy over the fireplace, and one brown sixteenth-century map with Tritons and little ships dotted about a curly sea. But such things were less prominent on the white panelling than some cases of quaint-coloured South American birds, very scientifically stuffed, fantastic shells from the Pacific, and several instruments so rude and queer in shape that savages might have used them either to kill their enemies or to cook them. But the alien colour culminated in the fact that, besides the butler, the Admiral's only servants were two Negroes, somewhat quaintly clad in tight uniforms of yellow. The priest's instinctive trick of analysing his own impressions told him that the colour and the little neat coat-tails of these bipeds had suggested the word "Canary", and so by a mere pun connected them with southward travel. Towards the end of the dinner they took their yellow clothes and black faces out of the room, leaving only the black clothes and yellow face of the butler.

"I'm rather sorry you take this so lightly," said Fanshaw to the host; "for the truth is, I've brought these friends of mine with the idea of their helping you, as they know a good deal of these things. Don't you really believe in the family story at all?"

"I don't believe in anything," answered Pendragon very briskly, with a bright eye cocked at a red tropical bird. "I'm a man of science."

Rather to Flambeau's surprise, his clerical friend, who seemed to have entirely woke up, took up the digression and talked natural history with his host with a flow of words and much unexpected information, until the dessert and decanters were set down and the last of the servants vanished. Then he said, without altering his tone, "Please don't think me impertinent,

Admiral Pendragon. I don't ask for curiosity, but really for my guidance and your convenience. Have I made a bad shot if I guess you don't want these old things talked of before your butler?"

The Admiral lifted the hairless arches over his eyes and exclaimed: "Well, I don't know where you got it, but the truth is I can't stand the fellow, though I've no excuse for discharging a family servant. Fanshaw, with his fairy tales, would say my blood moved against men with that black, Spanish-looking hair."

Flambeau struck the table with his heavy fist. "By Jove!" he cried; "and so had that girl!"

"I hope it'll all end tonight," continued the Admiral, "when my nephew comes back safe from his ship. You look surprised. You won't understand, I suppose, unless I tell you the story. You see, my father had two sons; I remained a bachelor, but my elder brother married, and had a son who became a sailor like all the rest of us, and will inherit the proper estate. Well, my father was a strange man; he somehow combined Fanshaw's superstition with a good deal of my scepticism; they were always fighting in him; and after my first voyages, he developed a notion which he thought somehow would settle finally whether the curse was truth or trash. If all the Pendragons sailed about anyhow, he thought there would be too much chance of natural catastrophes to prove anything. But if we went to sea one at a time in strict order of succession to the property, he thought it might show whether any connected fate followed the family as a family. It was a silly notion, I think, and I quarrelled with my father pretty heartily; for I was an ambitious man and was left to the last, coming, by succession, after my own nephew."

"And your father and brother," said the priest, very gently, "died at sea, I fear."

"Yes," groaned the Admiral; "by one of those brutal accidents on which are built all the lying mythologies of mankind, they were both shipwrecked. My father, coming up this coast out of the Atlantic, was washed up on these Cornish rocks. My brother's ship was sunk, no one knows where, on the voyage home from Tasmania. His body was never found. I tell you it was from perfectly natural mishap; lots of other people besides Pendragons were drowned; and both disasters are discussed in a normal way by navigators. But, of course, it set this forest of supersition on fire; and men saw the flaming tower everywhere. That's why I say it will be all right when Walter returns. The girl he's engaged to was coming today; but I was so afraid of some chance delay frightening her that I wired her not to come till she heard from me. But he's practically sure to be here some time tonight, and then it'll all end in smoke—tobacco smoke. We'll crack that old lie when we crack a bottle of this wine."

"Very good wine," said Father Brown, gravely lifting his glass, "but, as you see, a very bad wine-bibber. I most sincerely beg your pardon"; for he had spilt a small spot of wine on the table-cloth. He drank and put down the glass with a composed face; but his hand had started at the exact moment when he became conscious of a face looking in through the garden window just behind the Admiral—the face of a woman, swarthy, with southern hair and eyes, and young, but like a mask of tragedy.

After a pause the priest spoke again in his mild manner. "Admiral," he said, "will you do me a favour? Let me, and my friends if they like, stop in that tower of yours just for tonight? Do you know that in my business you're an exorcist almost before anything else?"

Pendragon sprang to his feet and paced swiftly to and fro across the window, from which the face had instantly vanished. "I tell you there is nothing in it," he cried, with ringing violence. "There is one thing I know about this matter. You may call me an atheist. I am an atheist." Here he swung round and fixed Father Brown with a face of frightful concentration. "This business is perfectly natural. There is no curse in it at all."

Father Brown smiled. "In that case," he said, "there can't be any objection to my sleeping in your delightful summer-house."

"The idea is utterly ridiculous," replied the Admiral, beating a tattoo on the back of his chair.

"Please forgive me for everything," said Brown in his most

sympathetic tone, "including spilling the wine. But it seems to me you are not quite so easy about the flaming tower as you try to be."

Admiral Pendragon sat down again as abruptly as he had risen; but he sat quite still, and when he spoke again it was in a lower voice. "You do it at your own peril," he said; "but wouldn't *you* be an atheist to keep sane in all this devilry?"

Some three hours afterwards Fanshaw, Flambeau and the priest were still dawdling about the garden in the dark; and it began to dawn on the other two that Father Brown had no intention of going to bed either in the tower or the house.

"I think the lawn wants weeding," said he dreamily. "If I could find a spud or something I'd do it myself."

They followed him, laughing and half remonstrating; but he replied with the most solemnity, explaining to them, in a maddening little sermon, that one can always find some small occupation that is helpful to others. He did not find a spud; but he found an old broom made of twigs, with which he began energetically to brush the fallen leaves off the grass.

"Always some little thing to be done," he said with idiotic cheerfulness; "as George Herbert says: 'Who sweeps an Admiral's garden in Cornwall as for Thy laws makes that and the action fine.' And now," he added, suddenly slinging the broom away, "let's go and water the flowers."

With the same mixed emotions they watched him uncoil some considerable lengths of the large garden hose, saying with an air of wistful discrimination: "The red tulips before the yellow, I think. Look a bit dry, don't you think?"

He turned the little tap on the instrument, and the water shot out straight and solid as a long rod of steel.

"Look out, Samson," cried Flambeau; "why, you've cut off the tulip's head."

Father Brown stood ruefully contemplating the decapitated plant.

"Mine does seem to be a rather kill or cure sort of watering," he admitted, scratching his head. "I suppose it's a pity I didn't find the spud. You should have seen me with the spud! Talking of tools, you've got that swordstick, Flambeau, you always carry? That's right; and Sir Cecil could have that sword the Admiral threw away by the fence here. How grey everything looks!"

"The mist's rising from the river," said the staring Flambeau.

Almost as he spoke the huge figure of the hairy gardener appeared on a higher ridge of the trenched and terraced lawn, hailing them with a brandished rake and a horribly bellowing voice. "Put down that hose," he shouted; "put down that hose and go to your——"

"I am fearfully clumsy," replied the reverend gentleman weakly; "do you know, I upset some wine at dinner." He made a wavering half-turn of apology towards the gardener, with the hose still spouting in his hand. The gardener caught the cold crash of the water full in his face like the crash of a cannon-ball; staggered, slipped and went sprawling with his boots in the air.

"How very dreadful!" said Father Brown, looking round in a sort of wonder. "Why, I've hit a man!"

He stood with his head forward for a moment as if looking or listening; and then set off at a trot towards the tower, still trailing the hose behind him. The tower was quite close, but its outline was curiously dim.

"Your river mist," he said, "has a rum smell."

"By the Lord it has," cried Fanshaw, who was very white. "But you can't mean——"

"I mean," said Father Brown, "that one of the Admiral's scientific predictions is coming true tonight. This story is going to end in smoke."

As he spoke a most beautiful rose-red light seemed to burst into blossom like a gigantic rose; but accompanied with a crackling and rattling noise that was like the laughter of devils.

"My God! What is this?" cried Sir Cecil Fanshaw.

"The sign of the flaming tower," said Father Brown, and sent the driving water from his hose into the heart of the red patch.

"Lucky we hadn't gone to bed!" ejaculated Fanshaw. "I suppose it can't spread to the house."

"You may remember," said the priest quietly, "that the wooden fence that might have carried it was cut away."

Flambeau turned electrified eyes upon his friend, but Fanshaw only said rather absently: "Well, nobody can be killed, anyhow."

"This is rather a curious kind of tower," observed Father Brown; "when it takes to killing people, it always kills people who are somewhere else."

At the same instant the monstrous figure of the gardener with the streaming beard stood again on the green ridge against the sky, waving others to come on; but now waving not a rake but a cutlass. Behind him came the two Negroes, also with the old crooked cutlasses out of the trophy. But in the blood-red glare, with their black faces and yellow figures, they looked like devils carrying instruments of torture. In the dim garden behind them a distant voice was heard calling out brief directions. When the priest heard the voice, a terrible change came over his countenance.

But he remained composed; and never took his eye off the patch of flame which had begun by spreading, but now seemed to shrink a little as it hissed under the torch of the long silver spear of water. He kept his finger along the nozzle of the pipe to ensure the aim, and attended to no other business, knowing only by the noise and that semi-conscious corner of the eye, the exciting incidents that began to tumble themselves about the island garden. He gave two brief directions to his friends. One was: "Knock these fellows down somehow and tie them up, whoever they are; there's rope down by those faggots. They want to take away my nice hose." The other was: "As soon as you get a chance, call out to that canoeing girl; she's over on the bank with the gipsies. Ask her if they could get some buckets across and fill them from the river." Then he closed his mouth and continued to water the new red flower as ruthlessly as he had watered the red tulip.

He never turned his head to look at the strange fight that followed between the foes and friends of the mysterious fire. He almost felt the island shake when Flambeau collided with the huge gardener; he merely imagined how it would whirl round them as they wrestled. He heard the crashing fall; and his friend's gasp of triumph as he dashed on to the first Negro; and the cries of both the blacks as Flambeau and Fanshaw bound them. Flambeau's enormous strength more than redressed the odds in the fight, especially as the fourth man still hovered near the house, only a shadow and a voice. He heard also the water broken by the paddles of a canoe; the girl's voice giving orders, the voices of gipsies answering and coming nearer, the plumping and sucking noise of empty buckets plunged into a full stream; and finally the sound of many feet around the fire. But all this was less to him than the fact that the red rent, which had lately once more increased, had once more slightly diminished.

Then came a cry that very nearly made him turn his head. Flambeau and Fanshaw, now reinforced by some of the gipsies, had rushed after the mysterious man by the house; and he heard from the other end of the garden the Frenchman's cry of horror and astonishment. It was echoed by a howl not to be called human, as the being broke from their hold and ran along the garden. Three times at least it raced round the whole island, in a way that was as horrible as the chase of a lunatic, both in the cries of the pursued and the ropes carried by the pursuers; but was more horrible still, because it somehow suggested one of the chasing games of children in a garden. Then, finding them closing in on every side, the figure sprang upon one of the higher river banks and disappeared with a splash into the dark and driving river.

"You can do no more, I fear," said Brown in a voice cold with pain. "He has been washed down to the rocks by now, where he has sent so many others. He knew the use of a family legend."

"Oh, don't talk in these parables," cried Flambeau impatiently. "Can't you put it simply in words of one syllable?"

"Yes," answered Brown, with his eye on the house. " 'Both eyes bright, she's all right; one eye blinks, down she sinks.' "

The fire hissed and shrieked more and more, like a strangled thing, as it grew narrower and narrower under the flood from the pipe and buckets, but Father Brown still kept his eye on it as he went on speaking:

"I thought of asking this young lady, if it were morning yet, to look through that telescope at the river mouth and the river. She might have seen something to interest her: the sign of the ship, or Mr. Walter Pendragon coming home, and perhaps even the sign of the half-man, for though he is certainly safe by now, he may very well have waded ashore. He has been within a shave of another shipwreck; and would never have escaped it, if the lady hadn't had the sense to suspect the old Admiral's telegram and come down to watch him. Don't let's talk about the old Admiral. Don't let's talk about anything. It's enough to say that whenever this tower, with its pitch and resin-wood, really caught fire, the spark on the horizon always looked like the twin light to the coast lighthouse."

"And that," said Flambeau, "is how the father and brother died. The wicked uncle of the legends very nearly got his estate after all."

Father Brown did not answer; indeed, he did not speak again, save for civilities, till they were all safe round a cigar-box in the cabin of the yacht. He saw that the frustrated fire was extinguished; and then refused to linger, though he actually heard young Pendragon, escorted by an enthusiastic crowd, come tramping up the river bank; and might (had he been moved by romantic curiosities) have received the combined thanks of the man from the ship and the girl from the canoe. But his fatigue had fallen on him once more, and he only started once, when Flambeau abruptly told him he had dropped cigar-ash on his trousers.

"That's no cigar-ash," he said rather wearily. "That's from the fire, but you don't think so because you're all smoking cigars. That's just the way I got my first faint suspicion about the chart."

"Do you mean Pendragon's chart of his Pacific Islands?" asked Fanshaw.

"You thought it was a chart of the Pacific Islands," answered Brown. "Put a feather with a fossil and a bit of coral and everyone will think it's a specimen. Put the same feather with a ribbon and an artificial flower and everyone will think it's for a lady's hat. Put the same feather with an ink-bottle, a book and a stack of writing-paper, and most men will swear they've seen a quill pen. So you saw that map among tropic birds and shells and thought it was a map of Pacific Islands. It was the map of this river."

"But how do you know?" asked Fanshaw.

"I saw the rock you thought was like a dragon, and the one like Merlin, and——"

"You seem to have noticed a lot as we came in," cried Fanshaw. "We thought you were rather abstracted."

"I was sea-sick," said Father Brown simply. "I felt simply horrible. But feeling horrible has nothing to do with not seeing things." And he closed his eyes.

"Do you think most men would have seen that?" asked Flambeau. He received no answer: Father Brown was asleep.

From *The Father Brown Stories*
(Cassell & Co. Ltd.)

The Bottomless Well

On an oasis, or green island in the red and yellow seas of sand that stretch beyond Europe towards the sunrise, there can be found a rather fantastic contrast which is none the less typical of such a place, since international treaties have made it an out-post of British occupation. The site is famous among archaeologists for something that is hardly a monument but merely a hole in the ground. But it is a round shaft like that of a well, and probably a part of some great irrigation works of remote and disputed date; perhaps more ancient than anything in that ancient land. There is a green fringe of palm and prickly pear round the black mouth of the well; but nothing of the upper masonry remains except two bulky and battered stones standing like the pillars of a gateway of nowhere; in which some of the more transcendental archaeologists, in certain moods at moon-rise or sunset, think they can trace the faint lines of figures or features of more than Babylonian monstrosity; while the more rationalistic archaeologists, in the more rational hours of day-light, see nothing but two shapeless rocks. It may have been noticed, however, that all Englishmen are not archaeologists. Many of those assembled in such a place for official and military purposes have hobbies other than archaeology. And it is a solemn fact that the English in this eastern exile have con-trived to make a small golf links out of the green scrub and sand; with a comfortable club house at one end of it and this primeval monument at the other. They did not actually use this archaic abyss as a bunker; because it was by tradition un-fathomable, and even for practical purposes unfathomed. Any sporting projectile sent into it might be counted most literally as a lost ball. But they often sauntered round it in their interludes of talking and smoking cigarettes, and one of them had just come down from the club house to find another gazing somewhat moodily into the well.

The two Englishmen both wore light clothes and white pith helmets and pugarees, but there for the most part their resemblance ended. And they both almost simultaneously said the same word; but they said it on two totally different notes of the voice.

"Have you heard the news?" asked the man from the club. "Splendid."

"Splendid," replied the man by the well. But the first man pronounced the word as a young man might say it about a woman; and the second as an old man might say it about the weather; not without sincerity but certainly without fervour.

And in this the tone of the two men was sufficiently typical of them. The first, who was a certain Captain Boyle, was of a bold and boyish type, dark and with a sort of native heat in his face that did not belong to the atmosphere of the East, but rather to the ardours and ambitions of the West. The other was an older man and certainly an older resident; a civilian official named Horne Fisher; and his drooping eyelids and drooping light moustaches expressed all the paradox of the Englishman in the East. He was much too hot to be anything but cool.

Neither of them thought it necessary to mention what it was that was splendid. That would indeed have been superfluous conversation about something that everybody knew. The striking victory over a menacing combination of Turks and Arabs in the north, won by troops under the command of Lord Hastings, the veteran of so many striking victories, was already spread by the newspapers all over the Empire, let alone to this small garrison so near to the battlefield.

"Now no other nation in the world could have done a thing like that," cried Captain Boyle emphatically.

Horne Fisher was still looking silently into the well; a moment later he answered:

"We certainly have the art of unmaking mistakes. That's where the poor old Prussians went wrong. They could only make mistakes and stick to them. There is really a certain talent in unmaking mistakes."

"What do you mean?" asked Boyle. "What mistake?"

"Well, everybody knows it looked like biting off more than we could chew," replied Horne Fisher. It was a peculiarity of Mr. Fisher that he always said that everybody knew things that about one person in two million was ever allowed to hear of. "And it was certainly jolly lucky that Travers turned up so well in the nick of time. Odd how often the right thing's been done for us by the second in command, even when a great man was first in command. Like Colborne at Waterloo."

"It ought to add a whole province to the Empire," observed the other.

"Well, I suppose the Zimmerns would have insisted on it as far as the canal," observed Fisher thoughtfully, "though everybody knows adding provinces doesn't always pay much nowadays."

Captain Boyle frowned in a slightly puzzled fashion. Being cloudily conscious of never having heard of the Zimmerns in his life, he could only remark stolidly:

"Well, one can't be a Little Englander."

Horne Fisher smiled; and he had a pleasant smile.

"Every man out here is a Little Englander," he said. "He wishes he were back in Little England."

"I don't know what you're talking about, I'm afraid," said the younger man rather suspiciously. "One would think you didn't really admire Hastings or—or anything."

"I admire him no end," replied Fisher. "He's by far the best man for this post; he understands the Moslems and can do anything with them. That's why I'm all against pushing Travers against him, merely because of this last affair."

"I really don't understand what you're driving at," said the other frankly.

"Perhaps it isn't worth understanding," answered Fisher lightly, "and, anyhow, we needn't talk politics. Do you know the Arab legend about that well?"

"I'm afraid I don't know much about Arab legends," said Boyle rather stiffly.

"That's rather a mistake," replied Fisher, "especially from your point of view. Lord Hastings himself is an Arab legend. That is perhaps the very greatest thing he really is. If his reputation went, it would weaken us all over Asia and Africa. Well, the story about that hole in the ground, that goes down nobody knows where, has always fascinated me rather. It's Mahomedan in form now; but I shouldn't wonder if the tale is a long way older than Mahomet. It's all about somebody they call the Sultan Aladin; not our friend of the lamp, of course, but rather like him in having to do with genii or giants or something of that sort. They say he commanded the giants to build him a sort of pagoda rising higher and higher above all the stars. The Utmost for the Highest, as the people said when they built the Tower of Babel. But the builders of the Tower of Babel were quite modest and domestic people, like mice, compared with old Aladin. They only wanted a tower that would reach heaven, a mere trifle. He wanted a tower that would *pass* heaven, and rise above it, and go on rising for ever and ever. And Allah cast him down to earth with a thunderbolt, which sank into the earth, boring a hole deeper and deeper, till it made a well that was without a bottom as the tower was to have been without a top. And down that inverted tower of darkness the soul of the proud Sultan is falling for ever and ever."

"What a queer chap you are," said Boyle, "you talk as if a fellow could believe those fables."

"Perhaps I believe the moral and not the fable," answered Fisher, "but here comes Lady Hastings. You know her, I think?"

The club house on the golf links was used, of course, for many other purposes besides that of golf. It was the only social centre of the garrison besides the strictly military headquarters; it had a billiard-room and a bar, and even an excellent reference library for those officers who were so perverse as to take their profession seriously. Among these was the great general himself, whose head of silver and face of bronze, like that of a brazen eagle, were often to be found bent over the charts and folios of the library. The great Lord Hastings believed in science and study, as in other severe ideals of life; and had given much paternal advice on the point to young Boyle, whose appearances in that place of research were rather more intermittent. It was from one of these snatches of study that the young man had just come out through the glass doors of the library on to the golf links. But above all the club was so appointed as to serve the social conveniences of ladies at least as much as gentlemen; and Lady Hastings was able to play the queen in such a society almost as much as in her own ballroom. She was eminently calculated, and, as some said, eminently inclined to play such a part. She was much younger than her husband; an attractive and sometimes dangerously attractive lady; and Mr. Horne Fisher looked after her, a little sardonically, as she swept away with the young soldier. Then his rather dreary eye strayed to the green and prickly growths round the well; growths of that curious cactus formation in which one thick leaf grows directly out of the other without stalk or twig. It gave his fanciful mind a sinister feeling of a blind growth without shape or purpose. A flower or shrub in the West grows to the blossom which is its crown, and is content. But this was as if hands could grow out of hands, or legs grow out of legs in a nightmare. "Always adding a province to the Empire," he said with a smile; and then added more sadly: "but I doubt if I was right after all."

A strong but genial voice broke in on his meditations; and he looked up and smiled, seeing the face of an old friend. The voice was indeed rather more genial than the face, which was at the first glance decidedly grim. It was a typically legal face, with angular jaws and heavy grizzled eyebrows; and it belonged to an eminently legal character, though he was now attached in a semi-military capacity to the police of that wild district. Cuthbert Grayne was perhaps more of a criminologist than either a lawyer or a policeman; but in his more barbarous surroundings he had proved successful in turning himself into a practical combination of all three. The discovery of a whole series of strange Oriental crimes stood to his credit; but as few people were acquainted with, or attracted to, such a hobby or branch of knowledge, his intellectual life was somewhat solitary. Among the few exceptions was Horne Fisher, who had a curious capacity for talking to almost anybody about almost anything.

"Studying botany, or is it archaeology?" inquired Grayne. "I shall never come to the end of your interests, Fisher. I should say that what you don't know isn't worth knowing."

"You are wrong," replied Fisher with a very unusual abruptness and even bitterness. "It's what I do know that isn't worth knowing. All the seamy side of things; all the secret reasons and rotten motives and bribery and blackmail they call politics. I needn't be so proud of having been down all these sewers that I should brag about it to the little boys in the street."

"What do you mean? What's the matter with you?" asked his friend. "I never knew you taken like this before."

"I'm ashamed of myself," replied Fisher. "I've just been throwing cold water on the enthusiasms of a boy."

"Even that explanation is hardly exhaustive," observed the criminal expert.

"Damned newspaper nonsense the enthusiasms were, of course," continued Fisher, "but I ought to know that at that age illusions can be ideals. And they're better than the reality, anyhow. But there is one very ugly responsibility about jolting a young man out of the rut of the most rotten ideal."

"And what may that be?"

"It's very apt to set him off with the same energy in a much worse direction," answered Fisher. "A pretty endless sort of direction—a bottomless pit, as deep as the Bottomless Well."

Fisher did not see his friend until a fortnight later, when he found himself in the garden at the back of the club house on the opposite side from the links—a garden heavily coloured and scented with semi-tropical plants in the glow of a desert sunset. Two other men were with him, the third being the now celebrated second in command, familiar to everybody as Tom Travers, a lean, dark man who looked older than his years, with a furrow in his brow and something morose about the very shape of his black moustache. They had just been served with black coffee by the Arab now officiating as the temporary

147

servant of the club, though he was a figure already familiar, and even famous, as the old servant of the General. He went by the name of Said, and was notable among other Semites for that unnatural length of his yellow face and height of his narrow forehead which is sometimes seen among them, and gave an irrational impression of something sinister, in spite of his agreeable smile.

"I never feel as if I could quite trust that fellow," said Grayne, when the man had gone away. "It's very unjust, I take it, for he was certainly devoted to Hastings, and saved his life, they say. But Arabs are often like that—loyal to one man. I can't help feeling he might cut anybody else's throat, and even do it treacherously."

"Well," said Travers, with a rather sour smile, "so long as he leaves Hastings alone the world won't mind much."

There was a rather embarrassing silence, full of memories of the great battle, and then Horne Fisher said quietly:

"The newspapers aren't the world, Tom. Don't you worry about them. Everybody in your world knows the truth well enough."

"I think we'd better not talk about the General just now," remarked Grayne, "for he's just coming out of the club."

"He's not coming here," said Fisher. "He's only seeing his wife to the car."

As he spoke, indeed, the lady came out on the steps of the club, followed by her husband, who then went swiftly in front of her to open the garden gate. As he did so she turned back and spoke for a moment to a solitary man still sitting in a cane chair in the shadow of the doorway, the only man left in the deserted club, save for the three that lingered in the garden. Fisher peered for a moment into the shadow and saw that it was Captain Boyle.

The next moment, rather to their surprise, the General reappeared, and remounting the steps, spoke a word or two to Boyle in his turn. Then he signalled to Said, who hurried up with two cups of coffee, and the two men re-entered the club, each carrying his cup in his hand. The next moment a gleam of

148

white light in the growing darkness showed that the electric lamps had been turned on in the library beyond.

"Coffee and scientific researches," said Travers grimly. "All the luxuries of learning and theoretical research. Well, I must be going, for I have my work to do as well."

And he got up rather stiffly, saluted his companions and strode away into the dusk.

"I only hope Boyle *is* sticking to scientific researches," said Horne Fisher. "I'm not very comfortable about him myself. But let's talk about something else."

They talked about something else longer than they probably imagined, until the tropical night had come and a splendid moon painted the whole scene with silver; but before it was bright enough to see by, Fisher had already noted that the lights in the library had been abruptly extinguished. He waited for the two men to come out by the garden entrance, but nobody came.

"They must have gone for a stroll on the links," he said.

"Very possibly," replied Grayne. "It's going to be a beautiful night."

A moment or two after he had spoken they heard a voice hailing them out of the shadow of the club house, and were astonished to perceive Travers hurrying towards them, calling out as he came:

"I shall want your help, you fellows," he cried. "There's something pretty bad out on the links."

They found themselves plunging through the club smoking-room and the library beyond in complete darkness, mental as well as material. But Horne Fisher, in spite of his affectation of indifference, was a person of a curious and almost transcendental sensibility to atmospheres, and he already felt the presence of something more than an accident. He collided with a piece of furniture in the library and almost shuddered with the shock; for the thing moved as he could never have fancied a piece of furniture moving. It seemed to move like a living thing, yielding and yet striking back. The next moment Grayne had turned on the lights; and he saw he had only stumbled against one of the

149

revolving book-stands that had swung round and struck him; but his own involuntary recoil had revealed to him his own sub-consciousness of something mysterious and monstrous. There were several of these revolving bookcases here and there about the library; on one of them stood the two cups of coffee, and on another a large open book. It was Budge's book on Egyptian hieroglyphics, with coloured plates of strange birds and gods; and even as he rushed past, he was conscious of something odd about the fact that this, and not any work of military science, should be open in that place at that moment. He was even conscious of the gap in the well-lined bookshelf from which it had been taken; and it seemed almost to gape at him in an ugly fashion, like a gap in the teeth of some sinister face.

A run brought them in a few minutes to the other side of the ground in front of the Bottomless Well; and a few yards from it, in a moonlight almost as broad as daylight, they saw what they had come to see.

The great Lord Hastings lay prone on his face, in a posture in which there was a touch of something strange and stiff, with one elbow erect above his body, the arm being doubled, and his big bony hand clutching the rank and ragged grass. A few feet away was Boyle, almost as motionless, but supported on his hands and knees, and staring at the body. It might have been no more than shock and accident; but there was something ungainly and unnatural about the quadrupedal posture and the gaping face. It was as if his reason had fled him. Behind there was nothing but the clear blue southern sky and the beginning of the desert, except for the two great broken stones in the front of the well. And it was in such a light and atmosphere that men could fancy they traced in them enormous and evil faces, looking down.

Horne Fisher stooped and touched the strong hand that was still clutching the grass; and it was as cold as a stone. He knelt by the body and was busy for a moment applying other tests; then he rose again and said with a sort of confident despair: "Lord Hastings is dead."

There was a stony silence; and then Travers remarked

gruffly: "This is your department, Grayne; I will leave you to question Captain Boyle. I can make no sense of what he says."

Boyle had pulled himself together and risen to his feet, but his face still wore an awful expression, making it like a new mask or the face of another man.

"I was looking at the well," he said, "and when I turned he had fallen down."

Grayne's face was very dark.

"As you say, this is my affair," he said. "I must first ask you to help me carry him to the library, and let me examine things thoroughly."

When they had deposited the body in the library, Grayne turned to Fisher, and said in a voice that had recovered its fullness and confidence: "I am going to lock myself in and make a thorough examination first. I look to you to keep in touch with the others, and make a preliminary examination of Boyle. I will talk to him later. And just telephone to headquarters for a policeman; and let him come here at once, and stand by till I want him."

Without more words, the great criminal investigator went into the lighted library, shutting the door behind him; and Fisher, without replying, turned and began to talk quietly to Travers.

"It is curious," he said, "that the thing should happen just in front of that place."

"It would certainly be very curious," replied Travers, "if the place played any part in it."

"I think," replied Fisher, "that the part it didn't play is more curious still."

And with these apparently meaningless words he turned to the shaken Boyle, and, taking his arm, began to walk him up and down in the moonlight, talking in low tones.

Dawn had begun to break abrupt and white when Cuthbert Grayne turned out the lights in the library and came out on to the links. Fisher was lounging about alone in his listless fashion; but the police messenger for whom he had sent was standing at attention in the background.

"I sent Boyle off with Travers," observed Fisher carelessly, "he'll look after him; and he'd better have some sleep, anyhow."

"Did you get anything out of him?" asked Grayne. "Did he tell you what he and Hastings were doing?"

"Yes," answered Fisher, "he gave me a pretty clear account after all. He said that after Lady Hastings went off in the car, the General asked him to take coffee with him in the library, and look up a point about local antiquities. He himself was beginning to look for Budge's book in one of the revolving bookstands, when the General found it in one of the bookshelves on the wall. After looking at some of the plates they went out, it would seem rather abruptly, on to the links and walked towards the old well; and while Boyle was looking into it, he heard a thud behind him and turned round to find the General lying as we found him. He himself dropped on his knees to examine the body, and then was paralysed with a sort of terror and could not come nearer to it or touch it. But I think very little of that; people caught in a shock of surprise are sometimes found in the queerest postures."

Grayne wore a grim smile of attention, and said after a short silence:

"Well, he hasn't told you many lies. It's really a creditably clear and consistent account of what happened, with everything of importance left out."

"Have you discovered anything in there?" asked Fisher.

"I have discovered everything," answered Grayne.

Fisher maintained a somewhat gloomy silence, as the other resumed his explanation in quiet and assured tones.

"You were quite right, Fisher, when you said that young fellow was in danger of going down dark ways towards the pit. Whether or no, as you fancied, the jolt you gave to his view of the General had anything to do with it, he has not been treating the General well for some time. It's an unpleasant business, and I don't want to dwell on it, but it's pretty plain that his wife was not treating him well either. I don't know how far it went, but it went as far as concealment anyhow; for when Lady Hastings spoke to Boyle, it was to tell him she had hidden a note in the Budge book in the library. The General overheard, or came somehow to know, and he went straight to the book and found it. He confronted Boyle with it, and they had a scene, of course. And Boyle was confronted with something else; he was confronted with an awful alternative; in which the life of one old man meant ruin, and his death meant triumph and even happiness."

"Well," observed Fisher at last. "I don't blame him for not telling you the woman's part of the story. But how do you know about the letter?"

"I found it on the General's body," answered Grayne, "but I found worse things than that. The body had stiffened in the way rather peculiar to poisons of a certain Asiatic sort. Then I examined the coffee cups, and I knew enough chemistry to find poison in the dregs of one of them. Now the General went straight to the bookcase, leaving his cup of coffee on the book-stand in the middle of the room. While his back was turned and Boyle was pretending to examine the book-stand, he was left alone with the coffee cups. The poison takes about ten minutes to act; and ten minutes' walk would bring them to the Bottom-less Well."

"Yes," remarked Horne Fisher, "and what about the Bottomless Well?"

"What has the Bottomless Well got to do with it?" asked his friend.

"It has nothing to do with it," replied Fisher. "That is what I find utterly confounding and incredible."

"And why should that particular hole in the ground have anything to do with it?"

"It is a particular hole in your case," said Fisher. "But I won't insist on that just now. By the way, there is another thing I ought to tell you. I said I sent Boyle away in charge of Travers. It would be just as true to say I sent Travers in charge of Boyle."

"You don't mean to say you suspect Tom Travers?" cried the other.

"He was a deal bitterer against the General than Boyle

153

ever was," observed Horne Fisher, with a curious indifference.

"Man, you're not saying what you mean," cried Grayne. "I tell you I found the poison in one of the coffee cups."

"There was always Said, of course," added Fisher, "either for hatred or for hire. We agreed he was capable of almost anything."

"And we agreed he was incapable of hurting his master," retorted Grayne.

"Well, well," said Fisher amiably, "I dare say you are right, but I should just like to have a look at the library and the coffee cups."

He passed inside, while Grayne turned to the policeman in attendance and handed him a scribbled note to be telegraphed from headquarters. The man saluted and hurried off; Grayne, following his friend into the library, found him beside the book-stand in the middle of the room, on which were the empty cups.

"This is where Boyle looked for Budge, or pretended to look for him, according to your account," he said.

As Fisher spoke he bent down in a half-crouching attitude, to look at the volumes in the low revolving shelf; for the whole book-stand was not much higher than an ordinary table. The next moment he sprang up as if he had been stung.

"Oh, my God!" he cried.

Very few people, if any, had ever seen Mr. Horne Fisher behave as he behaved just then. He flashed a glance at the door, saw that the open window was nearer, went out of it with a flying leap as if over a hurdle, and went racing across the turf in the track of the disappearing policeman. Grayne, who stood staring after him, soon saw his tall, loose figure returning, restored to all its normal limpness and air of leisure. He was fanning himself slowly with a piece of paper: the telegram he had so violently intercepted.

"Lucky I stopped that," he observed. "We must keep this affair as quiet as death. Hastings must die of apoplexy or heart disease."

"What on earth is the trouble?" demanded the other investigator.

154

"The trouble is," said Fisher, "that in a few days we should have a very agreeable alternative: of hanging an innocent man or knocking the British Empire to hell."

"Do you mean to say," asked Grayne, "that this infernal crime is not to be punished?"

Fisher looked at him steadily.

"It is already punished," he said.

After a moment's pause he went on.

"You reconstructed the crime with admirable skill, old chap, and nearly all you said was true. Two men with two coffee cups did go into the library and did put their cups on the bookstand and did go together to the well, and one of them was a murderer and had put poison in the other's cup. But it was not done while Boyle was looking at the revolving bookcase. He did look at it, though, searching for the Budge book with the note in it; but I fancy that Hastings had already moved it to the shelves on the wall. It was part of that grim game that he should find it first.

"Now how does a man search a revolving bookcase? He does not generally hop all round it in a squatting attitude, like a frog. He simply gives it a touch and makes it revolve."

He was frowning at the floor as he spoke, and there was a light under his heavy lids that was not often seen there. The mysticism that was buried deep under all the cynicism of his experience was awake and moving in the depths. His voice took unexpected turns and inflexions, almost as if two men were speaking.

"That was what Boyle did; he barely touched the thing, and it went round as easily as the world goes round. Yes, very much as the world goes round; for the hand that turned it was not his. God, who turns the wheel of all the stars, touched that wheel and brought it full circle, that his dreadful justice might return."

"I am beginning," said Grayne slowly, "to have some hazy and horrible idea of what you mean."

"It is very simple," said Fisher. "When Boyle straightened himself from his stooping posture, something had happened

155

which he had not noticed, which his enemy had not noticed, which nobody had noticed. The two coffee cups had exactly changed places."

The rocky face of Grayne seemed to have sustained a shock in silence; not a line of it altered, but his voice when it came was unexpectedly weakened.

"I see what you mean," he said, "and, as you say, the less said about it the better. It was not the lover who tried to get rid of the husband, but—the other thing. And a tale like that about a man like that would ruin us here. Had you any guess of this at the start?"

"The Bottomless Well, as I told you," answered Fisher quietly, "that was what stumped me from the start. Not because it had anything to do with it. Because it had nothing to do with it."

He paused a moment, as if choosing an approach, and then went on: "When a murderer knows his enemy will be dead in ten minutes, and takes him to the edge of an unfathomable pit, he means to throw his body into it. What else should he do? A born fool would have the sense to do it; and Boyle is not a born fool. Well, why did not Boyle do it? The more I thought of it the more I suspected that there was some mistake in the murder, so to speak. Somebody had taken somebody there to throw him in; and yet he was not thrown in. I had already an ugly unformed idea of some substitution or reversal of parts; then I stooped to turn the book-stand myself, by accident, and I instantly knew everything; for I saw the two cups revolve once more, like moons in the sky."

After a pause Cuthbert Grayne said: "And what are we to say to the newspapers?"

"My friend Harold March is coming along from Cairo to-day," said Fisher. "He is a very brilliant and successful journalist. But for all that he's a thoroughly honourable man; so you must not tell him the truth."

Half an hour later Fisher was again walking to and fro in front of the club house with Captain Boyle, the latter by this time with a very buffeted and bewildered air; perhaps a sadder and a wiser man.

"What about me, then?" he was saying. "Am I cleared? Aren't I going to be cleared?"

"I believe and hope," answered Fisher, "that you are not going to be suspected. But you are certainly not going to be cleared. There must be no suspicion against him, and therefore no suspicion against you. Any suspicion against him, let alone such a story against him, would knock us endways from Malta to Mandalay. He was a hero as well as a holy terror among the Moslems. Indeed, you might almost call him a Moslem hero in the English service. Of course he got on with them partly because of his own little dose of Eastern blood; he got it from his mother, the dancer from Damascus; everybody knows that."

"Oh," repeated Boyle mechanically, staring at him with round eyes. "Everybody knows that."

"I dare say there was a touch of it in his jealousy and ferocious vengeance," went on Fisher. "But for all that the crime would ruin us among the Arabs, all the more because it was something like a crime against hospitality. It's been hateful for you, and it's pretty horrid for me. But there are some things that damned well can't be done, and while I'm alive that's one of them."

"What do you mean?" asked Boyle, glancing at him curiously. "Why should you, of all people, be so passionate about it?"

Horne Fisher looked at the young man with a baffling expression.

"I suppose," he said, "it's because I'm a Little Englander."

"I can never make out what you mean by that sort of thing," answered Boyle doubtfully.

"Do you think England is so little as all that," said Fisher, with a warmth in his cold voice; "that it can't hold a man across a few thousand miles? You lectured me with a lot of ideal patriotism, my young friend; but it's practical patriotism now for you and me, and with no lies to help it. You talked as if everything went right with us, all over the world, in a triumphant crescendo culminating in Hastings. I tell you everything has gone wrong with us here, except Hastings. His was the one name we had left to conjure with; and that mustn't

157

go as well; no, by God! It's bad enough that a gang of infernal Jews should plant us here, where there's no earthly English interest to serve, and all hell beating up against us, simply because Nosey Zimmern has lent money to half the Cabinet. It's bad enough that an old pawnbroker from Baghdad should make us fight his battles; we can't fight with our right hand cut off. Our one score was Hastings and his victory; which was really somebody else's victory. Tom Travers has to suffer, and so have you."

Then, after a moment's silence, he pointed towards the Bottomless Well and said in a quieter tone:

"I told you," he said, "that I didn't believe in the philosophy of the Tower of Aladin. I don't believe in the Empire growing until it reaches the sky; I don't believe in the Union Jack going up and up eternally like the Tower. But if you think I am going to let the Union Jack go down and down eternally like the Bottomless Well, down into the blackness of the Bottomless Pit, down in defeat and derision amid the jeers of the very Jews who have sucked us dry—no, I won't, and that's flat; not if the Chancellor were blackmailed by twenty millionaires with their gutter rags, not if the Prime Minister married twenty Yankee Jewesses, not if Woodville and Carstairs had shares in twenty swindling mines. If the thing is really tottering, God help it, it mustn't be we who tip it over."

Boyle was regarding him with a bewilderment that was almost fear, and had even a touch of distaste.

"Somehow," he said, "there seems to be something rather horrid about the things you know."

"There is," replied Horne Fisher. "I am not at all pleased with my small stock of knowledge and reflection. But as it is partly responsible for your not being hanged, I don't know that you need complain of it."

And as if a little ashamed of his first boast, he turned and strolled away towards the Bottomless Well.

From *The Man Who Knew Too Much*
(Darwen Finlayson)

158

The Oracle of the Dog

"Yes," said Father Brown, "I always like a dog, so long as he isn't spelt backwards."

Those who are quick in talking are not always quick in listening. Sometimes even their brilliancy produces a sort of stupidity. Father Brown's friend and companion was a young man with a stream of ideas and stories, an enthusiastic young man named Fiennes, with eager blue eyes and blond hair that seemed to be brushed back, not merely with a hair-brush but with the wind of the world as he rushed through it. But he stopped in the torrent of his talk in a momentary bewilderment before he saw the priest's very simple meaning.

"You mean that people make too much of them?" he said. "Well, I don't know. They're marvellous creatures. Sometimes I think they know a lot more than we do."

Father Brown said nothing, but continued to stroke the head of the big retriever in a half-abstracted but apparently soothing fashion.

"Why," said Fiennes, warming again to his monologue, "there was a dog in the case I've come to see you about: what they call the 'Invisible Murder Case', you know. It's a strange story, but from my point of view the dog is about the strangest thing in it. Of course, there's the mystery of the crime itself, and how old Druce can have been killed by somebody else when he was all alone in the summer-house——"

The hand stroking the dog stopped for a moment in its rhythmic movement, and Father Brown said calmly: "Oh, it was a summer-house, was it?"

"I thought you'd read all about it in the papers," answered

Fiennes. "Stop a minute; I believe I've got a cutting that will give you all the particulars." He produced a strip of newspaper from his pocket and handed it to the priest, who began to read it, holding it close to his blinking eyes with one hand while the other continued its half-conscious caresses of the dog. It looked like the parable of a man not letting his right hand know what his left hand did.

"Many mystery stories, about men murdered behind locked doors and windows, and murderers escaping without means of entrance and exit, have come true in the course of the extraordinary events at Cranston on the coast of Yorkshire, where Colonel Druce was found stabbed from behind by a dagger that has entirely disappeared from the scene, and apparently even from the neighbourhood.

"The summer-house in which he died was indeed accessible at one entrance, the ordinary doorway which looked down the central walk of the garden towards the house. But, by a combination of events almost to be called a coincidence, it appears that both the path and the entrance were watched during the crucial time, and there is a chain of witnesses who confirm each other. The summer-house stands at the extreme end of the garden, where there is no exit or entrance of any kind. The central garden path is a lane between two ranks of tall delphiniums, planted so close that any stray step off the path would leave its traces; and both path and plants run right up to the very mouth of the summer-house, so that no straying from that straight path could fail to be observed, and no other mode of entrance can be imagined.

"Patrick Floyd, secretary of the murdered man, testified that he had been in a position to overlook the whole garden from the time when Colonel Druce last appeared alive in the doorway to the time when he was found dead; as he, Floyd, had been on the top of a step-ladder clipping the garden hedge. Janet Druce, the dead man's daughter, confirmed this, saying that she had sat on the terrace of the house throughout that time and had seen Floyd at his work. Touching some part of the time, this is again supported by Donald Druce, her brother—who overlooked the garden—standing at his bedroom window in his dressing-gown, for he had risen late. Lastly, the account is consistent with that given by Dr. Valentine, a neighbour, who called for a time to talk with Miss Druce on the terrace, and by the Colonel's solicitor, Mr. Aubrey Traill, who was apparently the last to see the murdered man alive—presumably with the exception of the murderer.

"All are agreed that the course of events was as follows: About half-past three in the afternoon, Miss Druce went down the path to ask her father when he would like tea; but he said he did not want any and was waiting to see Traill, his lawyer, who was to be sent to him in the summer-house. The girl then came away and met Traill coming down the path; she directed him to her father and he went in as directed. About half an hour afterwards he came out again, the Colonel coming with him to the door and showing himself to all appearances in health and even high spirits. He had been somewhat annoyed earlier in the day by his son's irregular hours, but seemed to recover his temper in a perfectly normal fashion, and had been rather markedly genial in receiving other visitors, including two of his nephews, who came over for the day. But as these were out walking during the whole period of the tragedy, they had no evidence to give. It is said, indeed, that the Colonel was not on very good terms with Dr. Valentine, but that gentleman only had a brief interview with the daughter of the house, to whom he is supposed to be paying serious attentions.

"Traill, the solicitor, says he left the Colonel entirely alone in the summer-house, and this is confirmed by Floyd's bird's-eye view of the garden, which showed nobody else passing the only entrance. Ten minutes later, Miss Druce again went down the garden and had not reached the end of the path when she saw her father, who was conspicuous by his white linen coat, lying in a heap on the floor. She uttered a scream which brought others to the spot, and on entering the place they found the Colonel laying dead beside his basket-chair, which was also upset. Dr. Valentine, who was still in the immediate neighbourhood, testified that the wound was made by some sort of stiletto, entering under the shoulder-blade and piercing the heart. The police have searched the neighbourhood for such a weapon, but no trace of it can be found."

"So Colonel Druce wore a white coat, did he?" said Father Brown as he put down the paper.

"Trick he learnt in the tropics," replied Fiennes, with some wonder. "He'd had some queer adventures there, by his own account; and I fancy his dislike of Valentine was connected with the doctor coming from the tropics, too. But it's all an infernal puzzle. The account there is pretty accurate; I didn't see the tragedy, in the sense of the discovery; I was out walking with the young nephews and the dog—the dog I wanted to tell you about. But I saw the stage set for it as described; the straight lane between the blue flowers right up to the dark entrance, and the lawyer going down it in his blacks and silk hat, and the red head of the secretary showing high above the green hedge as he worked on it with his shears. Nobody could have mistaken that red head at any distance; and if people say they saw it there all the time, you may be sure they did. This red-haired secretary, Floyd, is quite a character; a breathless, bounding sort of fellow, always doing everybody's work as he was doing the gardener's. I think he is an American; he's certainly got the American view of life—what they call the view-point, bless 'em."

"What about the lawyer?" asked Father Brown.

There was a silence and then Fiennes spoke quite slowly for him. "Traill struck me as a singular man. In his fine black clothes he was almost foppish, yet you can hardly call him fashionable. For he wore a pair of long, luxuriant black whiskers such as haven't been seen since Victorian times. He had rather a fine grave face and a fine grave manner, but every now and then he seemed to remember to smile. And when he showed his white teeth he seemed to lose a little of his dignity, and there was something faintly fawning about him. It may have been only embarrassment, for he would also fidget with his cravat and his tie-pin, which were at once handsome and unusual, like

162

himself. If I could think of anybody—but what's the good, when the whole thing's impossible? Nobody knows who did it. Nobody knows how it could be done. At least there's only one exception I'd make, and that's why I really mentioned the whole thing. The dog knows."

Father Brown sighed and then said absently: "You were there as a friend of young Donald, weren't you? He didn't go on your walk with you?"

"No," replied Fiennes smiling. "The young scoundrel had gone to bed that morning and got up that afternoon. I went with his cousins, two young officers from India, and our conversation was trivial enough. I remember the elder, whose name I think is Herbert Druce and who is an authority on horse-breeding, talked about nothing but a mare he had bought and the moral character of the man who sold her; while his brother Harry seemed to be brooding on his bad luck at Monte Carlo. I only mention it to show you, in the light of what happened on our walk, that there was nothing psychic about us. The dog was the only mystic in our company."

"What sort of a dog was he?" asked the priest.

"The same breed as that one," answered Fiennes. "That's what started me off on the story, your saying you didn't believe in believing in a dog. He's a big black retriever, named Nox, and a suggestive name, too; for I think what he did a darker mystery than the murder. You know Druce's house and garden are by the sea; we walked about a mile from it along the sands and then turned back, going the other way. We passed a rather curious rock called the Rock of Fortune, famous in the neighbourhood because it's one of those examples of one stone barely balanced on another, so that a touch would knock it over. It is not really very high but the hanging outline of it makes it look a little wild and sinister; at least it made it look so to me, for I don't imagine my jolly young companions were afflicted with the picturesque. But it may be that I was beginning to feel an atmosphere; for just then the question arose of whether it was time to go back to tea, and even then I think I had a premonition that time counted for a good deal in the business. Neither

Herbert Druce nor I had a watch, so we called out to his brother, who was some paces behind, having stopped to light his pipe under the hedge. Hence it happened that he shouted out the hour, which was twenty-past four, in his big voice through the growing twilight; and somehow the loudness of it made it sound like the proclamation of something tremendous. His unconsciousness seemed to make it all the more so; but that was always the way with omens; and particular ticks of the clock were really very ominous things that afternoon. According to Dr. Valentine's testimony, poor Druce had actually died just about half-past four.

"Well, they said we needn't go home for ten minutes, and we walked a little farther along the sands, doing nothing in particular—throwing stones for the dog and throwing sticks into the sea for him to swim after. But to me the twilight seemed to grow oddly oppressive, and the very shadow of the top-heavy Rock of Fortune lay on me like a load. And then the curious thing happened. Nox had just brought back Herbert's walking-stick out of the sea and his brother had thrown his in also. The dog swam out again, but just about what must have been the stroke of the half-hour, he stopped swimming. He came back again on to the shore and stood in front of us. Then he suddenly threw up his head and sent up a howl or wail of woe—if ever I heard one in the world.

" 'What the devil's the matter with the dog?' asked Herbert; but none of us could answer. There was a long silence after the brute's wailing and whining died away on the desolate shore; and then the silence was broken. As I live, it was broken by a faint and far-off shriek, like the shriek of a woman from beyond the hedges inland. We didn't know what it was then; but we knew afterwards. It was the cry the girl gave when she first saw the body of her father."

"You went back, I suppose," said Father Brown patiently. "What happened then?"

"I'll tell you what happened then," said Fiennes with a grim emphasis. "When we got back into that garden the first thing we saw was Traill, the lawyer; I can see him now with his black hat and black whiskers relieved against the perspective of the blue flowers stretching down to the summer-house, with the sunset and the strange outline of the Rock of Fortune in the distance. His face and figure were in shadow against the sunset; but I swear the white teeth were showing in his head and he was smiling.

"The moment Nox saw that man the dog dashed forward and stood in the middle of the path barking at him madly, murderously, volleying out curses that were almost verbal in their dreadful distinctness of hatred. And the man doubled up and fled along the path between the flowers."

Father Brown sprang to his feet with a startling impatience.

"So the dog denounced him, did he?" he cried. "The oracle of the dog condemned him. Did you see what birds were flying, and are you sure whether they were on the right hand or the left? Did you consult the augurs about the sacrifices? Surely you didn't omit to cut open the dog and examine his entrails. That is the sort of scientific test you heathen humanitarians seem to trust when you are thinking of taking away the life and honour of a man."

Fiennes sat gaping for an instant before he found breath to say: "Why, what's the matter with you? What have I done now?"

A sort of anxiety came back into the priest's eyes—the anxiety of a man who has run against a post in the dark and wonders for a moment whether he has hurt it.

"I'm most awfully sorry," he said with sincere distress. "I beg your pardon for being so rude; pray forgive me."

Fiennes looked at him curiously. "I sometimes think you are more of a mystery than any of the mysteries," he said. "But anyhow, if you don't believe in the mystery of the dog, at least you can't get over the mystery of the man. You can't deny that at the very moment when the beast came back from the sea and bellowed, his master's soul was driven out of his body by the blow of some unseen power that no mortal man can trace or even imagine. And as for the lawyer—I don't go only by the dog—there are other curious details, too. He struck me as a smooth, smiling, equivocal sort of person; and one of his tricks seemed like a sort of hint. You know the doctor and the police were on the spot very quickly; Valentine was brought back when walking away from the house, and he telephoned instantly. That, with the secluded house, small numbers, and enclosed space, made it pretty possible to search everybody who could have been near; and everybody was thoroughly searched—for a weapon. The whole house, garden and shore were combed for a weapon. The disappearance of the dagger is almost as crazy as the disappearance of the man."

"The disappearance of the dagger," said Father Brown, nodding. He seemed to have become suddenly attentive.

"Well," continued Fiennes, "I told you that man Traill had a trick of fidgeting with his tie and tie-pin—especially his tie-pin. His pin, like himself, was at once showy and old-fashioned. It had one of those stones with concentric coloured rings that look like an eye; and his own concentration on it got on my nerves, as if he had been a Cyclops with one eye in the middle of his body. But the pin was not only large but long; and it occurred to me that his anxiety about its adjustment was because it was even longer than it looked; as long as a stiletto in fact."

Father Brown nodded thoughtfully. "Was any other instrument ever suggested?" he asked.

"There was another suggestion," answered Fiennes, "from one of the young Druces—the cousins, I mean. Neither Herbert nor Harry Druce would have struck one at first as likely to be of assistance in scientific detection; but while Herbert was really the traditional type of heavy Dragoon, caring for nothing but horses and being an ornament to the Horse Guards, his younger brother Harry had been in the Indian Police and knew something about such things. Indeed, in his own way he was quite clever; and I rather fancy he had been too clever; I mean he had left the police through breaking some red-tape regulations and taking some sort of risk and responsibility of his own. Anyhow, he was in some sense a detective out of work, and threw himself into this business with more than the ardour of an amateur. And it was with him that I had an argument about the weapon—an argument that led to something new. It began by his countering my description of the dog barking at Traill; and he said that a dog at his worst didn't bark, but growled."

"He was quite right there," observed the priest.

"This young fellow went on to say that, if it came to that, he'd heard Nox growling at other people before then; and among others at Floyd, the secretary. I retorted that his own argument answered itself; for the crime couldn't be brought home to two or three people, and least of all to Floyd, who was as innocent as a harum-scarum schoolboy, and had been seen by everybody all the time perched above the garden hedge with his fan of red hair as conspicuous as a scarlet cockatoo. 'I know there's difficulties anyhow,' said my colleague; 'but I wish you'd come with me down the garden a minute. I want to show you something I don't think anyone else has seen.' This was on the very day of the discovery, and the garden was just as it had been. The step-ladder was still standing by the hedge, and just under the hedge my guide stopped and disentangled something from the deep grass. It was the shears used for clipping the hedge, and on the point of one of them was a smear of blood."

There was a short silence, and then Father Brown said suddenly. "What was the lawyer there for?"

"He told us the Colonel sent for him to alter his will," answered Fiennes. "And, by the way, there was another thing about the business of the will that I ought to mention. You see, the will wasn't actually signed in the summer-house that afternoon."

"I suppose not," said Father Brown; "there would have to be two witnesses."

"The lawyer actually came down the day before and it was signed then; but he was sent for again next day because the old man had a doubt about one of the witnesses and had to be reassured."

"Who were the witnesses?" asked Father Brown.

"That's just the point," replied his informant eagerly, "the witnesses were Floyd, the secretary, and this Dr. Valentine, the foreign sort of surgeon or whatever he is; and the two have a quarrel. Now I'm bound to say that the secretary is something of a busybody. He's one of those hot and headlong people whose warmth of temperament has unfortunately turned mostly to pugnacity and bristling suspicion; to distrusting people instead of to trusting them. That sort of red-haired, red-hot fellow is always either universally credulous or universally incredulous; and sometimes both. He was not only a Jack-of-all-trades, but he knew better than all tradesmen. He not only knew everything, but he warned everybody against everybody. All that must be taken into account in his suspicions about Valentine; but in that particular case there seems to have been something behind it. He said the name of Valentine was not really Valentine. He said he had seen him elsewhere known by the name of De Villon. He said it would invalidate the will; of course he was kind enough to explain to the lawyer what the law was on that point. They were both in a frightful wax."

Father Brown laughed. "People often are when they are to witness a will," he said; "for one thing, it means that they can't have any legacy under it. But what did Dr. Valentine say? No doubt the universal secretary knew more about the doctor's name than the doctor did. But even the doctor might have some information about his own name."

Fiennes paused a moment before he replied.

"Dr. Valentine took it in a curious way. Dr. Valentine is a curious man. His appearance is rather striking but very foreign. He is young but wears a beard cut square; and his face is very pale, dreadfully pale and dreadfully serious. His eyes have a sort of ache in them, as if he ought to wear glasses, or had given himself a headache with thinking; but he is quite handsome and always very formally dressed, with a top hat and a dark coat and a little red rosette. His manner is rather cold and haughty, and he has a way of staring at you which is very disconcerting. When thus charged with having changed his name, he merely stared like a sphinx and then said with a little laugh that he supposed Americans had no names to change. At that I think the Colonel also got into a fuss and said all sorts of angry things

168

to the doctor; all the more angry because of the doctor's pretensions to a future place in his family. But I shouldn't have thought much of that but for a few words that I happened to hear later, early in the afternoon of the tragedy. I don't want to make a lot of them, for they weren't the sort of words on which one would like, in the ordinary way, to play the eavesdropper. As I was passing out towards the front gate with my two companions and the dog, I heard voices which told me that Dr. Valentine and Miss Druce had withdrawn for a moment into the shadow of the house, in an angle behind a row of flowering plants, and were talking to each other in passionate whisperings —sometimes almost like hissings; for it was something of a lovers' quarrel as well as a lovers' tryst. Nobody repeats the sort of things they said for the most part; but in an unfortunate business like this I'm bound to say that there was repeated more than once a phrase about killing somebody. In fact, the girl seemed to be begging him not to kill somebody, or saying that no provocation could justify killing anybody; which seems an unusual sort of talk to address to a gentleman who has dropped in to tea."

"Do you know," asked the priest, "whether Dr. Valentine seemed to be very angry after the scene with the secretary and the Colonel—I mean about witnessing the will?"

"By all accounts," replied the other, "he wasn't half so angry as the secretary was. It was the secretary who went away raging after witnessing the will."

"And now," said Father Brown, "what about the will itself?"

"The Colonel was a very wealthy man, and his will was important. Traill wouldn't tell us the alteration at that stage, but I have since heard only this morning in fact—that most of the money was transferred from the son to the daughter. I told you that Druce was wild with my friend Donald over his dissipated hours."

"The question of motive has been rather over-shadowed by the question of method," observed Father Brown thoughtfully. "At that moment, apparently, Miss Druce was the immediate gainer by the death."

169

"Good God! What a cold-blooded way of talking," cried Fiennes, staring at him. "You don't really mean to hint that she——"

"Is she going to marry that Dr. Valentine?" asked the other.

"Some people are against it," answered his friend. "But he is liked and respected in the place and is a skilled and devoted surgeon."

"So devoted a surgeon," said Father Brown, "that he had surgical instruments with him when he went to call on the young lady at tea-time. For he must have used a lancet or something, and he never seems to have gone home."

Fiennes sprang to his feet and looked at him in a heat of inquiry. "You suggest he might have used the very same lancet——"

Father Brown shook his head. "All these suggestions are fancies just now," he said. "The problem is not who did it or what did it, but how it was done. We might find many men and even many tools—pins and shears and lancets. But how did a man get into the room? How did even a pin get into it?"

He was staring reflectively at the ceiling as he spoke, but as he said the last words his eye cocked in an alert fashion as if he had suddenly seen a curious fly on the ceiling.

"Well, what would you do about it?" asked the young man. "You have a lot of experience; what would you advise now?"

"I'm afraid I'm not much use," said Father Brown with a sigh. "I can't suggest very much without having ever been near the place or the people. For the moment you can only go on with local inquiries. I gather that your friend from the Indian Police is more or less in charge of your inquiry down there. I should run down and see how he is getting on. See what he's been doing in the way of amateur detection. There may be news already."

As his guests, the biped and the quadruped, disappeared, Father Brown took up his pen and went back to his interrupted occupation of planning a course of lectures on the Encyclical *Rerum Novarum*. The subject was a large one and he had to recast it more than once, so that he was somewhat similarly employed some two days later when the big black dog again came bounding into the room and sprawled all over him with enthusiasm and excitement. The master who followed the dog shared the excitement if not the enthusiasm. He had been excited in a less pleasant fashion, for his blue eyes seemed to start from his head and his eager face was even a little pale.

"You told me," he said abruptly and without preface, "to find out what Harry Druce was doing. Do you know what he's done?"

The priest did not reply, and the young man went on in jerky tones:

"I'll tell you what he's done. He's killed himself."

Father Brown's lips moved only faintly, and there was nothing practical about what he was saying—nothing that has anything to do with this story or this world.

"You give me the creeps sometimes," said Fiennes. "Did you —did you expect this?"

"I thought it possible," said Father Brown; "that was why I asked you to go and see what he was doing. I hoped you might not be too late."

"It was I who found him," said Fiennes rather huskily. "It was the ugliest and most uncanny thing I ever knew. I went down that old garden again, and I knew there was something new and unnatural about it besides the murder. The flowers still tossed about in blue masses on each side of the black entrance into the old grey summer-house; but to me the blue flowers looked like blue devils dancing before some dark cavern of the underworld. I looked all round, everything seemed to be in its ordinary place. But the queer notion grew on me that there was something wrong with the very shape of the sky. And then I saw what it was. The Rock of Fortune always rose in the background beyond the garden hedge and against the sea. And the Rock of Fortune was gone."

Father Brown had lifted his head and was listening intently.

"It was as if a mountain had walked away out of a landscape or a moon fallen from the sky; though I knew, of course, that a touch at any time would have tipped the thing over. Something possessed me and I rushed down that garden path like the wind and went crashing through that hedge as if it were a spider's web. It was a thin hedge really, though its undisturbed trimness had made it serve all the purposes of a wall. On the shore I found the loose rock fallen from its pedestal; and poor Harry Druce lay like a wreck underneath it. One arm was thrown round it in a sort of embrace as if he had pulled it down on himself; and on the broad brown sands beside it, in large crazy lettering, he had scrawled the words: 'The Rock of Fortune falls on the Fool.' "

"It was the Colonel's will that did that," observed Father Brown. "The young man had staked everything on profiting himself by Donald's disgrace, especially when his uncle sent for him on the same day as the lawyer, and welcomed him with so much warmth. Otherwise he was done; he'd lost his police job; he was beggared at Monte Carlo. And he killed himself when he found he'd killed his kinsman for nothing."

"Here, stop a minute!" cried the staring Fiennes. "You're going too fast for me."

"Talking about the will, by the way," continued Father Brown calmly, "before I forget it, or we go on to bigger things, there was a simple explanation, I think, of all that business about the doctor's name. I rather fancy I have heard both names before somewhere. The doctor is really a French nobleman with the title of the Marquis de Villon. But he is also an ardent Republican and has abandoned his title and fallen back on the forgotten family surname. 'With your Citizen Riquetti you have puzzled Europe for ten days.' "

"What is that?" asked the young man blankly.

"Never mind," said the priest. "Nine times out of ten it is a rascally thing to change one's name; but this was a piece of fine fanaticism. That's the point of his sarcasm about Americans having no names—that is, no titles. Now in England the Marquis of Hartington is never called Mr. Hartington; but in France the Marquis de Villon is called M. de Villon. So it might well look like a change of name. As for the talk about killing, I fancy that also was a point of French etiquette. The doctor was talking about challenging Floyd to a duel, and the girl was trying to dissuade him."

"Oh, I *see*," cried Fiennes slowly. "Now I understand what she meant."

"And what is that about?" asked his companion, smiling.

"Well," said the young man, "it was something that happened to me just before I found that poor fellow's body; only the catastrophe drove it out of my head. I suppose it's hard to remember a little romantic idyll when you've just come on top of a tragedy. But as I went down the lanes leading to the Colonel's old place I met his daughter walking with Dr. Valentine. She was in mourning, of course, and he always wore black as if he were going to a funeral; but I can't say that their faces were very funereal. Never have I seen two people looking in their own way more respectably radiant and cheerful. They stopped and saluted me, and then she told me they were married and living in a little house on the outskirts of the town, where the doctor was continuing his practice. This rather surprised me, because I knew that her old father's will had left her his property; and I hinted at it delicately by saying I was going along to her father's old place and had half expected to meet her there. But she only laughed and said: 'Oh, we've given up all that. My husband doesn't like heiresses.' And I discovered with some astonishment they really had insisted on restoring the property to poor Donald; so I hope he's had a healthy shock and will treat it sensibly. There was never much really the matter with him; he was very young and his father was not very wise. But it was in connexion with that that she said something I didn't understand at the time; but now I'm sure it must be as you say. She said with a sort of sudden and splendid arrogance that was entirely altruistic:

" 'I hope it'll stop that red-haired fool from fussing any more about the will. Does he think my husband, who has given up a crest and a coronet as old as the Crusades for his principles, would kill an old man in a summer-house for a legacy like that?' Then she laughed again and said, 'My husband isn't killing anybody except in the way of business. Why, he didn't even ask his friends to call on the secretary.' Now, of course, I see what she meant."

"I see part of what she meant, of course," said Father Brown. "What did she mean exactly by the secretary fussing about the will?"

Fiennes smiled as he answered. "I wish you knew the secretary, Father Brown. It would be a joy to watch him make things hum, as he calls it. He made the house of mourning hum. He filled the funeral with all the snap and zip of the brightest sporting event. There was no holding him, after something had really happened. I've told you how he used to oversee the gardener as he did the garden, and how he instructed the lawyer in the law. Needless to say, he also instructed the surgeon in the practice of surgery; and as the surgeon was Dr. Valentine, you may be sure it ended in accusing him of something worse than bad surgery. The secretary got it fixed in his red head that the doctor had committed the crime, and when the police arrived he was perfectly sublime. Need I say that he became, on the spot, the greatest of all amateur detectives? Sherlock Holmes never towered over Scotland Yard with more Titanic intellectual pride and scorn than Colonel Druce's private secretary over the police investigating Colonel Druce's death. I tell you it was a joy to see him. He strode about with an abstracted air, tossing his scarlet crest of hair and giving curt impatient replies. Of course it was his demeanour during these days that made Druce's daughter so wild with him. Of course he had a theory. It's just the sort of theory a man would have in a book; and Floyd is the sort of man who ought to be in a book. He'd be better fun and less bother in a book."

"What was his theory?" asked the other.

"Oh, it was full of pep," replied Fiennes gloomily. "It would have been glorious copy if it could have held together for ten minutes longer. He said the Colonel was still alive when they found him in the summer-house, and the doctor killed him with the surgical instrument on pretence of cutting the clothes."

"I see," said the priest. "I suppose he was lying flat on his face on the mud floor as a form of siesta."

"It's wonderful what hustle will do," continued his informant. "I believe Floyd would have got his great theory into the papers at any rate, and perhaps had the doctor arrested, when all these things were blown sky high as if by dynamite by the discovery of that dead body lying under the Rock of Fortune. And that's what we come back to after all. I suppose the suicide is almost a confession. But nobody will ever know the whole story."

There was a silence, and then the priest said modestly: "I rather think I know the whole story."

Fiennes stared. "But look here," he cried; "how do you come to know the whole story, or to be sure it's the true story? You've been sitting here a hundred miles away writing a sermon; do you mean to tell me you really know what happened already? If you've really come to the end, where in the world do you begin? What started you off with your own story?"

Father Brown jumped up with a very unusual excitement and his first exclamation was like an explosion.

"The dog!" he cried. "The dog, of course! You had the whole story in your hands in the business of the dog on the beach, if you'd only noticed the dog properly."

Fiennes stared still more. "But you told me before that my feelings about the dog were all nonsense, and the dog had nothing to do with it."

"The dog had everything to do with it," said Father Brown, "as you'd have found out if you'd only treated the dog as a dog, and not as God Almighty judging the souls of men."

He paused in an embarrassed way for a moment, and then said, with a rather pathetic air of apology: "The truth is, I happen to be awfully fond of dogs. And it seemed to me that in all this lurid halo of dog superstitions nobody was really thinking about the poor dog at all. To begin with a small point, about his barking at the lawyer or growling at the secretary. You asked how I could guess things a hundred miles away; but honestly it's mostly to your credit, for you described people so well that I know the types. A man like Traill, who frowns usually and smiles suddenly, a man who fiddles with things, especially at his throat, is a nervous, easily embarrassed man. I shouldn't wonder if Floyd, the efficient secretary, is nervy and jumpy, too; those Yankee hustlers often are. Otherwise he wouldn't have cut his fingers on the shears and dropped them when he heard Janet Druce scream.

"Now dogs hate nervous people. I don't know whether they make the dog nervous, too; or whether, being after all a brute, he is a bit of a bully; or whether his canine vanity (which is colossal) is simply offended at not being liked. But anyhow there was nothing in poor Nox protesting against those people, except that he disliked them for being afraid of him. Now I know you're awfully clever, and nobody of sense sneers at cleverness. But sometimes I fancy, for instance, that you are too clever to understand animals. Sometimes you are too clever to understand men, especially when they act almost as simply as animals. Animals are very literal; they live in a world of truisms. Take this case: a dog barks at a man and a man runs away from a dog. Now you do not seem to be quite simple enough to see the fact: that the dog barked because he disliked the man and the man fled because he was frightened of the dog. They had no other motives and they needed none; but you must read psychological mysteries into it and suppose the dog had super-normal vision, and was a mysterious mouthpiece of doom. You must suppose the man was running away, not from the dog but from the hangman. And yet, if you come to think of it, all this deeper psychology is exceedingly improbable. If the dog really could completely and consciously realize the murderer of his master he wouldn't stand yapping as he might at a curate at a tea-party; he's much more likely to fly at his throat. And on the other hand, do you really think a man who had hardened his heart to murder an old friend and then walk about smiling at the old friend's family, under the eyes of his old friend's daughter and post-mortem doctor—do you think a man like that would be doubled up by mere remorse because a dog barked? He might feel the tragic irony of it; it might shake his soul, like any other tragic trifle. But he wouldn't rush madly the length of a garden to escape from the only witness whom he knew to be unable to talk. People have a panic like that when they are frightened, not of tragic ironies, but of teeth. The whole thing is simpler than you can understand.

"But when we come to that business by the seashore, things are much more interesting. As you stated them, they were much more puzzling. I didn't understand that tale of the dog going in and out of the water; it didn't seem to me a doggy thing to do. If Nox had been very much upset about something else, he might possibly have refused to go after the stick at all. He'd probably go off nosing in whatever direction he suspected the mischief. But when once a dog is actually chasing a thing, a stone or a stick or a rabbit, my experience is that he won't stop for anything but the most peremptory command, and not always for that. That he should turn round because his mood changed seems to me unthinkable."

"But he did turn round," insisted Fiennes; "and came back without the stick."

"He came back without the stick for the best reason in the world," replied the priest. "He came back because he couldn't find it. He whined because he couldn't find it. That's the sort of thing a dog really does whine about. A dog is a devil of a ritualist. He is as particular about the precise routine of a game as a child about the precise repetition of a fairy-tale. In this case something had gone wrong with the game. He came back to complain seriously of the conduct of the stick. Never had such a thing happened before. Never had an eminent and distinguished dog been so treated by a rotten old walking-stick."

"Why, what had the walking-stick done?" inquired the young man.

"It had sunk," said Father Brown.

Fiennes said nothing, but continued to stare; and it was the priest who continued:

"It had sunk because it was not really a stick, but a rod of steel with a very thin shell of cane and a sharp point. In other words, it was a sword-stick. I suppose a murderer never gets rid of a bloody weapon so oddly and yet so naturally as by throwing it into the sea for a retriever."

"I begin to see what you mean," admitted Fiennes; "but even if a sword-stick was used, I have no guess of how it was used."

"I had a sort of guess," said Father Brown, "right at the beginning when you said the word summer-house. And another when you said that Druce wore a white coat. As long as everybody was looking for a short dagger, nobody thought of it; but if we admit a rather long blade like a rapier, it's not so impossible."

He was leaning back, looking at the ceiling, and began like one going back to his own first thoughts and fundamentals.

"All that discussion about detective stories like the Yellow Room, about a man found dead in sealed chambers which no one could enter, does not apply to the present case, because it is a summer-house. When we talk of a Yellow Room, or any room, we imply walls that are really homogeneous and impenetrable. But a summer-house is not made like that; it is often made, as it was in this case, of closely interlaced but separate boughs and strips of wood, in which there are chinks here and there. There was one of them just behind Druce's back as he sat in his chair up against the wall. But just as the room was a summer-house, so the chair was a basket-chair. That also was a lattice of loopholes. Lastly, the summer-house was close up under the hedge; and you have just told me that it was really a thin hedge. A man standing outside it could easily see, amid a network of twigs and branches and canes, one white spot of the Colonel's coat as plain as the white of a target.

"Now, you left the geography a little vague; but it was possible to put two and two together. You said the Rock of Fortune was not really high; but you also said it could be seen dominating the garden like a mountain-peak. In other words, it was very near the end of the garden, though your walk had taken you a long way round to it. Also, it isn't likely the young lady really howled so as to be heard half a mile. She gave an ordinary involuntary cry, and yet you heard it on the shore. And among other interesting things that you told me, may I remind you that you said Harry Druce had fallen behind to light his pipe under a hedge."

Fiennes shuddered slightly. "You mean he drew his blade there and sent it through the hedge at the white spot. But surely it was a very odd chance and a very sudden choice. Besides, he couldn't be certain the old man's money had passed to him, and as a fact it hadn't."

Father Brown's face became animated.

"You misunderstand the man's character," he said, as if he himself had known the man all his life. "A curious but not unknown type of character. If he had really *known* the money would come to him, I seriously believe he wouldn't have done it. He would have seen it as the dirty thing it was."

"Isn't that rather paradoxical?" asked the other.

"This man was a gambler," said the priest, "and a man in disgrace for having taken risks and anticipated orders. It was probably for something pretty unscrupulous, for every imperial police is more like a Russian secret police than we like to think. But he had gone beyond the line and failed. Now, the temptation of that type of man is to do a mad thing precisely because the risk will be wonderful in retrospect. He wants to say, 'Nobody but I could have seized that chance or seen that it was then or never. What a wild and wonderful guess it was, when I put all those things together; Donald in disgrace; and the lawyer being sent for: and Herbert and I sent for at the same time —and then nothing more but the way the old man grinned at me and shook hands. Anybody would say I was mad to risk it; but that is how fortunes are made, by the man mad enough to have a little foresight.' In short, it is the vanity of guessing. It is the megalomania of the gambler. The more incongruous the coincidence, the more instantaneous the decision, the more likely he is to snatch the chance. The accident, the very triviality of the white speck and the hole in the hedge intoxicated him like a vision of the world's desire. Nobody clever enough to see such a combination of accidents could be cowardly enough not to use them! That is how the devil talks to the gambler. But the devil himself would hardly have induced that unhappy man to go down in a dull, deliberate way and

179

kill an old uncle from whom he'd always had expectations. It would be too respectable."

He paused a moment, and then went on with a certain quiet emphasis.

"And now try to call up the scene, even as you saw it yourself. As he stood there, dizzy with his diabolical opportunity, he looked up and saw that strange outline that might have been the image of his own tottering soul; the one great crag poised perilously on the other like a pyramid on its point, and remembered that it was called the Rock of Fortune. Can you guess how such a man at such a moment would read such a signal? I think it strung him up to action and even to vigilance. He who would be a tower must not fear to be a toppling tower. Anyhow, he acted; his next difficulty was to cover his tracks. To be found with a sword-stick, let alone a blood-stained sword-stick, would be fatal in the search that was certain to follow. If he left it anywhere, it would be found and probably traced. Even if he threw it into the sea the action might be noticed and thought noticeable—unless indeed he could think of some more natural way of covering the action. As you know, he did think of one, and a very good one. Being the only one of you with a watch, he told you it was not yet time to return, strolled a little farther and started the game of throwing in sticks for the retriever. But how his eyes must have rolled darkly over all that desolate seashore before they alighted on the dog!"

Fiennes nodded, gazing thoughtfully into space. His mind seemed to have drifted back to a less practical part of the narrative.

"It's queer," he said, "that the dog really was in the story after all."

"The dog could almost have told you the story, if he could talk," said the priest. "All I complain of is that because he couldn't talk, you made up his story for him, and made him talk with the tongues of men and angels. It's part of something I've noticed more and more in the modern world, appearing in all sorts of newspaper rumours and conversational catchwords; something that's arbitrary without being authoritative.

People readily swallow the untested claims of this, that, or the other. It's drowning all your old rationalism and scepticism, it's coming in like a sea; and the name of it is superstition." He stood up abruptly, his face heavy with a sort of frown, and went on talking almost as if he were alone. "It's the first effect of not believing in God that you lose your common sense and can't see things as they are. Anything that anybody talks about, and says there's a good deal in it, extends itself indefinitely like a vista in a nightmare. And a dog is an omen, and a cat is a mystery, and a pig is a mascot and a beetle is a scarab, calling up all the menagerie of polytheism from Egypt and old India; Dog Anubis and great green-eyed Pasht and all the holy howling Bulls of Bashan; reeling back to the bestial gods of the beginning, escaping into elephants and snakes and crocodiles; and all because you are frightened of four words: 'He was made Man'."

The young man got up with a little embarrassment, almost as if he had overheard a soliloquy. He called to the dog and left the room with vague but breezy farewells. But he had to call the dog twice, for the dog had remained behind quite motionless for a moment, looking up steadily at Father Brown as the wolf looked at St. Francis.

From *The Father Brown Stories*
(Cassell & Co. Ltd.)

The Dagger With Wings

Father Brown, at one period of his life, found it difficult to hang his hat on a hat-peg without repressing a slight shudder. The origin of this idiosyncrasy was indeed a mere detail in much more complicated events; but it was perhaps the only detail that remained to him in his busy life to remind him of the whole business. Its remote origin was to be found in the facts which led Dr. Boyne, the medical officer attached to the police force, to send for the priest on a particular frosty morning in December.

Dr. Boyne was a big dark Irishman, one of those rather baffling Irishmen to be found all over the world, who will talk scientific scepticism, materialism and cynicism at length and at large, but who never dream of referring anything touching the ritual of religion to anything except the traditional religion of their native land. It would be hard to say whether their creed is a very superficial varnish or a very fundamental substratum; but most probably it is both, with a mass of materialism in between. Anyhow, when he thought that matters of that sort might be involved, he asked Father Brown to call, though he made no pretence of preference for that aspect of them.

"I'm not sure I want you, you know," was his greeting. "I'm not sure about anything yet. I'm hanged if I can make out whether it's a case for a doctor, or a policeman, or a priest."

"Well," said Father Brown with a smile, "as I suppose you're both a policeman and a doctor, I seem to be rather in a minority."

"I admit you're what politicians call an instructed minority," replied the doctor. "I mean, I know you've had to do a little in our line as well as your own. But it's precious hard to say whether this business is in your line or ours, or merely in the line of the Commissioners in Lunacy. We've just had a message from a man living near here, in that white house on the hill, asking for protection against a murderous persecution. We've gone into the facts as far as we could, and perhaps I'd better tell you the story, as it is supposed to have happened, from the beginning.

"It seems that a man named Aylmer, who was a wealthy landowner in the West Country, married rather late in life and had three sons, Philip, Stephen and Arnold. But in his bachelor days, when he thought he would have no heir, he had adopted a boy whom he thought very brilliant and promising, who went by the name of John Strake. His origin seems to be vague; they say he was a foundling; some say he was a gipsy. I think the last notion is mixed up with the fact that Aylmer in his old age dabbled in all sorts of dingy occultism, including palmistry and astrology, and his three sons say that Strake encouraged him in it. But they said a great many other things besides that. They said Strake was an amazing scoundrel, and especially an amazing liar; a genius in inventing lies on the spur of the moment, and telling them so as to deceive a detective. But that might very well be a natural prejudice, in the light of what happened. Perhaps you can more or less imagine what happened. The old man left practically everything to the adopted son; and when he died the three real sons disputed the will. They said their father had been frightened into surrender and, not to put too fine a point on it, into gibbering idiocy. They said Strake had the strangest and most cunning ways of getting at him, in spite of the nurses and the family, and terrorizing him on his deathbed. Anyhow, they seemed to have proved something about the dead man's mental condition, for the courts set aside the will and the sons inherited. Strake is said to have broken out in the most dreadful fashion, and sworn he would kill all three of them, one after another, and that nothing could hide them from his vengeance. It is the third or last of the brothers, Arnold Aylmer, who is asking for police protection."

"Third and last," said the priest, looking at him gravely.

"Yes," said Boyne. "The other two are dead."

There was a silence before he continued. "That is where the doubt comes in. There is no proof they were murdered, but they might possibly have been. The eldest, who took up his position as squire, was supposed to have committed suicide in his garden. The second, who went into trade as a manufacturer, was knocked on the head by the machinery in his factory; he might very well have taken a false step and fallen. But if Strake did kill them, he is certainly very cunning in his way of getting to work and getting away. On the other hand, it's more than likely that the whole thing is a mania of conspiracy founded on a coincidence. Look here, what I want is this. I want somebody of sense, who isn't an official, to go up and have a talk to this Mr. Arnold Aylmer, and form an impression of him. You know what a man with a delusion is like, and how a man looks when he is telling the truth. I want you to be the advance guard, before we take the matter up."

"It seems rather odd," said Father Brown, "that you haven't had to take it up before. If there is anything in this business, it seems to have been going on for a good time. Is there any particular reason why he should send for you just now, any more than any other time?"

"That had occurred to me, as you may imagine," answered Dr. Boyne. "He does give a reason, but I confess it is one of the things that make me wonder whether the whole thing isn't only the whim of some half-witted crank. He declares that all his servants have suddenly gone on strike and left him, so that he is obliged to call on the police to look after his house. And on making inquiries, I certainly do find that there has been a general exodus of servants from that house on the hill; and of course the town is full of tales, very one-sided tales I dare say. Their account of it seems to be that their employer had become quite impossible in his fidgets and fears and exactions; that he wanted them to guard the house like sentries, or sit up like night nurses in a hospital; that they could never be left alone because he must never be left alone. So they all announced in a loud voice that he was a lunatic, and left. Of course that does not prove he is a lunatic; but it seems rather rum nowadays for a man to expect his valet or his parlourmaid to act as an armed guard."

"And so," said the priest with a smile, "he wants a policeman to act as his parlour-maid because his parlour-maid won't act as a policeman."

"I thought that rather thick, too," agreed the doctor; "but I can't take the responsibility of a flat refusal till I've tried a compromise. You are the compromise."

"Very well," said Father Brown simply. "I'll go and call on him now if you like."

The rolling country round the little town was sealed and bound with frost, and the sky was as clear and cold as steel, except in the north-east, where clouds with lurid haloes were beginning to climb up the sky. It was against these darker and more sinister colours that the house on the hill gleamed with a row of pale pillars, forming a short colonnade of the classical sort. A winding road led up to it across the curve of the down, and plunged into a mass of dark bushes. Just before it reached the bushes the air seemed to grow colder and colder, as if he were approaching an ice-house or the North Pole. But he was a highly practical person, never entertaining such fancies except as fancies. And he merely cocked his eye at the great livid cloud crawling up over the house, and remarked cheerfully:

"It's going to snow."

Through a low ornamental iron gateway of the Italianate pattern he entered a garden having something of that desolation which only belongs to the disorder of orderly things. Deep-green growths were grey with the faint powder of the frost, large weeds had fringed the fading pattern of the flower-beds as if in a ragged frame; and the house stood as if waist-high in a stunted forest of shrubs and bushes. The vegetation consisted largely of evergreens or very hardy plants; and though it was thus thick and heavy, it was too northern to be called luxuriant. It might be described as an Arctic jungle. So it was in some sense with the house itself, which had a row of columns and a classical

185

façade, which might have looked out on the Mediterranean; but which seemed now to be withering in the wind of the North Sea. Classical ornament here and there accentuated the contrast; caryatides and carved masks of comedy or tragedy looked down from corners of the building upon the grey confusion of the garden paths; but the faces seemed to be frost-bitten. The very volutes of the capitals might have curled up with the cold.

Father Brown went up the grassy steps to a square porch flanked by big pillars and knocked at the door. About four minutes afterwards he knocked again. Then he stood still patiently waiting with his back to the door and looked out on the slowly darkening landscape. It was darkening under the shadow of that one great continent of cloud that had come flying out of the north; and even as he looked out beyond the pillars of the porch, which seemed huge and black above him in the twilight, he saw the opalescent crawling rim of the great cloud as it sailed over the roof and bowed over the porch like a canopy. The grey canopy with its faintly coloured fringes seemed to sink lower and lower upon the garden beyond, until what had recently been a clear and pale-hued winter sky was left in a few silver ribbons and rags like a sickly sunset. Father Brown waited, and there was no sound within.

Then he betook himself briskly down the steps and round the house to look for another entrance. He eventually found one, a side door in the flat wall, and on this also he hammered and outside this also he waited. Then he tried the handle and found the door apparently bolted or fastened in some fashion; and then he moved along that side of the house, musing on the possibilities of the position, and wondering whether the eccentric Mr. Aylmer had barricaded himself too deep in the house to hear any kind of summons; or whether perhaps he would barricade himself all the more, on the assumption that any summons must be the challenge of the avenging Strake. It might be that the decamping servants had only unlocked one door when they left in the morning, and that their master had locked that; but whatever he might have done it was unlikely that they, in the mood of that moment, had looked so carefully to the defences. He continued his prowl round the place; it was not really a large place, though perhaps a little pretentious; and in a few moments he found he had made the complete circuit. A moment after he found what he suspected and sought. The french window of one room, curtained and shadowed with creeper, stood open by a crack, doubtless accidentally left ajar, and he found himself in a central room, comfortably upholstered in a rather old-fashioned way, with a staircase leading up from it on one side and a door leading out of it on the other. Immediately opposite him was another door with red glass let into it, a little gaudily for later tastes; something that looked like a red-robed figure in cheap stained glass. On a round table to the right stood a sort of aquarium—a great bowl full of greenish water, in which fishes and similar things moved about as in a tank; and just opposite it a plant of the palm variety with very large green leaves. All this looked so very dusty and Early Victorian that the telephone, visible in the curtained alcove, was almost a surprise.

"Who is that?" a voice called out sharply and rather suspiciously from behind the stained-glass door.

"Could I see Mr. Aylmer?" asked the priest apologetically.

The door opened and a gentleman in a peacock-green dressing-gown came out with an inquiring look. His hair was rather rough and untidy, as if he had been in bed or lived in a state of slowly getting up, but his eyes were not only awake but alert, and some would have said alarmed. Father Brown knew that the contradiction was likely enough in a man who had rather run to seed under the shadow either of a delusion or a danger. He had a fine aquiline face when seen in profile, but when seen full face the first impression was of the untidiness and even the wilderness of his loose brown beard.

"I am Mr. Aylmer," he said, "but I have got out of the way of expecting visitors."

Something about Mr. Aylmer's unrestful eye prompted the priest to go straight to the point. If the man's persecution was only a monomania, he would be the less likely to resent it.

187

"I was wondering," said Father Brown softly, "whether it is quite true that you never expect visitors."

"You are right," replied his host steadily. "I always expect one visitor. And he may be the last."

"I hope not," said Father Brown, "but at least I am relieved to infer that I do not look very like him."

Mr. Aylmer shook himself with a sort of savage laugh. "You certainly do not," he said.

"Mr. Aylmer," said Father Brown frankly, "I apologize for the liberty, but some friends of mine have told me about your trouble, and asked me to see if I could do anything for you. The truth is, I have some little experience in affairs like this."

"There are no affairs like this," said Aylmer.

"You mean," observed Father Brown, "that the tragedies in your unfortunate family were not normal deaths?"

"I mean they were not even normal murders," answered the other. "The man who is hounding us all to death is a hell-hound, and his power is from hell."

"All evil has one origin," said the priest gravely. "But how do you know they were not normal murders?"

Aylmer answered with a gesture which offered his guest a chair; then he seated himself slowly in another, frowning, with his hands on his knees; but when he looked up his expression had grown milder and more thoughtful, and his voice was quite cordial and composed.

"Sir," he said, "I don't want you to imagine that I'm in the least an unreasonable person. I have come to these conclusions by reason, because unfortunately reason really leads there. I have read a great deal on these subjects; for I was the only one who inherited my father's scholarship in somewhat obscure matters, and I have since inherited his library. But what I tell you does not rest on what I have read but on what I have seen."

Father Brown nodded, and the other proceeded, as if picking his words:

"In my elder brother's case I was not certain at first. There were no marks or footprints where he was found shot, and the pistol was left beside him. But he had just received a threatening letter, certainly from our enemy, for it was marked with a sign like a winged dagger, which was one of his infernal cabalistic tricks. And a servant said she had seen something moving along the garden wall in the twilight that was much too large to be a cat. I leave it there; all I can say is that if the murderer came, he managed to leave no traces of his coming. But when my brother Stephen died it was different; and since then I have known. A machine was working in an open scaffolding under the factory tower; I scaled the platform a moment after he had fallen under the iron hammer that struck him; I did not see anything else strike him, but I saw what I saw.

"A great drift of factory smoke was rolling between me and the factory tower; but through a rift of it I saw on the top of it a dark human figure wrapped in what looked like a black cloak. Then the sulphurous smoke drove between us again; and when it cleared I looked up at the distant chimney—there was nobody there. I am a rational man, and I will ask all rational men how he had reached that dizzy unapproachable turret, and how he left it."

He stared across at the priest with a sphinx-like challenge; then after a silence he said abruptly:

"My brother's brains were knocked out, but his body was not much damaged. And in his pocket we found one of those warning messages dated the day before and stamped with the flying dagger.

"I am sure," he went on gravely, "that the symbol of the winged dagger is not merely arbitrary or accidental. Nothing about that abominable man is accidental. He is all design; though it is indeed a most dark and intricate design. His mind is woven not only out of elaborate schemes but out of all sorts of secret languages and signs, and dumb signals and wordless pictures which are the names of nameless things. He is the worst sort of man that the world knows: he is the wicked mystic. Now, I don't pretend to penetrate all that is conveyed by this symbol; but it seems surely that it must have a relation to all that was most remarkable, or even incredible, in his movements as he had hovered round my unfortunate family. Is there no connexion between the idea of a winged weapon and the mystery by which Philip was struck dead on his own lawn without the lightest touch of any footprint having disturbed the dust or grass? Is there no connexion between the plumed poignard flying like a feathered arrow and that figure which hung on the far top of the toppling chimney, clad in a cloak for pinions?"

"You mean," said Father Brown thoughtfully, "that he is in a perpetual state of levitation."

"Simon Magus did it," replied Aylmer, "and it was one of the commonest predictions of the Dark Ages that Antichrist would be able to fly. Anyhow, there was the flying dagger on the document; and whether or no it could fly, it could certainly strike."

"Did you notice what sort of paper it was on?" asked Father Brown. "Common paper?"

The sphinx-like face broke abruptly into a harsh laugh.

"You can see what they're like," said Aylmer grimly, "for I got one myself this morning."

He was leaning back in his chair now, with his long legs thrust out from under the green dressing-gown, which was a little short for him, and his bearded chin pillowed on his chest. Without moving otherwise, he thrust his hand in the dressing-gown pocket and held out a fluttering scrap of paper at the end of a rigid arm. His whole attitude was suggestive of a sort of paralysis, that was both rigidity and collapse. But the next remark of the priest had a curious effect of rousing him.

Father Brown was blinking in his short-sighted way at the paper presented to him. It was a singular sort of paper, rough without being common, as from an artist's sketch-book; and on it was drawn boldly in red ink a dagger decorated with wings like the rod of Hermes, with the written words, "Death comes the day after this, as it came to your brothers".

Father Brown tossed the paper on the floor and sat bolt upright in his chair.

"You mustn't let that sort of stuff stupefy you," he said sharply. "These devils always try to make us helpless by making us hopeless."

Rather to his surprise, an awakening wave went over the prostrate figure, which sprang from its chair as if startled out of a dream.

"You're right, you're right!" cried Aylmer with a rather uncanny animation; "and the devils shall find I'm not so hopeless after all, nor so helpless either. Perhaps I have more hope and better help than you fancy."

He stood with his hands in his pockets, frowning down at the priest, who had a momentary doubt, during that strained silence, about whether the man's long peril had not touched his brain. But when he spoke it was quite soberly.

"I believe my unfortunate brothers failed because they used the wrong weapons. Philip carried a revolver, and that was how his death came to be called suicide. Stephen had police protection, but he also had a sense of what made him ridiculous; and he could not allow a policeman to climb up a ladder after him to a scaffolding where he stood only a moment. They were both scoffers, reacting into scepticism from the strange mysticism of my father's last days. But I always knew there was more in my father than they understood. It is true that by studying magic he fell at last under the blight of black magic; the black magic of this scoundrel Strake. But my brothers were wrong about the antidote. The antidote to black magic is not brute materialism or worldly wisdom. The antidote to black magic is white magic."

"It rather depends," said Father Brown, "what you mean by white magic."

"I mean silver magic," said the other, in a low voice, like one speaking of a secret revelation. Then after a silence he said: "Do you know what I mean by silver magic? Excuse me a moment."

He turned and opened the central door with the red glass and went into a passage beyond it. The house had less depth than Brown had supposed; instead of the door opening into interior rooms, the corridor it revealed ended in another door on the garden. The door of one room was on one side of the passage; doubtless, the priest told himself, the proprietor's bedroom, whence he had rushed out in his dressing-gown. There was nothing else on that side but an ordinary hat-stand with the ordinary dingy cluster of old hats and overcoats; but on the other side was something more interesting: a very dark old oak sideboard laid out with some old silver, and overhung by a trophy or ornament of old weapons. It was by that that Arnold Aylmer halted, looking up at a long, antiquated pistol with a bell-shaped mouth.

The door at the end of the passage was barely open, and through the crack came a streak of white daylight. The priest had very quick instincts about natural things, and something in the unusual brilliancy of that white line told him what had happened outside. It was indeed what he had prophesied when he was approaching the house. He ran past his rather startled host and opened the door, to face something that was at once a blank and a blaze. What he had seen shining through the crack was not only the most negative whiteness of daylight but the positive whiteness of snow. All round, the sweeping fall of the country was covered with that shining pallor that seems at once hoary and innocent.

"Here is white magic anyhow," said Father Brown in his cheerful voice. Then, as he turned back into the hall, he murmured, "And silver magic too, I suppose," for the white lustre touched the silver with splendour and lit up the old steel here and there in the darkling armoury. The shaggy head of the brooding Aylmer seemed to have a halo of silver fire, as he turned with his face in shadow and the outlandish pistol in his hand.

"Do you know why I choose this sort of old blunderbuss?" he asked. "Because I can load it with this sort of bullet."

He had picked up a small apostle spoon from the sideboard, and by sheer violence broke off the small figure at the top. "Let us go back into the other room," he added.

"Did you ever read about the death of Dundee?" he asked when they had reseated themselves. He had recovered from his momentary annoyance at the priest's restlessness. "Graham of Claverhouse, you know, who persecuted the Covenanters and had a black horse that could ride straight up a precipice. Don't you know he could only be shot with a silver bullet, because he had sold himself to the Devil? That's one comfort about you; at least you know enough to believe in the Devil."

"Oh, yes," replied Father Brown, "I believe in the Devil. What I don't believe in is the Dundee. I mean the Dundee of Covenanting legends, with his nightmare of a horse. John Graham was simply a seventeenth-century professional soldier, rather better than most. If he dragooned them it was because he was a dragoon, but not a dragon. Now my experience is that it's not that sort of swaggering blade who sells himself to the Devil. The devil-worshippers I've known were quite different. Not to mention names, which might cause a social flutter, I'll take a man in Dundee's own day. Have you ever heard of Dalrymple of Stair?"

"No," replied the other gruffly.

"You've heard of what he did," said Father Brown, "and it was worse than anything Dundee ever did; yet he escapes the infamy by oblivion. He was the man who made the Massacre of Glencoe. He was a very learned man and lucid lawyer, a statesman with very serious and enlarged ideas of statesmanship, a quiet man with a very refined and intellectual face. That's the sort of man who sells himself to the Devil."

Aylmer half started from his chair with an enthusiasm of eager assent.

"By God! you are right," he cried. "A refined intellectual face! That is the face of John Strake."

Then he raised himself and stood looking at the priest with a curious concentration. "If you will wait here a little while," he said, "I will show you something."

He went back through the central door, closing it after him; going, the priest presumed, to the old sideboard or possibly to his bedroom. Father Brown remained seated, gazing abstractedly at the carpet, where a faint red glimmer shone from the glass in the doorway. Once it seemed to brighten like a ruby and then darkened again, as if the sun of that stormy day had passed from cloud to cloud. Nothing moved except the aquatic creatures which floated to and fro in the dim green bowl. Father Brown was thinking hard.

A minute or two afterwards he got up and slipped quietly to the alcove of the telephone, where he rang up his friend Dr. Boyne, at the official headquarters. "I wanted to tell you about Aylmer and his affairs," he said quietly. "It's a queer story, but I rather think there's something in it. If I were you I'd send some men up here straight away; four or five men, I think, and surround the house. If anything does happen there'll probably be something startling in the way of an escape."

Then he went back and sat down again, staring at the dark carpet, which again glowed blood-red with the light from the glass door. Something in that filtered light set his mind drifting on certain borderlands of thought, with the first white day-break before the coming of colour, and all that mystery which is alternately veiled and revealed in the symbol of windows and of doors.

An inhuman howl in a human voice came from beyond the closed doors, almost simultaneously with the noise of firing. Before the echoes of the shot had died away the door was violently flung open and his host staggered into the room, the dressing-gown half torn from his shoulder and the long pistol smoking in his hand. He seemed to be shaking in every limb, yet he was shaken in part with an unnatural laughter.

"Glory be to the White Magic!" he cried; "Glory be to the silver bullet! The hell-hound has hunted once too often, and my brothers are avenged at last."

He sank into a chair and the pistol slid from his hand and fell on the floor. Father Brown darted past him, slipped through the glass door and went down the passage. As he did so he put his hand on the handle of the bedroom door, as if half intending to enter; then he stooped a moment, as if examining something —and then he ran to the outer door and opened it.

On the field of snow, which had been so blank a little while before, lay one black object. At first glance it looked a little like an enormous bat. A second glance showed that it was, after all, a human figure; fallen on its face, the whole head covered by a broad black hat having something of a Latin-American look; while the appearance of bat-wings came from the two flaps or loose sleeves of a very vast black cloak spread out, perhaps by accident, to their utmost length on either side. Both the hands were hidden, though Father Brown thought he could detect the position of one of them, and saw close to it, under the edge of the cloak, the glimmer of some metallic weapon. The main effect, however, was curiously like that of the simple extravagances of heraldry; like a black eagle displayed on a white ground. But by walking round it and peering under the hat the priest got a glimpse of the face, which was indeed what his host had called refined and intellectual; even sceptical and austere: the face of John Strake.

"Well, I'm jiggered," muttered Father Brown. "It really does look like some vast vampire that has swooped down like a bird."

"How else could he have come?" came a voice from the doorway, and Father Brown looked up to see Aylmer once more standing there.

"Couldn't he have walked?" replied Father Brown evasively.

Aylmer stretched out his arm and swept the white landscape with a gesture.

"Look at the snow," he said in a deep voice that had a sort of roll and thrill in it. "Is not the snow unspotted—pure as the white magic you yourself called it? Is there a speck on it for miles, save that one foul black blot that has fallen there? There are no footprints, but a few of yours and mine; there are none approaching the house from anywhere."

Then he looked at the little priest for a moment with a concentrated and curious expression, and said:

"I will tell you something else. That cloak he flies with is too long to walk with. He was not a very tall man, and it would trail behind him like a royal train. Stretch it out over his body, if you like, and see."

"What happened to you both?" asked Father Brown abruptly.

"It was too swift to describe," answered Aylmer. "I had looked out of the door and was turning back when there came

195

a kind of rushing of wind all around me, as if I were being buffeted by a wheel revolving in mid-air. I spun round somehow and fired blindly; and then I saw nothing but what you see now. But I am morally certain you wouldn't see it if I had not had silver shot in my gun. It would have been a different body lying there in the snow."

"By the way," remarked Father Brown, "shall we leave it lying there in the snow? Or would you like it taken into your room—I suppose that's your bedroom in the passage?"

"No, no," replied Aylmer hastily; "we must leave it there till the police have seen it. Besides, I've had as much of such things as I can stand for the moment. Whatever else happens, I'm going to have a drink. After that, they can hang me if they like."

Inside the central apartment, between the palm plant and the bowl of fishes, Aylmer tumbled into a chair. He had nearly knocked the bowl over as he lurched into the room, but he had managed to find the decanter of brandy after plunging his hand rather blindly into several cupboards and corners. He did not at any time look like a methodical person, but at this moment his distraction must have been extreme. He drank with a long gulp and began to talk rather feverishly, as if to fill up a silence.

"I see you are still doubtful," he said, "though you have seen the thing with your own eyes. Believe me, there was something more behind the quarrel between the spirit of Strake and the spirit of the house of Aylmer. Besides, you have no business to be an unbeliever. You ought to stand for all the things these stupid people call superstitions. Come now, don't you think there's a lot in those old wives' tales about luck and charms and so on, silver bullets included? What do you say about them as a Catholic?"

"I say I'm an agnostic," replied Father Brown, smiling.

"Nonsense," said Aylmer impatiently. "It's your business to believe things."

"Well, I do believe some things, of course," conceded Father Brown; "and therefore, of course, I don't believe other things."

Aylmer was leaning forward, and looking at him with a strange intensity that was almost like that of a mesmerist.

"You do believe it," he said. "You do believe everything. We all believe everything, even when we deny everything. The deniers believe. The unbelievers believe. Don't you feel in your heart that these contradictions do not really contradict: that there is a cosmos that contains them all? The soul goes round upon a wheel of stars and all things return; perhaps Strake and I have striven in many shapes, beast against beast and bird against bird, and perhaps we shall strive for ever. But since we seek and need each other, even that eternal hatred is an eternal love. Good and evil go round in a wheel that is one thing and not many. Do you not realize in your heart, do you not believe behind all your beliefs, that there is but one reality and we are its shadows; and that all things are but aspects of one thing: a centre where men melt into Man and Man into God?"

"No," said Father Brown.

Outside, twilight had begun to fall, in that phase of such a snow-laden evening when the land looks brighter than the sky. In the porch of the main entrance, visible through a half-curtained window, Father Brown could dimly see a bulky figure standing. He glanced casually at the french windows through which he had originally entered, and saw they were darkened with two equally motionless figures. The inner door with the coloured glass stood slightly ajar; and he could see in the short corridor beyond, the ends of two long shadows, exaggerated and distorted by the level light of evening, but still like grey caricatures of the figures of men. Dr. Boyne had already obeyed his telephone message. The house was surrounded.

"What is the good of saying no?" insisted his host, still with the same hypnotic stare. "You have seen part of that eternal drama with your own eyes. You have seen the threat of John Strake to slay Arnold Aylmer by black magic. You have seen Arnold Aylmer slay John Strake by white magic. You see Arnold Aylmer alive and talking to you now. And yet you do not believe it."

"No, I do not believe it," said Father Brown, and rose from his chair like one terminating a visit.

"Why not?" asked the other.

The priest only lifted his voice a little, but it sounded in every corner of the room like a bell.

"Because you are not Arnold Aylmer," he said. "I know who you are. Your name is John Strake; and you have murdered the last of the brothers, who is lying outside in the snow."

A ring of white showed round the iris of the other man's eyes; he seemed to be making, with bursting eyeballs, a last effort to mesmerize and master his companion. Then he made a sudden movement sideways; and even as he did so the door behind him opened and a big detective in plain clothes put one hand quietly on his shoulder. The other hand hung down, but it held a revolver. The man looked wildly round, and saw plain-clothes men in all corners of the quiet room.

That evening Father Brown had another and longer conversation with Dr. Boyne about the tragedy of the Aylmer family. By that time there was no longer any doubt of the central fact of the case, for John Strake had confessed his identity and even confessed his crimes; only it would be truer to say that he boasted of his victories. Compared to the fact that he had rounded off his life's work with the last Aylmer lying dead, everything else, including existence itself, seemed to be indifferent to him.

"The man is a sort of monomaniac," said Father Brown. "He is not interested in any other matter; not even in any other murder. I owe him something for that; for I had to comfort myself with the reflection a good many times this afternoon. As has doubtless occurred to you, instead of weaving all that wild but ingenious romance about winged vampires and silver bullets, he might have put an ordinary leaden bullet into me, and walked out of the house. I assure you it occurred quite frequently to me."

"I wonder why he didn't," observed Boyne. "I don't understand it; but I don't understand anything yet. How on earth did you discover it, and what in the world did you discover?"

"Oh, you provided me with very valuable information," replied Father Brown modestly, "especially the one piece of information that really counted. I mean the statement that Strake was a very inventive and imaginative liar, with great presence of mind in producing his lies. This afternoon he needed it; but he rose to the occasion. Perhaps his only mistake was in choosing a preternatural story; he had the notion that because I am a clergyman I should believe anything. Many people have little notions of that kind."

"But I can't make head or tail of it," said the doctor. "You must really begin at the beginning."

"The beginning of it was a dressing-gown," said Father Brown simply. "It was the one really good disguise I've ever known. When you meet a man in a house with a dressing-gown on, you assume quite automatically that he's in his own house. I assumed it myself; but afterwards queer little things began to happen. When he took the pistol down he clicked it at arm's length, as a man does to make sure a strange weapon isn't loaded; of course he would know whether the pistols in his own hall were loaded or not. I didn't like the way he looked for the brandy, or the way he nearly barged into the bowl of fishes. For a man who has a fragile thing of that sort as a fixture in his rooms gets a quite mechanical habit of avoiding it. But these things might possibly have been fancies; the first real point was this. He came out from the little passage between the two doors; and in that passage there's only one other door leading to a room; so I assumed it was the bedroom he had just come from. I tried the handle; but it was locked. I thought this odd; and looked through the keyhole. It was an utterly bare room, obviously deserted; no bed, no anything. Therefore he had not come from inside any room, but from outside the house. And when I saw that, I think I saw the whole picture.

"Poor Arnold Aylmer doubtless slept and perhaps lived upstairs, and came down in his dressing-gown and passed through the red glass door. At the end of the passage, black against the winter daylight, he saw the enemy of his house. He saw a tall bearded man in a broad-brimmed black hat and a large flapping black cloak. He did not see much more in this world. Strake sprang on him, throttling or stabbing him; we cannot be sure till the inquest. Then Strake, standing in the narrow passage between the hat-stand and the old sideboard, and looking down in triumph on the last of his foes, heard something he had not expected. He heard footsteps in the parlour beyond. It was myself entering by the french windows.

"His masquerade was a miracle of promptitude. It involved not only a disguise but a romance—an impromptu romance. He took off his big black hat and cloak and put on the dead man's dressing-gown. Then he did a rather grisly thing; at least a thing that affects my fancy as more grisly than the rest. He hung the corpse like a coat on one of the hatpegs. He draped it in his own long cloak, and found it hung well below the heels; he covered the head entirely with his own wide hat. It was the only possible way of hiding it in that little passage with the locked door; but it was really a very clever one. I myself walked past the hat-stand once without knowing it was anything but a hat-stand. I think that unconsciousness of mine will always give me a shiver.

"He might perhaps have left it at that; but I might have discovered the corpse at any minute; and, hung where it was, it was a corpse calling for what you might call an explanation. He adopted the bolder stroke of discovering it himself and explaining it himself.

"Then there dawned on this strange and frightfully fertile mind the conception of a story of substitution; the reversal of the parts. He had already assumed the part of Arnold Aylmer. Why should not his dead enemy assume the part of John Strake? There must have been something in that topsy-turvy-dom to take the fancy of that darkly fanciful man. It was like some frightful fancy-dress ball to which the two mortal enemies were to go dressed up as each other. Only the fancy-dress ball was to be a dance of death: and one of the dancers would be dead. That is why I can imagine that man putting it in his own mind, and I can imagine him smiling."

Father Brown was gazing into vacancy with his large grey

eyes, which, when not blurred by his trick of blinking, were the one notable thing in his face. He went on speaking simply and seriously:

"All things are from God; and above all, reason and imagination and the great gifts of the mind. They are good in themselves; and we must not altogether forget their origin even in their perversion. Now this man had in him a very noble power to be perverted; the power of telling stories. He was a great novelist; only he had twisted his fictive power to practical and to evil ends; to deceiving men with false fact instead of with true fiction. It began with his deceiving old Aylmer with elaborate excuses and ingeniously detailed lies; but even that may have been, at the beginning, little more than the tall stories and tarradiddles of the child who may say equally he has seen the King of England or the King of the Fairies. It grew strong in him through the vice that perpetuates all vices, pride; he grew more and more vain of his promptitude in producing stories of his originality, and subtlety in developing them. That is what the young Aylmers meant by saying that he could always cast a spell over their father; and it was true. It was the sort of spell that the story-teller cast over the tyrant in the Arabian Nights. And to the last he walked the world with the pride of a poet, and with the false yet unfathomable courage of a great liar. He could always produce more Arabian Nights if ever his neck was in danger. And today his neck was in danger.

"But I am sure, as I say, that he enjoyed it as a fantasy as well as a conspiracy. He set about the task of telling the true story the wrong way round: of treating the dead man as living and the live man as dead. He had already got into Aylmer's dressing-gown; he proceeded to get into Aylmer's body and soul. He looked at the corpse as if it were his own corpse lying cold in the snow. Then he spread-eagled it in that strange fashion to suggest the sweeping descent of a bird of prey, and decked it out not only in his own dark and flying garments but in a whole dark fairy-tale about the black bird that could only fall by the silver bullet. I do not know whether it was the silver glittering on the sideboard or the snow shining beyond the door that suggested to his intensely artistic temperament the theme of white magic and the white metal used against magicians. But whatever its origin, he made it his own like a poet; and did it very promptly, like a practical man. He completed the exchange and reversal of parts by flinging the corpse out on to the snow as the corpse of Strake. He did his best to work up a creepy conception of Strake as something hovering in the air everywhere, a harpy with wings of speed and claws of death; to explain the absence of footprints and other things. For one piece of artistic impudence I hugely admire him. He actually turned one of the contradictions in his case into an argument for it; and said that the man's cloak being too long for him proved that he never walked on the ground like an ordinary mortal. But he looked at me very hard while he said that; and something told me that he was at that moment trying a very big bluff."

Dr. Boyne looked thoughtful. "Had you discovered the truth by then?" he asked. "There is something very queer and close to the nerves, I think, about notions affecting identity. I don't know whether it would be more weird to get a guess like that swiftly or slowly. I wonder when you suspected and when you were sure."

"I think I really suspected when I telephoned to you," replied his friend. "And it was nothing more than the red light from the closed door brightening and darkening on the carpet. It looked like a splash of blood that grew vivid as it cried for vengeance. Why should it change like that? I knew the sun had not come out; it could only be because the second door behind it had been opened and shut on the garden. But if he had gone out and seen his enemy then, he would have raised the alarm then; and it was some time afterwards that the fracas occurred. I began to feel he had gone out to do something . . . to prepare something . . . but as to when I was certain, that is a different matter. I knew that right at the end he was trying to hypnotize me, to master me by the black art of eyes like talismans and a voice like an incantation. That's what he used to do with old Aylmer, no doubt. But it wasn't only the way he said it, it was what he said. It was the religion and philosophy of it."

"I'm afraid I'm a practical man," said the doctor with gruff humour, "and I don't bother much about religion and philosophy."

"You'll never be a practical man till you do," said Father Brown. "Look here, doctor; you know me pretty well; I think you know I'm not a bigot. You know I know there are all sorts in all religions; good men in bad ones and bad men in good ones. But there's just one little fact I've learned simply as a practical man, an entirely practical point, that I've picked up by experience, like the tricks of an animal or the trade-mark of a good wine. I've scarcely ever met a criminal who philosophized at all, who didn't philosophize along those lines of orientalism and recurrence and reincarnation, and the wheel of destiny and the serpent biting its own tail. I have found merely in practice that there is a curse on the servants of that serpent; on their belly shall they go and the dust shall they eat; and there was never a blackguard or a profligate born who could not talk that sort of spirituality. It may not be like that in its real religious origins; but here in our working world it is the religion of rascals; and I knew it was a rascal who was speaking."

"Why," said Boyne, "I should have thought that a rascal could pretty well profess any religion he chose."

"Yes," assented the other; "he could profess any religion; that is he could pretend to any religion, if it was all a pretence. If it was mere mechanical hypocrisy and nothing else, no doubt it could be done by a mere mechanical hypocrite. Any sort of mask can be put on any sort of face. Anybody can learn certain phrases or state verbally that he holds certain views. I can go out into the street and state that I am a Wesleyan Methodist or a Sandemanian, though I fear in no very convincing accent. But we are talking about an artist; and for the enjoyment of the artist the mask must be to some extent moulded on the face. What he makes outside him must correspond to something inside him; he can only make his effects out of some of the materials of his soul. I suppose he could have said he was a Wesleyan Methodist; but he could never be an eloquent

Methodist as he can be an eloquent mystic and fatalist. I am talking of the sort of ideal such a man thinks of if he really tries to be idealistic. It was his whole game with me to be as idealistic as possible; and whenever that is attempted by that sort of man, you will generally find it is that sort of ideal. That sort of man may be dripping with gore; but he will always be able to tell you quite sincerely that Buddhism is better than Christianity. Nay, he will tell you quite sincerely that Buddhism is more Christian than Christianity. That alone is enough to throw a hideous and ghastly ray of light on his notion of Christianity."

"Upon my soul," said the doctor, laughing, "I can't make out whether you're denouncing or defending him."

"It isn't defending a man to say he is a genius," said Father Brown. "Far from it. And it is simply a psychological fact that an artist will betray himself by some sort of sincerity. Leonardo da Vinci cannot draw as if he couldn't draw. Even if he tried, it will always be a strong parody of a weak thing. This man would have made something much too fearful and wonderful out of the Wesleyan Methodist."

When the priest went forth again and set his face homeward, the cold had grown more intense and yet was somehow intoxicating. The trees stood up like silver candelabra of some incredible cold candlemas of purification. It was a piercing cold, like that silver sword of pure pain that once pierced the very heart of purity. But it was not a killing cold, save in the sense of seeming to kill all the mortal obstructions to our immortal and immeasurable vitality. The pale green sky of twilight, with one star like the star of Bethlehem, seemed by some strange contradiction to be a cavern of clarity. It was as if there could be a green furnace of cold which wakened all things to life like warmth, and that the deeper they went into those cold crystalline colours the more were they light like winged creatures and clear coloured glass. It tingled with truth and it divided truth from error with a blade like ice; but all that was left had never felt so much alive. It was as if all joy were a jewel in the heart of an iceberg. The priest hardly understood his own mood as he advanced deeper and deeper into the green gloaming, drinking deeper and deeper draughts of that virginal vivacity of the air. Some forgotten muddle and morbidity seemed to be left behind, or wiped out as the snow had painted out the footprints of the man of blood. As he shuffled homewards through the snow, he muttered to himself: "And yet he is right enough about there being a white magic, if only he knows where to look for it."

From *The Father Brown Stories*
(Cassell & Co. Ltd.)

The Mirror of the Magistrate

James Bagshaw and Wilfred Underhill were old friends, and were fond of rambling through the streets at night, talking interminably as they turned corner after corner in the silent and seemingly lifeless labyrinth of the large suburb in which they lived. The former, a big, dark, good-humoured man with a strip of black moustache, was a professional police detective; the latter, a sharp-faced, sensitive-looking gentleman with light hair, was an amateur interested in detection. It will come as a shock to the readers of the best scientific romance to learn that it was the policeman who was talking and the amateur who was listening, even with a certain respect.

"Ours is the only trade," said Bagshaw, "in which the professional is always supposed to be wrong. After all, people don't write stories in which hairdressers can't cut hair and have to be helped by a customer; or in which a cabman can't drive a cab until his fare explains to him the philosophy of cab-driving. For all that, I'd never deny that we often tend to get into a rut: or, in other words, have the disadvantages of going by a rule. Where the romancers are wrong is, that they don't allow us even the advantages of going by a rule."

"Surely," said Underhill, "Sherlock Holmes would say that he went by a logical rule."

"He may be right," answered the other; "but I mean a collective rule. It's like the staff work of an army. We pool our information."

"And you don't think detective stories allow for that?" asked his friend.

"Well, let's take any imaginary case of Sherlock Holmes, and

Lestrade, the official detective. Sherlock Holmes, let us say, can guess that a total stranger crossing the street is a foreigner, merely because he seems to look for the traffic to go to the right instead of the left. I'm quite ready to admit Holmes might guess that. I'm quite sure Lestrade wouldn't guess anything of the kind. But what they leave out is the fact that the policeman, who couldn't guess, might very probably know. Lestrade might know the man was a foreigner merely because his department has to keep an eye on all foreigners; some would say on all natives, too. As a policeman I'm glad the police know so much; for every man wants to do his own job well. But as a citizen, I sometimes wonder whether they don't know too much."

"You don't seriously mean to say," cried Underhill incredulously, "that you know anything about strange people in a strange street. That if a man walked out of that house over there, you would know anything about him?"

"I should if he was the householder," answered Bagshaw. "That house is rented by a literary man of Anglo-Roumanian extraction, who generally lives in Paris, but is over here in connexion with some poetical play of his. His name's Osric Orm, one of the new poets, and pretty steep to read, I believe."

"But I mean all the people down the road," said his companion. "I was thinking how strange and new and nameless everything looks, with these high blank walls and these houses lost in large gardens. You can't know all of them."

"I know a few," answered Bagshaw. "This garden wall we're walking under is at the end of the grounds of Sir Humphrey Gwynne, better known as Mr. Justice Gwynne, the old judge who made such a row about spying during the war. The house next door to it belongs to a wealthy cigar merchant. He comes from Spanish-America and looks very swarthy and Spanish himself; but he bears the very English name of Buller. The house beyond that—did you hear that noise?"

"I heard something," said Underhill, "but I really don't know what it was."

"I know what it was," replied the detective, "it was a rather heavy revolver, fired twice, followed by a cry for help. And it came straight out of the back garden of Mr. Justice Gwynne, that paradise of peace and legality."

He looked up and down the street sharply and then added:

"And the only gate of the back garden is half a mile round on the other side. I wish this wall were a little lower, or I were a little lighter; but it's got to be tried."

"It is lower a little farther on," said Underhill, "and there seems to be a tree that looks helpful."

They moved hastily along and found a place where the wall seemed to stoop abruptly, almost as if it had half-sunk into the earth; and a garden tree, flamboyant with the gayest garden blossom, straggled out of the dark enclosure and was gilded by the gleam of a solitary street-lamp. Bagshaw caught the crooked branch and threw one leg over the low wall; and the next moment they stood knee-deep amid the snapping plants of a garden border.

The garden of Mr. Justice Gwynne by night was rather a singular spectacle. It was large and lay on the empty edge of the suburb, in the shadow of a tall, dark house that was the last in its line of houses. The house was literally dark, being shuttered and unlighted, at least on the side overlooking the garden. But the garden itself, which lay in its shadow and should have been a tract of absolute darkness, showed a random glitter, like that of fading fireworks; as if a giant rocket had fallen in fire among the trees. As they advanced they were able to locate it as the light of several coloured lamps, entangled in the trees like the jewel fruits of Aladdin, and especially as the light from a small, round lake or pond, which gleamed with pale colours as if a lamp were kindled under it.

"Is he having a party?" asked Underhill. "The garden seems to be illuminated."

"No," answered Bagshaw. "It's a hobby of his, and I believe he prefers to do it when he's alone. He likes playing with a little plant of electricity that he works from that bungalow or hut over there, where he does his work and keeps his papers. Buller, who knows him very well, says the coloured lamps are rather more often a sign that he's not to be disturbed."

"Sort of red danger signals," suggested the other.

"Good Lord! I'm afraid they are danger signals!" and he began suddenly to run.

A moment after Underhill saw what he had seen. The opalescent ring of light, like the halo of the moon, round the sloping sides of the pond, was broken by two black stripes or streaks which soon proved themselves to be the long, black legs of a figure fallen head downwards into the hollow, with the head in the pond.

"Come on," cried the detective sharply, "that looks to me like——"

His voice was lost, as he ran on across the wide lawn, faintly luminous in the artificial light, making a bee-line across the big garden for the pool and the fallen figure. Underhill was trotting steadily in that straight track, when something happened that startled him for the moment. Bagshaw, who was travelling as steadily as a bullet towards the black figure by the luminous pool, suddenly turned at a sharp angle and began to run even more rapidly towards the shadow of the house. Underhill could not imagine what he meant by the altered direction. The next moment, when the detective had vanished into the shadow of the house, there came out of that obscurity the sound of a scuffle and a curse; and Bagshaw returned lugging with him a little struggling man with red hair. The captive had evidently been escaping under the shelter of the building, when the quicker ears of the detective had heard him rustling like a bird among the bushes.

"Underhill," said the detective, "I wish you'd run on and see what's up by the pool. And now, who are you?" he asked, coming to a halt. "What's your name?"

"Michael Flood," said the stranger in a snappy fashion. He was an unnaturally lean little man, with a hooked nose too large for his face, which was colourless, like parchment, in contrast with the ginger colour of his hair. "I've got nothing to do with this. I found him lying dead and I was scared; but I only came to interview him for a paper."

"When you interview celebrities for the Press," said

Bagshaw, "do you generally climb over the garden wall?"

And he pointed grimly to a trail of footprints coming and going along the path towards the flower bed.

The man calling himself Flood wore an expression equally grim.

"An interviewer might very well get over the wall," he said, "for I couldn't make anybody hear at the front door. The servant had gone out."

"How do you know he'd gone out?" asked the detective suspiciously.

"Because," said Flood, with an almost unnatural calm, "I'm not the only person who gets over garden walls. It seems just possible that you did it yourself. But, anyhow, the servant did; for I've just this moment seen him drop over the wall, away on the other side of the garden, just by the garden door."

"Then why didn't he use the garden door?" demanded the cross-examiner.

"How should I know?" retorted Flood. "Because it was shut, I suppose. But you'd better ask him, not me; he's coming towards the house at this minute."

There was, indeed, another shadowy figure beginning to be visible through the fire-shot gloaming, a squat, square-headed figure, wearing a red waistcoat as the most conspicuous part of a rather shabby livery. He appeared to be making with unobtrusive haste towards a side-door in the house, until Bagshaw halloed him to a halt. He drew nearer to them very reluctantly, revealing a heavy, yellow face, with a touch of something Asiatic which was consonant with his flat, blue-black hair.

Bagshaw turned abruptly to the man called Flood. "Is there anybody in this place," he said, "who can testify to your identity?"

"Not many, even in this country," growled Flood. "I've only just come from Ireland; the only man I know round here is the priest at St. Dominic's Church—Father Brown."

"Neither of you must leave this place," said Bagshaw, and then added to the servant: "But you can go into the house and ring up St. Dominic's Presbytery and ask Father Brown if he would mind coming round here at once. No tricks, mind."

While the energetic detective was securing the potential fugitives, his companion, at his direction, had hastened on to the actual scene of the tragedy. It was a strange enough scene; and, indeed, if the tragedy had not been tragic it would have been highly fantastic. The dead man (for the briefest examination proved him to be dead) lay with his head in the pond, where the glow of the artificial illumination encircled the head with something of the appearance of an unholy halo. The face was gaunt and rather sinister, the brow bald, and the scanty curls dark grey, like iron rings; and, despite the damage done by the bullet wound in the temple, Underhill had no difficulty in recognizing the features he had seen in the many portraits of Sir Humphrey Gwynne. The dead man was in evening-dress, and his long, black legs, so thin as to be almost spidery, were sprawling at different angles up the steep bank from which he had fallen. As by some weird whim of diabolical arabesque, blood was eddying out, very slowly, into the luminous water in snaky rings, like the transparent crimson of sunset clouds.

Underhill did not know how long he stood staring down at this macabre figure, when he looked up and saw a group of four figures standing above him on the bank. He was prepared for Bagshaw and his Irish captive, and he had no difficulty in guessing the status of the servant in the red waistcoat. But the fourth figure had a sort of grotesque solemnity that seemed strangely congruous to that incongruity. It was a stumpy figure with a round face and a hat like a black halo. He realized that it was, in fact, a priest; but there was something about it that reminded him of some quaint old black woodcut at the end of a Dance of Death.

Then he heard Bagshaw saying to the priest:

"I'm glad you can identify this man; but you must realize that he's to some extent under suspicion. Of course, he may be innocent; but he did enter the garden in an irregular fashion."

"Well, I think he's innocent myself," said the little priest in a colourless voice. "But, of course, I may be wrong."

"Why do you think he is innocent?"

"Because he entered the garden in an irregular fashion," answered the cleric. "You see, I entered it in a regular fashion myself. But I seem to be almost the only person who did. All the best people seem to get over garden walls nowadays."

"What do you mean by a regular fashion?" asked the detective.

"Well," said Father Brown, looking at him with limpid gravity, "I came in by the front door. I often come into houses that way."

"Excuse me," said Bagshaw, "but does it matter very much how you came in, unless you propose to confess to the murder?"

"Yes, I think it does," said the priest mildly. "The truth is, that when I came in at the front door I saw something I don't think any of the rest of you have seen. It seems to me it might have something to do with it."

"What did you see?"

"I saw a sort of general smash-up," said Father Brown in his mild voice. "A big looking-glass broken, and a small palm tree knocked over, and the pot smashed all over the floor. Somehow, it looked to me as if something had happened."

"You are right," said Bagshaw after a pause. "If you saw that, it certainly looks as if it had something to do with it."

"And if it had anything to do with it," said the priest very gently, "it looks as if there was one person who had nothing to do with it; and that is Mr. Michael Flood, who entered the garden over the wall in an irregular fashion, and then tried to leave it in the same irregular fashion. It is his irregularity that makes me believe in his innocence."

"Let us go into the house," said Bagshaw abruptly.

As they passed in at the side-door, the servant leading the way, Bagshaw fell back a pace or two and spoke to his friend.

"Something odd about that servant," he said. "Says his name is Green, though he doesn't look it; but there seems no doubt he's really Gwynne's servant, apparently the only regular servant he had. But the queer thing is, that he flatly denied that his master was in the garden at all, dead or alive. Said the old judge had gone out to a grand legal dinner and couldn't be home for hours, and gave that as his excuse for slipping out."

"Did he," asked Underhill, "give any excuse for his curious way of slipping in?"

"No, none that I can make sense of," answered the detective. "I can't make him out. He seems to be scared of something."

Entering by the side-door, they found themselves at the inner end of the entrance hall, which ran along the side of the house and ended with the front door, surmounted by a dreary fanlight of the old-fashioned pattern. A faint, grey light was beginning to outline its radiation upon the darkness, like some dismal and discoloured sunrise; but what light there was in the hall came from a single, shaded lamp, also of an antiquated sort, that stood on a bracket in a corner. By the light of this Bagshaw could distinguish the debris of which Brown had spoken. A tall palm, with long sweeping leaves, had fallen full length, and its dark red pot was shattered into shards. They lay littered on the carpet, along with pale and gleaming fragments of a broken mirror, of which the almost empty frame hung behind them on the wall at the end of the vestibule. At right angles to this entrance, and directly opposite the side-door as they entered, was another and similar passage leading into the rest of the house. At the other end of it could be seen the telephone which the servant had used to summon the priest; and a half-open door, showing even through the crack, the serried ranks of great leather-bound books, marked the entrance to the judge's study.

Bagshaw stood looking down at the fallen pot and the mingled fragments at his feet.

"You're quite right," he said to the priest; "there's been a struggle here. And it must have been a struggle between Gwynne and his murderer."

"It seemed to me," said Father Brown modestly, "that something had happened here."

"Yes; it's pretty clear what happened," assented the detective. "The murderer entered by the front door and found Gwynne; probably Gwynne let him in. There was a death grapple, possibly a chance shot, that hit the glass, though they might have broken it with a stray kick or anything. Gwynne

213

managed to free himself and fled into the garden, where he was pursued and shot finally by the pond. I fancy that's the whole story of the crime itself; but, of course, I must look round the other rooms."

The other rooms, however, revealed very little, though Bagshaw pointed significantly to the loaded automatic pistol that he found in a drawer of the library desk.

"Looks as if he was expecting this," he said; "yet it seems queer he didn't take it with him when he went out into the hall."

Eventually they returned to the hall, making their way towards the front door, Father Brown letting his eye rove around in a rather absent-minded fashion. The two corridors, monotonously papered in the same grey and faded pattern, seemed to emphasize the dust and dingy floridity of the few early Victorian ornaments, the green rust that devoured the bronze of the lamp, the dull gold that glimmered in the frame of the broken mirror.

"They say it's bad luck to break a looking-glass," he said. "This looks like the very house of ill-luck. There's something about the very furniture——"

"That's rather odd," said Bagshaw sharply. "I thought the front door would be shut, but it's left on the latch."

There was no reply; and they passed out of the front door into the front garden, a narrower and more formal plot of flowers, having at one end a curiously clipped hedge with a hole in it, like a green cave, under the shadow of which some broken steps peeped out.

Father Brown strolled up to the hole and ducked his head under it. A few moments after he had disappeared they were astonished to hear his quiet voice in conversation above their heads, as if he were talking to somebody at the top of a tree. The detective followed, and found that the curious covered stairway led to what looked like a broken bridge, over-hanging the darker and emptier spaces of the garden. It just curled round the corner of the house, bringing in sight the field of coloured lights beyond and beneath. Probably it was the relic of some abandoned architectural fancy of building a sort of terrace on arches across the lawn. Bagshaw thought it a curious cul-de-sac in which to find anybody in the small hours between night and morning; but he was not looking at the details of it just then. He was looking at the man who was found.

As the man stood with his back turned—a small man in light grey clothes—the one outstanding feature about him was a wonderful head of hair, as yellow and radiant as the head of a huge dandelion. It was literally outstanding like a halo, and something in that association made the face, when it was slowly and sulkily turned on them, rather a shock of contrast. That halo should have enclosed an oval face of the mildly angelic sort; but the face was crabbed and elderly with a powerful jowl and a short nose that somehow suggested the broken nose of a pugilist.

"This is Mr. Orm, the celebrated poet, I understand," said Father Brown, as calmly as if he were introducing two people in a drawing-room.

"Whoever he is," said Bagshaw, "I must trouble him to come with me and answer a few questions."

Mr. Osric Orm, the poet, was not a model of self-expression when it came to the answering of questions. There, in that corner of the old garden, as the grey twilight before dawn began to creep over the heavy hedges and the broken bridge, and afterwards in a succession of circumstances and stages of legal inquiry that grew more and more ominous, he refused to say anything except that he had intended to call on Sir Humphrey Gwynne, but had not done so because he could not get anyone to answer the bell. When it was pointed out that the door was practically open, he snorted. When it was hinted that the hour was somewhat late, he snarled. The little that he said was obscure, either because he really knew hardly any English, or because he knew better than to know any. His opinions seemed to be of a nihilistic and destructive sort, as was indeed the tendency of his poetry for those who could follow it; and it seemed possible that his business with the judge, and perhaps his quarrel with the judge, had been something in the anarchist line. Gwynne was known to have had something of a mania about Bolshevist spies, as he had about German spies. Anyhow, one coincidence, only a few moments after his capture, confirmed Bagshaw in the impression that the case must be taken seriously. As they went out of the front gate into the street, they so happened to encounter yet another neighbour, Buller, the cigar merchant from next door, conspicuous by his brown, shrewd face and the unique orchid in his buttonhole; for he had a name in that branch of horticulture. Rather to the surprise of the rest, he hailed his neighbour, the poet, in a matter-of-fact manner, almost as if he had expected to see him.

"Hullo, here we are again," he said. "Had a long talk with old Gwynne, I suppose?"

"Sir Humphrey Gwynne is dead," said Bagshaw. "I am investigating the case and I must ask you to explain."

Buller stood as still as the lamp-post beside him, possibly stiffened with surprise. The red end of his cigar brightened and darkened rhythmically, but his brown face was in shadow; when he spoke it was with quite a new voice.

"I only mean," he said, "that when I passed two hours ago Mr. Orm was going in at this gate to see Sir Humphrey."

"He says he hasn't seen him yet," observed Bagshaw, "or even been into the house."

"It's a long time to stand on the door-step," observed Buller.

"Yes," said Father Brown; "it's rather a long time to stand in the street."

"I've been home since then," said the cigar merchant. "Been writing letters and came out again to post them."

"You'll have to tell all that later," said Bagshaw. "Good night—or good morning."

The trial of Osric Orm for the murder of Sir Humphrey Gwynne, which filled the newspapers for so many weeks, really turned entirely on the same crux as that little talk under the lamp-post, when the grey-green dawn was breaking about the dark streets and gardens. Everything came back to the enigma of those two empty hours between the time when Buller saw Orm going in at the garden gate, and the time when Father

Brown found him apparently still lingering in the garden. He had certainly had the time to commit six murders, and might almost have committed them for want of something to do; for he could give no coherent account of what he was doing. It was argued by the prosecution that he had also the opportunity, as the front door was unlatched, and the side-door into the larger garden left standing open. The court followed, with considerable interest, Bagshaw's clear reconstruction of the struggle in the passage, of which the traces were so evident; indeed, the police had since found the shot that had shattered the glass. Finally, the hole in the hedge to which he had been tracked, had very much the appearance of a hiding-place. On the other hand, Sir Matthew Blake, the very able counsel for the defence, turned this last argument the other way: asking why any man should entrap himself in a place without possible exit, when it would obviously be much more sensible to slip out into the street. Sir Matthew Blake also made effective use of the mystery that still rested upon the motive for the murder. Indeed, upon this point, the passages between Sir Matthew Blake and Sir Arthur Travers, the equally brilliant advocate for the prosecution, turned rather to the advantage of the prisoner. Sir Arthur could only throw out suggestions about a Bolshevist conspiracy which sounded a little thin. But when it came to investigating the facts of Orm's mysterious behaviour that night he was considerably more effective.

The prisoner went into the witness-box, chiefly because his astute counsel calculated that it would create a bad impression if he did not. But he was almost as uncommunicative to his own counsel as to the prosecuting counsel. Sir Arthur Travers made all possible capital out of his stubborn silence, but did not succeed in breaking it. Sir Arthur was a long, gaunt man, with a long, cadaverous face, in striking contrast to the sturdy figure and bright, bird-like eye of Sir Matthew Blake. But if Sir Matthew suggested a very cocksure sort of cock-sparrow, Sir Arthur might more truly have been compared to a crane or stork; as he leaned forward, prodding the poet with questions, his long nose might have been a long beak.

"Do you mean to tell the jury," he asked, in tones of grating incredulity, "that you never went in to see the deceased gentleman at all?"

"No!" replied Orm shortly.

"You wanted to see him, I suppose. You must have been very anxious to see him. Didn't you wait two whole hours in front of his front door?"

"Yes," replied the other.

"And yet you never even noticed the door was open?"

"No," said Orm.

"What in the world were you doing for two hours in somebody else's front garden?" insisted the barrister. "You were doing something I suppose?"

"Yes."

"Is it a secret?" asked Sir Arthur, with adamantine jocularity.

"It's a secret from you," answered the poet.

It was upon this suggestion of a secret that Sir Arthur seized in developing his line of accusation. With a boldness which some thought unscrupulous, he turned the very mystery of the motive, which was the strongest part of his opponent's case, into an argument for his own. He gave it as the first fragmentary hint of some far-flung and elaborate conspiracy, in which a patriot had perished like one caught in the coils of an octopus.

"Yes," he cried in a vibrating voice, "my learned friend is perfectly right! We do not know the exact reason why this honourable public servant was murdered. We shall not know the reason why the next public servant is murdered. If my learned friend himself falls a victim to his eminence, and the hatred which the hellish powers of destruction feel for the guardians of law, he will be murdered, and he will not know the reason. Half the decent people in this court will be butchered in their beds, and we shall not know the reason. And we shall never know the reason and never arrest the massacre, until it has depopulated our country, so long as the defence is permitted to stop all proceedings with this stale tag about 'motive', when every other fact in the case, every glaring incongruity, every gaping silence, tells us that we stand in the presence of Cain."

"I never knew Sir Arthur so excited," said Bagshaw to his group of companions afterwards. "Some people are saying he went beyond the usual limit and that the prosecutor in a murder case oughtn't to be so vindictive. But I must say there was something downright creepy about that little goblin with the yellow hair, that seemed to play up to the impression. I was vaguely recalling, all the time, something that De Quincey says about Mr. Williams, that ghastly criminal who slaughtered two whole families almost in silence. I think he says that Williams had hair of a vivid unnatural yellow; and that he thought it had been dyed by a trick learned in India, where they dye horses green or blue. Then there was his queer, stony silence, like a troglodyte's; I'll never deny that it all worked me up until I felt there was a sort of monster in the dock. If that was only Sir Arthur's eloquence, then he certainly took a heavy responsibility in putting so much passion into it."

"He was a friend of poor Gwynne's, as a matter of fact," said Underhill, more gently; "a man I know saw them hobnobbing together after a great legal dinner lately. I dare say that's why he feels so strongly in this case. I suppose it's doubtful whether a man ought to act in such a case on mere personal feeling."

"He wouldn't," said Bagshaw. "I bet Sir Arthur Travers wouldn't act only on feeling, however strongly he felt. He's got a very stiff sense of his own professional position. He's one of those men who are ambitious even when they've satisfied their ambition. I know nobody who'd take more trouble to keep his position in the world. No; you've got hold of the wrong moral to his rather thundering sermon. If he lets himself go like that, it's because he thinks he can get a conviction, anyhow, and wants to put himself at the head of some political movement against the conspiracy he talks about. He must have some very good reason for wanting to convict Orm and some very good reason for thinking he can do it. That means that the facts will support him. His confidence doesn't look well for the prisoner." He became conscious of an insignificant figure in the group.

"Well, Father Brown," he said with a smile; "what do you think of our judicial procedure?"

219

"Well," replied the priest rather absently, "I think the thing that struck me most was how different men look in their wigs. You talk about the prosecuting barrister being so tremendous. But I happened to see him take his wig off for a minute, and he really looks quite a different man. He's quite bald, for one thing."

"I'm afraid that won't prevent his being tremendous," answered Bagshaw. "You don't propose to found the defence on the fact that the prosecuting counsel is bald, do you?"

"Not exactly," said Father Brown good-humouredly. "To tell the truth, I was thinking how little some kinds of people know about other kinds of people. Suppose I went among some remote people who had never even heard of England. Suppose I told them that there is a man in my country who won't ask a question of life and death, until he has put an erection made of horse-hair on the top of his head, with little tails behind, and grey corkscrew curls at the side, like an Early Victorian old woman. They would think he must be rather eccentric; but he isn't at all eccentric, he's only conventional. They would think so, because they don't know anything about English barristers; because they don't know what a barrister is. Well, that barrister doesn't know what a poet is. He doesn't understand that a poet's eccentricities wouldn't seem eccentric to other poets. He thinks it odd that Orm should walk about in a beautiful garden for two hours, with nothing to do. God bless my soul! a poet would think nothing of walking about in the same backyard for ten hours if he had a poem to do. Orm's own counsel was quite as stupid. It never occurred to him to ask Orm the obvious question."

"What question do you mean?" asked the other.

"Why, what poem he was making up, of course," said Father Brown rather impatiently. "What line he was stuck at, what epithet he was looking for, what climax he was trying to work up to. If there were any educated people in court, who know what literature is, they would have known well enough whether he had had anything genuine to do. You'd have asked a manu- facturer about the conditions of his factory; but nobody seems to consider the conditions under which poetry is manufactured. It's done by doing nothing."

"That's all very well," replied the detective; "but why did he hide? Why did he climb up that crooked little stairway and stop there; it led nowhere."

"Why, because it led nowhere, of course," cried Father Brown explosively. "Anybody who clapped eyes on that blind alley ending in mid-air might have known an artist would want to go there, just as a child would."

He stood blinking for a moment, and then said apologetically: "I beg your pardon; but it seems odd that none of them understand these things. And then there was another thing. Don't you know that everything has, for an artist, one aspect or angle that is exactly *right*? A tree, a cow, and a cloud, in a certain relation only, mean something; as three letters, in one order only, mean a word. Well, the view of that illuminated garden from that unfinished bridge was the right view of it. It was as unique as the fourth dimension. It was a sort of fairy foreshortening; it was like looking *down* at heaven and seeing all the stars growing on trees and that luminous pond like a moon fallen flat on the fields in some happy nursery tale. He could have looked at it for ever. If you told him the path led nowhere, he would tell you it had led him to the country at the end of the world. But do you expect him to tell you that in the witness-box? What would you say to him if he did? You talk about a man having a jury of his peers. Why don't you have a jury of poets?"

"You talk as if you were a poet yourself," said Bagshaw.

"Thank your stars I'm not," said Father Brown. "Thank your lucky stars a priest has to be more charitable than a poet. Lord have mercy on us, if you knew what a crushing, what a cruel contempt he feels for the lot of you, you'd feel as if you were under Niagara."

"You may know more about the artistic temperament than I do," said Bagshaw after a pause; "but, after all, the answer is simple. You can only show that he might have done what he did, without committing the crime. But it's equally true that he might have committed the crime. And who else could have committed it?"

"Have you thought about the servant, Green?" asked Father Brown, reflectively. "He told a rather queer story."

"Ah," cried Bagshaw quickly, "you think Green did it, after all."

"I'm quite sure he didn't," replied the other. "I only asked if you'd thought about his queer story. He only went out for some trifle, a drink or an assignation or what not. But he went out by the garden door and came back over the garden wall. In other words, he left the door open, but he came back to find it shut. Why? Because Somebody Else had already passed out that way."

"The murderer," muttered the detective doubtfully. "Do you know who he was?"

"I know what he looked like," answered Father Brown quietly. "That's the only thing I do know. I can almost see him as he came in at the front door, in the gleam of the hall lamp; his figure, his clothes, even his face!"

"What's all this?"

"He looked like Sir Humphrey Gwynne," said the priest.

"What the devil do you mean?" demanded Bagshaw. "Gwynne was lying dead with his head in the pond."

"Oh, yes," said Father Brown.

After a moment he went on: "Let's go back to that theory of yours, which was a very good one, though I don't quite agree with it. You suppose the murderer came in at the front door, met the judge in the front hall, struggling with him and breaking the mirror; that the judge then retreated into the garden, where he was finally shot. Somehow, it doesn't sound natural to me. Granted he retreated down the hall, there are two exits at the end, one into the garden and one into the house. Surely, he would be more likely to retreat into the house? His gun was there; his telephone was there; his servant, so far as he knew, was there. Even the nearest neighbours were in that direction. Why should he stop to open the garden door and go out alone on the deserted side of the house?"

"But we know he did go out of the house," replied his companion, puzzled. "We know he went out of the house, because he was found in the garden."

"He never went out of the house, because he never was in the house," said Father Brown. "Not that evening, I mean. He was sitting in that bungalow. I read *that* lesson in the dark, at the beginning, in red and golden stars across the garden. They were worked from the hut; they wouldn't have been burning at all if he hadn't been in the hut. He was trying to run across to the house and the telephone, when the murderer shot him beside the pond."

"But what about the pot and the palm and the broken mirror?" cried Bagshaw. "Why, it was you who found them! It was you yourself who said there must have been a struggle in the hall."

The priest blinked rather painfully. "Did I?" he muttered. "Surely, I didn't say that. I never thought that. What I think I said, was that something had happened in the hall. And something did happen; but it wasn't a struggle."

"Then what broke the mirror?" asked Bagshaw shortly.

"A bullet broke the mirror," answered Father Brown gravely; "a bullet fired by the criminal. The big fragments of falling glass were quite enough to knock over the pot and the palm."

"Well, what else could he have been firing at except Gwynne?" asked the detective.

"It's rather a fine metaphysical point," answered his clerical companion almost dreamily. "In one sense, of course, he was firing at Gwynne. But Gwynne wasn't there to be fired at. The criminal was alone in the hall."

He was silent for a moment, and then went on quietly. "Imagine the looking-glass at the end of the passage, before it was broken, and the tall palm arching over it. In the half-light, reflecting these monochrome walls, it would look like the end of the passage. A man reflected in it would look like a man coming from inside the house. It would look like the master of the house—if only the reflection were a little like him."

"Stop a minute," cried Bagshaw. "I believe I begin——"

"You begin to see," said Father Brown. "You begin to see why all the suspects in this case must be innocent. Not one of them could possibly have mistaken his own reflection for old Gwynne. Orm would have known at once that his bush of yellow hair was not a bald head. Flood would have seen his own red head, and Green his own red waistcoat. Besides, they're all short and shabby; none of them could have thought his own image was a tall, thin, old gentleman in evening-dress. We want another, equally tall and thin, to match him. That's what I meant by saying that I knew what the murderer looked like."

"And what do you argue from that?" asked Bagshaw, looking at him steadily.

The priest uttered a sort of sharp, crisp laugh, oddly different from his ordinary mild manner of speech.

"I am going to argue," he said, "the very thing that you said was so ludicrous and impossible."

"What do you mean?"

"I'm going to base the defence," said Father Brown, "on the fact that the prosecuting counsel has a bald head."

"Oh, my God!" said the detective quietly, and got to his feet, staring.

Father Brown had resumed his monologue in an unruffled manner.

"You've been following the movements of a good many people in this business; you policemen were prodigiously interested in the movements of the poet, and the servant, and the Irishman. The man whose movements seem to have been rather forgotten is the dead man himself. His servant was quite honestly astonished at finding his master had returned. His master had gone to a great dinner of all the leaders of the legal profession, but had left it abruptly and come home. He was not ill, for he summoned no assistance; he had almost certainly quarrelled with some leader of the legal profession. It's among the leaders of that profession that we should have looked first for his enemy. He returned, and shut himself up in the bungalow, where he kept all his private documents about

224

treasonable practices. But the leader of the legal profession, who knew there was something against him in those documents, was thoughtful enough to follow his accuser home; he also being in evening-dress, but with a pistol in his pocket. That is all; and nobody could ever have guessed it except for the mirror."

He seemed to be gazing into vacancy for a moment, and then added:

"A queer thing is a mirror; a picture frame that holds hundreds of different pictures, all vivid and all vanished for ever. Yet, there was something specially strange about the glass that hung at the end of that grey corridor under that green palm. It is as if it was a magic glass and had a different fate from others, as if its picture could somehow survive it, hanging in the air of that twilight house like a spectre; or at least like an abstract diagram, the skeleton of an argument. We could, at least, conjure out of the void the thing that Sir Arthur Travers saw. By the way, there was one very true thing that you said about him."

"I'm glad to hear it," said Bagshaw with grim good-nature. "And what was it?"

"You said," observed the priest, "that Sir Arthur must have some good reason for wanting to get Orm hanged."

A week later the priest met the police detective once more, and learned that the authorities had already been moving on the new lines of inquiry when they were interrupted by a sensational event.

"Sir Arthur Travers," began Father Brown.

"Sir Arthur Travers is dead," said Bagshaw, briefly.

"Ah!" said the other, with a little catch in his voice; "you mean that he——"

"Yes," said Bagshaw, "he shot at the same man again, but not in a mirror."

From *The Father Brown Stories*
(Cassell & Co. Ltd.)

The Yellow Bird

Five men had halted at the top of a hill overlooking a valley beautiful enough to be called a vision, but too neglected ever to have been vulgarized by being called a view. They were a sketching club on a walking tour; but when they had come to that place they did no more walking, and, strangely enough, very little sketching. It was as if they had come to some quiet end of the world; that corner of the earth seemed to have a curious effect on them, varying with their various personalities, but acting on all as something arresting and vaguely final. Yet the quality was as nameless as it was unique; there was nothing definably different from twenty other wooded valleys in those western shires upon the marches of Wales. Green slopes dived into a fringe of dark forests that looked black by comparison, but the grey columns of which were mirrored in the curving river like a long winding colonnade. Only a little way along, on one side of the river, the bank was cleared of timber, and formed a platform for old gardens and orchards, in the midst of which stood an old tall house, of a rich brown brick with blue shutters, and rather neglected creepers clinging to it, more like moss to a stone than like flowers to a flower-bed. The roof was flat, with a chimney near the centre of it, from which a thin thread of smoke was drawn up into the sky; the only sign that the house was not wholly deserted. Of the five men who looked down at the landscape, only one had any special reason for looking at the house.

The eldest of the artists, a dark, active, ambitious man in spectacles, destined to be famous afterwards under the name of Luke Walton, was affected by the place in a curious fashion.

It seemed to tease him like a fly or something elusive; he could not please himself with a point of view, but was perpetually shifting his camp-stool from place to place, crossing and re-crossing the theatre of these events amid the jeers of his companions. The second, a heavy, fair-haired man named Hutton, stared at the scene in a somewhat bovine fashion, made a few lines on a sketching block, and then announced in a loud voice that it was a good place for a picnic, and that he was going to have his lunch. The third painter agreed with him; but as he was said to be a poet as well as a painter, he was expected to show a certain fervour for any opportunities of avoiding work. Indeed, this particular artist, whose name was Gabriel Gale, did not seem disposed even to look at the landscape, far less to paint it; but after taking a bite out of a ham sandwich, and a swig at somebody else's flask of claret, incontinently lay down on his back under a tree and stared up at the twilight of twinkling leaves; some believing him to be asleep, while others more generously supposed him to be composing poetry. The fourth, a smaller and more alert man named Garth, could only be regarded as an honorary member of the artistic group; for he was more interested in science than in art, and carried not a paint-box but a camera. Nevertheless, he was not without an intelligent appreciation of scenery, and he was in the act of fixing up his photographic apparatus so that it covered the angle of the river where stood the neglected garden, and the distant house. And at that moment the fifth man, who had not yet moved or spoken, made so abrupt and arresting a gesture that one might say that he struck up the camera, like a gun pointed to kill.

"Don't," he said; "it's bad enough when they try to paint it."

"What's the matter?" asked Garth. "Don't you like that house?"

"I like it too much," said the other, "or rather, I love it too much to like it at all."

The fifth man who spoke was the youngest of the party, but he had already at least some local success and celebrity; partly because he had devoted his talent to the landscape and legends of that countryside, and partly because he came of a family of small squires whose name was historic in those hills. He was tall, with dark-brown hair and a long brown face, with a high-bridged nose that looked rather distinguished than handsome; and there was a permanent cloud of consideration on his brow that made him seem much older than his years. He alone of all these men had made no gesture, either of labour or relaxation, on coming to the crest of the hill. While Walton went to and fro, and Hutton started cheerfully on his meal, and Gale flung himself on the couch of leaves to look up into the tree-tops, this man had stood like a statue looking across the valley to the house, and it was only when Garth pointed his camera that he had even lifted a hand.

Garth turned on him a humorous face, in spite of its hard angular features; for the little scientist was a man of admirable good temper.

"I suppose there's a story about it," he said; "you look as if you were in quite a confidential mood. If you like to tell me, I assure you I can keep a secret. I'm a medical man and have to keep secrets, especially those of the insane. That ought to encourage you."

The younger man, whose name was John Mallow, continued to gaze moodily across the valley, but there was something about him that suggested that the other had guessed right, and he was about to speak.

"Don't bother about the others," said Garth, "they can't hear; they're too busy doing nothing. Hutton," he called out in much more strident tones, "Gale, are you fellows listening?"

"Yes; I'm listening to the birds," came the half-buried voice of Gale out of his leafy lair.

"Hutton's asleep," observed Garth with satisfaction. "No wonder, after all that lunch. Are you asleep, Gale?"

"Not asleep, but dreaming," answered the other. "If you look up long enough, there isn't any more up or down, but a sort of green, dizzy dream; with birds that might as well be fishes. They're just odd shapes of different colours against the green, brown and grey, and one of them looks quite yellow."

228

"A yellow-hammer, I suppose," remarked Garth.

"It doesn't look like a hammer," said Gale, sleepily; "not such an odd shape as all that."

"Ass!" said Garth briefly. "Did you expect it to look like an auctioneer's hammer? You poets who are so strong about Nature are generally weak in natural history. Well, Mallow," he added, turning to his companion, "you've nothing to fear from them, if you like to talk in an ordinary voice. What about this house of yours?"

"It's not mine," said Mallow. "As a matter of fact, it belongs to an old friend of my mother's, a Mrs. Verney, a widow. The place has very much run to seed now, as you see, for the Verneys have got poorer and poorer, and don't know what to do next, which is the beginning of the trouble. But I have passed happier times there than I shall probably ever have again."

"Was Mrs. Verney so enchanting a character?" asked his friend softly; "or may I take the liberty of supposing there was a rising generation?"

"Unfortunately for me, it is a very rising generation," replied Mallow. "It rises in a sort of small revolution; and it rises rather above my head." Then, after a silence, he said somewhat abruptly, "Do you believe in lady doctors?"

"I don't believe in any doctors," answered Garth. "I'm one myself."

"Well, it isn't exactly lady doctors, I believe, but it's something of that sort," went on Mallow; "study of psychological science, and so on. Laura has got it very badly, and is helping some Russian psychologist or other."

"Your narrative style is a little sketchy," remarked Dr. Garth, "but I suppose I may infer that Laura is a daughter of Mrs. Verney, and also that Laura has some logical connexion with the happy days that will not return."

"Suppose it all, and have done with it," replied the young man. "You know what I mean; but the real point is this. Laura has all the new ideas, and has persuaded her mother to come down off the high horse of genteel poverty in all sorts of ways. I don't say she's not right in that; but as it works out there are some curious complications. For one thing, Laura not only earns her own living but earns it in the laboratory of this mysterious Muscovite; and for another, she has bounced her mother into taking a paying guest. And the paying guest is the mysterious Muscovite again, who wants a quiet rest in the country."

"And I suppose, I may take it," said the doctor, "that you feel there is a little too much of the Muscovite in your young life?"

"As a matter of fact, he moved into the house late last night," continued Mallow, "and I suppose that's really why I drifted in this direction this morning, trailing you all at my heels. I said it was a beautiful place, and so it is; but I don't want to paint it, and I don't even want to visit it; but all the same, I had a vague sort of feeling I should like to be somewhere near."

"And, as you couldn't get rid of us, you brought us along," said Garth with a smile. "Well, I think I can understand all that. Do you know anything about this Russian professor?"

"I know nothing whatever against him," answered the other. "He is a very famous man both in science and politics. He escaped from a Siberian prison in the old days, by blowing up the wall with a bomb of his own construction; it's quite an exciting story, and he must at least be a man of courage. He has written a great book called *The Psychology of Liberty*, I believe; and Laura is very keen on his views. It's rather an indescribable thing altogether; she and I are very fond of each other, and I don't think she mistakes me for a fool, and I don't think I am a fool. But whenever we have met lately it has been literally like a meeting on a high road, when two people are going opposite ways. And I think I know what it is; she is always going outwards, and I am always going inwards. The more I see of the world, and the more men I meet or books I read or questions I answer, the more I come back with increased conviction to those places where I was born or played as a boy, narrowing my circles like a bird going back to a nest. That seems to me the end of all travel, and especially of the widest travel—to get home. But she has another idea in her mind. It's not only that she says that old brown brick house is like a prison, or that the hills are like walls shutting her in; I dare say things do get pretty dull in such a place. There's a theory in it, too, which I suppose she's got from her psychological friend. She says that even in her own valley, and in her own garden, the trees only grow because they radiate outwards, which is only the Latin for branching. She says the very word 'radiant' shows it is the secret of happiness. There is something in it, I suppose; but I radiate inwards, so to speak; that is why I paint all my pictures of this little corner of the world. If I could only paint this valley, I might go on to paint that garden; and, if only I could paint that garden, I might be worthy to paint the creeper under her window."

The sleeping Hutton awoke with an uproarious yawn, and lifting himself from his bed of leaves, wandered away to where the more industrious Walton had at last settled down to work on the other side of the hill. But the poet Gale still lay gazing at his topsy-turvydom of tree-tops. And the only reply he would make to a further challenge from Garth was to say heavily, "They've driven the yellow one away."

"Who have driven what away?" demanded Mallow, rather irritably.

"The other birds attacked the yellow one and drove it away," said the poet.

"Regarded it as an undesirable alien, no doubt," said Garth.

"The Yellow Peril," said Gale, and relapsed into his dreams.

Mallow had already resumed his monologue:

"The name of the psychologist is Ivanhov, and he's said to be writing another great book in this country retreat; I believe she is acting as his secretary. It is to embody some mathematical theory about the elimination of limits and——"

"Hullo!" cried Garth. "This moated grange of yours is actually coming to life. Somebody is actually beginning to open a window."

"You haven't been looking at it as I have," answered Mallow quietly. "Just round the angle on the left there's a little window that's been open all the time. That belongs to the little sitting-room out of the spare bedroom. It used to be Laura's room, and

231

still has a lot of her things in it; but I think they give it now to their guests."

"Including, doubtless, their paying guest," observed Garth.

"He's a queer sort of guest. I only hope he's a paying one," returned the other. "That big window where they just opened the shutters is at the end of the long library; all these windows belong to it. I expect they'll stick the philosopher in there if he wants to philosophize."

"The philosopher seems to be philosophical about draughts," observed Dr. Garth; "he or somebody else has opened three more windows, and seems to be struggling with another."

Even as he spoke the fifth window burst open, and even from where they stood they could see a creeper that had strayed across it snap and drop with the gesture. It had the look of the snapping of some green chain securing the house like a prison. It had almost the look of the breaking of the seal of a tomb.

For Mallow, against all his prejudices, felt the presence and pressure of that revolutionary ideal which he recognized as his rival. All along the shattered façade of the old brown house the windows were opening one after another like the eyes of an Argus waking from his giant sleep. He was forced to admit to himself that he had never seen the place thus coming to life from within, as a plant unfolds itself. The last three windows were now open to the morning; the long room must already be full of light, to say nothing of air. Garth had spoken of a philosopher enduring draughts; but it seemed more as if a pagan priest had been turned into a temple of the winds. But there was more in that morning vision than the mere accident of a row of windows open when they were commonly closed. The same fancy about unfolding life seemed to fill the whole scene like a new atmosphere. It was as if a fresh air had streamed out of the windows instead of into them. The sun was already fairly high, but it came out of the morning mists above the house with something of the silent explosion of daybreak. The very shapes of the forest trees, spreading themselves like fans, seemed to repeat the original word "radiant", which he had thought of almost as a Latin pun. Sailing over his head, as if sent flying by a sort of centrifugal force, the clouds still carried into the height of noon the colours of sunrise. He felt all the fresh things that he feared coming at him by an irrepressible expansion. Everything seemed to enlarge itself. Even when his eye fell on a stunted gate-post standing alone in the old garden, he could fancy that it swelled as he stared at it.

A sharp exclamation from his friend woke him from his unnatural day-dream, which might rather be called, by a contradiction, a white nightmare of light.

"By blazes! he's found another window," cried the doctor; "a window in the roof."

There was, indeed, the gleam of a skylight which caught the sun at an angle as it was forced upwards, and out of the opening emerged the moving figure of a man. Little could be seen of him at that distance, except that he was tall and slim and had yellow hair which looked like gold in the strong sun. He was dressed in some long, light-coloured garment, probably a dressing-gown, and he stretched his long limbs as if with the sleepy exultation of one arisen from sleep.

"Look here!" said Mallow suddenly, an indescribable expression flashing across his face and vanishing; "I'm going to pay a call."

"I rather thought you might," answered Garth. "Do you want to go alone?"

As he spoke he looked round for the rest of the company, but Walton and Hutton were still chatting some distance away on the other side of the hill, and only Gale still lay in the shadow of the thick trees staring up at the birds, as if he had never stirred. Garth called to him by name, but it was only after a silence that Gale spoke. What he said was:

"Were you ever an isosceles triangle?"

"Very seldom," replied Garth with restraint. "May I ask what the devil you are talking about?"

"Only something I was thinking about," answered the poet, lifting himself on to one elbow. "I wondered whether it would be a cramping sort of thing to be surrounded by straight lines,

233

and whether being in a circle would be any better. Did anybody ever live in a round prison?"

"Where do you get these cracked notions?" inquired the doctor.

"A little bird told me," Gale said gravely. "Oh, it's quite true."

He had risen to his feet by this time, and came slowly forward to the brow of the hill, looking across at the house by the river. As he looked his dreamy blue eyes seemed to wake up, like the windows opening in the house he gazed at.

"Another bird," he said softly, "like a sparrow on the housetops. And that fits in with it exactly."

There was some suggestion of truth in the phrase, for the strange figure was standing on the very edge of the roof, with space below him and his hands spread out almost as if he wished to fly. But the last sentence, and still more the strange manner in which it was spoken, puzzled the doctor completely.

"Fits in with what?" he asked, rather sharply.

"He's like that yellow bird," said Gale vaguely. "In fact, he is a yellow bird, with that hair and the sun on him. What did you say you thought it was—a yellow-hammer?"

"Yellow-hammer yourself," retorted Garth; "you're quite as yellow as he is. In fact, with your long legs and straw-coloured hair, you're really rather like him."

Mallow, in his more mystical mood, looked strangely from one to the other, for indeed there was a certain vague similarity between the two tall, fair-haired figures, the one on the house and the other on the hill.

"Perhaps I am rather like him," said Gale quietly. "Perhaps I'm just sufficiently like him to learn not to be like him, so to speak. We may both be birds of a feather, the yellow feather; but we don't flock together, because he likes to flock by himself. And as to being a hammer, yellow or otherwise, well, that also is an allegory."

"I decline to make head or tail of your allegories," said Dr. Garth shortly.

"I used to want a hammer to smash things with," continued

234

Gale; "but I've learnt to do something else with a hammer, which is what a hammer is meant for; and every now and then I manage to do it."

"What do you mean by that?" inquired the doctor.

"I can hit the right nail on the head," answered the poet.

It was not, in fact, until later in the day that Mallow paid his call at Mrs. Verney's house. Mrs. Verney was going up to the neighbouring village for the afternoon; and Mallow had more than one motive for making his attack when the stranger was alone with his secretary. He had a general idea of using his friends to detach or detain the stranger while he himself sought for explanation from the secretary; so he dragged Garth and Gale along with him to Mrs. Verney's drawing-room; or rather he would have done so if Gale had been an easy person to drag successfully anywhere. But Gale had a tendency to get detached from any such group, and was always being left behind. Large as he was, he had a way of getting mislaid. His friends forgot him as they had almost forgotten him when he was lying under the tree. It was not that he was unsociable; on the contrary, he was very fond of his friends and very fond of his opinions, and always delighted to detail the latter to the former. Strangers would have said that he was very fond of the sound of his own voice, but friends who were fond of him knew better. They knew that he had hardly ever heard his own voice, in the sense of listening to it. What made his movements incalculable was that his thinking or talking would start from any small thing that seemed to him a large thing. What are to most men impressions, or half impressions, were to him incidents; and the chief incidents of the day. Many imaginative people know what is meant by saying that certain empty rooms or open doors are suggestive; but he always acted on the suggestion. Most of them understand that there can be something vaguely inviting about a gap in a garden hedge, or the abrupt angle of a path; but he always accepted the invitation. The shape of a hill, or the corner of a house, checked him like a challenge. He wrestled with it seriously till it had given up something of its secret, till he could put something like a name to his nameless fancy; and these things were the active adventures of his life. Hence it was that he would sometimes follow one train of thought for hours, as steadily as a bird winging its way homewards. But it might start anywhere; and hence, in his actual movements, he looked more like a floating tuft of thistledown caught upon any thorn.

On this occasion his friends lost him, or left him behind, as they turned the corner of the house just after passing an old-fashioned bow-window looking out on the garden. Inside the window stood a small round table on which was a bowl of goldfish; and Gale stopped abruptly and stared at it as if he had never seen such a thing before. He had often maintained that the main object of man's life was to see a thing as if he had never seen it before. But in this case the twilight of the little empty room, touched here and there with the late afternoon sunlight, seemed somehow a subtle but suitable background for the thing that he saw. The heart of a dark green sphere was alive with little living flames.

"Why the devil do they call them goldfish?" he asked almost irritably. "They're a much more gorgeous colour than gold; I've never seen it anywhere except in very rare red clouds in a sunset. Gold suggests yellow, and not the best yellow either; not half so good as the clear lemon yellow of that bird I saw to-day. They're more like copper than gold. And copper is twenty times finer than gold. Why isn't copper the most precious metal, I wonder?"

He paused a moment and then said reflectively:

"Would it do, I wonder, when one changed a cheque into gold, to give a man coppers instead, and explain that they have more of the rich tones of sunset?"

His inquiry remained unanswered, for he made it to the empty air. His companions were deficient in his sense of the importance of goldfish, and had gone on impatiently to the main entrance of the house, leaving him lingering by the bowl near the bow-window. He continued to look at it for a considerable time, and when at last he turned away, it was not to follow his friends, but to pace the paths of the garden in the

236

deepening and darkening twilight, revolving in his mind some occult romance beginning with a bowl of fish.

Meanwhile, his more practical friends, pursuing the main purpose of the story, had penetrated into the house and found at least some members of the household. There had been many things in the garden or the gateway over which Mallow also might have been disposed to linger if his mood had been merely sentimental; an old swing standing by the corner of the orchard, the angle of a faded tennis lawn, the fork of a pear-tree, all of which had stories attached to them. But he was possessed of a passionate curiosity far too practical for sentiment of the merely reminiscent sort; he was resolved to run to earth the mystery of the new man in the old house. He felt that a change had come over everything with the man's mere presence; and wished to know how far that change had gone. He half expected to see those familiar rooms swept bare, or filled with strange furniture where the stranger had passed.

Accident, indeed, gave to their passage through those empty rooms an air of pursuit, as if something were escaping. For, as they passed from an outer room into the long library, the stranger, who was at the other end by the window, emphasized his restless love of the open air by putting one long leg over the low window-sill and stepping out on to the lawn. He had evidently, however, no real desire to avoid them, for he stood there smiling in the sunlight, and uttered some greeting very pleasantly with a slight foreign accent. He was still wearing the long lemon-coloured dressing-gown which, along with his yellow hair, had suggested the comparison of a yellow bird. Under the yellow hair his brow was broad but not high, and the nose was not only long and straight, but came down in a single line from the forehead in the manner that may be seen on many Greek coins and carvings, but which has an unnatural and even sinister symmetry when seen in real life. There was nothing else eccentric or exuberant about him; his manners were casual, but not ungraceful; and nothing contradicted the sunny ease of his situation and demeanour except, perhaps, a slightly strained look in the eyes, which were eager and promi-

237

nent. Until his acquaintances grew accustomed to it, as a fixed involuntary feature of his face, they occasionally had a sort of shock when catching his quiet face in shadow and realizing that the round eyes were standing out of his head.

The first thing the eyes seemed to encounter was Dr. Garth's hand-camera; and, as soon as introductions and salutations had passed, he plunged into talk about photography. He prophesied its extension at the expense of painting, and brushed aside the objection, which even the doctor offered, that painting had the superiority in colour.

"Colour-photography will soon be completed," he said hastily; "or rather, it will never be completed, but will always be improved. That is the point of science. You know more or less finally what can be done, well or ill, with a draughtsman's chalk or a sculptor's chisel. But with us the instruments themselves are always changing. That's the real triumph of a telescope—that it is telescopic."

"Well," said Mallow grimly, "I shall wait for one more change in the camera as a scientific instrument before I cut up my old easel for firewood."

"What change is that?" asked the Russian with a kind of eagerness.

"I shall wait till one of those tall cameras walks on its own three legs along a country lane to pick out the view it likes best."

"Even something like that may be more possible than you think," replied the other. "In these days when a man has his eyes and ears at the end of long wires; his own nerves, so to speak, spread over a city in the form of telephones and telegraphs. A great modern city will become a great machine with its handle in the human hand. Thus only can a man become a giant."

John Mallow looked at the man rather darkly for a moment, and then said:

"If you are so very fond of a big modern city," he said, "why do you hide yourself in such a quiet little hole in the country?"

For a flash the stranger's face seemed to wince and alter in the white sunlight; but the next instant he was still smiling, though he spoke a little more apologetically.

"There is certainly more space," he answered. "I confess I like a lot of space. But even there the science of the city will ultimately provide its own remedy. The answer is in one word—aviation."

Before the other could reply the speaker went on, his prominent eye kindling and his whole figure filling out with animation. He made a movement with his hand like a man throwing a stone into the air.

"It's upwards the new extension will be," he cried. "That road is wide enough, and that window is always open. The new roads will stand up like towers. The new harbours will stand far out in that sea above our heads—a sea you can never find the end of. It would only be a beginning to conquer the planets and colonize the fixed stars."

"I think," said Mallow, "that you will have conquered the remotest star before you really conquer this one old corner of the earth. It has a magic of its own which I think will outlast all such conjuring tricks. This was the house of Merlin; and, though they say Merlin himself fell under a spell, it was not that of Marconi."

"No," answered the stranger, still smiling. "We all know the spell under which Merlin fell."

Mallow knew enough about Russian intellectuals not to be surprised at the wide knowledge of the poetry and culture of the West; but here it seemed the almost satiric symbol of a deeper familiarity, and a mocking whisper told him what might have chained this magician in that western valley.

Laura Verney was coming across the garden towards them with some papers in her hand. She was of a red-haired, full-blooded type, handsome in a fashion which seemed to have a certain pagan exuberance till she came near enough to show the concentrated seriousness of her clear eyes; she might be called a pagan with the eyes of a puritan. She saluted her guests without any change of countenance, and handed the papers to the professor without any word of comment. Something in her automatic manner seemed to sting Mallow to a final impatience; and, picking up his hat from the window-sill, he called out in a loud and careless voice:

"Laura, will you show me the way out of this garden? I've forgotten the way."

It was some time afterwards, however, that he said any sort of final farewell to her, under the shadow of the outer wall, and near the ultimate gate of the garden. In the somewhat bitter intensity of his mood, he seemed rather to be exaggerating the finality of the farewell; not only touching herself, but all the things which he had always felt to be full of her presence.

"You will pull down that old swing, I suppose?" he had said as they went through the garden, "and put up an electric steel swing that will take anybody in ten seconds to the moon."

"I can't pull down the moon, anyhow," replied the girl, with a smile, "and I don't know that I want to."

"That's rather reactionary of you," remarked Mallow. "The moon is a very extinct volcano, valuable only to old-fashioned romanticists. And I suppose you'll turn our old lawn-tennis lawn into a place where tennis can be played by machinery, by pressing buttons a hundred miles away. I'm not sure whether they've yet finished the plans for a pear-tree that grows pears by electricity."

"But surely," she replied, looking a little troubled, "the world can go on without losing the things it seems to leave behind. And, after all, surely the world must go on; at least, it must go on growing. I think that's where you misunderstand. It isn't only going on; it's more like growing outwards."

"It's expansion, that's the word; growing broader, always describing wider and wider circles; but that only means more self-fulfilment, and therefore serenity and peace; it means——"

She stopped short, as if at a spoken answer, but it was only because the moon had flung a new shadow across her. It was from a figure standing on the wall. The moonshine made a halo of pale yellow round the head; and for a moment they thought it was the Russian, standing on the wall as he had stood on the roof. Then Mallow looked more closely at the face in shadow, and uttered, with some astonishment, the name of Gale.

"You must get away from here at once," said the poet sharply; "everybody who can must get away from this house. There's no time to explain."

As he spoke, he sprang from the wall and alighted beside them, and his friend, catching his face in a new light, saw that it was quite pale.

"What's the matter with you?" he demanded. "Have you seen a ghost?"

"The ghost of a fish," answered the poet; "three little grey ghosts of three little fishes. We must get away at once."

Without turning his head again, he led the way up the rising ground beyond the garden towards the clump of trees where the party had first encamped. Both Mallow and the girl pursued him with questions; but to only one of them did he give any answer. When Laura insisted on knowing whether her mother had come home yet, he answered shortly, "No; thank God! I sent Garth off to stop her on the road from the village. She's all right, anyhow."

But Laura Verney was a lady who could not be indefinitely dragged at the tail of a total stranger talking in a tone of authority; and by the time they came to the top of a hill, and the trees in whose shadow the poet had indulged in his meditations on birds, she halted and resolutely demanded his reasons.

"I won't go a step farther," she said firmly, "till you've given me some sort of proofs."

He turned with passion in his pale face.

"Oh, proofs!" he cried; "I know the sort of proofs you want. The foot-prints of the remarkable boots. The bloody finger-print carefully compared with the one at Scotland Yard. The conveniently mislaid matchbox, and the ashes of the unique tobacco. Do you suppose I've never read any detective stories? Well, I haven't got any proofs—of that sort. I haven't got any proofs at all, in that sense. If I told you my reasons, you'd think them the most rambling nonsense in the world. You must either do as I tell you and thank me afterwards; or you must let me talk as I like, and as long as I like, and thank your God you've come as far as this towards safety."

Mallow was looking at the poet in his quiet and intense fashion; and after a moment's pause, he said:

"You'd better tell us your own reasons in your own way. I know you generally have pretty good ones, really."

Gale's eyes wandered from the staring face of the girl to that of his friend, and then to the drift of dead leaves under the tree where he had once rested.

"I was lying there looking up at the sky, or, rather, the tree-tops," he said slowly. "I didn't hear what the others were talking about, because I was listening to the birds and looking at them. You know what happens when you go on staring at something like that; it turns into a sort of pattern like a wall-paper; and this was a quiet pattern of green and grey and brown. It seemed as if the whole world was that pattern; as if God had never made anything except a world of birds; of tree-tops hung in space."

Laura made a half-protest that sounded like a laugh, but Mallow said steadily: "Go on!"

"And then I slowly became conscious that there was a spot of yellow in the pattern. I slowly realized that it was another bird, and then what sort of bird. Somebody said it must be a yellow-hammer; but, little as I knew about it, I knew better than that. It was a canary."

The girl, who had already turned away, looked back at him with her first flash of interest.

"I wondered vaguely how a canary would get on in the world of birds, and how it had got there. I didn't think of any human being in particular. Only I saw in a sort of vision, somewhere against the morning sky, a window standing open, and the door of a cage standing open. Then I saw that all the brown birds were trying to kill the yellow one, and that started my thoughts off as it might anybody's. Is it always kind to set a bird at liberty? What exactly is liberty? First and foremost, surely, it is the power of a thing to be itself. In some ways the yellow bird was free in the cage. It was free to be alone. It was free to sing. In the forest its feathers would be torn to pieces and its voice choked for ever. Then I began to think that being oneself, which is liberty, is itself limitation. We are limited by our brains and bodies; and if we break out, we cease to be ourselves, and, perhaps, to be anything. That was when I asked you whether an isosceles triangle felt itself in prison, and if there were such a thing as a round prison. We shall hear more of the round prison before this story is over.

"Then I saw the man on the roof, with his hands spread like wings to the sky. I knew nothing of him; but I knew on the instant that he was the man who had given a bird its freedom at any risk. As we went down the hill I heard a little more about him; how he had escaped by blowing up his prison; and I felt that one fact had filled all his life with a philosophy of emancipation and escape. Always at the back of his mind, I was certain, was that one bursting moment when he saw white daylight shining through the shattered wall. I knew why he let birds out of cages and why he had written a book on the psychology of liberty. Then I stopped outside a window to stare at those gorgeous goldfish, merely because I had a fancy for such things; they coloured my thoughts, so to speak, with a sort of orange or scarlet, for long afterwards. And long afterwards I was again passing that window; and I found their colours were faded and their positions changed. At that time it was already dark, with a rising moon; and what forms I could see scattered in the shadow seemed almost grey, and even outlined in lines of grey light, which might have been moonlight, but I think was the corpse-light of phosphorescence. They lay scattered at random on the round table; and I saw by the faint glimmer that the glass bowl was broken. So I found my romance when I returned to it; for those fantastic fishes had been to me like the hieroglyphics of a message, which the fiery finger of God had thus written in red-hot gold. But when I looked again, the finger had written another lesson in letters of an awful and ashen silver. And what the new message said was: 'The man is mad.'

"Perhaps you think I am as mad as he; and I have told you that I am at once like him and unlike him. I am like him be-

243

cause I also can go on the wild journeys of such wild minds, and have a sympathy with his love of liberty. I am unlike him because, thank God, I can generally find my way home again. The lunatic is he who loses his way and cannot return. Now, almost before my eyes, this man had made the great stride from liberty to lunacy. The man who opened the bird-cage loved freedom; possibly too much; certainly very much. But the man who broke the bowl merely because he thought it a prison for the fish, when it was their only possible house of life—that man was already outside the world of reason, raging with a desire to be outside everything. In a most literal and living sense, he was out of his wits. And there was another thing revealed to me by the grey ghosts of the fishes. The rise of the insanity had been very rapid and steep. To send the bird into danger was only a disputable kindness, to fling the fish to death was a dance of raving destruction. What would he do next?

"I have spoken of a round prison. After all, to any mind that can move parallel to a mood like this, there really is a round prison. The sky itself, studded with stars, the serene arch of what we call infinity——"

As he spoke he staggered, clutched at the air, and fell all his great length on the grass. At the same moment Mallow was hurled against a tree, and the girl collapsed against him, clinging to him in a way which even in that blinding whirl, was an answer to many of his questionings. It was only when they had picked themselves up and pulled themselves together that they were fully conscious that the valley was still resounding with echoes of one hideous and rending uproar; or that the darkness had just shut down upon a blaze that blinded them like red lightning. For the instant that it lasted it was a standing glory, like a great sunrise. There rose to the surface of Mallow's memory only one word for it; the word radiant.

Mallow found himself reflecting in a dull fashion that it was lighter than it might have been at that hour, because of a friendly flame that was licking itself in a lively fashion a few yards away. Then he saw that it was the smouldering ruin of the blue wooden gate-post at which he had gazed that morning, flung all the way through the air like a flaming thunderbolt. They had come just far enough from the house to be out of danger. Then he looked again at the blue-painted wood curling with golden flames, and for the first time began to tremble.

The next moment he caught sight of the faces of his other friends, Walton and Hutton, pale in the flame as they hurried up the road from the remoter inn to which they had retired for the evening.

"What was it?" Walton was calling out.

"An explosion," said Hutton rather hazily.

"An expansion," replied Mallow, and mastered himself with the effort of a grim smile.

By this time, more people were running out from remote cottages, and Gabriel Gale turned his face to something like a small crowd.

"It was only the prison gun," he said, "the signal that a prisoner has escaped."

From *The Poet and the Lunatics*
(Darwen Finlayson)

The Blast of the Book

Professor Openshaw always lost his temper, with a loud bang, if anybody called him a Spiritualist; or a believer in Spiritualism. This, however, did not exhaust his explosive elements; for he also lost his temper if anybody called him a disbeliever in Spiritualism. It was his pride to have given his whole life to investigating Psychic Phenomena; it was also his pride never to have given a hint of whether he thought they were really psychic or merely phenomenal. He enjoyed nothing so much as to sit in a circle of devout Spiritualists and give devastating descriptions of how he had exposed medium after medium and detected fraud after fraud: for indeed he was a man of much detective talent and insight, when once he had fixed his eye on an object, and he always fixed his eye on a medium, as a highly suspicious object. There was a story of his having spotted the same Spiritualistic mountebank under three different disguises: dressed as a woman, a white-bearded old man, and a Brahmin of a rich chocolate brown. These recitals made the true believers rather restless, as indeed they were intended to do; but they could hardly complain, for no Spiritualist denies the existence of fraudulent mediums; only the Professor's flowing narrative might well seem to indicate that all mediums were fraudulent.

But woe to the simple-minded and innocent Materialist (and Materialists as a race are rather innocent and simple-minded) who, presuming on this narrative tendency, should advance the thesis that ghosts were against the laws of nature, or that such things were only old superstitions; or that it was all tosh, or, alternately, bunk. Him would the Professor, suddenly reversing all his scientific batteries, sweep from the field with a cannonade of unquestionable cases and unexplained phenomena, of which the wretched rationalist had never heard in his life, giving all the dates and details, stating all the attempted and abandoned natural explanations; stating everything, indeed, except whether he, John Oliver Openshaw, did or did not believe in Spirits; and that neither Spiritualist nor Materialist could ever boast of finding out.

Professor Openshaw, a lean figure with pale leonine hair and hypnotic blue eyes, stood exchanging a few words with Father Brown, who was a friend of his, on the steps outside the hotel where both had been breakfasting that morning and sleeping the night before. The Professor had come back rather late from one of his grand experiments, in general exasperation, and was still tingling with the fight that he always waged alone and against both sides.

"Oh, I don't mind you," he said laughing. "You don't believe in it even if it's true. But all these people are perpetually asking me what I'm trying to prove. They don't seem to understand that I'm a man of science. A man of science isn't trying to prove anything. He's trying to find out what will prove itself."

"But he hasn't found out yet," said Father Brown.

"Well, I have some little notions of my own, that are not quite so negative as most people think," answered the Professor, after an instant of frowning silence; "anyhow, I've begun to fancy that if there is something to be found, they're looking for it along the wrong line. It's all too theatrical; it's showing off, all their shiny ectoplasm and trumpets and voices and the rest; all on the model of old melodramas and mouldy historical novels about the Family Ghost. If they'd go to history instead of historical novels, I'm beginning to think they'd really find something. But not Apparitions."

"After all," said Father Brown, "Apparitions are only Appearances. I suppose you'd say the Family Ghost is only keeping up appearances."

The Professor's gaze, which had commonly a fine abstracted character, suddenly fixed and focused itself as it did on a dubious medium. It had rather the air of a man screwing a

247

strong magnifying-glass into his eye. Not that he thought the priest was in the least like a dubious medium; but he was startled into attention by his friend's thought following so closely on his own.

"Appearances!" he muttered, "crikey, but it's odd you should say that just now. The more I learn, the more I fancy they lose by merely looking for appearances. Now if they'd look a little into Disappearances——"

"Yes," said Father Brown, "after all, the real fairy legends weren't so very much about the appearance of famous fairies; calling up Titania or exhibiting Oberon by moonlight. But there were no end of legends about people *disappearing*, because they were stolen by the fairies. Are you on the track of Kilmeny or Thomas the Rhymer?"

"I'm on the track of ordinary modern people you've read of in the newspapers," answered Openshaw. "You may well stare; but that's my game just now; and I've been on it for a long time. Frankly, I think a lot of psychic appearances could be explained away. It's the disappearances I can't explain, unless they're psychic. These people in the newspapers who vanish and are never found—if you knew the details as I do . . . and now only this morning I got confirmation; an extraordinary letter from an old missionary, quite a respectable old boy. He's coming to see me at my office this morning. Perhaps you'd lunch with me or something; and I'd tell the results—in confidence."

"Thanks; I will—unless," said Father Brown modestly, "the fairies have stolen me by then."

With that they parted and Openshaw walked round the corner to a small office he rented in the neighbourhood; chiefly for the publication of a small periodical, of psychical and psychological notes of the priest and most agnostic sort. He had only one clerk, who sat at a desk in the outer office, totting up figures and facts for the purposes of the printed report; and the Professor paused to ask if Mr. Pringle had called. The clerk answered mechanically in the negative and went on mechanically adding up figures; and the Professor turned towards the inner room that was his study. "Oh, by the way, Berridge," he added, without turning round, "if Mr. Pringle comes, send him straight in to me. You needn't interrupt your work; I rather want those notes finished tonight if possible. You might leave them on my desk tomorrow, if I am late."

And he went into his private office, still brooding on the problem which the name of Pringle had raised; or rather, perhaps, had ratified and confirmed in his mind. Even the most perfectly balanced of agnostics is partially human; and it is possible that the missionary's letter seemed to have greater weight as promising to support his private and still tentative hypothesis. He sat down in his large and comfortable chair, opposite the engraving of Montaigne; and read once more the short letter from the Rev. Luke Pringle, making the appointment for that morning. No man knew better than Professor Openshaw the marks of the letter of the crank; the crowded details; the spidery handwriting; the unnecessary length and repetition. There were none of these things in this case; but a brief and businesslike typewritten statement that the writer had encountered some curious cases of Disappearance, which seemed to fall within the province of the Professor as a student of psychic problems. The Professor was favourably impressed; nor had he any unfavourable impression, in spite of a slight movement of surprise, when he looked up and saw that the Rev. Luke Pringle was already in the room.

"Your clerk told me I was to come straight in," said Mr. Pringle apologetically, but with a broad and rather agreeable grin. The grin was partly masked by masses of reddish-grey beard and whiskers; a perfect jungle of a beard, such as is sometimes grown by white men living in the jungles; but the eyes above the snub nose had nothing about them in the least wild or outlandish. Openshaw had instantly turned on them that concentrated spotlight or burning-glass of sceptical scrutiny which he turned on many men to see if they were mountebanks or maniacs; and, in this case, he had a rather unusual sense of reassurance. The wild beard might have belonged to a crank, but the eyes completely contradicted the beard; they were full of that quite frank and friendly laughter which is never found in the faces of those who are serious frauds or serious lunatics. He would have expected a man with those eyes to be a Philistine, a jolly sceptic, a man who shouted out shallow but hearty contempt for ghosts and spirits; but anyhow, no professional humbug could afford to look so frivolous as that. The man was buttoned up to the throat in a shabby old cape, and only his broad limp hat suggested the cleric; but missionaries from wild places do not always bother to dress like clerics.

"You probably think all this is another hoax, Professor," said Mr. Pringle, with a sort of abstract enjoyment, "and I hope you will forgive my laughing at your very natural air of disapproval. All the same, I've got to tell my story to somebody who knows, because it's true. And, all joking apart, it's tragic as well as true. Well, to cut it short, I was missionary in Nya-Nya, a station in West Africa, in the thick of the forests, where almost the only other white man was the officer in command of the district, Captain Wales; and he and I grew rather thick. Not that he liked missions; he was, if I may say so, thick in many ways; one of those square-headed, square-shouldered men of action who hardly need to think, let alone believe. That's what makes it all the queerer. One day he came back to his tent in the forest, after a short leave, and said he had gone through a jolly rum experience, and didn't know what to do about it. He was holding a rusty old book in a leather binding, and he put it down on a table beside his revolver and an old Arab sword he kept, probably as a curiosity. He said this book had belonged to a man on the boat he had just come off; and the man swore that nobody must open the book, or look inside it; or else they would be carried off by the devil, or disappear, or something. Wales said this was all nonsense, of course; and they had a quarrel; and the upshot seems to have been that this man, taunted with cowardice or superstition, actually did look into the book; and instantly dropped it; walked to the side of the boat——"

"One moment," said the Professor, who had made one or two notes. "Before you tell me anything else. Did this man tell

Wales where he had got the book, or who it originally belonged to?"

"Yes," replied Pringle, now entirely grave. "It seems he said he was bringing it back to Dr. Hankey, the Oriental traveller now in England, to whom it originally belonged, and who had warned him of its strange properties. Well, Hankey is an able man and a rather crabbed and sneering sort of man; which makes it queerer still. But the point of Wales's story is much simpler. It is that the man who had looked into the book walked straight over the side of the ship, and was never seen again."

"Do you believe it yourself?" asked Openshaw after a pause.

"Well, I do," replied Pringle. "I believe it for two reasons. First, that Wales was an entirely unimaginative man; and he added one touch that only an imaginative man could have added. He said that the man walked straight over the side on a still and calm day; but there was no splash."

The Professor looked at his notes for some seconds in silence; and then said: "And your other reason for believing it?"

"My other reason," answered the Rev. Luke Pringle, "is what I saw myself."

There was another silence; until he continued in the same matter-of-fact way. Whatever he had, he had nothing of the eagerness with which the crank, or even the believer, tried to convince others.

"I told you that Wales put down the book on the table beside the sword. There was only one entrance to the tent; and it happened that I was standing in it, looking out into the forest, with my back to my companion. He was standing by the table grumbling and growling about the whole business; saying it was tomfoolery in the twentieth century to be frightened of opening a book; asking why the devil he shouldn't open it himself. Then some instinct stirred in me and I said that he had better not do that, it had better be returned to Dr. Hankey. 'What harm could it do?' he said restlessly. 'What harm did it do?' I answered obstinately. 'What happened to your friend on the boat?' He didn't answer, indeed I didn't know what he

251

could answer; but I pressed my logical advantage in mere vanity. 'If it comes to that,' I said, 'what is your version of what really happened on the boat?' Still he didn't answer; and I looked round and saw that he wasn't there.

"The tent was empty. The book was lying on the table; open but on its face, as if he had turned it downwards. But the sword was lying on the ground near the other side of the tent; and the canvas of the tent showed a great slash, as if somebody had hacked his way out with the sword. The gash in the tent gaped at me; but showed only the dark glimmer of the forest outside. And when I went across and looked through the rent I could not be certain whether the tangle of the tall plants and the undergrowth had been bent or broken; at least not farther than a few feet. I have never seen or heard of Captain Wales from that day.

"I wrapped the book up in brown paper, taking good care not to look at it; and I brought it back to England, intending at first to return it to Dr. Hankey. Then I saw some notes in your paper suggesting a hypothesis about such things; and I decided to stop on the way and put the matter before you; as you have a name for being balanced and having an open mind."

Professor Openshaw laid down his pen and looked steadily at the man on the other side of the table; concentrating in that single stare all his long experience of many entirely different types of humbug, and even some eccentric and extraordinary types of honest men. In the ordinary way, he would have begun with the healthy hypothesis that the story was a pack of lies. On the whole he did incline to assume that it was a pack of lies. And yet he could not fit the man into his story; if it were only that he could not see that sort of liar telling that sort of lie. The man was not trying to look honest on the surface, as most quacks and impostors do; somehow, it seemed all the other way; as if the man *was* honest, in spite of something else that was merely on the surface. He thought of a good man with one innocent delusion; but again the symptoms were not the same; there was even a sort of virile indifference; as if the man did not care much about his delusion, if it was a delusion.

"Mr. Pringle," he said sharply, like a barrister making a witness jump, "where is this book of yours now?"

The grin reappeared on the bearded face which had grown grave during the recital.

"I left it outside," said Mr. Pringle. "I mean in the outer office. It was a risk, perhaps; but the less risk of the two."

"What do you mean?" demanded the Professor. "Why didn't you bring it straight in here?"

"Because," answered the missionary, "I knew that as soon as you saw it, you'd open it—before you had heard the story. I thought it possible you might think twice about opening it—after you'd heard the story."

Then after a silence he added: "There was nobody out there but your clerk; and he looked a stolid steady-going specimen, immersed in business calculations."

Openshaw laughed unaffectedly. "Oh, Babbage," he cried, "your magic tomes are safe enough with him, I assure you. His name's Berridge—but I often call him Babbage; because he's so exactly like a Calculating Machine. No human being, if you can call him a human being, would be less likely to open other people's brown paper parcels. Well, we may as well go and bring it in now; though I assure you I will consider seriously the course to be taken with it. Indeed, I tell you frankly," and he stared at the man again, "that I'm not quite sure whether we ought to open it here and now, or send it to this Dr. Hankey."

The two had passed together out of the inner into the outer office; and even as they did so, Mr. Pringle gave a cry and ran forward towards the clerk's desk. For the clerk's desk was there; but not the clerk. On the clerk's desk lay a faded old leather book, torn out of its brown-paper wrappings, and lying closed, but as if it had just been opened. The clerk's desk stood against the wide window that looked out into the street; and the window was shattered with a huge ragged hole in the glass; as if a human body had been shot through it into the world without. There was no other trace of Mr. Berridge.

Both the two men left in the office stood as still as statues;

253

and then it was the Professor who slowly came to life. He looked even more judicial than he had ever looked in his life, as he slowly turned and held out his hand to the missionary.

"Mr. Pringle," he said, "I beg your pardon. I beg your pardon only for thoughts that I have had; and half-thoughts at that. But nobody could call himself a scientific man and not face a fact like this."

"I suppose," said Pringle doubtfully, "that we ought to make some inquiries. Can you ring up his house and find out if he has gone home?"

"I don't know that he's on the telephone," answered Openshaw, rather absently; "he lives somewhere up Hampstead way, I think. But I suppose somebody will inquire here, if his friends or family miss him."

"Could we furnish a description," asked the other, "if the police want it?"

"The police!" said the Professor, starting from his reverie. "A description. . . . Well, he looked awfully like everybody else, I'm afraid, except for goggles. One of those clean-shaven chaps. But the police . . . look here, what *are* we to do about this mad business?"

"I know what I ought to do," said the Rev. Mr. Pringle firmly, "I am going to take this book straight to the only original Dr. Hankey, and ask him what the devil it's all about. He lives not very far from here, and I'll come straight back and tell you what he says."

"Oh, very well," said the Professor at last, as he sat down rather wearily; perhaps relieved for the moment to be rid of the responsibility. But long after the brisk and ringing footsteps of the little missionary had died away down the street, the Professor sat in the same posture, staring into vacancy like a man in a trance.

He was still in the same seat and almost in the same attitude, when the same brisk footsteps were heard on the pavement without and the missionary entered, this time, as a glance assured him, with empty hands.

"Dr. Hankey," said Pringle gravely, "wants to keep the book

254

for an hour and consider the point. Then he asks us both to call and he will give us his decision. He specially desired, Professor, that you should accompany me on the second visit."

Openshaw continued to stare in silence; then he said, suddenly:

"Who the devil is Dr. Hankey?"

"You sound rather as if you meant he was the devil," said Pringle, smiling, "and I fancy some people have thought so. He had quite a reputation in your own line; but he gained it mostly in India, studying local magic and so on, so perhaps he's not so well known here. He is a yellow skinny little devil with a lame leg, and a doubtful temper; but he seems to have set up in an ordinary respectable practice in these parts, and I don't know anything definitely wrong about him—unless it's wrong to be the only person who can possibly know anything about all this crazy affair."

Professor Openshaw rose heavily and went to the telephone; he rang up Father Brown, changing the luncheon engagement to a dinner, that he might hold himself free for the expedition to the house of the Anglo-Indian doctor; after that he sat down again, lit a cigar and sank once more into his own unfathomable thoughts.

Father Brown went round to the restaurant appointed for dinner, and kicked his heels for some time in a vestibule full of mirrors and palms in pots; he had been informed of Openshaw's afternoon engagement, and, as the evening closed-in dark and stormy round the glass and the green plants, guessed that it had produced something unexpected and unduly prolonged. He even wondered for a moment whether the Professor would turn up at all; but when the Professor eventually did, it was clear that his own more general guesses had been justified. For it was a very wild-eyed and even wild-haired Professor who eventually drove back with Mr. Pringle from the expedition to the North of London, where suburbs are still fringed with heathy wastes and scraps of common, looking more sombre under the rather thunderstorm sunset. Nevertheless, they had

255

apparently found the house, standing a little apart though within hail of other houses; they had verified the brass-plate duly engraved: "J. I. Hankey, M.D., M.R.C.S." Only they did not find J. I. Hankey, M.D., M.R.C.S. They found only what a nightmare whisper had already subconsciously prepared them to find: a commonplace parlour with the accursed volume lying on the table, as if it had just been read; and beyond, a backdoor burst open and a faint trail of footsteps that ran a little way up so steep a garden path that it seemed that no lame man could have run up so lightly. But it was a lame man who had run; for in those few steps there was the misshapen unequal mark of some sort of surgical boot; then two marks of that boot alone (as if the creature had hopped) and then nothing. There was nothing further to be learnt from Dr. J. I. Hankey, except that he had made his decision. He had read the oracle and received the doom.

When the two came into the entrance under the palms, Pringle put the book down suddenly on a small table, as if it burned his fingers. The priest glanced at it curiously; there was only some rude lettering on the front with a couplet:

> They that looked into this book
> Them the Flying Terror took;

and underneath, as he afterwards discovered, similar warnings in Greek, Latin and French. The other two had turned away with a natural impulsion towards drinks, after their exhaustion and bewilderment; and Openshaw had called to the waiter, who brought cocktails on a tray.

"You will dine with us, I hope," said the Professor to the missionary; but Mr. Pringle amiably shook his head.

"If you'll forgive me," he said, "I'm going to wrestle with this book and this business by myself somewhere. I suppose I couldn't use your office for an hour or so?"

"I suppose—I'm afraid it's locked," said Openshaw in some surprise.

"You forget there's a hole in the window." The Rev. Luke

Pringle gave the very broadest of all his broad grins and vanished into the darkness without.

"A rather odd fellow, that, after all," said the Professor, frowning.

He was rather surprised to find Father Brown talking to the waiter who had brought the cocktails, apparently about the waiter's most private affairs; for there was some mention of a baby who was now out of danger. He commented on the fact with some surprise, wondering how the priest came to know the man; but the former only said, "Oh, I dine here every two or three months, and I've talked to him now and then."

The Professor, who himself dined there about five times a week, was conscious that he had never thought of talking to the man; but his thoughts were interrupted by a strident ringing and a summons to the telephone. The voice on the telephone said it was Pringle; it was rather a muffled voice, but it might well be muffled in all those bushes of beard and whisker. Its message was enough to establish identity.

"Professor," said the voice, "I can't stand it any longer. I'm going to look for myself. I'm speaking from your office and the book is in front of me. If anything happens to me, this is to say good-bye. No—it's no good trying to stop me. You wouldn't be in time anyhow. I'm opening the book now. I . . ."

Openshaw thought he heard something like a sort of thrilling or shivering yet almost soundless crash; then he shouted the name of Pringle again and again, but he heard no more. He hung up the receiver, and, restored to a superb academic calm, rather like the calm of despair, went back and quietly took his seat at the dinner-table. Then, as coolly as if he were describing the failure of some small silly trick at a séance, he told the priest every detail of this monstrous mystery.

"Five men have now vanished in this impossible way," he said. "Every one is extraordinary; and yet the one case I simply can't get over is my clerk, Berridge. It's just because he was the quietest creature that he's the queerest case."

"Yes," replied Father Brown, "it was a queer thing for

Berridge to do, anyway. He was awfully conscientious. He was always so jolly careful to keep all the office business separate from any fun of his own. Why, hardly anybody knew he was quite a humorist at home and——"

"Berridge!" cried the Professor. "What on earth are you talking about? Did you know him?"

"Oh no," said Father Brown carelessly, "only as you say I know the waiter. I've often had to wait in your office, till you turned up; and of course I passed the time of day with poor Berridge. He was rather a card. I remember he once said he would like to collect valueless things, as collectors did the silly things they thought valuable. You know the old story about the woman who collected valueless things."

"I'm not sure I know what you're talking about," said Openshaw. "But even if my clerk was eccentric (and I never knew a man I should have thought less so), it wouldn't explain what happened to him; and it certainly wouldn't explain the others."

"What others?" asked the priest.

The Professor stared at him and spoke distinctly, as if to a child:

"My dear Father Brown, Five Men have disappeared."

Father Brown gazed back at his host with equal steadiness and spoke with equal distinctness. Nevertheless, the Professor required the words repeated, and they were repeated as distinctly.

"I say that no men have disappeared."

"My dear Professor Openshaw, no men have disappeared."

After a moment's silence, he added, "I suppose the hardest thing is to convince anybody that o + o + o = o. Men believe the oddest things if they are in a series; that is why Macbeth believed the three words of the three witches; though the first was something he knew himself; and the last something he could only bring about himself. But in your case the middle term is the weakest of all."

"What do you mean?"

"You saw nobody vanish. You did not see the man vanish from the boat. You did not see the man vanish from the tent.

All that rests on the word of Mr. Pringle, which I will not discuss just now. But you'll admit this; you would never have taken his word yourself, *unless* you had seen it confirmed by your clerk's disappearance; just as Macbeth would never have believed he would be king, if he had not been confirmed in believing he would be Cawdor."

"That may be true," said the Professor, nodding slowly. "But *when* it was confirmed, I knew it was the truth. You say I saw nothing myself. But I did; I saw my own clerk disappear. Berridge did disappear."

"Berridge did not disappear," said Father Brown. "On the contrary."

"What the devil do you mean by 'on the contrary'?"

"I mean," said Father Brown, "that he never disappeared. He appeared."

Openshaw stared across at his friend, but the eyes had already altered in his head, as they did when they concentrated on a new presentation of a problem. The priest went on:

"He appeared in your study, disguised in a bushy red beard and buttoned up in a clumsy cape, and announced himself as the Rev. Luke Pringle. And you had never noticed your own clerk enough to know him again, when he was in so rough-and-ready a disguise."

"But surely," began the Professor.

"Could you describe him for the police?" asked Father Brown. "Not you. You probably knew he was clean-shaven and wore tinted glasses; and merely taking off those glasses was a better disguise than putting on anything else. You had never seen his eyes any more than his soul; jolly laughing eyes. He had planted his absurd book and all the properties; then he calmly smashed the window, put on the beard and cape and walked into your study; knowing that you had never looked at him in your life."

"But why should he play me such an insane trick?" demanded Openshaw.

"Why, *because* you had never looked at him in your life," said Father Brown; and his hand slightly curled and clinched, as if he might have struck the table, if he had been given to gesture. "You called him the Calculating Machine, because that was all you ever used him for. You never found out even what a stranger strolling into your office could find out, in five minutes' chat: that he was a character; that he was full of antics; that he had all sorts of views on you and your theories and your reputation for 'spotting' people. Can't you understand his itching to prove that you couldn't spot your own clerk? He has nonsense notions of all sorts. About collecting useless things, for instance. Don't you know the story of the woman who bought the two most useless things: an old doctor's brassplate and a wooden leg? With those your ingenious clerk created the character of the remarkable Dr. Hankey; as easily as the visionary Captain Wales. Planting them in his own house——"

"Do you mean that place we visited beyond Hampstead was Berridge's own house?" asked Openshaw.

"Did *you* know his house—or even his address?" retorted the priest. "Look here, don't think I'm speaking disrespectfully of you or your work. You are a great servant of truth and you know I could never be disrespectful to that. You've seen through a lot of liars, when you put your mind to it. But don't *only* look at liars. Do, just occasionally, look at honest men— like the waiter."

"Where is Berridge now?" asked the Professor, after a long silence.

"I haven't the least doubt," said Father Brown, "that he is back in your office. In fact, he came back into your office at the exact moment when the Rev. Luke Pringle read the awful volume and faded into the void."

There was another long silence and then Professor Openshaw laughed; with the laugh of a great man who is great enough to look small. Then he said abruptly:

"I suppose I do deserve it; for not noticing the nearest helpers I have. But you must admit the accumulation of incidents was rather formidable. Did you *never* feel just a momentary awe of the awful volume?"

"Oh, that," said Father Brown. "I opened it as soon as I saw it lying there. It's all blank pages. You see, I am not superstitious."

From *The Father Brown Stories*
(Cassell & Co. Ltd.)

The Green Man

A young man in knickerbockers, with an eager sanguine profile, was playing golf against himself on the links that lay parallel to the sand and sea, which were all growing grey with twilight. He was not carelessly knocking a ball about, but rather practising particular strokes with a sort of microscopic fury; like a neat and tidy whirlwind. He had learned many games quickly, but he had a disposition to learn them a little more quickly than they can be learnt. He was rather prone to be a victim of those remarkable invitations by which a man may learn the Violin in Six Lessons—or acquire a perfect French accent by a Correspondence Course. He lived in the breezy atmosphere of such hopeful advertisement and adventure. He was at present the private secretary of Admiral Sir Michael Craven, who owned the big house behind the park abutting on the links. He was ambitious, and had no intention of continuing indefinitely to be private secretary to anybody. But he was also reasonable; and he knew that the best way of ceasing to be a secretary was to be a good secretary. Consequently he was a very good secretary; dealing with the ever-accumulating arrears of the Admiral's correspondence with the same swift centripetal concentration with which he addressed the golf-ball. He had to struggle with the correspondence alone and at his own discretion at present; for the Admiral had been with his ship for the last six months; and, though now returning, was not expected for hours, or possibly days.

With an athletic stride, the young man, whose name was Harold Harker, crested the rise of turf that was the rampart of the links and, looking out across the sands to the sea, saw a strange sight He did not see it very clearly; for the dusk was darkening every minute under stormy clouds; but it seemed to him, by a sort of momentary illusion, like a dream of days long past or a drama played by ghosts, out of another age in history.

The last of the sunset lay in long bars of copper and gold above the last dark strip of sea that seemed rather black than blue. But blacker still against this gleam in the west, there passed in sharp outline, like figures in a shadow pantomime, two men with three-cornered cocked hats and swords; as if they had just landed from one of the wooden ships of Nelson. It was not at all the sort of hallucination that would have come natural to Mr. Harker, had he been prone to hallucinations. He was of the type that is at once sanguine and scientific; and would be more likely to fancy the flying-ships of the future than the fighting-ships of the past. He therefore very sensibly came to the conclusion that even a futurist can believe his eyes.

His illusion did not last more than a moment. On the second glance, what he saw was unusual but not incredible. The two men who were striding in single file across the sands, one some fifteen yards behind the other, were ordinary modern naval officers; but naval officers wearing that almost extravagant full-dress uniform which naval officers never do wear if they can possibly help it; only on great ceremonial occasions such as the visits of Royalty. In the man walking in front, who seemed more or less unconscious of the man walking behind, Harker recognized at once the high-bridged nose and spike-shaped beard of his own employer the Admiral. The other man following in his tracks he did not know. But he did know something about the circumstances connected with the ceremonial occasion. He knew that when the Admiral's ship put in at the adjacent port, it was to be formally visited by a Great Personage; which was enough, in that sense, to explain the officers being in full dress. But he did also know the officers; or at any rate the Admiral. And what could have possessed the Admiral to come on shore in that rig-out, when one could swear he would seize five minutes to change into mufti or at least into undress uniform, was more than his secretary could conceive. It seemed some-

263

how to be the very last thing he would do. It was indeed to remain for many weeks one of the chief mysteries of this mysterious business. As it was, the outline of these fantastic court uniforms against the empty scenery, striped with dark sea and sand, had something suggestive of comic opera; and reminded the spectator of *Pinafore*.

The second figure was much more singular; somewhat singular in appearance, despite his correct lieutenant's uniform, and still more extraordinary in behaviour. He walked in a strangely irregular and uneasy manner; sometimes quickly and sometimes slowly; as if he could not make up his mind whether to overtake the Admiral or not. The Admiral was rather deaf and certainly heard no footsteps behind him on the yielding sand; but the footsteps behind him, if traced in the detective manner, would have given rise to twenty conjectures from a limp to a dance. The man's face was swarthy as well as darkened with shadow and every now and then the eyes in it shifted and shone, as if to accent his agitation. Once he began to run and then abruptly relapsed into a swaggering slowness and carelessness. Then he did something which Mr. Harker could never have conceived any normal naval officer in His Britannic Majesty's Service doing, even in a lunatic asylum. He drew his sword.

It was at this bursting-point of the prodigy that the two passing figures disappeared behind a headland on the shore. The staring secretary had just time to notice the swarthy stranger, with a resumption of carelessness, knock off a head of sea-holly with his glittering blade. He seemed then to have abandoned all idea of catching the other man up. But Mr. Harold Harker's face became very thoughtful indeed; and he stood there ruminating for some time before he gravely took himself inland, towards the road that ran past the gates of the great house and so by a long curve down to the sea.

It was up this curving road from the coast that the Admiral might be expected to come, considering the direction in which he had been walking, and making the natural assumption that he was bound for his own door. The path along the sands, under

264

the links, turned inland just beyond the headland and solidifying itself into a road, returned towards Craven House. It was down this road, therefore, that the secretary darted, with characteristic impetuosity, to meet his patron returning home. But the patron was apparently not returning home. What was still more peculiar, the secretary was not returning home either; at least until many hours later; a delay quite long enough to arouse alarm and mystification at Craven House.

Behind the pillars and palms of that rather too palatial country house, indeed, there was expectancy gradually changing to uneasiness. Gryce the butler, a big bilious man abnormally silent below as well as above stairs, showed a certain restlessness as he moved about the main front-hall and occasionally looked out of the wide windows of the porch, on the white road that swept towards the sea. The Admiral's sister Marion, who kept house for him, had her brother's high nose with a more sniffy expression; she was voluble, rather rambling, not without humour, and capable of sudden emphasis as shrill as a cockatoo. The Admiral's daughter Olive was dark, dreamy, and as a rule abstractedly silent, perhaps melancholy; so that her aunt generally conducted most of the conversation, and that without reluctance. But the girl also had a gift of sudden laughter that was very engaging.

"I can't think why they're not here already," said the elder lady. "The postman distinctly told me he'd seen the Admiral coming along the beach; along with that dreadful creature Rook. Why in the world they call him Lieutenant Rook——"

"Perhaps," suggested the melancholy young lady, with a momentary brightness, "perhaps they call him Lieutenant because he is a Lieutenant."

"I can't think why the Admiral keeps him," snorted her aunt, as if she were talking of a housemaid. She was very proud of her brother and always called him the Admiral; but her notions of a commission in the Senior Service were inexact.

"Well, Roger Rook is sulky and unsociable and all that," replied Olive, "but of course that wouldn't prevent him being a capable sailor."

"Sailor!" cried her aunt with one of her rather startling cockatoo notes, "he isn't my notion of a sailor. The Lass that Loved a Sailor, as they used to sing when I was young. . . . Just think of it! He's not gay and free and whatsitsname. He doesn't sing chanties or dance a hornpipe."

"Well," observed her niece with gravity. "The Admiral doesn't very often dance a hornpipe."

"Oh, you know what I mean—he isn't bright or breezy or anything," replied the old lady. "Why, that secretary fellow could do better than that."

Olive's rather tragic face was transfigured by one of her good and rejuvenating waves of laughter.

"I'm sure Mr. Harker would dance a hornpipe for you," she said, "and say he had learnt it in half an hour from the book of instructions. He's always learning things of that sort."

She stopped laughing suddenly and looked at her aunt's rather strained face.

"I can't think why Mr. Harker doesn't come," she added.

"I don't care about Mr. Harker," replied the aunt, and rose and looked out of the window.

The evening light had long turned from yellow to grey and was now turning almost to white under the widening moon-light, over the large flat landscape by the coast; unbroken by any features save a clump of sea-twisted trees round a pool and beyond, rather gaunt and dark against the horizon, the shabby fishermen's tavern on the shore that bore the name of the Green Man. And all that road and landscape was empty of any living thing. Nobody had seen the figure in the cocked hat that had been observed, earlier in the evening, walking by the sea; or the other and stranger figure that had been seen trailing after him. Nobody had even seen the secretary who saw them.

It was after midnight when the secretary at last burst in and aroused the household; and his face, white as a ghost, looked all the paler against the background of the stolid face and figure of a big Inspector of Police. Somehow that red, heavy, indifferent face looked, even more than the white and harassed one, like a mask of doom. The news was broken to the two women

266

with such consideration or concealments as were possible. But the news was that the body of Admiral Craven had been eventually fished out of the foul weeds and scum of the pool under the trees; and that he was drowned and dead.

Anybody acquainted with Mr. Harold Harker, secretary, will realize that, whatever his agitation, he was by morning in a mood to be tremendously on the spot. He hustled the Inspector, whom he had met the night before on the road down by the Green Man, into another room for private and practical consultation. He questioned the Inspector rather as the Inspector might have questioned a yokel. But Inspector Burns was a stolid character; and was either too stupid or too clever to resent such trifles. It soon began to look as if he were by no means so stupid as he looked; for he disposed of Harker's eager questions in a manner that was slow but methodical and rational.

"Well," said Harker (his head full of many manuals with titles like *Be a Detective In Ten Days*). "Well, it's the old triangle, I suppose. Accident, Suicide or Murder."

"I don't see how it could be accident," answered the policeman. "It wasn't even dark yet and the pool's fifty yards from the straight road that he knew like his own doorstep. He'd no more have got into that pond than he'd go and carefully lie down in a puddle in the street. As for suicide, it's rather a responsibility to suggest it, and rather improbable too. The Admiral was a pretty spry and successful man and frightfully rich, nearly a millionaire in fact; though of course that doesn't prove anything. He seemed to be pretty normal and comfortable in his private life too; he's the last man I should suspect of drowning himself."

"So that we come," said the secretary, lowering his voice with the thrill, "I suppose we come to the third possibility."

"We won't be in too much of a hurry about that," said the Inspector to the annoyance of Harker, who was in a hurry about everything. "But naturally there are one or two things one would like to know. One would like to know about his property, for instance. Do you know who's likely to come in for it? You're his private secretary; do you know anything about his will?"

"I'm not so private a secretary as all that," answered the young man. "His solicitors are Messrs. Willis, Hardman and Dyke, over in Suttford High Street; and I believe the will is in their custody."

"Well, I'd better get round and see them pretty soon," said the Inspector.

"Let's get round and see them at once," said the impatient secretary.

He took a turn or two restlessly up and down the room and then exploded in a fresh place.

"What have you done about the body, Inspector?" he asked.

"Dr. Straker is examining it now at the Police Station. His report ought to be ready in an hour or so."

"It can't be ready too soon," said Harker. "It would save time if we could meet him at the lawyer's." Then he stopped and his impetuous tone changed abruptly to one of some embarrassment.

"Look here," he said, "I want . . . we want to consider the young lady, the poor Admiral's daughter, as much as possible just now. She's got a notion that may be all nonsense; but I wouldn't like to disappoint her. There's some friend of hers she wants to consult, staying in the town at present. Man of the name of Brown; priest or parson of some sort; she's given me his address. I don't take much stock in priests or parsons, but——"

The Inspector nodded. "I don't take any stock in priests or parsons; but I take a lot of stock in Father Brown," he said. "I happened to have to do with him in a queer sort of society jewel case. He ought to have been a policeman instead of a parson."

"Oh, all right," said the breathless secretary as he vanished from the room. "Let him come to the lawyer's too."

Thus it happened that, when they hurried across to the neighbouring town to meet Dr. Straker at the solicitor's office, they found Father Brown already seated there, with his hands folded on his heavy umbrella, chatting pleasantly to the only available member of the firm. Dr. Straker also had arrived, but apparently only at that moment, as he was carefully placing his gloves in his top-hat and his top-hat on a side-table. And the mild and beaming expression of the priest's moonlike face and spectacles, together with the silent chuckles of the jolly old grizzled lawyer, to whom he was talking, were enough to show that the doctor had not yet opened his mouth to bring the news of death.

"A beautiful morning after all," Father Brown was saying. "That storm seems to have passed over us. There were some big black clouds, but I notice that not a drop of rain fell."

"Not a drop," agreed the solicitor toying with a pen; he was the third partner, Mr. Dyke; "there's not a cloud in the sky now. It's the sort of day for a holiday." Then he realized the newcomers and looked up, laying down the pen and rising. "Ah, Mr. Harker, how are you? I hear the Admiral is expected home soon." Then Harker spoke, and his voice ran hollow in the room.

"I am sorry to say we are the bearers of bad news. Admiral Craven was drowned before reaching home."

There was a change in the very air of the still office, though not in the attitudes of the motionless figures; both were staring at the speaker as if a joke had been frozen on their lips. Both repeated the word "drowned" and looked at each other, and then again at their informant. Then there was a small hubbub of questions.

"When did this happen?" asked the priest.

"Where was he found?" asked the lawyer.

"He was found," said the inspector, "in that pool by the coast, not far from the Green Man, and dragged out all covered with green scum and weeds so as to be almost unrecognizable. But Dr. Straker here has—— What is the matter, Father Brown? Are you ill?"

"The Green Man," said Father Brown with a shudder. "I'm so sorry . . . I beg your pardon for being upset."

"Upset by what?" asked the staring officer.

"By his being covered with green scum, I suppose," said the priest with a rather shaky laugh. Then he added rather more firmly, "I thought it might have been seaweed."

By this time everybody was looking at the priest, with a not unnatural suspicion that he was mad; and yet the next crucial surprise was not to come from him. After a dead silence, it was the doctor who spoke.

Dr. Straker was a remarkable man, even to look at. He was very tall and angular, formal and professional in his dress; yet retaining a fashion that has hardly been known since Mid-Victorian times. Though comparatively young, he wore his brown beard very long and spreading over his waistcoat; in contrast with it, his features, which were both harsh and handsome, looked singularly pale. His good looks were also diminished by something in his deep eyes that was not squinting, but like the shadow of a squint. Everybody noticed these things about him, because the moment he spoke, he gave forth an indescribable air of authority. But all he said was:

"There is one more thing to be said, if you come to details, about Admiral Craven being drowned." Then he added reflectively, "Admiral Craven was not drowned."

The Inspector turned with quite a new promptitude and shot a question at him.

"I have just examined the body," said Dr. Straker, "the cause of death was a stab through the heart with some pointed blade like a stiletto. It was after death, and even some little time after, that the body was hidden in the pool."

Father Brown was regarding Dr. Straker with a very lively eye, such as he seldom turned upon anybody; and when the group in the office began to break up, he managed to attach himself to the medical man for a little further conversation, as they went back down the street. There had not been very much else to detain them except the rather formal question of the will. The impatience of the young secretary had been somewhat tried by the professional etiquette of the old lawyer. But the latter was ultimately induced, rather by the tact of the priest than the authority of the policeman, to refrain from making a mystery where there was no mystery at all. Mr. Dyke admitted, with a smile, that the Admiral's will was a very normal and ordinary document, leaving everything to his only child Olive; and that there was really no particular reason for concealing the fact.

The doctor and the priest walked slowly down the street that struck out of the town in the direction of Craven House. Harker had plunged on ahead of him with all his native eagerness to get somewhere; but the two behind seemed more interested in their discussion than their direction. It was in rather an enigmatic tone that the tall doctor said to the short cleric beside him:

"Well, Father Brown, what do you think of a thing like this?"

Father Brown looked at him rather intently for an instant and then said: "Well, I've begun to think of one or two things; but my chief difficulty is that I only knew the Admiral slightly; though I've seen something of his daughter."

"The Admiral," said the doctor with a grim immobility of feature, "was the sort of man whom it is said that he had not an enemy in the world."

"I suppose you mean," answered the priest, "that there's something else that will not be said."

"Oh, it's no affair of mine," said Straker hastily but rather harshly. "He had his moods, I suppose. He once threatened me with a legal action about an operation; but I think he thought better of it. I can imagine his being rather rough with a subordinate."

Father Brown's eyes were fixed on the figure of the secretary striding far ahead; and as he gazed he realized the special cause of his hurry. Some fifty yards farther ahead the Admiral's daughter was dawdling along the road towards the Admiral's house. The secretary soon came abreast of her; and for the remainder of the time Father Brown watched the silent drama of two human backs as they diminished into the distance. The secretary was evidently very much excited about something; but if the priest guessed what it was, he kept it to himself. When he came to the corner leading to the doctor's house, he only said briefly: "I don't know if you have anything more to tell us."

"Why should I?" answered the doctor very abruptly; and striding off, left it uncertain whether he was asking why he should have anything to tell, or why he should tell it.

Father Brown went stumping on alone, in the track of the two young people; but when he came to the entrance and avenues of the Admiral's park, he was arrested by the action of the girl, who suddenly turned and came straight towards him; her face unusually pale and her eyes bright with some new and as yet nameless emotion.

"Father Brown," she said in a low voice, "I must talk to you as soon as possible. You must listen to me, I can't see any other way out."

"Why certainly," he replied, as coolly as if a gutter-boy had asked him the time. "Where shall we go and talk?"

The girl led him at random to one of the rather tumbledown arbours in the grounds; and they sat down behind a screen of large ragged leaves. She began instantly, as if she must relieve her feelings or faint.

"Harold Harker," she said, "has been talking to me about things. Terrible things."

The priest nodded and the girl went on hastily. "About Roger Rook. Do you know about Roger?"

"I've been told," he answered, "that his fellow-seamen call him The Jolly Roger, because he is never jolly; and looks like the pirate's skull and crossbones."

"He was not always like that," said Olive in a low voice. "Something very queer must have happened to him. I knew him well when we were children; we used to play over there on the sands. He was harum-scarum and always talking about being a pirate; I dare say he was the sort they say might take to crime through reading shockers; but there was something poetical in his way of being piratical. He really was a Jolly Roger then. I suppose he was the last boy who kept up the old legend of really running away to sea; and at last his family had to agree to his joining the Navy. Well. . . ."

"Yes," said Father Brown patiently.

"Well," she admitted, caught in one of her rare moments of mirth, "I suppose poor Roger found it disappointing. Naval officers so seldom carry knives in their teeth or wave bloody cutlasses and black flags. But that doesn't explain the change in him. He just stiffened; grew dull and dumb, like a dead man walking about. He always avoids me; but that doesn't matter. I supposed some great grief that's no business of mine had broken him up. And now—well, if what Harold says is true, the grief is neither more nor less than going mad; or being possessed of a devil."

"And what does Harold say?" asked the priest.

"It's so awful I can hardly say it," she answered. "He swears he saw Roger creeping behind my father that night; hesitating and then drawing his sword . . . and the doctor says father was stabbed with a steel point. . . . I *can't* believe Roger Rook had anything to do with it. His sulks and my father's temper sometimes led to quarrels; but what are quarrels? I can't exactly say I'm standing up for an old friend; because he isn't even friendly. But you can't help feeling sure of some things, even about an old acquaintance. And yet Harold swears that he——"

"Harold seems to swear a great deal," said Father Brown.

There was a sudden silence; after which she said in a different tone:

"Well he does swear other things too. Harold Harker proposed to me just now."

"Am I to congratulate you, or rather him?" inquired her companion.

"I told him he must wait. He isn't good at waiting." She was caught again in a ripple of her incongruous sense of the comic: "He said I was his ideal and his ambition and so on. He has lived in the States; but somehow I never remember it when he is talking about dollars; only when he is talking about ideals."

"And I suppose," said Father Brown very softly, "that it is because you have to decide about Harold that you want to know the truth about Roger?"

She stiffened and frowned, and then equally abruptly smiled, saying: "Oh, you know too much."

"I know very little, especially in this affair," said the priest gravely. "I only know who murdered your father." She started up and stood staring down at him stricken white. Father Brown made a wry face as he went on: "I made a fool of myself when I first realized it; when they'd just been asking where he was found, and went on talking about green scum and the Green Man."

Then he also rose; clutching his clumsy umbrella with a new resolution, he addressed the girl with a new gravity.

"There is something else that I know, which is the key to all these riddles of yours; but I won't tell you yet. I suppose it's bad news; but it's nothing like so bad as the thing you have been fancying." He buttoned up his coat and turned towards the gate. "I'm going to see this Mr. Rook of yours. In a shed by the shore, near where Mr. Harker saw him walking. I rather think he lives there." And he went bustling off in the direction of the beach.

Olive was an imaginative person; perhaps too imaginative to be safely left to brood over such hints as her friend had thrown out; but he was in rather a hurry to find the best relief for her broodings. The mysterious connexion between Father Brown's first shock of enlightenment and the chance language about the pool and the inn, hag-rode her fancy in a hundred forms of ugly symbolism. The Green Man became a ghost trailing loathsome weeds and walking the countryside under the moon; the sign of the Green Man became a human figure hanging as from a gibbet; and the tarn itself became a tavern, a dark subaqueous tavern for the dead sailors. And yet he had taken the most rapid method to overthrow all such nightmares, with a burst of blinding daylight which seemed more mysterious than the night.

For before the sun had set, something had come back into her life that turned her whole world topsy-turvy once more; something she had hardly known that she desired until it was abruptly granted; something that was, like a dream, old and familiar, and yet remained incomprehensible and incredible. For Roger Rook had come striding across the sands, and even when he was a dot in the distance, she knew he was transfigured; and as he came nearer and nearer, she saw that his dark face was alive with laughter and exultation. He came straight towards her, as if they had never parted, and seized her shoulders saying: "Now I can look after you, thank God."

She hardly knew what she answered; but she heard herself questioning rather wildly why he seemed so changed and so happy.

"Because I am happy," he answered. "I have heard the bad news."

All parties concerned, including some who seemed rather unconcerned, found themselves assembled on the garden path leading to Craven House, to hear the formality, now truly formal, of the lawyer's reading of the will; and the probable, and more practical, sequel of the lawyer's advice upon the crisis. Besides the grey-haired solicitor himself armed with the testamentary document, there was the Inspector armed with more direct authority touching the crime, and Lieutenant Rook in undisguised attendance on the lady; some were rather mystified on seeing the tall figure of the doctor, some smiled a little on seeing the dumpy figure of the priest. Mr. Harker, that Flying Mercury, had shot down to the lodge-gates to meet them, led them back on to the lawn, and then dashed ahead of them again to prepare their reception. He said he would be back in a jiffy; and anyone observing his piston-rod of energy could well believe it; but, for the moment, they were left rather stranded on the lawn outside the house.

"Reminds me of somebody making runs at cricket," said the Lieutenant.

"That young man," said the lawyer, "is rather annoyed that the law cannot move quite so quickly as he does. Fortunately, Miss Craven understands our professional difficulties and delays. She has kindly assured me that she still has confidence in my slowness."

"I wish," said the doctor, suddenly, "that I had as much confidence in his quickness."

"Why, what do you mean?" asked Rook, knitting his brows; "do you mean that Harker is too quick?"

"Too quick and too slow," said Dr. Straker, in his rather cryptic fashion. "I know one occasion at least when he was not so very quick. Why was he hanging about half the night by the pond and the Green Man, before the Inspector came down and found the body? Why did he meet the Inspector? Why should he expect to meet the Inspector outside the Green Man?"

"I don't understand you," said Rook. "Do you mean that Harker wasn't telling the truth?"

Dr. Straker was silent. The grizzled lawyer laughed with grim good humour.

"I have nothing more serious to say against the young man," he said, "than that he made a prompt and praiseworthy attempt to teach me my own business."

"For that matter, he made an attempt to teach me mine," said the Inspector, who had just joined the group in front. "But that doesn't matter. If Dr. Straker means anything by his hints, they do matter. I must ask you to speak plainly, doctor. It may be my duty to question him at once."

"Well, here he comes," said Rook, as the alert figure of the secretary appeared once more in the doorway.

At this point Father Brown, who had remained silent and inconspicuous at the tail of the procession, astonished everybody very much; perhaps especially those who knew him. He not only walked rapidly to the front, but turned facing the whole group with an arresting and almost threatening expression, like a sergeant bringing soldiers to the halt.

"Stop!" he said almost sternly. "I apologize to everybody; but it's absolutely necessary that I should see Mr. Harker first. I've got to tell him something I know; and I don't think anybody else knows; something he's got to hear. It may save a very tragic misunderstanding with somebody later on."

"What on earth do you mean?" asked old Dyke the lawyer.

"I mean the bad news," said Father Brown.

"Here, I say," began the Inspector indignantly; and then suddenly caught the priest's eye and remembered strange things he had seen in other days. "Well, if it were anyone in the world but you I should say of all the infernal cheek———"

But Father Brown was already out of hearing, and a moment afterwards was plunged in talk with Harker in the porch. They walked to and fro together for a few paces and then disappeared into the dark interior. It was about twelve minutes afterwards that Father Brown came out alone.

To their surprise he showed no disposition to re-enter the house, now that the whole company were at last about to enter it. He threw himself down on the rather rickety seat in the leafy arbour, and as the procession disappeared through the doorway, lit a pipe and proceeded to stare vacantly at the long ragged leaves about his head and to listen to the birds. There was no man who had a more hearty and enduring appetite for doing nothing.

He was apparently in a cloud of smoke and a dream of abstraction, when the front doors were once more flung open and two or three figures came out helter-skelter, running towards him, the daughter of the house and her young admirer Mr. Rook being easily winners in the race. Their faces were alight with astonishment; and the face of Inspector Burns, who advanced more heavily behind them, like an elephant shaking the garden, was inflamed with some indignation as well.

"What *can* all this mean?" cried Olive, as she came panting to a halt. "He's gone!"

"Bolted!" said the Lieutenant explosively. "Harker's just managed to pack a suitcase and bolted! Gone clean out of the back door and over the garden wall to God knows where. What *did* you say to him?"

"Don't be silly!" said Olive, with a more worried expression. "Of course you told him you'd found him out, and now he's gone. I never could have believed he was wicked like that!"

"Well!" gasped the Inspector, bursting into their midst. "What have you done now? What have you let me down like this for?"

"Well," repeated Father Brown, "what have I done?"

"You have let a murderer escape," cried Burns, with a decision that was like a thunderclap in the quiet garden; "you have *helped* a murderer to escape. Like a fool I let you warn him; and now he is miles away."

"I have helped a few murderers in my time, it is true," said Father Brown; then he added, in careful distinction, "not, you will understand, helped them to commit the murder."

"But you knew all the time," insisted Olive. "You guessed from the first that it must be he. That's what you meant about being upset by the business of finding the body. That's what the doctor meant by saying my father might be disliked by a subordinate."

"That's what I complain of," said the official indignantly. "You knew even then that he was the——"

"You knew even then," insisted Olive, "that the murderer was——"

Father Brown nodded gravely. "Yes," he said. "I knew even then that the murderer was old Dyke."

"Was *who*?" repeated the Inspector and stopped amid a dead silence; punctuated only by the occasional pipe of birds.

"I mean Mr. Dyke, the solicitor," explained Father Brown, like one explaining something elementary to an infant class. "That gentleman with grey hair who's supposed to be going to read the will."

They all stood like statues staring at him, as he carefully filled his pipe again and struck a match. At last Burns rallied his vocal powers to break the strangling silence with an effort resembling violence.

"But, in the name of heaven, *why*?"

"Ah, why?" said the priest and rose thoughtfully, puffing at his pipe. "As to why he did it. . . . Well, I suppose the time has come to tell you, or those of you who don't know, the fact that is the key of all this business. It's a great calamity; and it's a great crime; but it's not the murder of Admiral Craven."

He looked Olive full in the face and said very seriously:

"I tell you the bad news bluntly and in few words; because I

278

think you are brave enough, and perhaps happy enough, to take it well. You have the chance, and I think the power, to be something like a great woman. You are not a great heiress."

Amid the silence that followed it was he who resumed his explanation.

"Most of your father's money, I am sorry to say, has gone. It went by the financial dexterity of the grey-haired gentleman named Dyke, who is (I grieve to say) a swindler. Admiral Craven was murdered to silence him about the way in which he was swindled. The fact that he was ruined and you were disinherited is the single simple clue, not only to the murder, but to all the other mysteries in this business." He took a puff or two and then continued.

"I told Mr. Rook you were disinherited and he rushed back to help you. Mr. Rook is a rather remarkable person."

"Oh, chuck it," said Mr. Rook with a hostile air.

"Mr. Rook is a monster," said Father Brown with scientific calm. "He is an anachronism, an atavism, a brute survival of the Stone Age. If there was one barbarous superstition we all supposed to be utterly extinct and dead in these days, it was that notion about honour and independence. But then I get mixed up with so many dead superstitions. Mr. Rook is an extinct animal. He is a plesiosaurus. He did not want to live on his wife or have a wife who could call him a fortune-hunter. Therefore he sulked in a grotesque manner and only came to life again when I brought him the good news that you were ruined. He wanted to work for his wife and not be kept by her. Disgusting, isn't it? Let us turn to the brighter topic of Mr. Harker.

"I told Mr. Harker you were disinherited and he rushed away in a sort of panic. Do not be too hard on Mr. Harker. He really had better as well as worse enthusiasms; but he had them all mixed up. There is no harm in having ambitions; but he had ambitions and called them ideals. The old sense of honour taught men to suspect success; to say, 'This is a benefit; it may be a bribe.' The new nine-times-accursed nonsense about Making Good teaches men to identify being good with making

279

money. That was all that was the matter with him; in every other way he was a thoroughly good fellow, and there are thousands like him. Gazing at the stars and rising in the world were all Uplift. Marrying a good wife and marrying a rich wife were all Making Good. But he was not a cynical scoundrel; or he would simply have come back and jilted or cut you as the case might be. He could not face you; while you were there, half of his broken ideal was left.

"I did not tell the Admiral; but somebody did. Word came to him somehow, during the last grand parade on board, that his friend the family lawyer had betrayed him. He was in such a towering passion that he did what he could never have done in his senses; came straight on shore in his cocked hat and gold lace to catch the criminal; he wired to the police station, and that was why the Inspector was wandering round the Green Man. Lieutenant Rook followed him on shore because he suspected some family trouble and had half a hope he might help and put himself right. Hence his hesitating behaviour. As for his drawing his sword when he dropped behind and thought he was alone, well that's a matter of imagination. He was a romantic person who had dreamed of swords and run away to sea; and found himself in a service where he wasn't even allowed to wear a sword except about once in three years. He thought he was quite alone on the sands where he played as a boy. If you don't understand what he did, I can only say, like Stevenson, 'you will never be a pirate.' Also you will never be a poet; and you have never been a boy."

"I never have," answered Olive gravely, "and yet I think I understand."

"Almost every man," continued the priest musing, "will play with anything shaped like a sword or dagger, even if it is a paper-knife. That is why I thought it so odd when the lawyer didn't."

"What do you mean?" asked Burns, "didn't what?"

"Why, didn't you notice," answered Brown, "at that first meeting in the office, the lawyer played with a pen and not with a paper-knife; though he had a beautiful bright steel paper-knife in the pattern of a stiletto? The pens were dusty and splashed with ink; but the knife had just been cleaned. But he did not play with it. There are limits to the irony of assassins."

After a silence the Inspector said, like one waking from a dream: "Look here . . . I don't know whether I'm on my head or my heels; I don't know whether you think you've got to the end; but I haven't got to the beginning. Where do you get all this lawyer stuff from? What started you out on that trail?"

Father Brown laughed curtly and without mirth.

"The murderer made a slip at the start," he said, "and I can't think why nobody else noticed it. When you brought the first news of the death to the solicitor's office, nobody was supposed to know anything there, except that the Admiral was expected home. When you said he was drowned, I asked when it happened and Mr. Dyke asked where the corpse was found."

He paused a moment to knock out his pipe and resumed reflectively:

"Now when you are simply told of a seaman, returning from the sea, that he has been drowned, it is natural to assume that he has been drowned at sea. At any rate, to allow that he may have been drowned at sea. If he had been washed overboard, or gone down with his ship, or had his body 'committed to the deep,' there would be no reason to expect his body to be found at all. The moment that man asked where it was found I was sure he knew where it was found. Because he had put it there. Nobody but the murderer need have thought of anything so unlikely as a seaman being drowned in a land-locked pool a few hundred yards from the sea. That is why I suddenly felt sick and turned green, I dare say; as green as the Green Man. I never *can* get used to finding myself suddenly sitting beside a murderer. So I had to turn it off by talking in parables; but the parable meant something, after all. I said that the body was covered with green scum, but it might just as well have been seaweed."

It is fortunate that tragedy can never kill comedy and that

281

the two can run side by side; and that while the only acting partner of the business of Messrs. Willis, Hardman and Dyke blew his brains out when the Inspector entered the house to arrest him, Olive and Roger were calling to each other across the sands at evening, as they did when they were children together.

From *The Father Brown Stories*
(Cassell & Co. Ltd.)